5.10

Bad f

D0736123

By Christi Barth

Bad Boys Gone Good

BAD FOR HER

Coming Soon

NEVER BEEN GOOD • GOT IT BAD

Naked Men

RISKING IT ALL • WANTING IT ALL

GIVING IT ALL • TRYING IT ALL

Shore Secrets

UP TO ME • ALL FOR YOU

BACK TO US

Aisle Bound

PLANNING FOR LOVE

A FINE ROMANCE • FRIENDS TO LOVERS

A MATCHLESS ROMANCE

Bad Decisions

THE OPPOSITE OF RIGHT

THE REVERSE OF PERFECTION

CHECK MY HEART • LOVE AT HIGH TIDE

LOVE ON THE BOARDWALK

CRUISING TOWARD LOVE

ACT LIKE WE'RE IN LOVE

TINSEL MY HEART • ASK HER AT CHRISTMAS

Bad for Her

BAD BOYS GONE GOOD

CHRISTI BARTH

AVONIMPULSE
An Imprint of HarperCollins*Publishers*

Newmarket Public Library

R
PB -326
Barth

This is a work of fiction. Names, characters, places, and incidents are products of the author's imagination or are used fictitiously and are not to be construed as real. Any resemblance to actual events, locales, organizations, or persons, living or dead, is entirely coincidental.

Excerpt from *Never Been Good* copyright © 2018 by Christi Barth.

BAD FOR HER. Copyright © 2017 by Christi Barth. All rights reserved. Printed in the United States of America. No part of this book may be used or reproduced in any manner whatsoever without written permission except in the case of brief quotations embodied in critical articles and reviews. For information, address HarperCollins Publishers, 195 Broadway, New York, NY 10007.

Digital Edition OCTOBER 2017 ISBN: 978-0-06-268563-6
Print Edition ISBN: 978-0-06-268564-3

Cover design by Nadine Badalaty
Cover photograph © g-stockstudio/Shutterstock

Avon Impulse and the Avon Impulse logo are registered trademarks of HarperCollins Publishers in the United States of America.

Avon and HarperCollins are registered trademarks of HarperCollins Publishers in the United States of America and other countries.

FIRST EDITION

FEB 10 2018

17 18 19 20 21 HDC 10 9 8 7 6 5 4 3 2 1

If you purchased this book without a cover, you should be aware that this book is stolen property. It was reported as "unsold and destroyed" to the publisher, and neither the author nor the publisher has received any payment for this "stripped book."

For my husband,
who is the complete opposite of a bad boy,
which is why I married him.

Acknowledgments

My first and biggest thank you has to go to my brilliant editor, Nicole Fischer, who made me dig deeper than I ever have before to do justice to Rafe and Mollie. This book wouldn't be what it is without your insights. Hugs to Jessica Alvarez for championing this entire series and graciously putting up with my constant questions. A plate of brownies each to Misty Waters and Lea Nolan for their beta reading—wait'll you get a load of the final version! Immeasurable thanks to Laura Kaye and Stephanie Dray for helping me come up with the idea for WITSEC hotness.

And my absolute most sincere thanks go to you, the readers, for taking a chance on my Bad Boys!

Prologue

Silent Springs County Jail, 3:00 a.m.
Mood in the room—pissed as fuck

RONAN CONNOLLY HAD a talent for sizing up the mood in a room. More than once, hell, more times than the thirty-one years under his belt, it had saved his life. Because when you worked for the Chicago mob, sometimes all the heads-up you got that a situation was going south was a squinted eye or a tightened mouth.

Right now? He could get all fancy-pants and notice the tense hush that crammed the interrogation room with a shit-ton of unsaid words. He could get all shrink-y and assume that U.S. Marshal Delaney Evans's ramrod straight posture meant she was taut with anger. Or he could just look over at the two sets of blue eyes that matched his own, spitting fire. Kevin and Fallon, his brothers, were mad. Furious. Oh, yeah—he knew this because he felt exactly the same thing.

He spun the ladder-back chair around and straddled

it. Probably thumped it harder against the floor than necessary. But since he couldn't punch the wall, or a face, or even a god damned pillow, Ronan settled for slamming the chair.

"I came into the Witness Security Program of my own free will. You people didn't arrest me and cut a deal. I sought you out and offered to testify against the fucking Chicago mob. That's supposed to afford me and mine some protection. It's not supposed to get us dragged out of bed at the ass-end of the night and thrown into jail."

"You're not *in* jail." Delaney's boots clomped hard against the concrete as she walked to the door, opened it, and purposefully left it ajar. "See? Not locked. No guards."

"If that's true, how about you slide that gun out of your holster and put it on the table," Kevin suggested.

Ronan had to hand it to his brother. The guy thought like a lawyer, even though he was still one semester shy from a JD. He didn't ask the marshal to hand off the weapon to any of them. No, Kevin had just asked her to take it out of play.

"For God's sake." Delaney rolled her pretty blue eyes. "Do you really not trust me? After six months of shepherding your asses all around this country?"

Ronan didn't trust anyone.

Not anymore.

Nobody except his brothers. No matter how good the marshal had been to them.

With a lazy twist of his wrist, Kevin pointed one finger at the weapon. "A gun destabilizes the power dynamic.

Remove it, and any threat—perceived or otherwise—diminishes."

Delaney held his gaze as she slid it out of the holster and emptied the bullets into her hand. Then she put the now-useless gun in the middle of the scarred wooden table. "There. Happy?"

Kevin shrugged. "I won't be *happy* until I've tasted your lips. Until I've had them on me. But I do feel prepared to continue the conversation."

Unbelievable. If Ronan had told his brother once, he'd told the little pip-squeak a hundred times not to antagonize their protection agent. And she'd made it clear that she took Kevin's constant flirtation as an annoyance. Doing it now, when they'd been rousted out of bed and brought here in a squad car for some reason he couldn't begin to guess, was downright stupid. Ronan kicked him under the table. Twice.

"We might not be behind bars, but this is a county jail." Ronan knew he was repeating himself. But he was pissed. Tired. And feeling out of control, which he didn't do. Ever.

"Ronan's right." Fallon planted his forearms on the table and leaned forward. "Now, I built birdhouses in shop class better than that shithole apartment you stuck us in, but at least it had beds. Pillows. And, speaking for myself, a really hot dream about two redheads in a hot tub. Yanking us out of there with no explanation and bringing us to jail isn't playing fair."

Delaney shook back her long blond hair. And nailed

Fallon with an icy glare. "You're here, as it so happens, for your own protection. Because your house isn't safe anymore. Bringing you to, yes, the county jail, is merely a stopgap before we move you again."

"No." Ronan didn't like this town any better than the last three. But he damn well didn't want to move again. To pick a new name and a new job that sucked and learn the streets and try to fit in—which was so far proving impossible no matter where they went. "No freaking way."

"I warned you. I warned all of you. Screw up, break the rules, and we move you. Start picking out new names, fellas."

Ronan shot out of his chair. Then he grabbed Fallon and Kevin by their collars, lifting them halfway to their feet. "What the fuck did you do?"

"Let them go. It's you this time, Ronan."

The shock of her assertion was as much a punch to the gut as the elbow Fallon planted in his belly. He let go and reeled back a step to sag against the cinderblock wall. Because he'd fucking given up *everything*, turned his life inside out to keep his brothers safe. Not himself.

"I would never put them in danger," he said flatly.

"Not on purpose, no." Delaney's steely gaze softened. "I don't doubt that for a second."

Kevin sneered at him. It was a look he'd aimed at Ronan more in the past six months than in all the previous twenty-five years put together. The little snot held a grudge like nobody's business. And since he blamed

Ronan for getting him yanked out of law school, out of life, not to mention hiding their family's deep mob connections . . . well, that chip on his shoulder probably wasn't going away anytime soon. "What'd you do—call up one of your ex-skirts for some phone sex?"

"I wouldn't put your lives at risk for that." Ronan waggled his fingers. "I've got a hand, don't I?"

"Eww." Delaney shook her head. "No more guesses. I can't take it. Look, Ronan, you logged on to a certain Italian cooking website that's a known message board for the mob."

"I didn't leave a message. Didn't talk to anyone. I just looked around . . ." He let his voice trail off.

How did she know? That quick dip into his old life had been done from the privacy of his bedroom. On his laptop. Not at a coffeehouse where any passing busybody could peer over his shoulder. Not at a library where the system could be hacked. No, he'd surfed from the so-called comfort of his lumpy bed. The same place he'd searched a few other sites that a man only looked at in the privacy of his own room.

Son of a bitch. Ronan pushed off the wall and stalked forward. He braced one palm on the table and the other on the back of Delaney's chair, caging her in so that she had no choice but to look him in the eye. "You hacked my computer."

Had to give the lady credit. Ronan's menacing glare was usually all it took to make a grown man pee his pants and rush to both name names and hand over money. Sure, he'd carried a tire iron to send a message, but he'd rarely had to use it. Blondie, however, didn't look at all intimidated. The woman had a brass pair, that was for sure.

"I did no such thing."

Ronan's lips parted on a low growl.

That did it. She looked away. Just for a second, but that was all it took. She'd talk now.

"I didn't have to hack your government-provided computer because we already had a tap on it," the marshal said, as slick as January ice on Lake Michigan. "On all of them, actually."

Kevin thumped his fist on the table. "You can't do that. There's no way you had a warrant. No cause. Zero."

"I can do it because it is standard procedure with protectees until we're certain they don't pose a threat to themselves. You guys . . . well, you haven't exactly taken to your new lives. Any of them, so far. We watch for your own good. So we can yank you to safety when you do something boneheaded."

With a look of disgust, Fallon said, "You got on *Italiano Cucina Casalinga*? I don't care how much you craved a good bolognese sauce. There are a million other recipe sites out there that aren't full of secret messages."

"Wait—you hid mob business on an Italian home cooking site?" Kevin's head fell back until he stared at the ceiling. "God, is that where the family lasagne recipe comes from? Is there any part of our life that wasn't touched by the mob?"

Back in the day, Ronan never had to explain himself. He'd been second in command to McGinty. The fixer. Everyone looked up to him, and his word was the last word.

It was just one more thing that had changed. Along with his name, his job, and the stupid, scratchy goatees they'd all grown after the last middle-of-the-night move. He hadn't allowed himself the luxury of talking to a pretty woman—let alone romancing one—since they'd entered the program. Every hour of every day was spent second-guessing and safeguarding and holding all their shit together. So having to justify his actions to his younger brothers didn't just sting. It *sucked.*

But he'd do it. He'd swallow his pride and do it, to keep them from splintering apart anymore. Because keeping the three of them together? Safe and healthy? It was the only thing that mattered.

Ronan sat back down. Spread his hands wide, palms up, like he was doing penance. "I caught the tail end of a piece on the morning news about Danny McGinty. How he was taken from his jail cell and rushed to the hospital. I had to find out more. Was he attacked? Were they trying to take him out? Was he sick? If he dies, I can't testify against him. Would that change our whole situation? I thought I could nose around on the site, see if there was mention of a hit, or a change in leadership, and then I'd get out with no one being the wiser."

"Except they have programs on their end. Like the ones that show you nonstop travel ads on social media after you peek at one little beach hotel to de-stress after a long day." Delaney cleared her throat, winced, and then continued. "They can monitor who comes onto the site. Which means they could know that someone from this town, which has zero ties to any version of organized crime, was on there for some reason. It is a neon sign leading them to you."

His stomach churned, the way it did after eating too many Johnnie's Italian sausages topped with shredded beef. "I didn't know."

Delaney patted his arm. "I get it. But we told you when you joined the program not to do so much as a search on a one-night stand from high school. *Nothing* from your former lives can touch these new ones."

Ronan looked at his brothers. "I'm sorry." Then he looked over at Delaney. Kevin's flirting might annoy the shit out of her, but Ronan knew he could work his own magic to smooth out the frown lines on her face. So he aimed one of his patented panty-dropping smiles at her, full force. "And thank you, Marshal. For keeping watch. For having our backs. Wish you'd been up front about it, though."

"Reaaally?" She drawled the word out so long that Ronan knew he'd hate whatever came out next. The smile was clearly wasted on the pissed-off woman. "You're squeamish that I know you occasionally watch porn? Or is it the fact that you've been studying up on the Arizona Diamondbacks that embarrasses you?"

Shit.

Both, actually.

Kevin's neck actually snapped, he jerked it forward so fast. "Dude. The Diamondbacks? They're the dirtiest team in baseball."

Pointing at Delaney, Ronan said, "She told us that we can't be Cubs fans anymore. Not in public. I'm trying to find a new team."

"Try harder," Fallon said, tongue in his cheek.

Delaney stood, scraping her chair back. "You're right. I should've told you we were keeping an eye on you. Heads-up—we're going to keep doing it in this next town. For a while. Your phones, too."

He dipped his head. As much as it rankled, it also made sense. "Okay."

"We are monitoring the McGinty situation. When there's something to tell you, I will. Until then, there's no reason to send you into an uproar that maybe breaks your cover. That's why I didn't tell you. But next time, whether you have a question or get into trouble, you call me. It's my job to protect you—even if that means protecting you from yourself."

"Okay." Ronan would swallow that bitter pill. He'd try harder. He'd make sure his brothers toed the line, too.

Her boots thudded heavily as she walked the circumference of the room from each brother to the next. "Because—and this isn't a threat, just a warning—if you guys can't make it work in this next town, that's it. You're out of the program. The word came down from the top brass when they heard about this latest stunt. I mean, the unfortunate albeit unknowing *poor choice*." She put air quotes around the words. The marshal could be a hard ass.

"We'd be on our own?"

Delaney nodded. "No sweet monthly check, no help setting up new identities, no perfectly polished fake job references. If you blow it again, we drop Kevin first. Screw up after that and the two of you are out, too. We're well aware how badly you want to stay together, so that's our bargaining chip. Kick him out of the program and move you two out of his life forever. He's only along for the ride as a favor, since he's not testifying. And that means he'll be found. Probably killed."

Yeah. Like that possibility didn't already wake Ronan up a couple dozen times a week in a cold sweat.

"At least promise to wear something short and backless to my funeral," Kevin said with a wink. He tossed one of her bullets high up, then snatched it out of the air.

Idiot.

This wasn't going to be easy. But if Ronan could keep Chicago's criminal underbelly in line, he could damn well make sure he and his brothers behaved.

Probably.

Chapter One

Some stretch of Oregon freeway
Mood behind the wheel—free
. . . not that it'd last

Every time they'd been dumped in a new town, the Maguire brothers made a list of all the ways the new town sucked compared to Chicago. Rafe didn't like much about this new placement. Probably. Hell, he'd only been in Bandon for forty-eight hours. It'd rained for forty-seven of those hours, here on the Oregon coast. Seemed like everyone always bitched about the constant rain, and Rafe was happy to jump on the bandwagon. Even though it just made puddles, which cleaned themselves up. As opposed to the annual or three epic Chicago blizzards that broke your back with two solid days of shoveling out.

Rafe stopped himself. That wasn't the happy, perky mindset Marshal Evans preferred. The one he'd promised her—again—an hour ago when he'd picked up the final version of his brother's new license. It'd pissed him off to have to meet Delaney halfway between her office up in Eugene and his town. But it kept their cover secure. And part of him felt sorry for the government hack who'd spelled Kellan's new name wrong the first time around. Guess they changed 'em so often it was hard to keep track. Hadn't stopped his youngest brother from being pissy about the slipup, though.

The good thing about the almost pointless drive was his sweet-as-fuck ride. The one he'd conned the government into buying for him by pointing out that it cost less than an *actual* new car. Rafe had a sweet spot for classic cars. If he truly had to hunker down and build a life here? He'd damn well do it with his dream car.

A 1970 Chevrolet Camaro. With T-tops. The same blue as Lake Michigan on an August day.

Rafe wasn't even speeding. For once. It was too much fun to listen to the smooth rumble of the engine, feel the cool May wind rushing in the open windows, and not worry about anything waiting for him back in their new town. No worries about remembering his name or his brothers' names. No worries about doing a job he'd only played with as a hobby for fifteen years. No worries about whether anyone from their old life was on their trail.

For right now, he'd enjoy another half hour of pure freedom. The only thing that could make this better would be a hot blonde in the bucket seat next to him.

Hang on.

Rafe slowed. Then he stomped on the brakes. Because a Jeep sat half off the shoulder with a dark-haired woman kicking the flat tire.

A curvy brunette would do just fine.

It'd be wrong to drive past. Ungentlemanly. If Marshal Evans were here, wouldn't she tell him to do his civic god damned duty and help his fellow Oregonian?

Sure she would.

Parking right at the nose of her Jeep, he got out. Tried to appear non-menacing. Which was the complete opposite of how he'd approached pretty much every situation for half his life. Hell, even the women he'd dated had known what he did and gotten off on the idea of his dangerous life.

The marshal had given him some pointers on how to come off as normal. One thumb tucked into the waist of his jeans, so it didn't look like his fist was braced for action. Other arm relaxed at his side. She'd said something about a loose walk, but Rafe only knew one way to walk. To be safe, he stopped almost immediately.

"Hey there. Do you need some help?"

She turned to him with a whirl of her olive-colored skirt. It was too long to flash him any leg. But the motion did part her denim jacket to reveal a skin-tight orange tank. Too bad a green scarf covered what Rafe expected to be pretty spectacular breasts. "Only if you've got some sort of magic wand that'll fix my tire."

"I don't like to talk about my magic wand before I buy a girl dinner."

She cocked her head. Looked left, then right, then back at him. "You know, we're all alone on a forested stretch of highway. Maybe save the sexual innuendo for a better time and place?"

"Name it, and I will." Because she wasn't scared of him. Nothing about her posture had gone defensive after he'd made his comment. Which, yeah, was sleazy and cheap. Rafe had to remember that he wasn't in a big city with nine million people anymore. The disposable dating pool was limited. Probably not even eight thousand.

Sauntering forward—which *proved* the woman wasn't scared of him—she gave him an up-and-down stare. Fair enough. Rafe did the same to her. Except he didn't make it even partway down. He stalled out at her eyes. They were a smoky green; the color of the pine trees behind them, wrapped in fog. Bedroom eyes. Yeah, he could stare into those all night . . . and all the way through to breakfast.

"Okay," she finally said. "You're cute. But why should I give you a chance?"

Rafe liked that she went toe-to-toe with him. "I'm the one doing you the favor, remember? Turnabout is fair play."

"What favor?"

"I'm going to fix your car."

"Really?" She brightened all over, from her suddenly sparkling eyes to a bounce in her hair and a twitch in her ass as she rushed back to the tire. "I called for a tow truck, but they said it'd be more than an hour."

"I don't have a magic wand, but if you hand me that jack, I'll get that flat off and the spare on in less than ten minutes."

She shot him a sassy smirk. "This is one time when speed won't count against you, I promise." Which then turned into a frown. "Except that the tire won't come off. I tried."

"*You* tried. With those arms." Rafe snorted. The woman was on the taller side and skinny. He had no doubt she could roll a suitcase through an airport. But he had every doubt that she could hold her own against a guy who worked out in the boxing ring with his brothers every week. "What do you do for a living? Unless the answer is *work for UPS*, my case is closed."

Her chin shot up. Guess she didn't like being challenged. That was okay. Neither did Rafe. "I'm a doctor."

"That means you lift a one-pound stethoscope, right?" he teased.

"I work out," she shot back. *Now* she was super defensive. Arms crossed. Shoulders hunched. "I have muscles."

Rafe unzipped his black leather jacket. He draped it over the hood of the car while pretending not to hear her indrawn hiss of breath. It wasn't the first time a woman had ogled the biceps popping from beneath his tight black tee. It never got old, though. "Not like mine."

"So I see. What do *you* do for a living?"

Whatever the U.S. Marshals Service told him to do.

But Rafe went with a simpler answer as he crouched

by the rear tire. *This* week's answer, anyway. "I'm a mechanic."

"Wow. I really hit the jackpot when you stopped, didn't I?"

Rafe craned his neck up to look at the delighted smile that transformed her from pretty to gorgeous. "Would it make me sound like a cocky jackass if I say yes?"

"Cocky, yes. Jackass . . . well, time will tell."

"Fair enough."

"So what should I call you when I tell my friends how you saved me?"

"Mr. Wonderful?"

"Seriously. I'm Mollie Vickers." She thrust her hand right in front of his nose.

Standing, wiping his hands on his jeans afforded him the few extra seconds to ensure he'd get the name right that had only been his for two days. "Rafe Maguire."

"Nice to meet you. Extremely nice to meet you, as it so happens."

As an excuse to keep holding it, he swung her hand toward the tire. "You didn't take off the lug nuts."

"Is that a technical term? Like when I tell a patient that his proximal interphalangeal joint is suffering from longitudinal compression?"

"Dunno. What is that?"

"A jammed finger."

"Then no. Lug nuts are these things." He pointed as he rummaged back through her trunk for the necessary bits and pieces. "Think of them as the screw holding your tire to the car."

"Oh." She bent at the waist to look at the nuts. It gave him one heck of a sightline down her cleavage. "Is that why the tire didn't come off?"

Rafe wanted to laugh. He definitely would, later, when he told his brothers the story. "That, and you didn't jack up the car. So there's still four thousand pounds, give or take, pressing down to keep that tire in place. Did you think you could just pop it off like getting a Life Saver out of a roll?"

"Can I tell you a secret?" she whispered in his ear. "I don't know how to change a tire."

This time there was no stopping the laughter. It rolled out of him, long and loud, startling a flock of who the hell knew what kind of birds out of the pine trees lining the road. "Babe, that's no secret."

"I left Oregon for college at sixteen, so, of course, I only had a provisional license."

"Uh, right." What kind of idiots ran this state if they made you wait past your sixteenth birthday to get a real license? "Sixteen, huh? I suppose I should be impressed?" What he actually felt was seven kinds of stupid. Since McGinty had made him drop out halfway through senior year to work for him full-time and just get a GED.

"Don't be. I skipped second grade. Just about anyone could do that, if they wanted to, honest." The way she dismissed her obviously genius-sized brain put Rafe back at ease. "I did college and med school in Boston, and then my residency in Chicago. They've got some of the best public transit in the country." Leaning sideways against the door to watch him, she trailed her fingers along the handle. "I'm not really used to driving."

Chicago.

Dr. Mollie with the pretty green eyes had lived in Chicago. Rafe white-knuckled the lug wrench. The marshal had been way beyond specific about not contacting anyone from his hometown.

Wait.

The doc with the forest-secret eyes wasn't *from* Chicago. It sounded like she'd grown up right here, and then came back once her shit-ton of schooling was done. Rafe had binged his way through a couple of medical shows while healing from his last gunshot wound. He knew residency meant working thirty-six hours straight with no sleep. The shows also made it look like any time grabbed on mattresses was to knock boots, but that part was less believable.

The point being, she'd been too busy to roam around Chicago. Too busy to notice Rafe amidst nine million other people clogging up the city streets. And the only time he took the elevated train was to go to Wrigley Field and lose money betting on the Cubs.

It was safe.

He was safe.

His brothers were safe.

Rafe put all that pent-up adrenaline of the last sixty seconds into spinning the lug wrench and jacking up the car. He suddenly wasn't sure if he wanted to get this whole business over with and get away from her ASAP, or linger with the prettiest woman he'd talked to in weeks. Excluding the hot marshal, who would a) be nothing but trouble, b) be the stupidest thing he'd ever done aside from joining the mob in the first place, and c) was already spoken for by his idiot youngest brother, who now called himself Kellan. Rafe kept repeating his and Flynn's name a half-dozen times a day, still getting used to them.

Harsher than he intended, Rafe said, "You should learn a few things, Doc. The basics. How to change a tire, check your oil, swap out wiper blades. Why didn't you learn all that the same time you learned to pump your own gas?"

"Ha ha. Very funny."

"What's funny?" He pulled the spare off the back gate of the Jeep.

"You know we can't pump our own gas in Oregon."

Aaaand Rafe almost dropped the damn tire. "You're shitting me."

First the no-driving-at-sixteen thing, and now this? Clearly the marshal had forgotten to give them a really important background info file on the weirdness of their new state. As soon as he got home, he'd have to fill in the others. Right after bitching out the marshal in an email about how she hadn't "prepared them sufficiently for success in their new life"—a phrase she freaking loved to spout.

Lips pursed, Mollie asked, "You're not from here, are you?"

"No." He hadn't needed tips from the marshal on how to lie well. Rafe had learned the two basic rules of lying before he rolled on his first rubber. Keep it short, and stick to the truth as much as possible.

"But you live here now?"

He jerked his thumb some direction up or down the road. No idea which. The wall of pines on both sides of the highway made everything look the same. "That way, about ten miles."

"Same here. Except in the opposite direction." Those flat orange shoes of hers toe-heeled it out of his way. "Should I be helping?"

"Hell, no." But it made her as cute as could be for offering. So far she'd shown him sass, strength, stubbornness, and now a sweet side. Along with sexy when she'd given him that unintentional boob shot. Yeah, the doctor was the whole package. The only thing missing—by a mile—was street smarts. God knew Rafe had enough of those for both of them. "You save lives. That's important. Let me save your fingers."

"Mechanics are important, too. You're rescuing me from an hour of sheer boredom right now."

"Yeah. That really stacks up against straddling a guy, reaching into his blood-spurting chest, and plugging a hole in his heart with your finger *without* compressing the spinal cord and accidentally paralyzing him." The tire came off with one smooth pull. Rafe might've put a little more effort—and biceps—into it than strictly required. He'd decided that he did want to impress the doc. And from the way her eyes didn't leave his biceps, impressing her didn't take too much extra effort.

"That's oddly specific." Her dark brows drew together. "So specific that I think I can quote the episode of *Heartbeat* it came from." She slapped the door several times. It made a tinny, stinging noise, probably from the silver ring on her right forefinger. "Omigod. You watch cheesy medical dramas!"

Rafe jacked the car up a little more to fit the fully inflated spare. "I do not."

Chortling, she danced around him in a semicircle. "I am not letting you get away with this. What you just described is not an ordinary occurrence. My aforementioned proximal interphalangeal joint suffering from longitudinal compression is common. A gusher of an aortic tear is not. Especially not to laymen. *Very* much especially not to laymen mechanics who wear leather jackets. Admit it. You watch."

What he wanted to admit was how cute she looked, prancing around trying to make him feel like an idiot. Mollie wasn't all that graceful. Clearly she'd spent any ballet classes as a kid on the sidelines with her nose in a book. But her glee was adorable. The flailing arms she kept pointing at him with stretched her shirt even tighter across her nicely large breasts. And the bouncing made her long hair move like dark, sensual water.

Okay. He'd toss her a bone.

"I watched. Past tense. When I was, ah, sick." He'd had an IV, a button to push for morphine, and a post-surgical infection from falling in the Chicago River after getting shot. That should count as "sick." Not a lie at all. "Daytime television is either courtroom crap or five-year-old reruns. So, yeah, I chose the smaller risk. Still killed off a few brain cells watching it. Probably gave my eyeballs whiplash from rolling them so many times. And once I was all better, I didn't think about it again."

"Riiiiight." She picked up the lug nuts and handed them over, one at a time.

As if he'd let her have the last word. "You're the one who should be ashamed to admit you even got my reference."

"Why?"

He tightened everything in an *X* pattern, just the way his dad taught him decades ago. "Isn't a show like that beneath someone with all your smarts? And all your *real* medical know-how?"

"Well, sure. When you put it that way. But I watch it as a stress reliever. Stress kills. That's a medical fact. And I'd rather watch every week while really hot guys rip off their scrub tops every fifteen minutes than meditate."

Rafe made a mental note that apparently the lady

liked ripped abs as much as she liked popped biceps. He also filed away jacking off as a medically certified stress-buster. Less boring than meditating, and he sure felt relaxed afterward. Flynn would get a kick out of that. "What color scrubs do you wear, Doc?"

"Me?" She pulled her jacket tighter and crossed her arms over it. "How do you know I don't wear a starched white lab coat over pearls and a pencil skirt?"

Hot. If she took his blood pressure in that getup, he'd start having a fantasy about bending her over the exam table. Still in her heels. And he'd probably bust right out of the cuff. Hell, he was starting to get hard right now.

"I'd be fine with either scenario. But the way you look today—casual but put together—makes me think you're the kind of person who appreciates the perk of wearing more or less pajamas to work."

Mollie burst out laughing. "You've got me there. I actually said that on my first day of med school. And I say it again every time I eat too many slices of pizza and get to slide into that drawstring waistband the next morning."

"Color?" he prompted her. Rafe suddenly needed the visual.

"Hunter green. To match my surroundings," she said grandly, throwing her arms wide to indicate the forest. "I overdosed on the boring blue during my internship and residency. There are just a few of us on staff at the hospital, so I pulled rank to choose. I think next year we may go bright red, to switch it up. But I'll say it's for heart disease awareness. Turn it into a teaching tool, instead of letting everyone know I did it because I look rocking in red."

Rafe was learning important stuff here. Mollie liked pizza and wasn't embarrassed to eat more than one piece. That alone put her up a few pegs from at least a quarter of the women he'd dated in Chicago. She had confidence. Not boringly overmodest. It'd been so long that it took him a minute to realize he was having *fun* with her.

"I'd call that a good use of your power. It makes me want to accidentally jam my proximal interphalangeal joint next year just to see you in them." There. Low-dose flirting. Nothing too cocky or dangerous. He should be freaking taping this whole encounter to earn a gold star from the marshal.

After laughing again, Mollie asked, "Do you like it here?"

Shit. Talk about a loaded question.

No.

Rafe hated it here, because it wasn't Chicago. Because he heard freaking crickets at night instead of traffic and people hustling. Because there wasn't any deep-dish pizza. Because of no jazz clubs like the Green Mill.

Because it wasn't home.

But . . . yes.

Because this new place would keep his brothers alive. It was their shot. Their best shot. Their only shot. And if he didn't somehow find a reason to like it here, Rafe was screwed.

None of which he could say to Mollie. So he kept it simple. Shifted one knee to the ground so he could twist to look up at her and said, "I'm a big fan of the roadside attractions."

She pursed her lips, slicked the same orange as her top and shoes. "Before you were hitting on me. Now you're flirting with me. What's with the change in tactics?"

"Figure I'll just throw everything at the wall until something sticks." He stood. Crowded right up into her space. Used his thumb to tuck a long strand of hair behind her ear. Watched her chest rise and fall twice in rapid succession before continuing. "You let me know when that happens, Doc."

"I will," she said. Pretty much breathlessly.

This had all the markings of a slam dunk. "You're good."

"How do you know? You haven't even kissed me yet."

That was it. He could hear the swish of the ball going through the net. "Your car." Rafe edged to the right to kick the replaced tire. "The tire's changed out. You're good to hit the road."

"Oh." Her eyelids fluttered down.

"But now that it's on the table, I want to know."

"What?" And back up those long, dark lashes came. She had him locked in her sights like a laser.

Rafe moved to cage her against the car with his arms. They weren't touching anywhere, but he hadn't left room between for daylight to pass. "How good you are. Better yet, how *bad* you are."

Then he waited. Didn't move a muscle. Because it needed to be Mollie's choice. Mostly because they were on the side of a semi-deserted highway. The sun—or Oregon's pale version of it—was streaming down from overhead, and they were still on the blacktop. Rafe knew, though, that it could be seen as a potentially risky situation. He didn't want her to feel pressured or scared. He just wanted to keep having fun with her.

But he'd read all the signals right and didn't have to wait long.

"Stop flirting. Start doing," she ordered. And then Mollie crooked her leg around his calf in an invitation about as subtle as a gun to the head.

Rafe was a big fan of going for the obvious. It made life easier. So he leaned forward the extra eighth of an inch to bring their bodies flush. Waited again. The second she tipped her chin up in anticipation, *then* it was go time.

He took her mouth. This wasn't a good night kiss at the front door with her parents watching. It was two strangers on the side of the damn road who were into each other. So he showed her his heat, showed her what she'd stirred up in him. Rafe molded her lips with his. Instantly, he discovered that Mollie's lips were made for kissing. They were wide and warm and matched him move for move. Nip for nip.

Mollie's sucking sweetness shot desire through him. Mostly straight to his dick, though. He rocked it against her. No reason to keep it a secret how much he wanted her. In response, she slapped a palm against the seat of his jeans and held on tight.

Okay.

Game on.

He threaded his fingers through her waterfall of soft hair, tilting her head to the perfect angle. Tightened his other hand over the curve of her hip. Then he plunged into her mouth. Her hot, wet, sweet-as-sin mouth. Mollie's tongue met his, like two silken swords clashing for supremacy.

Ha. He'd win. He always did.

Rafe liked being in control in the bedroom. The women he was with liked it, too. But he also enjoyed the process of getting there. Of turning a woman inside out with passion and want until she begged for his cock. Nothing turned him on like the sound of a woman moaning in desire.

Right now, Mollie wasn't moaning yet. They were both gasping pretty hard for air in between kisses, though. Because she'd melted against him like butter. Her rockin' body flowed, breast to hips to legs. They moved back and forth in a copy of the rhythm he'd started in the *V* between her slim thighs. And this time, when he explored along the silk of her cheek and pulled her bottom lip like taffy with his teeth, she did moan.

A rule in Rafe's life—well, his *former* life—was pretty simple. Get in, do what you had to (or get what you came for), and get out. Time spent thinking about things or talking them to death was time wasted. Time that usually screwed your original plan six ways from Sunday. He'd learned a long time ago that his rule wasn't just good for mob business. It worked everywhere—at the grocery store, at a bar, and definitely with women.

Or when some four-legged little forest fuck might be about to bite an ankle. Rafe still didn't trust all this animal and plant life in his new space. The concrete and steel jungle of Chicago was his comfort zone. All this thick green foliage and rustling in the shadows frankly freaked him out way more than a gang huddle in a back alley on the South Side. Not that he'd ever admit it.

Rafe knew it was time he eased back before his dick burst through his jeans. He brushed over Mollie's swollen lower lip with the side of his thumb and then licked the taste of her from it, keeping his eyes on hers the whole time. A taste was all he'd gotten, and Rafe wasn't a one-nibble type of guy. He needed more.

He hadn't hooked up with a woman since leaving Chicago, and a tune-up for his gears sounded like just what the doctor should order. Nothing complicated. Just sex and fun, seeing as how that was all Rafe could offer with his whole life up in the air.

"Go out with me."

Mollie took a step back and tightened her ponytail. "When?"

He liked that she didn't play any stupid games. No asking why or being coy. They both knew they wanted each other. "Friday night. I'll come to your town."

"Convenience and chivalry. That's a combination I can't resist."

"Give me your phone." Mollie grabbed it from the front seat of the car. Rafe put in his number. "There. The ball's in your court. If this was weird, you can walk away, no questions asked. If you want a good time, text me where to meet you."

She stopped him with a hand on his arm. "Can I pay you for the tire change?"

Rafe was insulted for a split second before he realized she wasn't being stiffly polite. Her open smile was full of pure gratitude, like she actually thought it was a hardship to twirl a lug wrench for ten minutes.

"Would you ask for a couple of Jacksons if I'd cut my finger and you wrapped it up?"

"Of course not."

"Same thing," he said with a shrug.

Mollie dipped her head in acknowledgment. "I guess you're a genuinely good guy, Rafe Maguire."

Good thing he'd turned away to pick up his jacket. Because he just about convulsed with laughter at the thought. As would all his friends back home. And his brothers. And definitely Marshal Evans.

On the other hand, it was the ex-Chicago mobster with a name he'd given up who wasn't a good guy. Maybe, just maybe, Rafe Maguire *could* be one.

"No promises," he said over his shoulder.

Chapter Two

MOLLIE STOOD WITH one hand braced on her closet door. Dressing for a date with a near stranger was surprisingly hard. The easy part, the no-thought-required part, had been slipping into a matched blue lace bra and panties set. Not because she planned to have sex tonight. That'd be hasty.

Reckless.

Stupid.

No, she'd chosen the underwear because it was the exact shade of Rafe's eyes. Minus the black flecks that gave them depth and darkness and smolder.

That was it. Rafe Maguire *smoldered.* She closed her eyes and indulged in a quick sigh at the memory. Even if their date went horribly tonight, even if their chemistry fizzled at a regular old two-top, trying to engage in chit-chat, she'd always have the memory of their roadside kiss.

That was enough to see her through a long Oregon winter.

Although she very much hoped for more . . .

A loud wolf whistle almost pierced her ears. "Lookin' hot, Mollie."

Times like this Mollie wished she spoke a foreign language. Not the two years of Latin she took to make med school an iota easier, but something relevant and meaty, like Portuguese. That way she could let fly a string of curses without anyone knowing. Especially not a certain annoying cousin who had just interrupted a rather delightful smolder rerun.

With a sigh, she grabbed a kimono from the hook on the door and tied it around herself. "Jesse, that's inappropriate. I'm your cousin."

"You're standing there in just your lady bits." The tall man-boy shrugged, stuffing his hands into the pockets of his way-too-low-riding jeans. "Thought you'd want the compliment. Since, you know, usually you look all tired after your shift."

A compliment wrapped in an insult. The specialty of seventeen-year-old hooligans, apparently. Mollie knew the kid was merely trying to push her buttons. It worked a lot more often than she let him know. She backed farther into the closet, hoping it would give him a hint to vamoose. "Saving lives isn't always a cakewalk. It is, in fact, a lot more draining than sitting on the couch playing video games all day. Just as an example."

"Did you save a life today? Did you have to crack

someone's chest? Was there lots of blood? Was there an impalement?"

Bloodthirsty little troll. Or, again, just trying to get a rise out of her. Maybe both. "I started Lucien's dad on Lipitor, which should lower his cholesterol and, long-term, help save his life."

"So, no impalement?"

"Not yet," she said menacingly, whirling around to jab at him with a hanger. It surprised a squeak out of Jesse that sounded far more childish than the man he pretended to be. And made him jump back half a foot. Mollie grinned and called it a win. "You know you're supposed to knock before coming into my room."

"Why? We're family." There was an innocence to his tone that answered her earlier question. He wasn't truly ogling her—*thank God!*—but had just been yanking her chain. Hopefully the fifteen-year age gap between them would always keep her in his mind only as the indulgent older cousin who gave him candy and Matchbox cars every time she visited.

"Yes, but not the kind of family that ends up with three-toed children." Mollie tightened her belt and sat on the bed. So much for giving out candy. Looked like it was time for another dishing out of discipline. With a stern glare—the one she used on patients who begged for antibiotics for a simple head cold—she said, "You're not a little boy anymore. Things were different when I was in med school back in Boston and we hung out on my days off. You've got to follow the rules."

He dug a scuffed sneaker toe into the pink carpet. "I wish you were still living in Boston."

Oh, no. She'd made a promise to herself not to dismiss her cousin, no matter how busy. Care and attention was the obvious prescription for turning this troubled teen around. But did he have to pick the worst possible time to need that attention?

Getting ready for a date was, okay, not half the fun, but at least an eighth of the fun. The anticipation. The ubiquitous changing of outfits and primping and, yes, dancing in front of the mirror to Katy Perry to get pumped up.

Mollie shook her head. "Not this again, Jesse. Please. Have a heart. I'm running late."

"If you'd stayed in Boston, I could still be living with you there. In a real city. With my friends. Instead, I'm stuck in this armpit of a town in Nowheresville with Gran." The words came out in a rush. It was a familiar theme she'd heard at least twenty times since he moved in a week ago. And it sure didn't get any less annoying with each repeat.

At least Mollie had the answer down pat. Practice makes perfect, after all. And Jesse was giving her a heck of a lot of practice. She patted the pink and green patchwork quilt until he sat next to her.

"You're here because you screwed up. You're here because you got kicked out of high school and your mother wants you to have another chance at graduating. Being here is wholly your fault. She sent you to be in

Gran's care. My sharing Gran's house is just temporary." Well, coming up on eight months now. But telling herself it was temporary allowed Mollie to hold on to her sanity the days when her grandmother drove her nuts. Not to mention that it wasn't ideal to be a thirty-two-year-old single woman sharing a house with two other generations. Especially tonight. When the possibility of *where* to have a hot fling burned in her brain. "I don't have time to be your guardian, no matter where I live."

The pout had disappeared from his almost always surly face. Real regret mixed with panic-widened eyes the same color as her own. "You don't want me to live with you?"

Sheesh. If there was any chance she'd had this many mood swings as a teenager, Mollie owed her gran . . . well, a lot. A trip to Bermuda. A diamond bracelet. Neither of which her hippie-dippie grandmother would particularly want, but it was all that sprang to mind in terms of good guilt-relieving presents. Neither of which she could afford, thanks to paying off her med school loans for, oh, the rest of her life.

She grabbed for his hand. And was surprised when, for once, the snarky cactus of a man-boy actually allowed her to hold on to him for more than a nanosecond. "Jesse, I love you. You could get kicked out of five schools, and I'd still love you. I'm thrilled we get to spend time with each other. But no, I don't want to be your guardian, because I wouldn't be able to do it right.

I want you to have the best possible shot at life. Right now, that's staying with Gran. And I'll keep squeeing a little each morning that I get to gulp down cereal across from your handsome mug, for as long as it lasts."

Jesse dipped his head. Squeezed her hand back for a long moment that squeezed straight through to her heart, too. Then—because God forbid the emotional sharing *last*—he wrinkled his nose and said, "Can we have something besides stupid cereal tomorrow? Maybe French toast?"

No wonder people with kids didn't have sex. Mollie couldn't even scrape together ten minutes to make herself *look* ready for sex. She stood, hoping he'd take the hint that she wanted her bedroom back. "I don't have time to prep the bread tonight. Ask your gran. Or be satisfied with waffles from me on Sunday. That's my next day off."

"'kay," Jesse muttered, all rolling eyes and hunched shoulders. As if she'd deprived him of cake on his birthday, for crying out loud.

Ruffling his hair just like she did a decade ago with his ridiculous bowl cut, Mollie added, "But if we have waffles on Sunday, I'll be teaching you to make them yourself."

He ducked and spun out of her reach. "Geez, Mollie, I'm not a cook."

"Keep getting kicked out of high schools and you might be stuck pouring waffles the rest of your life. So learn to do that, and hedge your bets by doing your homework tonight. You've got some catching up to do at this new school, I hear."

"You don't understand Friday nights at all. They're supposed to be sacred."

Yep. Sacred to the ritual of primping for a date. With the sexiest man she'd ever met. Still, Jesse had a point. "Don't get grounded, get at least a B on your trig test next week, and we'll do something fun the next Friday. Deal?"

"Deal." He slouched his way to the door before tossing out the last word. "Don't wear your blue pants. They make your ass look flat."

At least he shut the door behind him. Impossible, really, to have hoped for more. Although, she certainly hoped she'd gotten through to him about why she couldn't be his guardian . . . without stooping to disparaging his mom in the process.

Because her aunt Angela had pretty much followed the perfect formula for turning her son into a teenaged delinquent. She'd made him a latchkey kid in grade school, went out every night once Jesse hit middle school, and then remarried and ignored him in high school. Which hit way too close to home and how her own mother abandoned her, come to think of it. Mollie started to scrub at the stress pounding in her temples, until she remembered the half-hour wrestling match with the flatiron.

It was okay. She could get this night back on track.

Starting with pumping Rachel Platten's "Fight Song" at full volume. Scrabbling in her ceramic jewelry box with the ballerina on top for a funky ring of interwoven silver threads. And thinking about Rafe some more. Rafe of the smoldering stare and the wonderfully oversized biceps—which, as a doctor, she was clinically able to state.

Mollie danced from her iPhone back over to the closet, hung up her robe, and tossed three shirts in a row onto the bed. They all had potential. Maybe. Sort of. The problem was that she'd spent the last ten years in scrubs during med school and residency, and yoga pants and hoodies when studying. Which was about ninety-nine percent of her life.

Rats.

Getting asked out on Wednesday for a Friday date and accepting it on Thursday via text hadn't left her any time to forage in her friends' closets for something sexy. And borrowing from Gran was out of the question.

Not because she was seventy-three.

But because everything that came from Gran's bedroom reeked of pot. Pot that the older woman grew, cooked with, and sold. Which was yet another problem on Mollie's plate. Hard to feel okay about moving out when the "responsible adult" in charge of Jesse was often more than half-stoned.

The door snicked open with zero warning. Again. "Mollie, would you be a dear and run Jesse to the store? The batteries in the remote just died."

"You don't keep batteries in the house?" The only

thing that stayed the same with Oregon weather was that it could be counted on to change. Or so her older patients delighted in telling her on an almost daily basis. Funny how her patients in Chicago used to say exactly the same thing. Still, storms came in off the ocean all the time. Electricity came and went at will during those storms, with so many trees crowding up against power lines. Batteries were, well, common sense.

Oh. *There* was her problem. Ex-Gunnery Sergeant Norah Vickers had left common sense behind the day she resigned her commission in the Navy after being grievously injured. She'd lost her right hand in a shipboard bombing off the coast of Libya and subsequently took up every woo-woo, half-baked trend that hit her. This no-battery thing must be the latest one.

The older woman gave a brisk shake of her head. It set the mostly gray hair streaked with brown and white tumbling over her shoulders. Streaked because hair dye was "full of toxic chemicals." Or so said the woman who inhaled a hand-rolled joint at least twice a day, every day.

"Absolutely not. They dull my aura. Unless they're being used and behind a casing, it simply isn't worth the drain on my personal vibrational energy to have them around."

"Gran, they're so weak that it takes two of them to power a vibrator. I really think you're worked up over nothing."

"Nothing is right, as I'll continue to not keep unused batteries in my house."

Mollie tossed another shirt onto the bed. She'd lived with her grandmother on and off since the age of three, which meant she knew it wasn't worth wasting her time to argue about whatever new weirdness the woman adopted. Mollie never won. And she loved her gran way too much to seriously argue with her. No matter how nutso bonkers her latest theory might be.

"Fine. But I can't drive Jesse to the store."

"Well, I can't drive him. I've got bingo."

She should've guessed. Gran was wearing her good prosthetic, the one that actually looked like a hand instead of her other super useful pincer. Bingo night had always been sacred to Norah. Sacred to most residents of Bandon, in fact. Small-town people had to make their own fun. Not that Mollie saw bingo as fun, but she certainly wouldn't rain on her gran's parade.

She had no trouble raining on her cousin's, though. Jesse's license was suspended. Yanked for a laundry list of offenses. Minor, but still things that deserved punishment. He's supposed to suffer a little from being without it, not simply use his relatives as his on-call chauffeurs. "He'll live."

Norah twitched her full, pleated fuchsia skirt in a sure sign of disappointment. A signal she thought Mollie was being all uptight and conformist. It was a back and forth between them as habitual as breathing. "You are aware that it's Friday night, dear?"

"Yes." Her hands fell to slap against her bare thighs in exasperation. "I'm well aware, as I have a date to which both you and Jesse seem intent on making me either show up late or naked."

"Hmm." Norah paced a semicircle on the bare pine floorboards, clearly zeroing in on Mollie's obvious *please fuck me* lingerie. Then she gave an approving nod. "Those could both work in your favor. Depending on the man."

"This isn't a show-up-naked sort of date." Not that she'd complain if they got there sooner rather than later. Her self-imposed *no dating potential patients* rule had left her in a serious dry spell. It was no coincidence she knew just how many batteries it took to keep a vibrator going. She'd already turned down all the eligible local men fifteen years ago. And it just seemed weird to contemplate getting frisky with a tourist who might get sick and need to see Mollie as a professional, instead of someone who filled out a lacy bra well. Mollie was in desperate need of a night out, a few laughs, and a questing hand down her shirt. Rafe looked like just the man for the job. "It's a first date."

"So?" Norah slowly moved her left arm in a circle. At least five bracelets of different colored crystals clinked down to her wrist. "Is he not attractive enough to deserve your beauteous nudity?"

Oh, crap. Sure, her gran was able and willing to have frank conversations about dating and sex any day of the week. Which freaked Mollie out no less now than it had when she'd been a teenager. But this felt like something more than frank. Especially coupled with the blown-wide pupils. "Gran, are you high right now?"

Another slow wave of her hand. "I'm just taking the edge off. It's Friday night, after all."

"So you say." Talk about a crappy behavior model for the angry and impressionable Jesse. It was time to put her foot down, even if it meant delaying the big outfit decision. Maybe she'd tell Rafe exactly *why* she'd stood, mostly naked, in her closet for half an hour. Or at least keep it in her back pocket in case conversation lagged at dinner. "You know what? You're not driving to bingo. Go call Ruth and tell her to swing by and get you on the way."

With a mischievous eyebrow waggle, Norah said, "Nice try, spoilsport. But I'm not on her way."

Great. Norah was high, playful, and stubborn. Jesse was moody and sullen. Mollie wanted to toss their words back at both of them and point out that *she* deserved a Friday night, too. With exaggerated patience, she put a hand in the small of her grandmother's back and steered her toward the door.

"Bandon is small. You live exactly one block out of her way, and less than a mile from bingo. I think she can handle the hit to her gas tank of picking you up."

"You think you're so smart."

"Because you raised me to believe in myself. Plus, I have half a wall of diplomas that sort of bolsters that belief."

"Smart-ass." But that was pride, rather than heat, in her tone.

Mollie couldn't help but grin. "You raised me to be *that* way, too."

"I don't think I raised you to strut around in the altogether. Why aren't you wearing clothes? You know we're sharing the house with a boy."

The woman ran hot and cold on propriety. It'd make Mollie laugh if she wasn't so darned frustrated. And late. "Yes, I know, Gran. Trust me when I tell you that I want to get dressed more than anything. But I can't find the right outfit."

Norah whirled around, dug in the far recesses of the closet, and then triumphantly shook a dress at her. It was forest green and made of a fuzzy jersey that clung in all the right places. In other words, it was perfect. "You wore this when you flew home for Lucien's engagement party three years ago. And singlehandedly broke up their engagement."

How did she remember that? More importantly, how did she know exactly where it was in Mollie's closet, when Mollie didn't even know? Not that she'd ask, in case Gran claimed the dress itself "gave off an aura." That'd result in an eye roll big enough to sprain her ocular muscles, which would make her late and give her a lazy eye. Every man's dream date.

Meanwhile, she had to defend herself. Again. Since nobody, not even her own flesh and blood, evidently believed it possible that she and Lucien could be BFFs without sharing some deep, dark desire for each other.

"I merely explained to Lucien that Brittney was only in it for his bank account, and not for his better-than-average physique and love of kayaking. That was my job as his best friend. Their breakup was all his idea."

"Tomato, tomahtoh," Norah said with yet another annoying hand wave. But then she hinged forward to buss Mollie on the cheek. "Have fun tonight. You deserve it." Then she was out the door in a swirl of skirts that left a strong scent of pot in her wake.

Mollie grabbed for her phone. Her thumbs whizzed over the keyboard.

I could be working at a prestigious hospital and sipping champagne on the 95th floor of the Hancock Building. But I moved back home. Where my non-leg-shaving grandmother has better fashion sense stoned than I do dead sober. My cousin thinks I don't want to spend time with him. And there's only diet ginger ale in my glass. Fuck my life.

Lucien's response was swift.

Not your whole life. You just need to get laid.

Although she agreed, Mollie couldn't let him get away with saying that.

> Did you forget that your best friend is of the female persuasion? Because we don't consider sex to be the be-all and end-all solution like you men do.

She snagged a wide brown belt and knee-high boots to finish the outfit. Once dressed, she checked for his answer.

> You ought to at least try it. If you pick the right guy, you might be pleasantly surprised at its efficacy. Take two orgasms and call me in the morning, Dr. Vickers.

What sort of doctor would she be if she didn't at least *try following* the recommended treatment?

Chapter Three

716 Spruce Lane, 7:00 p.m.
Mood on the porch—too frigging nervous

RAFE BRACED ONE hand on Mollie's doorjamb. This was his first date in his new persona. Hell, it was his first date in any of his assumed personas. Everything had been too weird, too different to try it before. Plus, it didn't seem right to seriously date someone when he had to lie about everything in his life. At thirty-one, he knew anything deeper than a hookup required actual sharing and communication. Hard to do with a made-up backstory, career, and his fifth fake name.

But the marshal insisted they start making the rounds. Loners stood out in a small town. Kellan had pointed out that Delaney was all but pimping them out, and she came back with the rebuttal that dating was a way to put down roots. All three of the Maguire brothers made gagging noises at that thought, because she'd made it sound like she was ordering them to get married. At which point she'd rolled her eyes and slammed out of the room.

It was pretty much how all their interactions with the marshal ended.

No way was he getting married. Rafe wouldn't saddle a woman with his shitstorm of a life, but he could play at following the rules to get the marshal off their backs. Dating? Nope. Sexcapades with a hot doctor? You bet . . . and the marshal wouldn't know the difference. Rafe would do just about anything to keep them all in the WITSEC program, and Delaney's advice on how to fit in boiled down to acting normally. Well, non-mobster normal. And normal for a thirty-one-year-old guy meant spending time with a hot woman.

So he wouldn't worry about blowing his cover. Wouldn't worry about how to make up lies on the fly if Mollie asked a question he hadn't prepped for. Not that he'd prepped for many, since Rafe had never been one to do his homework, even back in the day. He wouldn't worry about what trouble Flynn and Kellan might be getting into while he was trying to get it on. Because the depths of Mollie's green eyes would be a more than good enough distraction from all that.

Eyes were his weakness. Yeah, Rafe appreciated tits and ass as much as any other guy. But he'd spent a bunch of years doing business in strip clubs and all the naked parts flashing eventually became a sort of flesh-colored wallpaper to him. A good, deep set of eyes a man could drown in, though? That was something that always caught his interest. And the pretty doctor had a pair of eyes he could stare into for hours.

While running his hands over her very fine ass. Because he still had a dick, after all.

It only took two knocks before the door flew open. Mollie nipped out and shut it behind her in a flurry.

Rafe chuckled. "That hot for me already, huh?"

"No, I . . . I mean, yes, but . . ." Mollie bit her upper lip and shook her head. It sent her hair spilling down onto the creamy skin of her chest and the darkness against all the white turned him on like a match strike to his libido. Without even touching her yet.

Yeah, he'd clearly waited too long to have a woman beneath him.

If he played his cards right, that'd change. Tonight.

"How about we start over?" Rafe snaked an arm around her waist, dragging her up to her toes. Mollie's neck tilted back the second before he pressed his lips to hers.

Hot.

Hard.

A kiss to ground her in the moment. A kiss to clear out whatever had fuzzed her head on the way out the door and get her focused solely on him.

The kiss started out being for Mollie. But it didn't take more than a nip at her soft lower lip, sinking his teeth into it until she pressed even harder against him, before Rafe knew the kiss was for his benefit, too. A way to prove that whatever had flared between them on the side of the road wasn't an accident. That it wasn't a one-time thing. A way to prove to himself that it'd be worth sitting through an undoubtedly painful burger-and-beer's worth of small talk to get to the dessert of her sweet lips.

Rafe palmed her ass. God, it was sweet; firm and round and he couldn't wait to see it naked and facing him while she knelt on a bed with all that dark hair streaming down her pale back. Just touching it wasn't enough. So Rafe squeezed, molding the lusciously round globe with his fingers until Mollie's hips tilted forward. Then he felt her leg twine up and around the back of his.

Yeah. This was definitely a two-way super highway of lust.

That was the signal he needed to back off. So he eased his tongue out of her mouth with a final, teasing swipe along the smooth skin on the back of her lower lip. Her leg slid back down. Rafe took her hand, smiling right into those eyes full of secrets and sex. "Hi, Doc. You look great."

"You do, too." The blatant admiration in her gaze made him glad he'd pulled out a shirt with a collar. Glad he'd made Kellan iron it, too.

"Ready to go?"

Her gaze skittered to the door, and then back to him with an almost audible screech. "You have no idea."

Instead of leading her off the porch, Rafe froze. Because he didn't like the tone of her voice. Lots of unhappiness there. He didn't know her living situation, but if she had a dad or a roommate who was treating her like shit, they'd have to start the date over for a *third* time. Right after he went inside and made clear the rules of respecting a woman to whoever sent her running out the door to him.

Rafe curled his hand around her elbow. He put his mouth right at her ear and said in a low, harsh growl, "If there's a problem, Doc, you can tell me. And I promise you I'll handle it."

"What kind of a problem?"

"Anything. Anything that you don't like. I can make it right."

After a heavy silence, Mollie laughed. Laughed and laughed like he'd just told her the joke about the three-legged gigolo, the virgin, and the horse. She laughed so hard that she leaned her whole body into him. As though she'd fall over from the sheer force of whatever the hell had a grip on her funny bone.

Eventually the laughter tapered off to giggles, and then whimpering little sighs that made Rafe think of sex. Made him wonder how many more outdoors, over-the-clothes make out sessions they'd have before he teased them out of her indoors, without laughter or clothes.

"Thank you for the offer, Rafe. It's very gallant of you. But I don't think you're equipped."

Pride and anger flared up in his chest with the fire of heartburn. Nobody in Chicago would dare question his manhood like that. Dare to question if he was the one to get the job done. Rafe was the guy who *got* things done. Always. The go-to, the fixer.

So where did she get off laughing at him?

"Believe me when I say I can take care of anything you need." The promise tore out of him, low and gravelly.

It sure as hell wiped the smile off her face. But Mollie didn't look intimidated. No, she licked that kiss-swollen bottom lip of hers like he'd given her the sort of ideas that drenched her panties.

Huh.

Rafe hadn't meant it that way. Seeing as how he was trying to be on his best, normal-guy behavior.

Didn't make it any less true, though. No matter which way she interpreted it.

She laid a hand on the stiff fabric of his sleeve. "I don't question your abilities, Rafe. Not when it comes to showing me a good time, or changing spark plugs. In fact, I'm more than eager to put that promise of yours to the test. I just don't think you're the man to handle my current problem." Mollie drew them down the steps and onto the gravel driveway before continuing with a quick look over her shoulder at the house. "It's a seventeen-year-old juvenile delinquent of a cousin who moved in with me and my gran a couple of weeks ago."

Now he got why she'd bolted out of the house. Probably trying to outrace the shitty attitude that poured off teenaged boys more strongly than cheap cologne. Rafe snorted. Because this one was a piece of cake. "I've got two younger brothers. That I more or less raised."

"Oh. Then I take it all back." With a tug at his sleeve, she said, "We can walk to dinner. It's just a few blocks, if you're up for it."

That seriously cut down on the possibility of a post-dinner car fuck. But hey, he was stuck here indefinitely. Rafe had all the time in the world to seal the deal. Didn't mean he couldn't plant a sex seed in her brain, though. He draped an arm around her shoulder, letting his fingers dangle just above that exposed crescent of breast that he hungered to touch. Then he said, "I've got the stamina for *whatever* you want to do, Doc."

HOLY CRAP. RAFE'S voice rasped like a saw cutting through a plaster cast. It sliced through her reserve and any hesitation just as easily. Mollie had dithered about texting him to agree to the date for a whole day. What would they talk about? She was so darned rusty at this whole dating thing. What kind of connection did she have with a stranger who changed her tire?

But she'd been *yearning* to meet a stranger. To talk to someone who didn't already know her life story, who hadn't held the same opinion of her for decades. And then she'd thought about the heat of their kiss. Thought about how she hadn't dated since moving back to Bandon, and had been too busy at the hospital in Chicago for anything more than a quick grope in the on-call room for months before that. After that, Mollie's thumbs couldn't text Rafe back fast enough.

He'd caught her off guard tonight. The rough, lust-wrapped-in-leather guy she'd fantasized about had been replaced by a powerfully sleek man. Dark and wavy hair slicked back, all those bunched muscles hidden beneath a starched gray dress shirt and slacks, Rafe looked like a corporate pirate. All business, all polished, and completely different.

Until the kiss on her porch. Then she'd recognized him. *Then* she'd known, without a doubt, that they had a connection. And yes, his hotter-than-hell innuendos were exactly what the doctor ordered.

Mollie almost skipped as they started down the street. Not just because that might jiggle Rafe's fingers into grazing her boob. She had a shiny new person to talk to, to learn all about. The ubiquitous nightly fog hadn't rolled in off the ocean yet, making for a crisp, clear twilight. A snowy white owl hooted as it glided past—Gran swore they were a good luck omen—and the piney scent of Rafe's cologne made all her nerve endings quiver to attention.

Sex was on her horizon. Sex that she had no doubt would be off-the-charts amazing. The more she thought about it, the more Mollie had to admit Lucien was right. She did need to get laid. Desperately.

But first there was small talk and dinner to get through. Which couldn't all be about flirting and sex, or she'd internally combust.

"If you got your brothers to adulthood safe and sound, maybe I should pick your brain on what to do with Jesse."

Rafe choked out a half laugh. "Safe and sound. That's a good one. Flynn will bust a gut over it."

"Why, what happened? Lots of broken bones or something?"

"Uh . . . it's not important." Then, more firmly, almost as if convincing himself, he added, "They're fine now, which is all that matters."

That was oddly evasive. Who didn't like telling stories that threw their little brothers under the bus? What the heck had happened in the Maguire family? "Then tell me how to help Jesse."

Rafe hip-checked her. "Keep him busy."

That was . . . succinct. There was an entire shelf devoted to decoding the teenaged brain at the bookstore, and Rafe distilled it down to three words? Even the clinical description of how to excise a hangnail took more words. There had to be more.

"That's it? That's the great secret to getting a kid back on the straight and narrow? One who cut so many classes he got expelled from his last high school? Who got his license yanked? Who shoplifted undoubtedly many more times than the three he got caught?"

Rafe swatted away her objections like they were sand gnats. "Kids that age are like puppies. You need to feed them, train 'em, and wear them out so they don't have any energy left to cause trouble."

Okay. The stretched-out version did make sense. Mollie just didn't know how to put it into action. She leaned into Rafe's side. It was a relief to unburden her worries to someone who sounded like he'd gone through something similar.

"We sweet-talked the high school here into accepting him. He's smart, really smart, so it doesn't come close to wearing him out. And the rest of the time he sits on the couch playing video games until Gran or I come home."

"You feel guilty about leaving him alone after school." It was a statement, not a question. One that held zero judgment. Clearly Rafe had walked in her shoes. Even if he wouldn't fill her in on the details.

"I really do. He's not even my responsibility, legally, but I do. Gran runs a shop, so she can't cut out early. I help pick up the slack with errands, but it isn't the same as actually *helping* to turn Jesse around."

"Is he worth the effort? Or too far gone already?"

Some people might've taken offense at the question. But Mollie had lived in two big metropolises, watched the evening news, seen the GSWs and strung-out meth heads. She knew exactly what Rafe meant, and respected him for asking so matter-of-factly.

At the corner, she turned them onto the main street into Old Town. Even on a Friday night, traffic wasn't busy. That's what came of living in a town of three thousand, give or take the tourists.

"Jesse's a good kid. I see flashes of his inner self poking through the snark more often than not. But he hasn't been here long enough to make friends. Not to mention being grounded for all the aforementioned, ah, poor choices. I think he deserves the chance for a fresh start. To turn himself around. To make better choices and discover that they fit him. Everyone deserves that."

Rafe got a hitch in his step at her words. He dropped his arm off of her shoulder and Mollie wondered if he'd dismiss her as hopelessly naïve. But as he recovered and moved forward smoothly, he said, "I could help him."

"You? How?" His offer shocked her. Because nobody else *had* offered. The entire town knew the circumstances behind Jesse's move here. Knew he'd been thrown out of school and—albeit briefly—thrown in jail. So now, they all seemed to be scared to death of Jesse, which just alienated the poor kid even more.

"There's always scut work to be done around a garage. Jesse could earn a little money. That'd give him some self-worth. He could start to learn a trade. Not that he has to be a mechanic, but it's something that could maybe help him pay for college down the road. It'd keep him busy and be worthwhile."

"I can't believe you'd be willing to do that. For someone you don't even know."

Rafe lifted her hand to his lips and pressed a soft kiss on her knuckles. "You said he needs a second chance. That's a good enough reason." Then he looked at her from beneath half-lidded eyes that made her think of tousled sheets and dark desires. Desires she wanted to play out with Rafe more and more. "Well, that and it might get me in good with his smoking-hot cousin."

Mollie laughed. But also sent him a sideways glance

full of promise. Hopefully. Maybe it just looked like she was shifty. Yes. It was *definitely* past the time to get down and dirty with a man. Her moves were waaaay past rusty.

"You know what? It just might."

As he started to lower her hand, Rafe twisted it to look at the underside of her wrist. "That's an interesting tattoo. A caduceus, right?"

Jerking her hand away, she said, "Absolutely not. It's the Rod of Asclepius, which is the true symbol of medicine."

"Hey, I'm no doctor, but I know about a caduceus. Everyone does."

"You *think* you do." Mollie absolutely loved sharing the real story behind her tattoo. "The U.S. Army Medical Corps put the caduceus on their uniforms. But it was a mistake. One that nobody wanted to own up to, so it stuck."

"Government bureaucracy fucked things up, huh? There's a shocker."

She traced the purple staff with the single blue snake winding around it. "The Greek god Asclepius was associated with healing—he had a whole cult. His name is even in the first line of the original Hippocratic Oath. A whole group of us went out and got this done the night of med school graduation."

"Symbolic." Now Rafe traced the design with the blunt tip of his finger. It sent goose bumps rising from her wrist right up to her clavicle. "You inked yourself, to last for a lifetime, because you'll always be a doctor."

It was so nice that he got it. That it wasn't a status symbol to flash, but a deeply personal reminder. "Exactly." Linking her fingers through his, she asked, "Do you have any tattoos?"

"Yeah."

Oooh. That meshed perfectly with the whole bad boy vibe he had going when they met. "What are they?"

Rafe smirked down at her. "Telling's not as fun as showing."

"True." Her mouth watered at the thought. Where could they be on his oh-so-ripped body? "So . . . I showed you mine. Now you show me yours."

"Nope."

"Why not?"

His full lips parted, then closed, as if the wrong words had started to come out. Then he firmed them into a thin line and whizzed a side glance her way. "Once the clothes come off? What happens next will be a marathon. I need fuel for that. Burgers. Fries. Hopefully washed down with some real beer. None of that light and fruity shit."

A marathon, huh? Now her mouth wasn't the only place moisture was gathering. Mollie stopped, then pointed across the street. "Good thing that's our destination, then. The Gorse Lounge. It has the best burgers in town, and enough different beers to keep the tourists happy."

Instead of charging forward, Rafe winced. "Is there a second-best burger joint we could try?"

"Why?"

"My middle brother's the new bartender there. It'd be weird to have him watching us."

"Rafe, there are only three thousand people who live in Bandon full-time. Trust me when I say that everyone is always watching you." Then a horrible possibility hit her, with the strength of a bone-splitter right to her sternum. "Don't tell me that you live *here*? In Bandon?"

"Yeah." He hooked his thumb toward the water. "About a mile that way."

Except the last time he pointed directionally, on the highway, it had been to indicate that he lived in Coos Bay. Not Bandon. Which was a big part of why she'd agreed to a date with him. "You said you lived *up* the road!"

"Everything looks the same here. Trees. Sand. Beach. Whatever." Rafe shrugged. Clearly he didn't comprehend what a big deal this was to her.

Well, she'd sure as heck spell it out for him.

"I don't want to date a local." In a measured tone, Mollie calmly laid out her case. "People will tell you about me, once they know we're dating. They all have the same one-dimensional view of me because they helped raise me. You won't get to form your own opinion. Nothing will be new and shiny."

Rafe curled his fingers beneath her chin, and held on to it with his thumb. Then those piercing blue eyes locked onto hers. "Sweetheart, I don't want to date you. I just want to screw you."

Her mouth opened, but Mollie couldn't figure out which words to say. *Oh? What the hell? Are you always this rude on a first date?* If she'd been in a soap opera, her character probably would've hauled off and slapped him for being so blatantly ballsy. If her best friend was a woman instead of a man, Mollie might get the advice to knee him in the balls for being so aggressive.

But . . . that statement alone showed him to be more honest, more forthright than the last handful of men she'd dated.

Snagging a diamond solitaire wasn't on her to-do list for this month, or even this year.

Having some no-stress orgasms *was* on her to-do list for the month. If not sooner.

If they weren't *really* dating, then she wouldn't have to worry about Rafe leaving her. If they weren't *really* together, there was zero potential for heartbreak. Which the shrink she'd been required to see during her psych rotation said was Mollie's biggest issue. So avoiding that was just clinically smart. Just sex was the smartest thing she could do for her psyche.

Plus? Technically? Rafe was still new and shiny. Probably not too tainted by small-town gossip about her yet. He didn't seem like the type to hang out at her gran's coffee shop eating up the local dirt as fast as the donuts.

All the mental dithering boiled down to an attempt at being super casual. In a low murmur, she said, "That's an unusual and borderline insulting statement."

"It's the truth. Dating sounds like two people who

want to work toward a future together. I just want a little fun. Straight talk? It's all I'm up for." Then he lifted his thumb to brush the pad of it along her bottom lip. "And I think you want to screw me, too."

Damn it. The man was right.

"I'm tempted." When a smug smirk broke across his face, Mollie added, "But I won't do a one-night stand. I don't need roses or daily phone calls or a romantic getaway to Portland. I would, however, accept a friends-with-benefits arrangement. A fun, no-strings, no-expectations fling."

"Works for me. Your place or mine?"

"Neither." She crossed the street, knowing Rafe would follow. They were equally caught in each other's nets. "We're going to the Gorse for dinner."

"Ah. So I can fuel up?"

Mollie had to admire his one-track mind. Or was it perseverance? Either way, she had a feeling it'd play to her advantage once they got naked. "No. Just dinner tonight. So I can decide if we can actually be friends. I want to be able to relax and be comfortable with you, or the sex won't be as good."

"Let's get something straight." Rafe slammed a hand against the rough-hewn wooden door to the bar before she could open it. "The sex—which *will* happen—is going to be fucking phenomenal."

His words chased a shiver up one side of her spine and back down the other. A good shiver. The kind that moved her body right into the inner hunch of his chest and shoulders before her brain noticed. Mollie curved a palm along the thick ridge of muscles leading to his neck. "Is that a promise?"

"It's a damned fact." He spat the words out. Like he was ticked off that she even had to ask. "The heat between us is obvious. And that's with clothes on. When I get you out of yours, and that tight body comes to life under my hands and my tongue and I get my cock in you, then we're both going to explode."

Wow.

If Rafe lived up to even half of his own hype, Mollie would be *fine* with just sex. Beyond fine.

Fantastic.

Chapter Four

The Gorse, 10:30 p.m.
Mood in the pisser—horny as hell

THE BATHROOM DOOR creaked open and Rafe's whole body tightened as he looked up from washing his hands. He knew he didn't have any reason to be on alert 24/7 like back in Chicago. But old habits died hard. Especially habits that kept you alive and without *too* many bullet wound scars.

"Hey." Flynn leaned against the stall door, arms crossed.

It looked like he'd come in here to chat. Which was weird, since it was 1) a bar bathroom, and 2) they fucking lived together. Easy enough to talk at home. Who wanted to inhale the scent of urinal cakes any longer than absolutely necessary?

On the other hand, Flynn didn't *chat*. Not since leaving Chicago, anyway. His now surly, silent brother didn't initiate conversations with him or Kellan. So Rafe tossed him a softball. "Thanks for the beer pick. Tasted like beer, instead of seventeen different kinds of fruit."

"Did you catch the name of it? Sierra was supposed to tell you."

"The waitress?" She'd probably tried. Rafe had been pretty focused on flirting the pants off of Mollie. "I didn't pay attention."

"Rogue Dead Guy Ale." Flynn smirked. "Seemed like a good fit for you."

"Very funny." And it was. The gallows humor was the first hint of Flynn's old personality coming back. Rafe was happy to have it aimed at him as long as it kept coming. "Remember, the point of all this is to avoid getting whacked. The Maguires are not dead men walking."

Flynn shrugged. "Time will tell."

So . . . willing to crack jokes, but not willing to actually have hope. Flynn was in one hell of a six-month sulk. Rafe was equal parts pissed about it, and desperate to find a way to knock Flynn *out* of it. What was the point of going to these lengths to save him if his brother didn't *live* his life anymore?

Problem for another day. Rafe had a hot brunette waiting for him, and Flynn was still on the clock. His piss-poor attitude wasn't going to change tonight. "What's so urgent you had to follow me back here?"

"Are you having fun? On your date?"

"It's not a date," Rafe said automatically. He waved

his hand to get the paper towel machine to spit out more than one sheet, which barely dried a single finger.

Flynn straightened, a surprising smile lighting up his face. "You bought her dinner. You've been fucking her with your eyes all night. What about that isn't a date?"

The fact they both swore it wouldn't be. "Hanging out." He one-shotted the paper towel into the trash. "We're going for the friends-with-benefits thing."

"Sounds like dating—without the commitment. It also sounds too good to be true."

Beautiful and down-to-earth, smart, funny—yeah, he'd pegged Dr. Mollie Vickers as too good to be true from the first moment he'd laid eyes on her. Consciously echoing his brother, Rafe said, "Time will tell."

"Funny."

Rafe met his brother's gaze in the mirror. And looking at him—aside from Flynn's way shorter hair, was a lot like, well, looking in a mirror. "What do you care about Mollie?"

"It looked like you guys were having a good time."

"Perv. You were watching us?"

"Just glanced up a couple of times in between pouring drafts." Flynn crossed his arms. Shifted his weight back and forth in the running shoes he wore to stand behind the bar all night. "Seemed like you were having fun. Something that's been in short supply for half a year now. I'm glad, is all. Wanted to tell you." He clapped Rafe on the side of his arm and rushed out the door.

Talk about a surprise. Flynn, making an effort to be

nice. Making an effort for two whole minutes to act like a brother again.

Whaddya know? Bandon might be good for the Maguires after all.

If it lasted . . .

MOLLIE LOOKED UP at the stars winking between the tall canopies of pine trees. The night was clear. The sea air was soft. It was all too romantic for words. How on earth was a determined-not-to-have-sex woman supposed to resist jumping the hot hunk walking her home?

Desperate to find a non-sexy topic, she said, "Your brother seemed nice."

"Flynn literally said hello and goodbye. That's one hell of an assumption you're making off of two words."

"He looks like you."

"Yeah. Kellan does, too. Hard to tell who's who in the baby pictures." Then Rafe stopped, shook his head, and winced.

"What's wrong?"

"Nothing."

What was it with men thinking that *not* sharing made them seem tough? When it took a lot more strength, in fact, to open up and be real? "Come on. I can tell whatever you just said upset you. What was it?"

"I, uh, remembered that all our baby pictures are gone."

"That's horrible. How did it happen?"

Another too-long beat of silence, which was weird. Almost like Rafe was figuring out what to say. "Basement flood. Scrapbooks, yearbooks—everything from our childhood is gone."

Mollie didn't have any baby pictures, either. No milestones in her life captured until she'd been left with her grandmother. But she didn't want to harp on her own regrets. Not when Rafe was still frowning and visibly bothered.

"Lucky that you're still living together. Plenty of opportunity to capture memories today."

"You're a glass-half-full person, aren't you?" Rafe reached over to hold a tree branch out of her way. He walked on the outside, too, in an old-school, gentlemanly move that impressed her.

"Not always. You see a lot of bad things happen to good people in emergency medicine. Along with some seriously bad people. So I know to find the good where I can, and glom on to it."

"I dunno, Doc. I might be too dark for you, then."

Really? This coming from the smooth operator who'd kept her laughing all through dinner? Who'd shared hilarious stories of the trouble he and his brothers used to get into as children? Who had pushed his plate back in the middle of dinner to take her hand and slowly kiss the back of each knuckle?

Rafe Maguire was no dark and tortured soul. If he was, he wouldn't be dallying in the moonlight with her. Mollie shook her head. "Nope. You may have dark spots, but I'll bet I can shine a light in and find the good parts."

Rafe stopped, bent in half, and braced his hands on his thighs. Low laughter rumbled out of him. "What's so funny?" she demanded.

"Let's just say you'd be the first person to try."

If that was true, it was just sad. "No time like the present. How about you make me a promise? When you get home, take a picture with your brothers. Something silly, with all three of you mugging for the camera. It'll start your new cache of memories."

"We're doing a night out at the Gorse tomorrow. I could make sure their beers are full of foam and blow it in their faces."

His tone said Rafe was joking, but Mollie kind of loved the idea. "That'd be adorable. But I fear it might not be worth the inevitable retribution they'd rain down on you."

"Or maybe I'll wake them up at dawn so everyone has bedhead." He tugged on that longish curl that dipped onto his forehead like Superman. "Make it really ugly."

"No chance of that. You're all so handsome, I'll bet when you post a photo on Instagram you get hit on by total strangers."

"I don't post." And he sounded deadly serious. Like it was a vow of internet silence that he'd taken.

"At all? Anywhere?"

A quick, hard shake of his head. "Social media isn't my thing. I don't need the world knowing my business."

That was kind of . . . refreshing. Mollie had sat through countless dates, dinners with friends, and even meetings where conversation ground to a halt so everyone could post a status update. Come to think of it, Rafe hadn't checked his phone once during dinner.

Mollie wanted him to check his phone. In oh, say, about an hour. Because her house loomed in front of them and she wasn't ready for whatever was bubbling between them to end. The thought of texting a hot man for fun from under the bedcovers appealed to her.

"Do you text?"

His side-eye pricked at her, it was so sharp. "I'm not Amish. Texted you about tonight, didn't I?"

That's right. She stopped on the bottom step leading up to her porch. Rested a hand on her hip and shot him a come-hither smile. "Maybe you should text me later."

His lips curled up at the corners. One eyebrow arched. Smugness rolled off him like fog off the ocean. As did interest. But Rafe played it cool. Played along. "About what?"

"I'll be mulling my review of tonight. While the Maguires are getting their drink on at the Gorse tomorrow night, I've got my very sacred biweekly girls' night. I need to figure out what kind of a grade to give you."

"I'll bet you're a grade obsessed overachiever."

She was noticing that he liked to classify things. "Rafe, I was in colleges and med school for about a billion years. You don't get through without worrying about grades."

"I never did. Found a way to work around boring things like tests and studying." He stepped closer. Put one hand up on the column above her head, giving the impression she was boxed in. Not that Mollie wanted to go *anywhere* right now. "For example, how do you feel about giving extra credit for life skills?"

A shiver of excitement danced along her nerves like a hot breeze. No, Mollie needed to self-diagnose properly. It was pure lust. "I'm open to the possibility."

Rafe put his thumb and forefinger on her chin, tilting her head a bare inch up. Her eyelids shut, and her lips parted in anticipation. Every sense revved hot—Mollie felt the sharp corner of the column against her shoulder blade. Heard the crickets' constant chirping layered below the hollow hoots of an owl. Smelled the fresh layer of cedar chips Gran had laid out in the garden this week.

But no kiss. Mollie's eyes popped back open. Yep, Rafe was right there, face shrouded in darkness, all hard planes and shadows. *Aka* soooo darn tingle-inducing. "Did you get lost on the way to my lips?"

"Sometimes it's about the journey, not the destination." The hand holding her chin moved to push a strand of hair behind her ear. But he did it in super slo-mo. The rough drag of his calloused skin up her cheek, across her cheekbone, brought goose bumps to the surface. When his fingertip barely grazed over the top of her ear, another set of goose bumps formed, this time *inside* her body.

Mollie knew it wasn't medically possible. She also knew what she felt. What Rafe *made* her feel. A sigh slipped between her lips.

Then Rafe squeezed her hip. It was a firm squeeze that wrapped his big hand around to the top of her butt. One that made her realize just how large in spread and length his fingers really were. He began an excruciatingly slow glide up her rib cage. Halfway, he flipped his hand over. So just the back of his knuckles glanced along the side of her breast.

It was enough.

It was more than enough. Mollie's eyes fluttered shut again in sheer pleasure. Rafe could take all the time he wanted if it was going to feel this bone-meltingly good. She reached out and got a handful of his shirt. Not so much because she needed to anchor herself (although she *did*, truth be told), but because she needed to touch him, too. To feel the breadth of his body beneath her fingers.

So Mollie stretched her fingers and stroked past his scapula, over as much of that ridged, taut-as-rebar trapezius as she could get to. Rafe's muscles were spectacular. As a physician, it was a fact. As a woman, he was a fantasy come true.

Another gentle pull on her ponytail tipped her head to the side. Finally, Rafe bent his neck to bring his head down to the crook right where her carotid pulse throbbed hard just beneath her skin. Lips and tongue danced in a triple step over her throat. Mollie dug her fingers into his back.

A loud squeak of the front door barely registered before Jesse's voice did. "Hey. Quit with the vampire action on my cousin."

If the column hadn't been behind her, Mollie probably would've stumbled backward in surprise. Not that he'd caught her making out. Surprise that Jesse was actually trying to watch out for her.

Rafe straightened the neckline of her dress before stepping back, hands up. "Just saying good night. No actual vein puncturing occurred."

Mollie giggled.

"Good." Jesse banged out the screen door, hands fisted on his hips in what he probably saw as an attempt to look . . . scarier? Bigger? More menacing? She loved him for the attempt. "I'm Jesse Vickers. Mollie's cousin."

"Rafe Maguire." He strode forward, hand extended, and gave Jesse a couple of hard pumps. Rafe played it straight, as respectful as if Jesse were fully grown. Guess he *did* know how to deal with teenagers. "I heard a lot about you tonight."

Just like that, Jesse's whole attempt to look like an adult faded away. His shoulders hunched, his head drooped, and his expression turned into his usual *why is the world against me* sullenness. "Geez, no. What did you tell him, Moll? Can't there be one person in this whole town who doesn't know I got kicked out of school?"

"You just shared that little nugget all by yourself, Mr. Suave." Mollie poked him in the stomach.

Mollie sure dodged that bullet. Impressive how she backfired the blame onto Jesse without revealing that she'd spilled his secret earlier. Better for the kid to take responsibility for it himself.

Rafe spread his hands, palms up, at waist level. "She said you're new here, just like me. That you'd maybe have some time to do me a favor."

"What kind of a favor?" Skepticism and the usual teenage disinterest made Jesse's tone blander than hospital cafeteria custard.

"I'm the mechanic over at Wick's Garage. We need some part-time help. No experience required. I'll teach you everything you need to know. If you could come over after school a couple of days a week, and a weekend here and there, I'd appreciate it. The owner had a heart attack, and we're backed up with work."

Ohhhh, Rafe was good. Smooth. Mollie had to hand it to him.

"Would I get paid?"

"Not enough to put away for a car of your own. Probably enough to go nuts on iTunes once a week and get a new Xbox game every so often."

Jesse straightened. Leaned his whole body toward Mollie. "Would I get to keep the money?"

Aha. He was putting the pieces together. "Ultimately, yes. But only after you hand over all the money Gran and I fronted to pay back the shopkeepers you stole from."

"I knew it. This is a punishment, isn't it? Like being grounded, but with hard work?"

Before Mollie could try and reason/negotiate/finagle/plead with him to see the upside to a job, Rafe stepped in. Literally. He took the three steps to the top of the porch to tower over Jesse. Then he crossed his arms over his wide chest.

"It's not a punishment. It's a second chance. A chance to show your family that you can be trusted. That you're responsible. I've had a few of these myself. When someone gives you a second chance? That's a freaking *gift*. It'll be the first step to showing your maturity if you're smart enough to take it."

Jesse looked back and forth between them a couple of times. Mollie held her breath. The job offer was all Rafe's—his idea and his burden to bear. She wouldn't interfere. Finally, Jesse jammed his hands into his jeans pockets. "Okay."

"Okay, what?" Even in the dim porch light, it was easy to tell that Rafe was staring him down. Waiting for more. And that he wouldn't accept anything less than the proper answer.

After taking a big sigh, her cousin took his hands right back out. He extended one to Rafe. "Okay, I'll be happy to take the job. And thank you for giving me the opportunity." They shook on it.

"What else?" Rafe prompted.

Jesse turned to Mollie. "Thanks for letting me do this. I guess, in the long run, it'll be better than just being grounded." He surprised her with a fast side hug, then went inside.

"Well done."

"Don't jinx it. We had one conversation. In front of a family member he loves and respects. When he walks into the garage on Monday, there's no telling how things will go."

"Keep your expectations low," she warned.

"This, from the glass-half-full woman?"

"I *try* to see the good in everyone. That doesn't mean that I turn a blind eye to the bad parts."

"Speaking of eyes, I'd bet you another dinner at the Gorse that your cousin has his eyes glued to whatever crack you've got in your blinds." He went back down the steps.

Rafe was undoubtedly right. That meant their night had to be at an end. Mollie looked at her watch. She'd planned to wrap it up at a decent hour anyway, since she had to be at the hospital early. "You got me home before I turned into a pumpkin," she joked.

"Fat chance." Rafe snagged her by the waist and lifted her against his chest with just the one arm. "You're definitely the kind and beautiful princess in this story." He kissed her, hard and fast, and then set her back down. "G'night, Doc."

That compliment caught her totally off guard.

Mollie stared as he walked off into the darkness. Their can-we-be-friends test dinner had gone . . . well.

So well, that it rivaled a lot of *actual* dates that she'd had. Which concerned her more than a little. But that was a worry for another night, when her lips weren't still tender and warm from his.

Add a very fun dinner to the stellar kissing and masterful handling of her cousin, and Rafe Maguire had just earned himself an *A+* for the night.

She couldn't wait to see what his next move would be.

Chapter Five

Coquille Point, 11:45 p.m.
Mood on the beach—still horny as hell

RAFE KNEW THREE ways to deal with stress. Screw it off, drink it off, or run it off.

Options one and two were out.

His erection had never fully subsided since Mollie slammed out of her front door earlier that night. If he could screw her, if he was inside her right now, everything would be fine. Instead, he felt like his skin was three sizes too small. His dick felt four sizes too big. All of his stress came from the fact that they weren't naked and sweaty together.

Because he wanted this woman with an intensity Rafe couldn't explain.

Couldn't ignore, either.

If he drank at the Gorse, Flynn would shoot him the same mocking looks he'd thrown all during their dinner. If he drank at home, Kellan would tease the living shit out of him for having blue balls so bad they'd sent him straight into a bottle. Then he'd be forced to beat up the little shit, and that'd make for more stress.

So he'd thrown on sweats and a hoodie and hit the beach. Which was weird at night. Spooky. Having that unease hang over him didn't fit Rafe one damn bit. He used to run the streets of Chicago at three in the morning. He knew the slap of rubber against concrete. The stale tang of spilled beer on the sidewalk. The way shadows flickered at the edge of an alley if someone was dumb enough to try and jump him. The squeal of tires and skitter of rats and harsh stench of whatever the homeless and meth heads burned in trash cans to stay warm. There was a comfort to his world. Rafe was never on edge while running. He owned those streets, and they calmed him.

Now? To himself—and nobody else, *ever*—he'd admit the truth.

The beach at night freaked him the fuck out. Rafe was a city guy, through and through. He didn't know the outdoors. Didn't know how to reason with it or coerce it and he damn well didn't trust it.

He ran at the water's edge where the sand was packed flat. It crunched underfoot, almost like snow. The surf hissed as it advanced and retreated with every three steps. Fog—mist?—hung at kneecap level, swirling around him like short ghost farts. And the whole damn ocean was to his left. Dark. Loud. Unknowable. Anything could lurch out of it and swallow him whole. Or worse, gnaw on him for a while as he drowned.

Yeah, it was time to pick up the pace. He wouldn't quit. Wouldn't let the great outdoors send him running indoors screaming like a girl. And he sure as hell wouldn't text Delaney and offer her five hundred dollars to move them to a city. A real city. A city where the only noise came from traffic and drunks.

But he *would* run faster. Give up on trying to de-stress and just run his normal three miles and call it a win. All this new-to-him nature stuff would take some getting used to. Like how running on sand made his calves burn with the added effort. Which just pissed Rafe off more. Nature wouldn't beat him. It could try to beat him down, but it wouldn't win. Nobody beat Rafe Maguire.

"Hey, stranger."

Rafe did not scream. Another win for the night. He did, however, slam on the brakes and drop into a fighting crouch, weight forward and ready to whale on the dark shadow materializing around a giant-ass rock formation. "Who the hell are you?"

"Does it matter? Seeing as how you don't know anyone in town? I could tell you I'm General David Petraeus and you'd have to believe me."

Rafe unclenched his fists, let them fall to his sides. The man in the ball cap and fatigues moved stiffly, favoring one side. Plus, he looked to be over sixty. Overall, way easier to handle than potential ocean monsters on the attack.

"Being new in town doesn't make me an idiot. Petraeus? He was the one in that sex scandal who had to resign from leading the CIA. You're not him."

It wasn't that Rafe watched the news all that often. But when the FBI took credit for bringing down the director of their crosstown rival, agents talked about it. FBI agents, marshals, cops all talked about it, even a handful of years later. And Rafe had spent a god-awful amount of time in planes and cars and boring-ass rooms with all of the above for the past six months.

The man limped closer. Lifted the brim of his cap to give Rafe an assessing look. "You just might be worth my time to get to know."

Skulking beachcomber weirdo.

At least, that's what Rafe *wanted* to say. But Delaney's dire threats circled in his head. Fit in. Make friends. Play nice.

Or get yanked. Because apparently his and Flynn's testimony against McGinty was only worth so much money, time, and effort to the government. They were almost at that limit. There was no way in hell he'd let her just yank Kellan out of the program. The Maguires were a package deal—exactly as he'd said to her from day one. Staying with his brothers, well, and staying alive, was all that mattered.

They'd lose the legit credentials, lose the sweet monthly check, lose the house, lose the jobs. And without the protection of the feds, it wasn't too much of a stretch to assume he and his brothers would lose their lives soon after.

Trying to appear friendly, Rafe pocketed his hands in his hoodie. "Don't make a snap judgment based on my general trivia knowledge. But if you need a real reason to get to know me, I do mix one hell of a Horse's Neck with a Kick."

The nameless guy grimaced. "Is that a drink? Or a boxing combination?"

"It'll knock you out either way. But it's a drink. Old school."

The kind of old-school cocktail you got served in Chicago's legendary steakhouses. The kind your boss mixed you when he made you his second in command, in front of all his *lieutenants*. The boss who'd stepped in, acted like a father when your own was killed.

It was the one drink that always sprang immediately to mind . . . but Rafe wouldn't touch again with a ten-foot pole. Now it'd taste of nothing but betrayal.

Mad that he'd brought it up, that he'd let it slip back into his consciousness, Rafe hurried through the explanation. "It's got bourbon, bitters, ginger ale. Then you spiral the entire rind of a lemon into the glass and hang it over the rim."

"That'll put hair on your chest."

With a shrug, Rafe said, "You show me yours, I'll show you mine."

The old guy barked out a half laugh that turned into more of a wheeze. Then, a cough wracked his thin frame. Finally, he got out, "Damned fog. Keeps my lungs wet. The beach is no good for me."

Rafe knew the feeling. He doubted he'd be comfortable with the beach anytime soon. Of course, Rafe also knew that he'd be out here every damn night, trying to conquer it. Damned if he'd live with any shred of weakness. Weakness equaled danger. "Then why are you out here?"

"I'm patrolling."

"For what?" Rafe shook his head. "No. Back up. Who are you?"

He'd need the man's name for when he described the old coot to Flynn and Kellan.

He drew himself up ramrod straight. Tossed off a salute crisper than a potato chip. "Colonel Mick O'Keefe, USMC retired."

"Retired how long?"

"Too long," he snapped out. Then hacked a couple of more times, clutching at his chest.

That big rock thing would protect the colonel from the brunt of the damp wind. Rafe slowly eased toward it, hoping he'd follow. "Don't bite my head off. You're the one who ambushed me in the pitch dark. I'm being polite as hell over here."

"That's an effort for you, is it?"

Rafe leaned back against what had to be seven feet of mounded granite. Crossed his arms and sighed. "You have no idea."

Laughing again—but not coughing this time—the older man joined him on the leeward side. "Don't feel like you need to spit polish your manners on my account."

"Good to know, Colonel."

After a brief hesitation, he extended a hand. "It's Mick."

"Nice to meet you." Rafe wasn't annoyed anymore. Just pissed that he almost defended himself right into getting drop-kicked from the program. He didn't want it to happen again. And if he wouldn't cede this beach to whatever sea monsters lurked, he sure as hell wasn't ceding it to some gimpy old-timer. So he'd just issue a warning. Pull the punch, as it were. "Next time, don't sneak up on me, Mick. It's a good way to get yourself clocked in the eye."

With a shoulder bump, he settled onto the rock next to Rafe. "I would've accepted that challenge ten years ago."

"Ten years wouldn't have mattered. You still would've walked away with a shiner."

"Cocky bastard, aren't you?"

"No. Not one damn bit." Because cockiness could get you killed faster than drinking bleach. Or a one-way ticket to jail. Rafe honestly wasn't sure which would be worse. He did know that he got up every morning and did everything in his power to avoid both possibilities. "Just dead certain of my abilities."

Not that they mattered here, in his new life. Not officially, anyway. Since he was supposed to trust the U.S. Marshals Service would keep their lips zipped.

Still, no reason to let them get rusty because the Maguire brothers might not be staying long. The next place they landed might not be so peaceful.

Mick's appearance had caught him by surprise—something that never, *ever* would've happened in Chicago. The constant battering of the ocean against land had pulled his focus. Now he knew. Next time, he'd be prepped for it. Ears cocked, eyes more vigilant in scanning ahead and to the sides to compensate.

Because you never knew who'd sneak up on you. Might be a woman, ready to slide her hands down your pants. Or it might be a mobster hell-bent on getting revenge. McGinty's crew got disassembled, thanks to Rafe's testimony. So he couldn't let his guard down for a second. Just in case.

"I remember that feeling." Mick sucked in a fat string of air around his eyetooth. "It's a good one. Not invincible, exactly. Just sure down to the marrow of your bones."

"Exactly." Rafe hadn't expected to find understanding in a jarhead, of all people. On the other hand, the armed forces were a lot like the mob. There were ranks. Rules. Expectations.

An ex-colonel would understand Rafe's old rank. Would share his outrage at being outflanked and double-crossed. Would understand what he'd left behind, what he'd given up to save his own tight family squadron.

Not that he could ever tell Mick, oh, *any* of it.

Or anybody else, for that matter. Not even a green-eyed girl who Rafe already felt like he could tell anything to, and she'd happily listen.

Nope.

The marshal wanted him to fit in here. Did Delaney have any idea how damned hard that was when he had to lie to everyone 24/7?

"You're Rafe Maguire."

The statement startled him out of the quicksand of his thoughts. "Yeah." Polite or not, years of habit kicked in, and he had to ask, "How'd you know?"

"You didn't think three men could appear in a town as small as ours and not be the main topic of conversation, did you?"

"Never thought about it. I'm not much of a small-town guy."

"So Frieda tells me."

Ah. His boss. Half owner of Wick's Garage where he put in his eight solid, five days a week. Rafe almost rolled his eyes at the sliver of moon above. Then he remembered that Delaney had warned them that people being up in your business wasn't considered gossip in a town like Bandon. Sharing news was considered looking out for each other. Caring, for fuck's sake.

Well, he'd play along. "Frieda's good people for giving me a shot. Guess it makes sense she'd want to spread the word that her garage has a kick-ass new mechanic. It's a smart way to drum up business."

"What big town are you from? Your accent's faint, but it isn't West Coast."

"Nope. It's not." To evade more probing, Rafe bent to tighten an already perfectly secure shoelace. "How'd you guess I'm Rafe and not Kellan or Flynn?"

"I stopped in at the Gorse two nights ago. It's less lonely eating at a bar. There are so many people around, you feel like you're part of something."

"Yeah." Rafe got it. He used to go to the bar to watch baseball games. Football, too. He'd get swept up in cheering or cussing out the home team with everyone else lifting their beers and staring at the TV. It'd been fun. But he could easily see why someone Mick's age would want the noise and light and busyness of a bar as a refuge from loneliness.

He should probably ask why Mick was lonely. It was the kind of thing men shared after midnight, in the dark, braced on a big-ass rock against the wind. But that might make a connection between them.

Rafe couldn't risk forging a connection. All he could do was try to make the illusion of one. That was safest. It almost broke him to leave behind his life in Chicago. If he started to care about people here, it'd suck donkey balls if they had to go on the run and leave them behind.

"Your brother Flynn was tending bar." Mick stabbed a stubby finger that stopped short an inch from Rafe's face. "He's got the look of you, with the eyes and hair. He doesn't talk much, does he?"

"Not until he's got something to say. Then you can't shut him the hell up. Not even for a stripper and five Franklins. Believe me, I've tried." Rafe regretted the honesty the moment it escaped his lips. He knew a major portion of America would go right on red alert at his mention of a stripper. Shit. But if you couldn't talk strippers around soldiers, who was left?

Plus, it pulled another raspy laugh out of Mick. To Rafe's great relief. "I've got some friends like that. Used to, anyway. Flynn gave me a fine pour—not too much head on my Guinness. I liked him."

"He'll be thrilled to hear he's got a fan club of one."

"Anyway, Frieda told me her new hire at the garage was the oldest of the three brothers. You've got shadows in your eyes, secrets of a life lived, that put you at least a couple of years older than Flynn. That's how I figured out which one you were."

Damn it to hell. How was he supposed to guard against something as half-baked as shadows in his eyes? "It's after midnight. Whatever you thought you saw, I guarantee they were *actual* shadows. Moon, stars, and darkness. That's it," Rafe said roughly. "I don't have any secrets to hide."

"That's a load of bullshit. We all have secrets."

"I guess mine is that I need to start using face cream around my eyes." As if challenging him, Rafe held the old man in a stare.

After wavering between squinted eyes of disapproval and a lip that just kept curving upward, Mick slapped his thigh and hooted. "You're a smart-ass, aren't you?"

"On my better days. The rest of the time, I'm told I'm just an ass."

"I'd believe that."

That easy acceptance, the lack of any attempt to politely disagree, put Rafe back at ease. Made him feel like he was actually hanging with someone at his level. Even if he was thirty years older. "What were you doing out here tonight? You said patrolling? For what? 'Cause you, me, and the sea are the only things out here."

"That you know of . . ."

Rafe's eyes cut right. He couldn't help himself from a quick check on the unfurling wave about to hit the shore. Big, loud, but, you know, normal. Not belching out a giant squid or anything. Then he realized the ex-Marine probably meant he was patrolling for bad guys. Not scary-ass sea creatures that only existed in horror movies on crappy cable channels. And, of course, in Rafe's imagination.

He gave Mick a soft punch through the upper sleeve of his camo jacket. "Cut that out. Bandon is too quiet for crime."

"You'd better believe it," the old man said with an exuberant thumbs-up. "That's because I'm vigilant. There's no chance for criminals to spot a weakness and swoop in to cause trouble."

"Uh-huh." There was always a chance. A good criminal said to hell with chance and made his own luck. Usually by using money, influence, or both. God knew Rafe had done just that more times than he could count.

"What are you doing out here at this time of night?" Mick challenged.

Rafe pushed off the rock to pace to a big piece of driftwood draped in seaweed. It looked like something that should hang on the wall of a beach cabin. It was so iconic that seeing it up close and personal surprised him. Kind of squishy, too. Maybe from, oh, drifting through the water?

"I had a date." Yeah, his tone made it sound like he'd spent the evening in line at the DMV.

"Did it go in the crapper?"

"Nah. It went well." He winged the driftwood high over the rock and back out to sea. "Too well."

Understanding turned Mick's forehead and mouth down into a pained grimace. "Ah. Blue balls?"

"Like you wouldn't fucking believe."

"A beach run's a smart way to deal with 'em. Or, instead of annoying me with it, you could use that smart mouth of yours to charm the lady into bed sooner rather than later. Who was it?"

Dozens of people probably saw them in the Gorse. No point hiding it. "Mollie Vickers."

"Ah. Again, I don't mind saying that if I was ten years younger, I might've challenged you for her."

Rafe appreciated Mick's stubbornness and willingness to fight. No matter how hopeless it was in this particular situation. "And again, I don't mind saying that it wouldn't have mattered. I'd get the girl."

"If you were so sure of that, you wouldn't be out here running off a stiffy."

Guess he deserved that. Rafe shook his head. "She needs time. I'm happy to give it to her."

"Happy?"

Yeah, he didn't believe it, either. But this was a small town. Women were not a dime a dozen here the way they'd been in Chicago. And he respected her enough to wait. Rafe wasn't a desperate twenty-two-year-old. He knew that she was right—sex *was* better when you liked the person. "Willing, anyway."

"I'll buy that. You be good to poor Mollie."

"*Poor* Mollie? What's the story there?" Because he thought the doc had a perfect life. Mollie loved being a doctor. Loved helping people. Lived with a family she clearly adored, even if her little shit of a cousin didn't deserve it. From the number of people who'd stopped by their table to say hi in the bar, the whole town frigging loved her.

"Her mother abandoned her. Just walked out, almost before Mollie could walk. Decided she was too much work and left her with her grandmother." Mick wiped his hand through the air. "That woman had her own issues."

And there it was. The small-town avalanche of oversharing and gossip. Thank God Rafe had no official backstory for the town to pick apart to this extent. "Issues? Abandonment? This sounds like a remote therapy session."

"The way I heard it, the whole town pitched in to help raise her. They did what they could. What Norah would let them do. Not sure it was enough, though."

"I'd say she turned out great." Why did he have to defend her to someone who'd known Mollie what sounded like her whole life?

"She's a lovely woman. We're all proud. But," Mick limped over to Rafe and leaned in to half whisper, "dating's not her strong suit. Because of the abandonment thing, according to Norah."

Rafe stalked away a few steps. He needed space. Suddenly, the beach wasn't big enough for him. "Jesus Christ. You scare all her dates off with this speech?"

"No need. Everybody around here knows about Mollie."

"Well, I don't want to date her," he yelled a little too loudly over his shoulder. And how many times would he have to make that statement?

Shit.

It was probably not the right thing to say to a man who felt even a little pseudo-paternal toward Mollie. It was *definitely* not a good way to make a positive impression. To fit in. To come off as totally normal.

Rafe dug his toe into the sand, then sent a clump of it flying toward the breaking surf. He'd have to fix this. Which was ironic, given that Mollie seemed pretty much on board with the no-dating idea.

"What do you want to do with her?" Mick asked quietly.

He took his own sweet time turning around. Enough time to notice a sand crab breaking through where he'd disturbed its rest. And the way the starlight glistened on the water as though each individual star landed on it.

Okay. Maybe the beach at night had its good points.

Plus, talking to Mick had totally killed off the lingering lust from his date. Mission accomplished.

Maybe he'd swing by the hospital tomorrow. See how the doctor responded to his version of a house call. As his own test to see how the friends-with-benefits thing would work. Yeah. It was good to have a plan.

A little calmer, Rafe said, "I don't know. I don't know what's going to happen with her. To be fair, Mollie doesn't know, either."

After another one of those long damn looks, Mick nodded. "Probably suits her just fine."

"I think it does."

Resettling his cap, Mick said, "You tell her I was looking out for her, though." The older man walked off, down the beach, with a half salute as he passed Rafe.

"I'm not playing messenger boy. Tell her yourself." But there wasn't any heat fueling his words. It was normal banter. Guy talk. The kind of thing he'd say to a friend.

Shit.

How did that happen?

Chapter Six

Mollie loved her job. She loved having her regular patients at the primary care clinic, charting the growth of the kids and ultimately being a part of the lives of the adults. She loved that the hospital rotated her into the emergency department as well. Being able to walk to work was a huge plus.

What she didn't love? Showing up the morning after a date to do rounds at 6:00 a.m.—even if there were only fifteen beds in the whole hospital—and then moving on to a shift in the clinic. Because she'd gotten no sleep last night. None. Zero.

She wasn't of any use to her patients walking around like a zombie. That was why she'd ended the date by exactly eleven o'clock last night. Because that was what mature adults did when faced with having to save lives the next day.

But Mollie had been too busy thinking about Rafe to sleep.

Which both excited her and pissed her off to no end.

Mature adults did not run their fingertips across their lips, reliving the feel of a kiss. Except for, apparently, Mollie. She'd done that for each kiss Rafe gave her. Which, by the end of the night, added up to quite a few. Mature adults did not toss and turn for hours on end, thinking about the unusual offer of sex with no strings. Thinking of the breathtakingly sexy man who'd made it.

But Mollie did.

Rafe came off tough as nails, but he'd offered to help Jesse, which was *huge*. It showed he had a soft heart underneath all that muscle and sinew. He'd made it clear that sex was the only thing he offered, but then he'd been so much fun at dinner. He laughed, he listened, he didn't scope out the room to look for other women (something that seemed to be a habit with men of her generation). Rafe had been the perfect date.

Not that she'd let herself fall for him. That would be stupid. Self-sabotaging. Number one, because he lived here, in Bandon. He'd get an earful about poor, pitiful Mollie sooner rather than later. A story that didn't exactly inspire sexy times. Number two, because she didn't *want* to fall for him.

Mollie wanted to date, sure. She liked sex. Liked some laughs with a man who hopefully called her pretty once or twice. It was good for the ego. But she didn't want to *date* date. She didn't want to open herself up to another person. To be vulnerable. Because besides being humiliating and pathetic? The town lore of "that poor Mollie Vickers" happened to be true.

Yup, even though she was absent for most of her life, Mollie's mom still managed to impart one life lesson to her daughter. People can abandon you. And when they do, it hurts like hell. And if her own mother hadn't wanted her, why would a man? Especially in today's world, when hookups were plentiful and divorce as easy to get as a belly button piercing.

Even with all that in her head, it had been impossible to stop thinking about Rafe—the way he *got* her blunt humor, the way his eyes darkened when he touched her, the aura of total confidence he exuded about everything—and fall asleep. *That* frustrated Mollie on a whole new level, and—

"Hey. Paging Dr. Vickers. You're holding a sharp implement over my barely stitched together body. A body that I hone very carefully to attract the opposite sex. How about a little attention?"

Her best friend's voice brought her back to the exam room with the force of a swinging door to the head. Not that she'd admit it to him. Mollie ignored the hazel eyes she could all but feel boring into her and bent lower over the neatly closed gash in his leg.

"Lucien, I can do stitches in my sleep. Internal stitches. Ones that have to hold organs and nerves and arteries together. I'm giving you a whopping four stitches in your calf. They don't even have to be pretty. I have it on good authority that women find scars on a man hot."

He batted at the swoop of blond bangs on his forehead that the ever-present ocean wind must've mussed out of his usual gelled perfection. "What good authority?"

"Mine. Not to mention Lily, Karen, and Elena," she countered, listing off her closest friends here in town. "And in just about every romance novel I've ever read." She let the suture needle clatter onto the tray. Then grabbed an alcohol wipe to remove the bright orange Betadine from around his cut. Blood, stitches, pain, Lucien really didn't care. But if she stained his designer clothes with the antiseptic, there'd be hell to pay.

"You're saying my cut will get me laid?"

No need to look up to see the smug grin curving across his surfer good looks. It oozed out of his voice like jelly from her donut this morning. "Well, it doesn't come with a money-back guarantee or anything. But I think you'll do okay. If you play it right. Mostly, if you make up a better story than what actually happened."

"I saved one of my own employees from impalement." Mollie's snort barely disrupted Lucien's self-important rant. "When that angry idiot snapped his golf club in half and tossed it, it could've speared right through Javier like a harpoon. I risked my own life to save his."

Sooo melodramatic. As though Hollywood would

knock on his door to make a biopic out of his life because of it. Mollie stripped off her gloves. "You dropped a lawn mower blade on your leg."

"I chose to let it dangerously fall on me so that my hands would be free to catch the jagged half of a club."

Not that Lucien knew squat about repairing lawn mowers. He shouldn't have been holding the thing in the first place. But his father insisted that he spend time shadowing all the workers at their world-famous set of golf courses this summer. Here it was, only week two, and it'd already cost him blood and skin and an hour with no repair of said lawn mower, since Javier refused to leave the clinic without Lucien. Plus, Mollie was quite sure she'd have to sit through the retelling of the epic golf club harpoon save at least three more times this week.

Her only hope was to shut it down *now.* Before Lucien developed it into a well-rehearsed monologue that popped out every time he lifted a beer bottle to his lips. Mollie shook her head and winced. Maybe too dramatically, but you had to fight fire with fire. "Nope. All I hear is rusty, filthy lawn mower blade. Work on the story, dude. Trust me."

The paper on the exam table rustled as he shifted to grip the edge of it with both hands. Eagerness brightened his blue eyes. Eyes that Mollie couldn't help noticing weren't quite as blue as Rafe's . . . "You tell me a story instead. Tell me what happened with your down and dirty mechanic. Did he tune you up? Lube you up?

Rotate your—nah, that's no good." Laughter doubled him over as he continued. "Lemme have another shot at it."

Mollie whisked the drape off his leg and dropped it into the trash. This was her workplace. She didn't show up at *his* office and ask if he'd . . . um . . . putted through with his latest girl of the hour. "I'm not giving you any more time to come up with disgusting metaphors for sex with a mechanic."

"But it's so much more fun now. When you were a resident and never left the hospital, you only gave me doctors to use in sexy metaphors. Rattling your bones and suturing your sex drive never really hit the nail on the head."

"No. They absolutely did not." But the ridiculous conversation relaxed her. It made her happy as all get-out to be home. She'd missed Lucien a ton. Getting video chatted from club bathrooms when he needed dating advice wasn't the same as actually *being* here with him.

"Dr. Vickers?" Sakiko poked her head and half of her purple scrub top covered with teddy bears through the doorway. "I've got a child—Olivia Sebor—in for her immunizations who's refusing to leave the waiting room. She's too scared. And she's screaming."

"Yikes. I can't have that going down on my watch. She'll freak out the other patients." It certainly wasn't the first time, though. Mollie knew exactly what to do. She didn't want anyone, no matter what their age, to be scared of anything doctor related. Hospitals and medical staff should be seen as reassuring, as a place full of people who fixed things. People who made the pain go away. "Grab two hypos, the vaccine, and a Tdap. We'll be right out."

As the door closed behind the nurse, Lucien asked, "We? Do I get to wear a white coat and a stethoscope and act all medicinal?"

"You need a shot."

Lucien turned sheet white. Then he tried to scoot back, out of her reach, but he only succeeded in bonking his head on the wall. "No, I don't. I finished all my vaccines years ago. And you promised that you'd sneak my flu shot in one night when I was good and plastered so I wouldn't feel it."

"No flu shot until October. Geez, you're such a baby." Rafe would probably handle a shot without so much as blinking. If she could even get the needle into his rock-hard biceps. "But the lawn mower blade doesn't exactly cut in sterile conditions. You need your tetanus updated. And you're going to be a very, very brave model of good behavior for this frightened child."

"I hate shots."

Since her hand was banded around his wrist and she'd still barely managed to tug him toward the door, that much was obvious. "Help me and I'll dish on what went down with my mechanic."

"That's a sham of a deal. I'm your best friend. You were going to tell me anyway."

"Yes, but I promise to use dirty words instead of clinical ones."

"Sold." At least, that's what Lucien said. But it still took considerable yanking on Mollie's part to get him down the hallway and into the waiting room.

Its green-and-blue-striped walls were soothing. Just not to the six-year-old screaming her head off. The adults in the room looked annoyed and the one other child looked petrified. Great. Mollie rushed over, dragging Lucien in lockstep with her.

"Olivia, I'm so glad you came in today. I need your help." Mollie dropped to a crouch. Olivia stopped screaming, but sniffled and hiccupped and clearly was ready to burst into more tears.

Luckily, her mom played along. "Olivia's only six. Isn't she too little to help a doctor?"

"Nope. She's perfect." A sharp yank on Lucien's wrist dropped him to his knees beside her. "This man cut himself today. By being careless." Yes, it was petty to get in a poke at him. And totally worth it. "He needs a tetanus shot, but he's too scared. I told him that I have a six-year-old patient who can show him how easy it is to be brave. He didn't believe me."

"Boys are stupid." White teeth flashed as a surprisingly knowing smile widened her plump brown cheeks.

"They can be. But they can also learn pretty fast. Especially from a really smart, brave girl. Do you think you could show Mr. Dumont how to do it?"

Olivia shoved up the cap sleeve to her pink shirt. Then she shook her arm wordlessly at Lucien until he did the same to his sky-blue polo. Luckily, Sakiko was right there, with both hypos. Mollie left Lucien to the perfectly capable sticking capabilities of the nurse.

"By the time you name five animals, we'll be done. Why don't you take turns? Olivia can start."

Full of self-importance, Olivia shouted out "Camel!"

"Ostrich," Lucien responded, gritting his teeth. And then he turned it into a crossed-eyed grimace to make Olivia laugh. Mollie knew he'd come through. Who could resist a girl with seven pink bows twisted into her curls and a missing front tooth?

"El-lelephant." She stumbled over the word as the needle went in, but kept going. Mollie couldn't be prouder. The girl had grit.

"Octopus."

"That's a fish, silly." Olivia kicked her legs and squealed at besting the fully grown man. "Not an animal."

"Guess you showed him how to be brave and taught him a lesson. I may have to ask you for help the next time you come in, too." Mollie slapped on the bandage after showing Olivia the SpongeBob characters printed on it. "Would you be my official special helper?"

"Yes, Dr. Vickers." The little girl flung her arms around Mollie's neck in a fast hug.

Lucien then shook her hand with utter solemnity. "Thanks, Olivia. I'm not scared of shots anymore."

"Me, neither."

"Me, neither," a deep voice echoed.

Mollie spun around on one heel and almost fell out of her crouch. Because it was the last voice she expected to hear at nine on a Saturday morning. She had to crane her neck back to look up at Rafe's stubbled jaw. It went well with the faded gray tee that hugged every single ripple of lean muscle in his washboard abs. Which is where she'd keep her gaze at or above. No matter what. Since her eyes were directly level with a bulge in his jeans she *would not* so much as notice while in close proximity to a girl wearing light-up sneakers.

"Rafe?" Mollie cleared her throat. Because his name had come out in an excited squeak. Very undignified and un-doctor-like. "Did you have an appointment?"

"It's a walk-in clinic, right? I just walk in when I need medical attention?"

"Technically, yes."

"Rafe, huh?" Lucien started to rise with a very inquisitive gleam in his eye. Mollie leaned—hard—on his shoulder as she got up to keep him from following. Or asking anything else.

"Sakiko, would you discharge both Mr. Dumont and Olivia?" She dug a sheet of stickers out of the pocket of her lab coat and folded it into Olivia's damp palm. "I'm going to take Mr. Maguire on back."

Again, she found herself dragging a man by the wrist double-time down the long, eau-de-antiseptic-scented hallway of the clinic. "Are you hurt? Sick?"

"It's more that I've got a burning question. And my

last doctor chewed me out good when I googled for an answer instead of going in to the office."

"Rightly so." Mollie tried to lead him into an exam room. Instead, Rafe shifted his hand so that he now led her. And he pulled her right through the connecting door at the end of the hallway that joined the clinic wing with the actual hospital. "Uh, where are we going?"

"I did a little recon." He pulled her into the laundry room. The hospital was so small that although they sent a big load out twice a week, they had their own laundry room as well. Mollie liked it because nothing soothed an achy, irritable patient in the middle of the night like a blanket right out of the dryer. Then Rafe shoved a full laundry hamper against the door.

"Rafe, what's going on?"

He turned, locking the full intensity of his stare onto her. Enough so that her pulse picked up and her panties dampened beneath its blue heat. "You said you'd be open to a friends-with-benefits arrangement. Once you decided if we could actually be friends."

"Right." And their dinner had worked. She'd had a great time. From the way Rafe laughed and flirted and, frankly, eye-fucked her, so had he.

"Well, *I* don't want to enter into this arrangement until I'm sure the benefits will be good. For both of us." He shoved up his long sleeves, exposing forearms dusted with dark black hair. Forearms that literally made her mouth water. And Rafe wasn't even touching her. "That's the question I need answered."

Mollie backed up until her heels hit the dryer. Because she suddenly didn't have the space to catch a full breath. His broad shoulders took up so much room. The lust emanating off of him in waves took up even more, sucking up all the oxygen in the tiny space.

"You're kidding. Right now? I have a waiting room full of patients. Hacking coughs to medicate, vaccinations to give, and rheumatoid arthritis liver enzyme levels to review." And that was only the next hour of her packed schedule.

Fists braced on the dryer at her hips caged Mollie in. Not that it was necessary. Not like she was going anywhere. Not with her knees this wobbly and her arousal already spiking just from Rafe's nearness. Not that she could possibly ignore the forbidden excitement of his proposition.

It barely took a nudge from his heavy black boots to spread her legs. To create room between her thighs for Rafe to step closer. To nestle the bulge in his jeans against her abdomen. "If I was actually here as a patient, how long would you spend with me?"

"Ten minutes."

"That's all I'll need." Rafe's voice dropped to a near whisper right in her ear. The whorls of his breath raced chills down her spine. "You think I can't get you in the mood fast enough?"

"I didn't say that."

"Let's be clear—when we have sex, it'll take a while. Because I plan to take my time. Drawing a connecting line with my tongue between each of your freckles. Giving you ample opportunity to decide if you prefer clockwise or counterclockwise circles on your nipples. Discovering what pushes you over the line from panting to moaning. It'll be a whole-night deal. One that'll probably pick up again before the sun breaches the horizon." He pushed back the starched lapels of her lab coat.

"Is that so?" Mollie never knew she liked dirty talk. Now she *knew*. For sure. Or, at least, she knew that when Rafe did it, every nerve in her body came to attention and waved, frantically, in a silent plea for him to continue. Count that as her self-actualization for the day.

Rafe didn't answer. He couldn't. His mouth was full, clamped on to her breast over her scrub top. Using only his teeth, he bit down on her nipple just hard enough to make her toes tighten. At the same time, he used his hand to squeeze the other breast. The combination of the hard pinch and the firm but soft pressure rolled her eyes back in her head. Fully clothed goodness. Oh-so-goodness.

Ten minutes. Ten little minutes. Technically, just long enough to run to the bathroom, grab another jelly donut, and gulp down a coffee. Not an exorbitant or irresponsible amount of time at all. Plus, she'd finished with Olivia in record time. That ought to give her at least seven extra minutes? To balance being a good doctor against resolving too many months of sexual frustration?

Damn it, she'd rationalize—or not—later. Because

right now, Rafe was untying the knot holding her pants up.

"I like the way you move against me. I'll like it even more when we're naked."

"Agreed." Although Mollie hadn't even noticed the undulation of her hips until Rafe pointed it out. The motion had been an unconscious reflex. Cause and effect from his burning, knowing touch.

He curved his fingers into a claw shape and lightly raked them down her satin panties. This time, Mollie was *very* conscious of rocking her hips forward to meet him. To get more pressure to relieve the skyrocketing ache between her legs.

Instead, Rafe scraped lightly again. Which was teasing and wonderful and utterly insufficient. Mollie threaded her fingers through his thick hair, trying to pull him closer. All it did was pull a chuckle out of him. "Trust me, babe. I'll get you there."

"Oh, I do. I most definitely do." She might not know . . . well, much of *anything* about the dark-haired man with his hands down her pants. But Mollie did, one hundred percent trust that Rafe knew his way around a woman's body. That he knew it as libidinously as she knew it anatomically.

His mouth moved up to hers. When his tongue invaded with a swift plunge, so did his finger. It slipped beneath the elastic gather and went right inside her wetness. Right where she *craved* him.

Every stroke of his finger mimicked that of his

tongue. At every pause, the fingers of his other hand tightened to just the right side of firmness on her nipple. Through her bra. Since technically, Mollie was still fully clothed. Yet, she already hovered on the edge of orgasm.

Mollie went up on tiptoe, trying to give him better access. Rafe boosted her with just one muscular arm to teeter on the edge of the dryer. And then rewarded her by adding a second finger.

Breath coming as fast as if she'd just run a mile down the beach, Mollie offered, "Let me do something for you. I want to touch you, too."

He wrenched his mouth away. "Next time. Your test for me was dinner. This one's mine."

"I've always excelled at tests." Then she whimpered with desire. This was all so good. Yet it was all *sooo* not enough.

"You're already passing with flying colors, Doc." A third finger pressed tightly against the other two. It curved, pressing against the fleshy spot where so many nerves clustered. At her moan, Rafe rocked the heel of his palm firmly against her clitoris.

Once.

Twice.

The third time, Mollie simply broke apart into pulsing bliss.

Her head dropped to his shoulder as she waited for her heartbeat to slow and the white spots to stop dancing behind her closed lids. Beating around the bush wouldn't serve either of them. So she gulped in enough air to say, "That was fantastic. Beyond fantastic, actually. Thank you."

Rafe scooted her back on the dryer until she was stable. He dropped a kiss on her forehead, her nose, and then a more lingering one on her lips as her head tilted upright. Once her eyes fluttered open, he brought his fingers to his mouth. The fingers that had been inside of her. Licked them, one by one. "Thank *you*, Doc."

Omigod. The raw sensuality of this man just undid her.

Then he carefully retied her scrub pants with a perfect bow. Which undid her even more.

"So . . . we're going to do this?" she asked.

Rafe lifted her back onto her feet. Straightened her lapels. Then put his hand on the back of Mollie's neck while he crushed his mouth to hers for another few seconds.

With a flourish, he opened the door and waved her into the hallway. "We've already started."

Unable to resist, Mollie asked, "Was it better than going on the internet to answer your question?"

"The entire world wide web's got nothing on you." Rafe dipped into her pocket to steal a Tootsie Pop as they strolled down the hallway. "Plus, I get a double dose of sweetness. Talk about a great start to the day."

"Better than a chocolate muffin with honey?"

"Hmmm. You're giving me a good idea. Honey. Forget the muffin." He walked two fingers down the center of her body. "I'm going to drizzle it down your belly and—"

Mollie whacked the back of her hand against his flat stomach, practically bouncing off of its tautness. "Shhh. We're not behind closed doors anymore. Go on. Shoo. Before anyone gets suspicious."

"But I think I've got a fever now." He gently butted his forehead against hers.

She'd thought his sexy side was enough. But playful Rafe was too many kinds of adorable not to appreciate as well. "There's an entire ocean out there. Go cool off in it."

"Hmmm. The ocean. You're chock-full of good ideas this morning. How do you feel about skinny dipping?"

Like she'd be willing to try any dangerous and decadent thing Rafe Maguire suggested.

Twice.

Chapter Seven

The Gorse, 7:00 p.m.

Mood in the sad-ass excuse for a bar—frustrated

RAFE LIFTED HIS frosted beer mug. "To Saturday night."

Then he waited. Because neither Flynn nor Kellan lifted their mugs. They just stared at him. Flynn, with his jaw practically wired shut, he'd clamped down so hard. Kellan with his typical-for-the-last-six-months sneer curling his lip.

"Come on," Rafe urged. Purposely, he kept it light. Like he was trying to talk them into ordering the four-meat stuffed deep dish pizza at Giordano's, instead of the pansy-ass classic with green peppers. Who needed to ruin good 'za with freaking vegetables? "Don't leave a brother hanging."

Kellan's lip curled down even farther. "Not gonna clink your glass. Not for a fake toast."

Damn it. Rafe knew Kellan was pissing all over this small-town, quiet-as-a-Monday excuse for a bar. But if he played dumb—and kept at it—maybe he could still get them to lift their damn beers. "Uh, check out your calendar app. It's Saturday. The sun has set. We're good to toast."

"No way. This is a crappy excuse for a Saturday night." Kellan leaned back. Kicked the table leg enough to make it jump in the process and crossed his arms over his green plaid-covered chest.

Rafe almost laughed out loud. Did that idiot think he'd *won*? Think that the second highest ranking mobster in Chicago—*ex*-mobster, whatever—kept a stranglehold on the riffraff that filled the Second City by being outplayed by a pissant pout? Did he think Rafe would shrug and give up now that Kellan had pretended to lay down the law? Good thing they'd kept the kid away from the racket. He didn't have the *cojones*.

Rafe started and ended each day with fifty one-armed push-ups. He could hold his beer in midair until the Gorse closed down and not even blink. This time, he aimed his glass at Flynn. "You're a bartender now. You know it's bad luck to toast and not drink."

"Bad luck?" A harsh laugh grated from his brother's throat. Practically the same noise a drawbridge over the Chicago River made when its gears ground together to lift it. "You really think we could have any more bad luck rain down on us?"

That did it. Rafe thumped his glass so hard against the scarred wooden table that foam flew off the top. Because Flynn *knew* better. He knew the answer to that question. It was hard to believe he needed to be reminded.

Sure, he'd been protected from the worst of the violence. After all, Flynn used to sit behind a desk all day running the legit cover business for the organization. The one they could launder money through, when necessary. With books that could be legit audited. The one that supplied paychecks on the up-and-up to everyone in McGinty's crew so that they all looked like taxpaying, law-abiding citizens.

As long as you didn't look too hard.

The U.S. government was now doing exactly that: combing over the construction company's books and its employees with a magnifying glass, thanks to Rafe's pointing a spotlight on it. Which meant there were a shitton of pissed-off, vengeful, violent people just looking for someone to unleash all that anger on. Mainly, them.

He put his arm back up in the air and would keep it there until somebody god damned clinked his glass. Then Rafe leaned forward. All the way until his chin was practically over the center of the table. It clued his brothers to lean in, too. Almost under his breath, Rafe growled, "We could be at the bottom of Lake Michigan right now. In cement shoes. Or full of bullet holes. Or both. So, yeah, things could be a lot worse. Don't you fucking forget that for a minute."

Flynn gave in fast. He nodded, his gaze skittering away to the cranberry red wall with the jukebox. "You're right."

"I wish to hell I wasn't." Rafe meant that. With all

his heart. And was glad it hadn't taken much to remind Flynn of the life-and-death severity of their situation.

Kellan, however, was more stubborn. And in this family, that was saying something. He squinted. Gave actual side-eye. "You're sure you're not exaggerating?"

The temptation to drag him outside and slap him around for even asking the question was . . . strong. But it didn't fit their marshal's strict instruction to fly under the radar. To go unnoticed and be model citizens.

Christ, but it was hard work.

Yet again, Rafe tried to tease Kellan out of his funk. And dial him in to the harsh but undeniable truth of their new lives. "You think the US Marshals Service would be going to all this trouble to keep us safe if I was *exaggerating*?"

"Or spending all this money on us," Flynn added. About time he pulled his weight with straightening Kellan out. "They funded this blend-in-with-the-locals makeover." Then he sneered down at his own flannel shirt like it was covered in dog shit.

Not helpful.

Yeah, Flynn had been big into clothes. His weakness was expensive/trendy workout gear. The guy was into the gym scene. It kept him in fighting form for when he participated in the underground MMA circuit.

It'd reminded everyone that sitting behind a desk didn't mean Flynn was weak. Didn't mean he couldn't hold his own and then some.

Now? The closest he got to a good, head-clearing fight would be if things got wild here at the Gorse.

Which was unlikely.

Or Delaney wouldn't have placed him here.

Rafe missed his custom-tailored suits, too. His weekly shoe shine. The guys all respected him more for *looking* like McGinty's right-hand man. It hadn't sucked. The slick duds got him women, which also didn't suck.

On the other hand, it seemed like all it took to catch Mollie's eyes was a flex of his biceps. Luckily, Rafe carried those guns under whatever he wore.

"Can we be real for a minute?"

Uh-oh. Kellan had avoided asking questions for the last six months, which worked well for all three of them. This would be a truly shitty time to reverse that trend. But Rafe couldn't say no. The stewing anger that rode beneath almost everything that came out of his brother's mouth since they'd joined the witness protection program was gone. His face was curious, unguarded. A bit like when he'd asked Rafe all those years ago if there was really a Santa Claus.

Of course Rafe had told him the truth back then. That was before he'd learned to lie to his brother on a daily basis. Plus, knowing it was their parents who wrapped the presents made it easier to get what you really wanted. He did Kellan a favor by busting that myth.

He'd tell him the truth now, too. Because he'd sworn, from the day he and Delaney snatched Kellan outside his law school, shoved him into a big black SUV, and took the kid's whole life away, that he'd never lie to him again.

Enough was fucking enough.

"Yeah. Ask me anything, K."

"You claim these people, these guys from your organization, they'd kill us if they had the chance. But from what you said, you were in charge. Does that mean . . ." his Adam's apple worked up and down a couple of times, ". . . did you ever kill? Anyone? For your job?"

Fuck.

The Maguire brothers didn't do the hugging thing. Except at their mom's funeral, and then their dad's a year later. Now, though? Rafe wanted to sweep the kid into the kind of a hug they hadn't shared since his voice changed and he broke out a razor.

It hadn't occurred to him Kellan could be wondering about *that*. From the total lack of color in Flynn's face, it hadn't occurred to him, either. No wonder Kellan had been so pissy since they'd told him the truth about their lives. He thought the brothers he'd lived with for twenty-five years were fucking murderers.

That'd be enough to scare the shit out of anyone. Let alone being marooned with them after learning just enough to lead to that assumption.

That did it. Rafe put his beer down. Gripped Kellan's arm, right above the blue-and-silver Movado watch they'd given him for college graduation. It was classy. The kind of thing a soon-to-be lawyer needed. But now he'd never be a lawyer. When they hustled out of Chicago, Kellan was forced to leave his law books behind, his Northwestern sweatshirts, and the promise he'd made to their dad right before he died. That watch was the only thing left of the life he'd planned.

The life that his brothers had wanted so damn bad for him to have.

The life they'd abruptly ripped away.

"No. Never." God, Rafe hoped Kellan heard the sincerity and absolute fucking truth in the words he almost grunted out, they felt so raw.

"Same goes here," said Flynn. And son of a bitch, if he didn't reach out to grab Kellan's other wrist. Like they were squeezing their honest admission deep into their little brother's skin to make sure he believed.

Looking from one brother to the other, Kellan stayed quiet for a minute. Then he looked over Rafe's head to the tiny stage where some local hack was plugging guitars into amps. And he pulled out of their grips to cross his arms over his chest.

"I don't want to say that's how it always goes down in the movies. That sounds dumb. But if you're worried we've got a target on our backs, clearly, killing people is a thing. A real as fuck thing. And you said you were a big shot, Rafe. Didn't you have to, ah, get initiated and shoot at least a few people to advance up the career ladder?"

Flynn snorted. "Do you think Darth Vader's real, too?"

"Asshole," Kellan popped back automatically.

Jesus H.

Bad enough they had Kellan way the hell up on his high horse about how they'd ruined his life. Which, technically, was as true as it got. So Rafe gave him *some* leeway—that was overdue to run out—with the attitude. But Flynn became more and more of a pain in the ass with every passing month. Flynn used to be as even as a level. A rule follower. A peacemaker.

One little double-cross, one single god damned near miss of being thrown in jail, and suddenly Flynn transformed. Like he'd given up.

Getting the three of them into WITSEC was supposed to keep them alive and together. Only getting one out of two of those things . . . *sucked.*

Rafe rammed the tip of his boot against Flynn's ankle. Then two more times, until he finally clued in and spit out a mumbled, "Sorry," to their younger brother.

Okay. Back to the real problem. How to explain that they'd knowingly jumped into a profession famous for being both violent and fatal?

Rafe made a fist. Realized that sent the wrong message, and consciously splayed his fingers flat against the sticky wood. "Yeah, I bashed some heads over the years. Knocked people around who weren't pulling their weight or paying their way. Ones who knew exactly what they were getting into, and the price they'd have to pay if they screwed up. They all deserved it. Had all crossed a line." Maybe not a line the Chicago P.D. would approve of—but rules were rules.

Even in a lawless organization, there was respect.

Rules.

Consequences.

Eyes squinting, mouth screwed up like he'd just done a shot of straight lemon juice, Kellan said, "I guess I get that. I don't condone it. But I get it. You were a . . . what, an enforcer?"

"For a while. As I worked my way up." Not like there was an org chart. You did what the boss asked. Period. "Think of me more as a debt collector. People agreed to pay us. I collected—and if they were late, I made sure they knew not to slide again."

Kellan drained half his beer in three hard swallows. "So . . . why didn't you have to kill anyone?"

Guess the kid would've made a good lawyer. Because Rafe sure as hell felt like he was on the stand getting the third degree. But before he could figure out how to get that shadowed look of mistrust out of the blue eyes locked on his, Flynn jumped in.

"This isn't the movies, K. It doesn't happen so much anymore. Because we're not fucking animals. And in the wired-up, dialed-in internet era, you know how hard it is to make someone disappear?"

Flynn was not helping. Whining that it was hard to get rid of a corpse didn't send anywhere close to the right message. Especially since Flynn had not one fucking clue about what it took. Running the legit cover business meant his hands never, *ever* got dirty. Or even smudged.

He kicked Flynn under the table again. To shut him up. And, yeah, because it released a little bit of his frustration. Rafe wrapped both hands around his mug. "The truth? I told Danny McGinty when I joined, when I took the oath, that I wouldn't. Ever."

"How come?" Kellan's words sounded . . . challenging. Like Rafe still needed to prove to him that he wasn't a fucking murderer.

The way he kept pushing this topic? Showed it'd been eating at him for a long time. Rafe just wished his brother had spoken up sooner. Gotten this all out in the open. Because if the three of them couldn't trust each other, this whole witness protection thing would never work.

It blistered his heart a little that his kid brother would think he was capable of *killing* someone. No way could Rafe let that stand.

"Come on, K. How can you even ask that? You've known me your whole life. I taught you to save part of your allowance for the collection plate. To defend the weak kid on the playground against bullies. Killing people is hands-down wrong. You know it, and I sure as shit know it." He thumped his chest for good measure.

The brackets around Kellan's mouth smoothed out. He jerked a shoulder in what Rafe chose to call acceptance. "Thought maybe you'd forgotten. Good to know you haven't."

They could let it lie right there. Get up and play some darts. Shake off the heaviness of the conversation. But

Rafe *couldn't.* He'd promised to come clean with the whole truth, even though talking about this was as painful as a kick to the nuts.

"There was a bigger reason I told Danny I wouldn't kill. I'd carry a gun, I'd protect him, shoot to wound, but never, *ever* go out and so much as help to execute anyone."

"What was it?" For the first time all night, Flynn's interruption was actually helpful. Rafe had never told him this secret, either.

The Maguires weren't talkers. They'd shoot the shit, but they didn't *share,* for fuck's sake. The best way—or at least the one that worked for them—to deal with their parents dying was to not talk about it. They'd talk about the Bulls' chances in the finals, or if Flynn had a shot with the waitress at the diner they hit every Sunday morning. The casual stuff that filled a day. Never the things that went deep and dark and mattered.

Guess this new life, the new names, the new jobs, meant a new approach to being brothers, too.

"With Mom and Dad gone, I was responsible for both of you. I couldn't risk doing anything that would get me put away for life. My number one priority was providing for you guys, being there for you. That's a hundred times more important to me than any oath I took, than any money I could make. Being your brother comes first."

He didn't expect them to do a pansy-ass group hug or anything. Rafe just had to get it off his chest. He needed them to know that, no matter what, they'd always be his first consideration.

After a couple of too-long, too-quiet beats, Flynn slowly raised his mug into the air. "To Saturday night."

Kellan clinked his glass, and then Rafe's.

It was enough.

For now.

Rafe wiped the foam from his mouth with the back of his hand. "We're alive. All three of us. We're not in jail. That's only true because we're here. In Bandon. And it doesn't exactly suck to have to work our way through pint after pint until we find a local beer we like."

"The beer's the least of our problems," Flynn muttered.

He should've known one and a half minutes of peace was the maximum he could expect. But they were going to sit here and fucking enjoy a Saturday night together if it killed all of them.

Around a smile that felt more like a grimace, Rafe asked, "Now what?"

Frowning, Flynn said, "Everything about this town is small—including the dating pool. No point getting buzzed at a bar if we can't end the night with our hands down a pretty girl's bra."

Fair point. "Bandon isn't that small. Not with all the tourists that I'm told will flood in for the next six months. You might have to put some effort into it, for once, instead of just flexing your muscles in the gym, but you'll find a woman."

Kellan flipped him off. "You're only cocky because you've already scored with the hot doc."

"I haven't scored." Not that Rafe planned for that to be the case much longer. But the blue-balled truth would score him some sympathy cred with his brothers. "Just rounded a few bases."

"The women in Chicago couldn't resist your moves." Kellan rolled his eyes. "This small-town doc doesn't stand a chance."

He didn't like the implied dig at Mollie. And he wouldn't let it stand unchallenged. "She's not small-town. Or at least, she is, but by choice. She's smart. She could've worked anywhere."

Flynn did a slow roll of his head, taking in the less than two dozen tables, the obviously hand-painted (*aka* crappily so) picture of a gorse bush over the stage, and the lack of a crowd at the bar. On a Saturday freaking night. "She can't be that smart if she came back here of her own free will."

"Cut it out. No bashing Mollie."

Flynn jammed his forearms onto the table's edge. Squinted at him the way he used to squint at contracts behind his big glass-and-chrome desk. "You're awfully protective. Is this turning into more than a dine and dash with her?"

No. No way. Not in a million years.

Couldn't a man go back for thirds on lasagna at dinner without promising to only eat pasta for the rest of his life?

Rafe drained his beer. Raised his hand to signal for another round. "Please. I don't plan ahead with women. I sure as hell don't commit." Never seemed like an option as a mobster. Seemed like even less of one as an ex-mobster in hiding. It was impossible to build a relationship based on a whole life of lies. "Trying for something serious with Mollie would be stupid. It'd never work. Not with our background."

With both eyebrows raised almost to his hairline, Kellan murmured, "If you say so."

"No bashing Bandon, either. It's our home now." Their last chance at a real home without being on the run. "So you'd damn well better find something to like about it."

"Find me a better job, and I will." Kellan worked in the giant cranberry plant that employed more than half of the town. Rafe didn't think he was being a snob about the manual labor; the kid truly just missed using his giant brain.

After too many silent seconds went by, it was obvious Flynn wasn't going to jump in and do anything to put out this brush fire, either. Even though he knew the WITSEC rules as well as Rafe. Even though it was just as much *his* fault they were stuck here.

Fucknut.

Great. He got to play bad cop. *Again*. "Delaney only promised us jobs. She didn't say they'd be good. If you don't like it, look for something else."

"Flynn seems to be doing enough looking for both of us," Kellan teased.

Rafe swung around to follow the direction of his middle brother's locked-and-loaded stare. It was at the waitress headed over with three more beers and a basket of chips. Long brown hair. Nothing exceptional. No dramatic curves or coloring like Mollie.

What the hell? Mollie wasn't the only woman in the world. She sure as hell wasn't the only woman to ever make his dick hard. How'd she suddenly become a measuring stick for hotness? Rafe forced himself to take another look at the waitress. To try and get turned on by her.

As she served them, he said, "Hey, I'm Rafe. New in town."

Her eyelashes fluttered up, but she didn't meet his gaze. "Me, too."

"Look at us, already having something in common. That's Kellan, and I'm sure you already know Flynn. What's your name?"

"Sierra."

"Nice."

"It's weird." She crinkled her nose—cutely, Rafe had to admit. "Do you want to order some food?"

"You bet. Just give us two minutes." Then he shot her one of his *guaranteed to make the bras unsnap themselves* smiles. Only worked if she looked, though, and Sierra hurried away—if somebody could hurry and drift at the same time.

Rafe didn't feel any interest. Looking at Sierra just made him think about wanting to get back to Mollie.

The taste of her in the hospital had only whetted his appetite. Revved his motor. No one else would do.

Kellan nudged his elbow. "Look at that."

Huh. Flynn was still locked on the skinny girl. Even frowned a little when a guy by the bar tugged on her apron string.

"Planning to make a move on Sierra? It'd make your shifts here more fun."

"No," Flynn said flatly. "You don't piss where you eat."

Kellan threw out his arms to the sides. "Ah, the great romantic. Shakespeare's rolling over in his grave, wishing he could've come close to approaching your eloquence about the fairer sex."

Oh, yeah.

This would be a Saturday night for the Maguire brothers' record book.

Definitely made the top five *worst*.

Rafe knew a way to make it at least a little better, though. He pulled out his phone, swiping over Mollie's number . . .

Chapter Eight

RM: How's girls' night going? You having a pillow fight in your panties yet?

Pervert. Or just a big male cliché. Or maybe yanking her chain to get a rise out of her. Mollie bit back a smile. Her thumbs raced across the screen of her phone. Are you really picturing my friends in their lingerie?

RM: Nope. Only you. 'Cause if you are stripped down, I'll come over, toss them out, and we can get down to business.

This was fun. And a great way to soothe the itch of wanting that had chased across her brain since he'd left the hospital this morning. What about your brothers?

RM: They're not invited. I can get the job done all by myself. Halfway there myself just thinking about you. Your mossy eyes and breathtaking smile and breasts that fill my hands perfectly.

I wouldn't want you to embarrass yourself at the bar. Maybe we should go on radio silence. Even though she really hoped he wouldn't agree to it . . .

RM: Won't stop me from thinking about you. Can't stop thinking about you. You're like a sexual earworm.

Worse than "All About That Bass?"

RM: Worse than "Can't Stop The Feeling." And if you tell anyone I know a song by JT, punishment will be swift and severe.

"I thought you weren't on call tonight?" Lily, one of her oldest friends, gave her a frown of concern. "Do you need to go talk to a patient?"

Rats. They'd caught her. Not that she'd admit she was flirting with a sexy mechanic instead of listening to the conversation. Mollie dropped the phone onto the side of the chair. "All done."

"I think I should learn to play golf," Elena Guerrero announced as she wiggled her butt deeper into the black leather club chair in the middle of the Saturday-night-full restaurant.

Mollie didn't want to kibosh her dream. She got accused all the time by her girls—her friends since childhood—of being too literal, too black and white. Her medical friends never said any such thing, because they all saw the world the same way. Life or death. Sick or healthy. No gray areas in between.

Still, Elena had zero athletic ability. She'd worked the front desk at Lucien's family golf resort since high school, and had never once, in all that time, expressed any interest in the sport.

Trying to comment without being a *complete* buzzkill, Mollie said, "I thought you claimed your boobs got in the way of holding any sports equipment."

"True." She pulled out the edge of her low-cut, stretchy red top and tucked the stem of her martini glass into her cleavage. Then let go. The glass didn't even bobble. Twisting sideways over the arm of the chair, Elena then tipped backward enough to take a sip. Still without hands.

"Impressive trick." Lily flicked Elena's long black hair over her shoulder. Smirked when the tip of it landed in the martini. "If we were guys and cared *at all* about your big boobs." Which had been a bone of contention between the curvy Elena and Lily with the lean, swimmer's build since puberty hit. Funny how it never got old watching the two of them zing each other. "Since we're not? Let's go back to the question at hand. Why on earth do you want to learn golf?"

"Same reason I learned to ski two years ago."

Mollie remembered that trip. She hadn't been on it, of course. She'd been deep in her trauma rotation, getting texts every half hour of bearded men in sweaters and designs in the cocoa. Texts that made her miss her friends like crazy and start the plan to come back to Bandon. "You spent one hour on skis, and the rest of the time in Mammoth at the lodge drinking spiked cocoa by the fire."

"Exactly. The *amenities.* Look at where we are. This amazing lounge in the golf club, and we're the only women in it. We've got hot and cold running men, nineteen different flavors of martinis to try, a fireplace, and I heard a rumor there are duck nachos coming later."

Martini glass back in hand like a normal person—or a person without D cups and a push-up bra—Elena sighed. "If I golfed, I'd have a reason to hang out here all the time."

"You work here. All the time." Karen didn't roll her brown eyes, but her voice sure did the equivalent.

"I work at the front desk. That's vastly different. Especially the whole *having people wait on me* deliciousness. And I'm not stuffed into a uniform tonight. It's very freeing."

"Your breasts certainly seem to think so."

Mollie almost did a spit take with her martini. Lily and Elena were in fighting form tonight. She loved it.

She loved them. Beneath all the sniping, she knew they loved each other, too.

Her friends were all smart enough to have been successful at lives outside Bandon. Elena could be working at a swanky resort in a town with actual nightclubs. Karen could be managing payroll at a Fortune 500 company instead of the very small empire Lucien's family ran along the shore. And Lily was a firm but fair teacher who cared immensely about her kids. They'd all chosen to stay. They'd chosen each other, the town.

Just like Mollie had.

It melted her heart a little.

After another long sip, Elena said, "The point is, I'm very glad you had Lucien sneak us in for our girls' night, Mollie."

"Why *are* we here?" Karen gestured at the wall of floor-to-ceiling windows that, in daylight, overlooked the dunes of the twelfth hole. "Don't get me wrong—I'm a huge fan of this strawberry lemon drop martini. But girls' night at the Gorse is our tradition. What's with the relocate?"

Because it was hard to spill sex details with the sex-ee within hearing distance. Or worse yet, his *brothers* within hearing distance. As soon as Rafe had mentioned his intent to live it up at the Gorse with his brothers? That place became automatically off-limits for Mollie's Saturday night.

"I have something big to share. The Plover Lounge, as Elena pointed out, has all the amenities to give us a stellar girls' night."

"I like one particular amenity." Elena twisted around so far that it looked like she was posing for a yoga video. Then she tossed her hair and gave a little half wave toward the long mahogany bar before turning back. "That waiter, Victor. Six feet of dark hair and lean muscle?" Mollie shook her head. All that brought to mind were the six-plus feet of muscles who'd brought her to orgasm in the hospital laundry. Elena clarified further. "He brought us that bowl of mixed nuts without being asked. I'd like to mix it up with *his* nuts."

Karen's mouth dropped open with an audible click of her jawbones. Mollie would have to remember to ask her tomorrow if she'd been checked for TMJ. "Elena. It is girls' night. That means no hookups."

"I can still flirt, though, right? Flirt enough that he'll ask me out for another night?"

Karen pressed her fingertips to her forehead right below her straight brown bangs as though she had brain freeze. It was the same pained look she got the third week in January when she was responsible for getting the W-2s out for all the employees of the resort and the golf clubs. "I repeat, you work here. Every damn day. Can't you get your flirt on with a fellow employee at a more mutually agreeable time?"

"You work here, too. Why didn't you tell me about Victor?" An accusatory frown drew a straight line between her impeccably shaped brows. "Trying to keep him for yourself?"

Mollie's phone vibrated against the back of her hand. She tuned out her squabbling friends.

RM: My brother's a pain in the ass.

Which one?

RM: Grammar stickler, huh? My BROTHERS are a pain in the ass.

It wasn't just that he used all caps. Mollie could hear the frustration in Rafe's words. Not having a good night? She shifted the napkin over her jeans to better hide her surreptitious texting.

RM: There are times I feel like this family is like a rusted-out tailpipe. All it would take to make us fall apart is one good bump in the road.

Mollie wished she could race over there, pull him into a hug, and stroke his hair. It meant a lot that he was opening up to her. Now that he was, she couldn't give him a pat response. He deserved an equal measure of honesty. I'm sorry. Family can be a real challenge. My cousin and your brothers are poster children for the word "difficult."

RM: I'd add a few other choice words to that poster.

I wouldn't stop you. We're frustrated because you and I are the ones absorbing the hits. If you can hang in there, it's usually worth it in the end, though.

RM: You always see the best in people?

I try. You're a strong guy. I'll bet you can hold them together.

RM: You sure you should have that much faith in me already?

I don't know anywhere close to everything about you. But I can already swear, beyond the shadow of a doubt, that you'd move mountains to keep your brothers happy. Think of whatever you're going through tonight as warming up the bulldozer.

RM: Thanks. You helped. Nothing like a good farm implement metaphor to lift a guy's spirits.

Mollie lifted a hand to cover her mouth—and her smile. Then she lifted her martini glass high in the air to mask the gesture. "Let's circle back to my big thing I want to share." Big didn't begin to describe what she'd felt Rafe press against her in the laundry room at the hospital. Mollie almost giggled. But her days of giggling over anything remotely anatomical pretty much ended the first time she dissected a cadaver in med school.

Strawberry blonde wisps of hair fluttered against Lily's chin as she leaned forward. "You won a trip to Paris and you're taking all of us with you."

"No. And that's a very random guess." Mollie didn't even have a passport.

Suddenly, though, the thought of getting a passport appealed to her. Because then she and Rafe could have hot, dirty, filthy beach sex in Tulum. At night, they'd sit in the sultry air of the town square drinking margaritas and eating shrimp as big as her fist. They'd be the only two who spoke English, so they wouldn't have to whisper when they talked about all the borderline unspeakable things they planned to do to each other.

Between the fog and the rain and her family and work, that fantasy couldn't come true here in Oregon.

How long did it take to get a passport, anyway?

"You go to work." Lily thrust up her index finger, tipped in hot pink gels. "Then you hang out with your grandmother, your cousin, or your outrageously hot BFF." Three more fingers popped up in quick succession. Then Lily took her other hand and covered the fingers like a wet blanket. "There isn't anything big that *could* happen in your life. So I took a wild shot in the dark."

Med school, residency, and then trying to establish herself as a doctor people *wanted* to see didn't leave time for spontaneity. No blips. No excitement.

Which is why she was dancing on the inside with

glee right now. Smugly, Mollie said, "That's how much *you* know."

The leather of Karen's chair made a squelching noise as she wriggled to the edge of the seat. "You have a secret? You actually did something big?"

"You didn't have to bail Jesse out of jail, did you?" Elena asked in a half-jaded, half-resigned tone.

"No. Not . . . yet." Although Mollie wouldn't bet against it happening. The poor kid was so bored, lonely, and angry. That trifecta usually added up to trouble sooner rather than later. Hopefully Rafe's letting him work at the garage would make a difference.

Karen threw her hands in the air and a bejeweled charm bracelet slid down her arm. She claimed that since she could see her wrists all day long at her keyboard, she wanted something pretty to look at. The woman had more bracelets than Mollie had pairs of yoga pants. Which was saying *a lot*. "I give up."

"But you didn't even guess!"

"Didn't need to. Lily's right. Nothing big happens to you. Especially not here in Bandon."

Challenge . . . accepted. Mollie pushed to her feet. Put her arms out to the sides, and spun in a slow circle like she was the prize on a game show. Except without any bling, since she was just in jeans and a gray hemp sweater. Gran had insisted she try it out before it got ordered for an expansion into clothing at her increasingly marijuana-based coffee shop. "I'm having a fling."

"With what? Internet gambling?" Karen drawled.

"Seriously, you people are horrible guessers. And you ought to have more faith in me." That echo of Rafe's question made her breath catch in her throat. Because it wasn't logical that she'd feel such a strong connection with him after only a few days.

On the other hand, she'd known men for months, tried dating, and felt zero connection. Maybe she shouldn't look a gift horse in the mouth and just take the sexy gift that Fate had handed her on the side of the road.

"You really mean it?" Lily pushed her hot-pink cat eye glasses to the tip of her nose to eagle-eye Mollie over the rims. "You're having an actual, *sexual* fling? Hairy chest, bulging muscles, penis of steel, sexcapades fling?"

"Yes." To all of it. A thousandfold. Rafe Maguire was one of the most masculine, primal specimens of man she'd ever met. Let alone one with which she was well on the way to seeing naked. Mollie dropped back into the chair. Because it was comfortable. Not at all because her phone was there and she didn't want to miss a text.

Oh, who was she kidding?

"Victor!" Elena's arm shot up in the air as she yelled for the waiter. "We're going to need another round of martinis. Immediately." Then she tapped the tips of her fingers together. "This has to be one heck of an amazing stud to get you out of your rut."

"I wasn't in a rut. I dated in Chicago."

Karen drained her glass and set it down with a faint tinkle from her bracelet. "Did you? Or did you occasionally relieve stress with a quickie in a supply closet?"

Clearly everyone and their dog watched medical dramas and bought in to the fantasy of doctors hooking up in weird places. They also—clearly—overlooked the fact that working a thirty-six-hour shift was draining and left no energy for quickies.

Most of the time.

Casual dating at least got you sex—in a bedroom—every couple of months, albeit in a crowded triplex with too many roommates who could easily overhear.

But Mollie had no intention of defending or explaining her lack of relationship status over the past six years. So she shrugged and said, "There are no locks on the inside of a supply closet. That'd just be stupid and risky."

"You're avoiding the question. Which means you didn't really date. And God knows you haven't seen any action since moving back home."

That accusation she could easily rebut. "My rule makes that difficult."

"Your rule makes *you* difficult," Lily shot back. "There's nowhere in the Hippocratic Oath that says you can't date someone that maybe, if there's a catastrophic accident, you might have to slap some stitches into someday. A relationship is for every day. Whoever you end up with can hit the highway once a year to see a different doctor."

Well. That was a rant and a half. It dumped ice water all over her big reveal. Lily must've had it primed and loaded to go for a while. Probably waiting for a night when

Mollie's defenses were down. It seemed like she wouldn't be able to get on with raving about Rafe's muscles and the way he oh-so-sexily took charge until she cleared the air.

And if she had to do that, the duck nachos were *definitely* not happening. A girl could only force herself to do so many unpleasant things in one night.

Calling on the same patience she used when insisting that antibiotics were useless against the common cold, Mollie said calmly, "You know my rule isn't solely about not wanting to date a potential patient. That's just the fast-and-easy line I toss out to keep from being pestered—or worse, set up."

All four women gave a full body shudder at the mention of a setup. The track record on setups in Bandon—no matter how well-intentioned, was at a whopping 0.01% success rate. The only known success had come in passing off Mrs. Herbert's Labrador to Oswald Sturfins when she died.

"Everybody loves you here." Karen reached over to pat Mollie on the knee. "It's a big part of why you came back. I don't understand why you think you're seen as tainted goods."

"Not tainted." Great. Now she'd think of herself as smelly, two-week-old egg salad. Not sexy *at all.* "I just don't see myself the way most of the town does. You know, a pathetic, wounded victim of my mother's desertion? Not that you guys do, of course."

"Weeeeeel," Elena dragged the word out into three

syllables. Then she added insult to injury by flip-flopping her hand back and forth.

Wait . . . what? Mollie shoved up the sleeves of her sweater. She was getting her fight on, and they'd better be ready. "You really think I'm too much work for a man to jump into a relationship with because of my stupid, unimportant emotional scars?"

Even though her words peppered the air like verbal buckshot, all loud and harsh, none of them looked even the tiniest bit remorseful. No, they all looked straight at Elena, waiting for her to continue leading the charge.

She wrinkled her nose, as if smelling an old shoe. "I wouldn't call them unimportant. I'd also point out that your dating history isn't chock-full of long-term relationships."

So what? It in no way proved Elena's point. "That's not a character flaw. If you try a new shade of lipstick, and it doesn't make you feel like a better version of yourself, you stop wearing it. Men are the same way."

Lily snorted. "Your defense is that you're holding out for His Royal Highness, Perfect Prince Charming?"

Yup. The people who knew you best knew just where to find the chinks in your armor. Chipping away with, of all things, *logic* at every one of her rationalizations made her lemon drop martini suddenly not sit as well in her stomach. Could they be right?

No.

Or if they were, even a little bit, Mollie wouldn't

think about it tonight. Definitely not until she was done enjoying Rafe.

"I don't need to defend myself. Especially to you guys, I hope." A little bit of her self-doubt came through in her embarrassingly shaky voice.

"We're picking at you, aren't we?" Karen moved to sit on the arm of Mollie's chair. She gave her a one-armed hug.

Mollie didn't want to admit how much she needed one right at that moment. "Mmm-hmm."

Lilly rolled her lips in, and then firmed them. "We're sorry. It's just . . . don't you want someone to cuddle up and watch movies with on a Friday night?"

A new text vibrated against her palm. Mollie would rather text with Rafe than cuddle anyone else right now. "Look, I know you all mean well. But Rafe is the bad boy fling of my dreams. He's a living, breathing male fantasy. He's hot. He's uncomplicated. He's fun. He's drop-dead sexy."

"Uh, you already mentioned that he's hot," Karen said as she went back to her own club chair.

Saying it every hour *on* the hour wouldn't begin to encapsulate his hotness. "Trust me, it bears repeating."

Lily made frantic jazz hands in front of her chest. "You said Rafe? As in the tall, dark, and dreamy new mechanic over at Wick's Garage?"

"That's him."

"Omigod, he's so yummy!" Mollie's eyes must've

narrowed into a totally unconscious death glare, because Lily hastily backpedaled. "For *you*, I mean. Yumminess strictly for *you* to lap up."

Lap up was right. Mollie couldn't wait to trace her tongue over all those tattoos he'd mentioned—whatever and *wherever* they were. "He's delicious. Intense and with a hard, dangerous edge that I can't explain but makes me shiver. And yet he's got the manners of a high-powered broker at the Chicago Board of Trade. Much more polished than you think of a mechanic."

"What exactly have you let him polish?" Elena punctuated her question with an eyebrow waggle.

"A lot." Not nearly enough. "A lot that happened crazy fast, so we're in a holding pattern. I don't want to plan for the future, but I do want to be with someone I can talk to between all the copious rounds of hot, dirty sex."

"Of course." Three heads bobbed in agreement.

Mollie said lightly, "There wasn't time for fun in med school. Now I'm only looking as far into the future as my next, oh, dozen orgasms."

Lily ticked off a few fingers, then looked up. "Which should take about six months?"

Hardly. An incredibly smug grin stretched her lips sideways. "I get the feeling Rafe could get it done in six hours. Definitely within six days."

Elena raised her glass. "On behalf of all womankind, let me say *wow*. And congratulations. If you keep him around long enough, he'll be one hell of a date for the Cranberry Festival. Everyone will be jealous."

"Now tell us *everything*," Karen gushed.

"And start with how you met." Lily tapped her lips with one finger. "How good a kisser he is. If he used tongue on the first kiss."

Mollie could tell her friends were going overboard with their enthusiasm to balance against their airing of concerns. Which was fine with her.

Focusing, or even wishing for a future with someone? That was just a hop, skip, and a jump to thinking about when said hot person, say, a mechanic, would inevitably leave her.

Thinking about the *now* was a much better way to go.

She'd ride that orgasm train until it ran out of track. And try super hard to jump off before it crashed.

Another buzz. "I'll tell you everything. I just remembered that I have to, ah, return one message from a patient first." Mollie jumped out of the chair and hurried out of the room.

RM: The burgers are here and we're all still at the table and talking. So I guess the night's not going so badly.

Oh, good. Maybe you guys aren't so rusty after all.

RM: I sure felt a crack coming on tonight. But I think you helped me hold it together.

That's what us doctors do. Patch things up.

RM: I'm not used to leaning on people. Leaning on you isn't so bad, though. Thank you. Seriously.

Mollie leaned against the sea-grass papered wall with a sigh. A sincere thank you from a man was every bit as knee-weakening as a dozen red roses. Just in case, maybe I should resort to the old-fashioned kiss it and make it better?

RM: Tease. You and I both know you aren't bailing on girls' night. I hear that's sacred.

True. But Mollie refused to take any more than fifty percent of the blame. You wouldn't bail on your brothers, either.

RM: Does it count that I want to?

It counted for a lot.

Chapter Nine

Wick's Garage, 11:30 a.m.
Mood under the car—chilling to tunes with a wrench in his hand = pretty damned peaceful for once

FRIEDA WICK SQUEAKED every time she walked. In Rafe's first five minutes at the garage, he'd been borderline ape-shit with annoyance from it. She'd discovered Crocs the day he started. Loved 'em. Bought five pair in different, butt-ugly colors she loved them so much. She wore a new pair every day to break them in, and it was sure as hell breaking Rafe's spirit.

But hey, squeaky shoes weren't the worst thing in the world. His old boss? Tried to frame Flynn to get five years in the slammer. He was definitely involved in the deaths of both of their parents, and may have even pulled the trigger on Rafe's dad himself.

So Rafe could put up with some squeaky rubber shoes from his new boss.

Today's pair—bright yellow rain boots, because the sky had been pissing for the last four hours—stopped right next to his head. "How's that engine coming along?"

He didn't bother telling her he'd been changing the oil. If Frieda knew her way around cars, she wouldn't have needed to hire him when her husband had a heart attack. Rafe pushed his creeper out from underneath the Jeep and sat up on it. "Purring as sweetly as every woman that gets into my bed."

"You're just full of it, aren't you?"

"Full of the truth."

That got a bark of a laugh out of her. "I swear I don't know if I hired you for your looks, your skills beneath a hood, or the sheer entertainment factor."

"I'm a triple threat." Rafe actually liked Frieda. A whole lot. If he'd been in the Al Capone-era Chicago mob, he'd have called Frieda an honest-to-god *dame*. You could tell from her bright orange, spiked-up hair that the middle-aged woman had spunk. The way she'd held together two businesses with her husband in the hospital and then rehab without breaking or even slowing down showed her steel-hard spine. And no matter how outrageously he flirted with her, she just laughed and took it in stride.

It'd been six days since Frieda became his boss.

Rafe already hated lying to her.

The marshal insisted that they weren't supposed to think of it as lying to people 24/7. Delaney said their old lives, who they used to be, no longer existed. The only reality was who they were right now, which made it not a lie at all.

With that kind of smooth-talking ability to explain away anything, Delaney would've been a great criminal. Working for the feds was a waste of her natural talent.

Frieda tossed a rag at him. "Clean yourself up. You're going to lunch."

Eyeing the clock over the battered metal desk in the corner, Rafe said, "It's too early. I can get halfway through the tire rotation on that MINI Cooper before breaking." Talk about an awesome car. It wasn't a '64 Aston Martin, but it was the star of one of the best heist films of all time, *The Italian Job.*

"You're not listening. You're *going* to lunch. You have to leave now to get over to Billy Smoothboar's by noon."

"Who? Where? And, here's the big one, *why*?"

"Chamber of Commerce meeting. You're representing the garage."

Rafe stood, crossed to pause the Paramore blaring out of the iPod. "No."

Hell, no. A bunch of small-town saps sitting around jawing over tuna salad? It sounded like hell on earth, and a punishment he didn't deserve. He'd sat through more than his fair share of meetings back in Chicago. As Danny McGinty's right-hand man, he'd led more than a few of them. Amazing how even with hard-ass mobsters a meeting could easily degenerate into jaw-fests. Or arguments. Or both. The only thing that made it tolerable was caring about getting the job done.

He didn't care about the Chamber of Commerce.

Wasn't entirely sure what it did, but knew he didn't give two shits about it. Small-town politics. God help him.

"Wick's Garage and the Coquille River Creamery are both long-standing members in the Chamber." The Creamery was Frieda's other business. A freaking cheese shop. Apparently, this pimple on the Oregon coast was famous for cheese. He'd gotten an earful about it his first day.

If it was so damn famous, how come he'd never heard of it before moving here?

"Fine. So you go."

"I can't. We're short-staffed at the Creamery today. Besides, Neil always went and represented both of us. He's all torn up about not going."

Was she really playing the guilt card? Using her husband still in recovery from the triple bypass as leverage to get his ass to the meeting?

Frieda was *good.*

But Rafe had once stared down a coked-up human trafficker with a gun. Gotten the gun, gotten some licks in on behalf of humankind, and left him tied up on the steps of the CPD. He could say no to a middle-aged woman and make it stick. "I've only been here a week. I don't know enough to be your representative."

"You've got ears, don't you? Common sense, too. That's all it takes. Then report back to me. It'll get you the added bonus of a prime rib sandwich at the best steak joint in town, on me."

Rafe toed the creeper across the concrete to the edge

of a wall. Everything had its place in a garage. Out of place equaled danger. He hadn't dodged bullets in Chicago to crack his skull tripping over a loose tool and slamming into a hydraulic lift.

"What if they ask me—you—to vote on something? Or sign up for a sponsorship? I don't want to spend your money."

Frieda crossed her arms over her green Coquille River Creamery button-down. "You'll do this because it truly is part of the job. You'll do it because I asked. Most of all, you'll do it because you owe me for hiring Jesse Vickers without asking first."

Shit. She'd just turned over an ace-high flush on the river. Kicked a fifty-yard field goal in the last second on the clock. Rafe was stuck now.

Both going to the damn meeting—and giving an apology.

"Look, this place had been shut down for three weeks when I came on board. We've got cars backlogged *and* a wait list. Kenny only helps out part-time." Frieda called it paternity leave, letting the other mechanic downshift his hours since his son was born last month. Rafe called it bad business without a plan to pick up the slack. So he'd done just that—and made Mollie happy in the process. "We need another pair of hands. Jesse can fill the gap."

"I didn't say it was a bad idea," she said calmly. "Just that you should've asked me first. As you pointed out, you've only been here a week."

In Rafe's old life, he was the problem solver. Big or

small. People came to him, or he noticed things. Put a problem within his view, and it'd be worked through and solved. Period. Running his plan past somebody wasn't part of his routine.

Bypassing Frieda wasn't intentional. It wasn't a sign of disrespect. It was just how he did business. No middleman. No reporting. Just fixing.

But his new life had new rules.

Why hadn't the marshal given them a rulebook?

He unzipped his coverall. "You're right. I'm sorry. I knew we needed help and took a step. I should've taken a moment, too, and consulted with you."

"Glad we're clear. It's a good temporary fix. It'll be good for the little hooligan, too. From what Norah tells me, he's got a hard row to hoe, with all the damage his idiot mother did. The influence of a decent, stand-up man could make all the difference. You did the right thing."

Decent. Rafe Maguire had been called a lot of things in his life. Decent, though? This was a first.

"Now remove whatever bug crawled up your butt today and get to that meeting. I texted you the address." She handed him a key, attached to a fuzzy bumblebee key ring. "Take the brown Mazda in the lot. Listen for the 'weird, clacking, rolling noise' that Delia Chung described."

Huh. Maybe he *did* have a bug up his ass. Holding it together for Flynn and Kellan was hard fucking work. The garage was the only place he could let go and relax into the rhythm of what was black and white. An engine needed a tune-up, he did the required steps, and it ran well. No emotions. No hand-holding. No guessing three steps ahead for what might set off his brothers next. No hiding his own feelings about being dropped into this town and being forced to pimp it out to the others like it was Miss America and Miss Universe mud wrestling in bikinis.

Here, surrounded by harsh metal and the stink of oil, he'd let himself think about what he'd given up. What he didn't like about Bandon. What he missed from Chicago. Worry about them being tracked down by someone from McGinty's organization, then killed, one by one. Everything that couldn't be said to his brothers.

Everything he couldn't say to Mollie in their nightly texts.

Texts that made him want her more. Made him want to see her more, talk to her more.

Which hadn't been the plan at all. Shit.

Their texts weren't about sex. Well, not *just* about sex, anyway. The nights they texted were already more interesting than any of the nights he'd spent with a woman back in Chicago in years. Just texts—and Mollie—stacking up against nights out at clubs with free-flowing booze and gropes and craziness. She didn't just listen. Not just a string of emojis. She volleyed back, which Rafe wasn't used to at all.

How much he liked texting with her was . . . surprising. Rafe was still wrapping his head around it.

Rafe tossed the silly key ring in the air. Well, the prime rib sandwich alone would make the meeting worthwhile. He'd never say no to a thick slab of meat. Whatever inane weirdness got discussed would at least get him out of his own head. Distract him from worrying about being found.

Killed.

Or worse yet, seeing one of his brothers killed—and living to remember it the rest of his life.

ONE THING WAS for damned sure: the Irish mob would never, *ever* look for Rafe Maguire in this restaurant.

The walls were covered in diagonal wood paneling that maybe flew as a style in a 1970s basement rec room. Nowhere else. A couple of older guys were rocking knit caps against the thick mist hanging in the air. Lots of layers and a couple of shapeless knitted things he thought were called ponchos. They looked like the plastic cover-ups they passed out at Bears games in the rain. But none of the tables held anything more exciting than tea and coffee.

A summit meeting without booze never worked. If you didn't get people lubricated, they wouldn't screw up and be totally honest. Or totally embarrassing, which worked equally well in long-term negotiations.

No. He'd sworn to leave his mood at the garage.

Delaney hounded him to at least pretend to fit in,

find ways to make Bandon his own, and town leadership fit the bill pretty well. But pretending to care wasn't good enough. If the Maguires were spending the next fifty years here, Rafe might as well make it more to his liking. Take a stand. Take charge. So he'd stop counting the rows in the blue fishing net tacked up on the wall and tune in to the conversation. Hell, maybe he'd even find Kellan a better job.

Then his brother couldn't be mad at him anymore.

Now he'd pay attention.

"Hey, there. Thanks for saving me a few square inches." Mollie wheeled a chair into the catty-corner space at the edge of the table.

Still paying attention. Just not to the meeting. Now it was to the gorgeous woman who smelled of antiseptic, wore scrubs and sneakers, and had him at half-chub underneath his napkin. Rafe shifted to mutter against her cheek. "What are you doing here?"

"The hospital belongs to the Chamber of Commerce. I volunteered to be their rep. Can't beat the excitement of all the town's movers and shakers in one place!"

Mollie didn't just love her hometown. She lived, breathed, and *believed* in it. That made her the perfect person to smother his inner skeptic/smart-ass/big-city groupie and convert him.

Plus, he got to rest his hand on her thigh. Which skyrocketed this into one of the top ten meetings ever. Right below the one with the U.S. Marshals Service that promised him they'd keep Flynn and Kellan out of McGinty's grasp.

"Want me to flag down a waitress so you can order?"

"No." She flashed him a cheery smile of thanks. "Cheryl saw me come in. She'll bring my usual."

He moved his hand in slow, deliberate strokes up and down her thigh. She immediately responded by crooking her ankle around his. It gave his hand more room to roam. God, he could sit here touching her like this all damn day. Trying to keep things looking normal *above* the table, Rafe said, "You have a usual?"

"We meet here every month. When I find something I like, I stick with it."

If any other woman had said that, Rafe would've assumed it was a dig. A hint that they wanted, no, *expected* a long-term thing with him. But Mollie didn't play those games. She said what she meant, with no hidden meanings or double-talk to figure out. God knew she'd been up front about just wanting a fling from the start. Rafe had no doubt she'd be equally up front if she changed her mind. It was a fucking relief after years of examining every conversation for double-crossing and lies, too. With Mollie you got what you saw. Period.

Not that he gave her anywhere close to the same.

Squeezing her hand, he dialed back in to the guy in the fisherman's cap still yapping.

"I know you've all been waiting with baited breath—get it?" he said, tapping the double row of hooks and lures hanging from his floppy brim.

Great. Puns. Another reason why this meeting needed booze.

"Floyd, get on with it." Mick whipped off his faded gray USMC cap. Whapped it against his palm, re-creased the brim, then resettled it over the messy strands that didn't so much cover his scalp. "The May meeting is when you kick off discussions on the Cranberry Festival. There's no drumroll or surprise. Just a hope that you'll wrap it up before my burger comes."

If Rafe didn't already—grudgingly—like Mick, he would now. Any man who could cut through the bullshit and move things along was aces in his book.

"What's Mick's business?" he asked Mollie.

"None. He's here on behalf of the public. To make sure the business owners don't forget who keeps their doors open."

Rafe didn't buy it. "He showed up one day and nobody shooed him away."

"More or less," she said as a smile quirked up the corners of her mouth. "But he's smart. Always wants what's in the town's best interest. Mick has a good hand at reining people in, too. Tempers, ideas, you name it."

Making it to full colonel in the Marine Corps required a cool head. Rafe felt another ping of recognition for the fellow soldier. He'd always thought of himself as half soldier, half businessman.

Until now.

Now he was . . .

A mechanic? A whole new man? A guy holding his

family together with nothing more than hope and a shit-ton of cussing?

Floyd was now brandishing several clipboards. Jesus. Clipboards? Had they traveled back in time when he crossed the border into Oregon? If the Irish mob could use Google Docs, so could the Bandon Chamber of Commerce. "As usual, in addition to the manpower each business contributes, we'll need volunteers from the community."

Mollie waved her hand in the air. "To do what? Remember, we've had some newbies join in the past few months. Let's be sure to give them the full picture."

Great. Why not write *new guy* on his forehead with a Sharpie to really get their attention? Putting down roots and staying under the radar—per Delaney's instructions—seemed impossible to accomplish simultaneously. Too bad he couldn't tell which one gave them a better chance of surviving here.

"Right you are, Dr. Vickers. I wouldn't want anyone to be at sea with all the wonders," Floyd swooshed his hand into a large arc, "that the Cranberry Festival has in store."

The *wonders in store*? That did it. No doubt in Rafe's mind. Floyd lived with his mother. Probably had three cats, too. This guy was a trip.

"It is a multiday event celebrating our region's most famous crop. It all begins with a blessing of the cranberry harvest. We'll be choosing which local bog gets that particular privilege this year, so submit your nominations here." He handed off a clipboard to make the rounds of the two big tables. "There's the crowning of the queen and court, the hotly contested Food Fair for the best cranberry dish, a pancake breakfast, bake sale, bazaar, games, live music, the Cranberry Bowl, and of course, the parade."

Multiday event? This thing sounded like it lasted for a whole month. Rafe leaned in to Mollie. "Why all the hoopla?" he whispered. She gave a full body shiver as his breath tickled over her ear. Good to know she was as revved up as he was. He'd have to drag her away soon to take the edge off of all this heat between them. "Who even eats cranberries, aside from the can of stuff on Thanksgiving?"

Her deep pools of green rounded so wide that her upper lashes brushed her skin. "Shhhh! Are you looking to be blackballed out of the C of C on your first day? You can't say something like that in Bandon."

Rafe thought of the huge variety of festivals that dominated almost every weekend, spring through fall, in Chicago. You couldn't turn a corner without hearing bands, smelling charcoal and spices, and stepping in puddles of beer. There was no way this half-assed excuse for a town could throw a decent festival. "This sounds like a whole lot of excitement over nothing."

"Do you know how many pounds of cranberries Americans eat in a year?" Her whisper sliced back, as sharp as her scalpel.

"No." Rafe barely stopped before rolling his eyes.

Instead, he just muttered, "Not sure I give a rat's ass, either."

"Four hundred million pounds. Every year." Her ponytail jerked as her head bobbed on each word, driving the point home. "Cranberries are a very big deal, and they are *everything* to the people of Bandon. They are our livelihood, our purpose. And yes, for a few days every September, they're a heck of a lot of fun, too."

Shit. Cranberries evidently made the earth turn here, so he'd need to get on board. Well, first, he'd have to dial back his natural inclination to mock this piss-ant "festival." *Then* he'd get on board.

But damned if he'd suffer by himself.

Rafe shot his hand in the air. "I've got three volunteers for you."

"Wonderful." Floyd rushed at him like a quarterback aiming for the goal posts. "To do what?"

How the fuck should he know? Forcing his gritted teeth open into *maybe* a smile, Rafe said, "Whatever you need. My brothers and I are good with our hands. Flynn can build anything. Kellan could help write press releases. I just want to be a part of the action."

Especially if volunteering got him more action with Mollie. If it made him look like a good guy, a decent guy, in her eyes. Mollie, who was now patting his thigh in approval. Now her hand was moving up, up, to something that wasn't his thigh. Rafe jerked his chair farther forward to hide her wandering fingers from Floyd.

"You're the new mechanic over at Wick's, aren't you?" Instead of looking at Rafe, he skimmed his gaze over everyone else at the long table, as though looking for them to agree. He hooked a thumb into the gap between the pearlized snaps of his graph paper shirt.

Deciding he didn't want anyone else to speak for him, Rafe grunted out a, "Yeah."

"That skill set will come in very handy on our parade committee. Put your contact info on the sheet. Bandon's lucky to have transplants that already care so much about the town." Floyd pulled another clipboard from under his arm and waved it. "All right, moving on. Who wants to track down some new bands this year?"

If Bandon knew who the Maguire brothers really were?

They wouldn't feel lucky at all.

But Rafe felt damn lucky. Signing all three of them up for this so-called festival would satisfy the marshal's insistence that they do community service and the Maguires didn't mind giving back . . . in theory.

Their mom had insisted on helping others, even when they were little. Dad didn't care, but Rafe made sure to pass it down as his mom's legacy. Back in Chicago, Flynn mentored kids at a gym. Kellan tutored. Rafe did Habitat for Humanity. Figured it was the least he could do to tip the scales back the right way to putting the city together that he was occasionally responsible for pulling apart.

It was the government more or less *ordering* them to do it that chafed like a starched jock strap.

"I had no idea my bad boy was such a do-gooder," Mollie teased, nosing at his neck. It shot up the tiny hairs there.

Who knew being good had so many rewards? If it wasn't for Mick eagle-eyeing them across the room, Rafe would've turned the bare half inch to take her mouth. Instead, he ran a hand down her ponytail and gave it a tug at the bottom. Zeroed in on her smoky green eyes like they were totally alone. Eyes that darkened with some serious want the longer he stared at her. "Whatever it takes to keep you turned on."

"Apparently, that's very little when it comes to you." Her hand caressed his forearm. Not anything so sexy it'd be in a porno script. But the way Mollie did it had him almost leaping out of his chair. Rafe was so aware of her, aware of where they touched at the sides of their feet, their knees, their arms. Aware of the combo scent of forest air and hospital sterile scrub that was so *her*.

No need to pay attention to Floyd now that he had Rafe's slave labor lined up. But their suggestive whispers ended when a waitress slung plates down in front of them. The shift in their positions made Rafe aware of someone staring at them.

Staring daggers.

A man, his own age, way too handsome for Rafe's taste, what with the possessive way his eyes all but shot handcuffs around Mollie's arms.

Fat chance.

The best prime rib sandwich in town would have to wait a couple of minutes. Apparently Rafe needed to send a message.

Because he didn't believe in sharing. Not a pen, not his clothes, and damn sure not his woman. The mob had taught him to cling to what was his. If you loosened your grasp, even a little, someone would snatch away whatever was precious to you.

This thing with Mollie was casual. Temporary. A flash in the pan. But while they were in it? He was all in. One hundred percent.

So hands fucking off, you nameless, nosy bastard.

Chapter Ten

"COME WITH ME." Even before he finished the order, Rafe pulled Mollie from her seat.

It was kind of fun, how effortlessly he lifted her to her feet. Sexy, of course. But sex wasn't the uppermost need in her body right now. Flirting was fun. Food was a *necessity* after starting her shift two hours early to vaccinate the high school band for their upcoming trip to Brazil. "But my Bogwich is here."

"Your what?" he asked, still leading her out of the dining room toward the bar.

"The Hounddog Bogwich. My sandwich." The one she'd dreamed of all morning. Stabbing teenagers in the arm, it turned out, worked up quite an appetite. "Turkey, swiss, and cream cheese with Bogworks cranberry sauce."

He stopped without any warning. Mollie tripped

over his size humungous feet in hard-tipped work boots and fell against his side. Not that she was complaining about the full body slam. Any time she could rub up against Rafe Maguire and his six-plus feet of lean muscle, she would certainly jump on it. On him.

Except . . . those blue eyes squinted down at her, almost . . . pissed off? At her sandwich? Geez, if he had that much buyer's remorse over his own sandwich, she'd split hers with him.

After demanding at least a half-dozen kisses as payment. Because Mollie clearly had the leverage in this situation.

"No. Tell me you made that up." Rafe's hoarse plea sounded as serious as Jesse's unadulterated horror at her suggestion he put bananas on his waffle last weekend.

"The Bogwich? I told you, we live, breathe, and yes, *eat* cranberries here in Bandon." Not to mention its complete, tongue-melting deliciousness. Mollie had dreamt about this sandwich all through her residency. The mere thought of it got her through some endless thirty-six-hour shifts. It was the first thing she ordered when she got back to town.

"It's an abomination." The harsh words dragged out of him like tires over gravel.

That got her off of his chest. And made her mentally scroll through a few other casual comments in which Rafe had revealed Bandon was far from his dream destination. Mollie got that small-town life could require . . . an *adjustment*. It could be intrusive. It felt claustrophobic even to her the first few weeks after coming back from residency, and she loved Bandon more than ice cream.

She'd take a wild guess that the small-town charm hadn't drawn him here. Rafe wore big-city slick all over him like an invisible hand-tailored suit. It was in the way he walked and moved and talked. Which was unusual for a mechanic. His job also led her to believe he didn't come to golf every day at one of Lucien's world-famous resorts—not at the $250 a pop greens fees.

Mollie threw her hands up in the air in mock frustration. Which mostly covered her actual confusion. "Why on earth stay in Bandon if you don't like cranberries?"

Rafe was silent for a moment. A long enough moment for her to register the clatter of dishes in the wait station. The drone of local news on the television over the bar. Floyd's loud and impossible to ignore nasal voice still droning on and on and—

"I like . . . other things about the town." Rafe slid a finger along the *V* of her scrub top. Even though she wore a long-sleeved tee underneath, and he wasn't touching skin at all, the heat burning through the thin cotton seared straight through to her spine.

As a doctor, Mollie knew that wasn't actually possible.

As a woman, Mollie knew that it absolutely *was*.

"I'll tell you what I don't like." The hand cuffing her wrist was gentle, but firm as it pulled her the final few steps into the bathroom hallway.

"Not a surprise. I don't really see you holding back on your dislikes at all."

A sharp, deep laugh bounced off the acoustic tiles above and the cracked linoleum below. "Oh, I think you'd be surprised."

"Okay. Rock my world," she challenged.

"That comes later." His voice stayed deep on those words, but with none of the humor of his laugh. It was deep and dark and rich and oozed its sexual promise all over her. Rafe backed her against the wood paneling. "Right now, tell me about the guy."

"What guy?"

First one fist went onto the wall next to her head. Then the other one caged her in. Even though they weren't actually touching, Mollie *felt* Rafe. Felt the solid wall of his body throwing off heat and want and strength and edgy power.

He was almost unbearably sexy. Even though the vibes he threw off felt way closer to unsettled and ticked off. "The one I don't like. The one staring at you with ownership. And staring at me with an obvious urge to kick my ass right off the chair next to yours and all the way out the door."

"Nobody owns me. Certainly no man in this town even has dibs on me. Aside from you, and that's up for reevaluation depending on how this conversation progresses." Because, in theory, it was none of his business who ogled her across a room.

In reality? Mollie did sort of revel in this whole primal, possessive thing. It was the most fun she'd had in a long time. Definitely the most *wanted* that she'd ever felt. Weird, though. There wasn't a single man in that room who should've put Rafe's hackles up. He was fierce, harsh, rugged . . . for crying out loud, she could go on for days . . .

Rafe took home the trophy for best of everything. Period. Nobody else she'd ever met came close to stacking up to his potent mix of in-your-face sensuousness, muscled athleticism, dry humor, and easy charm.

Not that Mollie was comparing. Or that those attributes made him sound like the ultimate boyfriend. Nope. This was just a fling. A fun fling. Anything else would be crazy.

But being pressed up against the wall next to the bathroom door by his sheer presence would stay on her list of hottest encounters for an undoubtedly long time.

"The guy." Rafe's eyes darkened, as did his expression. All the rain clouds in Oregon seemed to have coalesced in his now deep indigo eyes. "The only one wearing a tie."

A belly laugh would've folded her in half if not for Rafe's more than six feet of solid muscle keeping her vertical. "Oh, that's just Lucien. I told you about him."

Not a single one of the hard lines on his face relaxed an iota. "You told me that you were just friends with him."

"Well, best friends, but yes. Nothing more. Nothing like . . . this." She waved her hand back and forth between them. "No chemistry."

"You sure about that? I know the look when a man

knows that he's lost and has to walk away without the prize."

Damn.

Her inner feminist rose up in protest at the terminology. And yet again, Mollie was simultaneously more than a little flattered that Rafe considered her a prize. "I'm positive. He's probably just feeling protective. In a big brother way. You *are* a stranger here, you know. That raises suspicions."

"About what?"

"He was all for me having a fling. But your approval rating dropped considerably when I mentioned that you picked me up on the side of the highway." That was totally her fault for over sharing.

Rafe's mouth turned down at one side. In a sneer. An actual, Al Pacino-esque sneer. "Big fucking deal. I'm employed. I put my ass to sleep at this meeting. I've got the responsible citizen thing down cold."

"I'm sure Frieda appreciates your ass's great sacrifice." Instantly, Mollie regretted the sarcasm. Because Floyd could be overbearing and managed to hold court for twenty minutes on what should've been a two-minute announcement. Fearful that Rafe would walk away with a negative impression of the monthly meetings she adored, Mollie added, "Once we get into the actual festival planning, things will pick up, I promise."

"I don't want to wait. Let's pick things up right now." Rafe crowded in on her.

His eagerness to kiss her again, to erase the entirely

imaginary threat of Lucien from her mind, was sweet. But the look on Rafe's face was anything but sweet. Dark brows knitted together, a vein pumping on his temple, and his clenched jaw all but screamed that he was still pissed at the totally erroneous idea that Lucien wanted her.

At first, it was only Rafe's lips that touched her. There was maybe an inch of air between the rest of them, but only those softly firm lips actually made contact. Mollie tipped her head back, trying to capture more, trying to get as much of him as possible. Hot, heady licks all along the seam of her lips. As soon as she opened for him, Rafe switched to nips along the edges. Laughing, she palmed the small of his back to pull him closer.

It was like the time she removed a clamp from a femoral artery. What happened next was powerful—and totally out of her control.

Rafe surged forward. No, first he put a hand behind her head to cushion it from the wall. It was the kind of thoughtful gesture that weakened her knees. But half a second behind that move? His entire body crushed Mollie against the wall. Against *him*.

Against his hardness.

Hardness everywhere. His thighs, his abs, pecs, his tight denim-clad ass beneath her hand, and most of all, the thick hardness between her legs. *Right* between her legs, because somehow she was up on her toes to notch him there. To rub against him right there.

Rafe's mouth dominated hers. There was no other

word for it. He tasted and licked and swirled inside. Every molecule of tissue was touched, was taken, was owned by him. His tongue demanded that she respond. That she burn up from the inside out.

With a tug on her ponytail, Rafe tipped her head to the side. He strafed her neck with searing kisses that followed the line of her carotid. It had to be pulsing against his lips as strongly as his cock throbbed against her core.

She bit his earlobe. It was all Mollie could reach as he laved the thin skin of her neck, each tiny taste bud just rough enough to set all her nerve endings to *yes, please, more*. Rafe needed to be as electrified as she was, darn it.

No way would she be *seduced* in the bathroom hallway at Billy Smoothboars. This had to be a give-and-take. Equal lust on both sides. Equal surrender to the liquid heat fueled by every kiss, every squeeze. Scraping her teeth down the fleshy part of his ear, she flicked her tongue rapidly along the edge.

That bucked his hips hard enough to bounce her off the wall. Which was gratifying. Also very useful to file away for later. When they were naked. When cheesy pop tunes from the nineties weren't blaring out of the speaker a foot overhead.

"Christ, I could sink my teeth into you."

"Nobody's saying you shouldn't," she murmured into his thick, wavy hair.

Rafe popped his head up. He wore a loose, teasing smile. One that said he didn't believe her at all but

would play along just for fun. "I can give the town doc a hickey with no objections?"

Why not? Why not have a souvenir? Something she could look at in the mirror after showering and trigger a memory strong enough to make her thighs tremble in want. Proof, too, that his exemplary control slipped. Slipped enough to let the leading edge of his lust take over.

Yes, the more Mollie thought about it, the more a hickey sounded like a thoroughly reasonable next step. It was a bad girl move. One that was to be expected from her bad boy hookup/fling. One that Elena, Lily, and Karen would no doubt applaud.

They might even order champagne to toast her boldness. There was zero downside to this.

"This is the Oregon coast. Cold, misty, rainy Oregon. It's always scarf season," she said lightly. "A hickey won't be a problem to hide."

Rafe slid his hand down her body. Fast, past her shoulder to her lats. A little slower as he approached the curve of her hip. Then he turned his hand so his whole palm dragged forward. Over the crest of her pelvis but acres—seemingly—away from where she burned hottest for his touch. One by one his fingers curled back until only his index finger continued its now torturously slow path to stop about an inch below the inseam of her scrubs.

"Here. This is where I'll give you a hickey. You'll scream. I'll have to think about when I saw my grandpa's dentures in a glass to stop from coming against the

sheets just from how soft your skin is. And we'll be the only two who know."

There he went. Being thoughtful. Protecting her reputation. "You're on," Mollie said with more breath than voice. Because his version of a hickey sounded way hotter than what she'd originally imagined.

Reaching around, he tightened her ponytail. Smoothed a few loose strands behind her ears. Then he tugged at the bottom of her top until it hung straight. "Let's go eat our lunch."

"Thanks for making me look respectable."

Smugly, he said, "Not a chance. Your lips are swollen from kisses and rubbing against my stubble. Your cheeks are red and your eyes look like you almost got fucked against a wall. Anyone with half a brain won't think 'respectable' when they look at you."

"Trying to send a message?"

"Only to you." Rafe's eyes burned, drew her focus until they could've been by the bathroom or in the middle of the Oregon Ducks homecoming game, and Mollie wouldn't know the difference. "Doesn't matter what anyone else thinks."

"Message received."

"MESSAGE RECEIVED, MOLL." Lucien bit off his words more sharply than the lawn mower blade that cut him last week. His polished patent leather loafers clicked hard against the cement sidewalk.

"I don't know what you're talking about." Mollie adjusted the napkin around the ice-cream cone she'd badgered him into buying them at the Coquille River Creamery.

"That mechanic just staked his claim on you. More to the point, you let him."

Whoa. Mollie stopped right in front of the diamond-paned windows of Coffee & 3 Leaves. Which wasn't ideal, as her gran would undoubtedly spot them and come out to chat and then she'd be late getting back to the hospital. But Lucien's dig had to be dealt with immediately.

"Did you just say 'that mechanic'? Because that's the sort of snobby thing your mom might say. Not my egalitarian best friend."

"I don't give a rat's farting ass if he's a mechanic or a NASA engineer." Using his cranberry-orange triple scoop waffle cone as a pointer, Lucien jabbed in her direction. "His job isn't what's got me in a lather."

"Why don't you spell it out for me? Because when I was stitching you up, you were all about the fun of my fling. You were rooting for me. You wrote two dirty limericks about mechanics and doctors on the back of your discharge instructions and left them on my desk."

"What can I say—I miss the old days of passing notes to you."

Did he really think reminiscing about high school would miraculously smooth things over? They weren't wearing nametags and chugging cheap wine at a reunion.

Mollie glanced over her shoulder at the display of what could be glass tea canisters in the window—if you didn't know they were full of marijuana. The threat of her grandmother emerging was too high for comfort. Pinching the heavy cream linen of his sleeve between her fingers, Mollie led Lucien across the street.

"The only notes you ever passed were so I'd fix the spelling before passing them *on* to girls you wanted to kiss."

He licked a flattened path across the top scoop. Gave her the big eyes that tried to sell innocence. But Mollie knew better. She knew *him* far, far better. "Like I said, I miss you fine-tuning my approach. You were a solid Cyrano to my Christian."

"You just compared me to a seventeenth-century coward with a hideous nose. Are you trying to make me more pissed off at you?"

"No. Of course not. But if that's the outcome from my caring about my best friend, so be it."

Par for the course from the man who'd pulled off her bathing suit top on a dare her first day in summer camp. She'd burst into tears of embarrassment—and then socked him in the jaw. Lucien had apologized smoothly, a charmer even back then. And he'd been so impressed by her right hook that he promised to be her best friend. Somehow, they stuck.

But *only* as friends. Mollie took an extra large bite of her margarita sherbet to purposely cause brain freeze. That was the only way to *not* double over in laughter at Rafe's worry of Lucien wanting to hook up with her. Rafe was so far down the wrong path on that one he might as well be in Antarctica.

Not that she minded, *at all*, their discussion about it and the subsequent kissing.

A jealous not-quite-boyfriend. That was a new experience.

Lucien turned them away from the water, toward Ferry Creek and the hospital. "Look, Moll, I did want you to have a fun fling. A stress reliever, like a night hitting the bars in Portland with me."

"And I took your advice. So why are your tighty-whities in a bunch over it?"

"I don't want you to get hurt. The way Rafe looked at you? It didn't look like a fling. For God's sake, you've never macked on someone in the middle of a crowded restaurant before."

Was that disapproval in his tone? She hoped it curdled his ice cream because Lucien Dumont was a fine one to talk. He wasn't throwing stones from inside a glass house on this topic. He was sitting poolside, lobbing them. Not even under an umbrella.

But she just didn't care. It was fun. *Lots* of fun. After all the years spent with her nose to the grindstone to become a doctor, didn't she deserve a little fun? "We didn't strip and do the horizontal tango on the table in front of Floyd. We were fully clothed, two rooms away, in a semiprivate hallway."

"*Semi* is the keyword. Waitresses walked by and saw

you, and it's not like they signed NDAs. Remy left the men's room, got an eyeful, and immediately texted his partner over at—"

"—at the hospital," she finished for him. Remy's guy managed the kitchen. They were two of the biggest gossips in Bandon. Sweet, bitingly funny, but unadulterated gossips.

Funny, Mollie didn't remember seeing anyone walk past them.

Guess that was a side effect of having your eyes squeezed shut in glorious, sexalicious bliss. She should've worried about being seen, about being the target of gossip. But Rafe wiped all those normal thoughts out of her mind.

Moving on to his second scoop, Lucien said, "The way you two were acting? It reeks of a relationship."

"Bite your tongue." Mollie couldn't even look at him after that accusation. To avoid biting his head off, she focused on the stand of pine trees bordering Mrs. Collier's house. Tested her mental patient database. Broken rib from a puppy training incident in the park involving a jungle gym. Asthma. And a daughter in the Navy.

"You're not a relationship girl." Lucien continued to bombard her with his ridiculous allegations and total misinterpretation of the facts. "They scare you, the same way they scare me."

"Ever since I passed the medical boards, I'm not scared of anything," she scoffed.

Not that he'd fall for it.

Mollie was scared of lots of things, and Lucien knew it. Losing her gran. Letting down Jesse and not keeping him out of trouble. Losing a patient. Never trying on a pair of Jimmy Choos. Slugs, which packed a double whammy of scaring her and grossing her out.

Relationships, though? They didn't inspire fear in her. There was no point fearing something you'd never encounter. It was like saying she'd be scared of dying on a spacewalk. Just not gonna happen.

Thanks to her mom's abandonment, Mollie had vowed to never open herself up to the pain of being left again. Ergo, no relationships allowed. Since also thanks to dear old mom, she was certain that a man would inevitably leave her. If her own mom didn't see Mollie as reason enough to stick around, why would anyone else?

After a calm lick at her cone, Mollie said, "You're jumping to conclusions. Erroneous ones, at that."

"I'm not taking a leap in a vacuum here. I'm telling you, the whole town is talking."

"You're the expert in that." Mollie immediately regretted slipping that verbal scalpel between his ribs. But for crying out loud, Lucien Dumont was a man-whore. She knew because he detailed more than she usually wanted to know about his conquests. *Everyone* in town knew because they had eyes and ears, and they whispered about him incessantly. He'd used his family golf resorts as his own personal hunting ground since long before he should've been able to get away with it.

Which meant she didn't need to take any guff from him. No, sir, and good day.

The sun glinted off his Patek Philippe watch as he crumpled up his napkin. "Not gonna deny it. The point is that you and your fling are big news. And I'm worried about you."

"You're worried. About something you *think* you saw a whole hour ago?"

Lucien didn't try to dodge her unassailable logic. He stood his ground, literally and figuratively. "Yes. I know I may not check all the boxes of a standard best friend. But I know my number one job is to look out for you. Protect you. And despite all your shallow, seedy intentions, I'm worried this isn't a fling. Because if it gets serious, you'll get hurt."

Okay. That was kind of sweet. Good intentions and all that. But enough was enough. "I appreciate your concern. The situation is under control."

"Opposites might attract, but they don't last."

"That explains your parade of brainless bimbettes that disappear faster than a pimple," she said with a snicker.

"What are you and a mechanic going to talk about over dinner?"

Why wouldn't he let up? Mollie chuffed out a breath. "Lots of things. What on earth do I have in common with the heir to a golf course empire . . . when I don't golf? Our disparate careers haven't clammed the two of us up at all."

He smoothed a hand over his wind-ruffled hair. "Thanks to me. Thanks to my scintillating small talk."

The brain freeze must've finally thawed, because Mollie had a great idea. One that would get her best friend to stop hounding her, and have the added bonus of helping a newcomer. Cocking her head, she flashed Lucien a disarming smile. One he'd see right through, but was necessary nonetheless. "Why don't you try lobbing some of that Rafe's way and see what you two have in common?"

"You know lobbing is a tennis term, not golf."

"Whatever." The smile was too much work if he was going to nitpick. "I'm saying Rafe's a fun guy. You'd like him. As long as you make it clear up front that you have not now, or ever, harbored any intention to get into my panties."

"What the ever loving fuck is that about?"

He looked equally as horrified as she'd found it hysterically funny. "Nothing. Forget I mentioned it."

"That's like asking me to forget when my frat brothers swapped out my bottle of Grey Goose with Everclear." He gave a full-body shudder.

Mollie squeezed his forearm. "I promise that this thing with Rafe is just sex. Or at least, it will be soon . . ."

"You'd better be right."

A fling wasn't *an* option.

It was the *only* option that worked for Mollie. She was certain of that. Because every other option scared the pants off of her—and not in a good way.

Chapter Eleven

Historic Old Town Bandon, 7:00 p.m.
Mood for all the Maguires—not too bad. For once.

"I CAN'T BELIEVE you're letting us leave the house for dinner." Kellan walked backward in front of his brothers. First Street wasn't the most direct route, but it took them next to the marina and steps away from the Pacific Ocean. Which Rafe had to admit beat Lake Michigan all to hell. "It was starting to feel like we were under house arrest."

Rafe waved away the accusation—and its more than partial truth—with a lazy swipe of his hand. "Just getting the lay of the land."

He always cased a place, a situation, before making himself a part of it. He'd needed his brothers to just go to work and take stock of their new surroundings. Now that the shock of moving was behind them, he could trust them not to flap their gums in a restaurant.

"We went out Saturday night," Flynn pointed out. Nice that he finally had Rafe's back again.

"Barely. And we used to go out for dinner all the time. We'd hit the Italian Village once a week, swing by Greektown for souvlaki, get Stilton burgers at Goose Island—"

Raising a hand in the air, Flynn cut him off. "We used to have more money," he said flatly.

"Oh, yeah." Kellan waved his hands in the air. "All those illegally gotten gains. Living the high life off of other people's money that you extorted from them."

Son of a bitch. One night. That's all Rafe wanted. One night without reminders of everything they'd left behind in Chi-town that made his mouth water. One fucking night without Kellan or Flynn making him feel like shit for saving their sorry asses and dragging them out of there. Now he had a food craving that couldn't be filled, and a little brother full of righteous anger.

He squinted over at the glints of early evening sunshine on the water. Thought about how good it'd feel to toss Kellan in. Wash off some of that self-righteousness or at least make him squeal like a girl from the cold.

But grown men didn't throw their brothers in the drink. No matter how much they *wanted* to. When he'd left Mollie at the C of C meeting after lunch, she'd reminded him to be patient with his brothers. And promised to reward him for it her next night off of ER rotation.

Rafe locked his jaw and barely ground out the words between his gritted teeth. "With Flynn off from the bar tonight, we deserve to get out of the house."

A siren went off. "Check that out. Your edict gets its own soundtrack," Kellan joked.

Rafe looked around. It sounded like a burglar alarm. Definitely not a cop siren. Or a car alarm. He could identify any variation of those in his sleep. But everything in sight seemed . . . fucking postcard-perfect as usual.

Turning his head back and forth, Flynn then stopped, on alert like a hunting dog. "It's coming from inland."

"No shit, Sherlock." Kellan gestured to the expanse of nothing but water to their right. "You think boats have burglar alarms?"

"I don't know and I'm not fucking arguing it with you right now."

Really? They were going to fight over boat alarms? Rafe jogged forward, both to get away from his brothers and to see if there was any unusual . . . anything in the row of storefronts with weathered shingles and brightly painted awnings lining both sides of the street.

Yeah. Two guys crawling out of what used to be a glassed-in window qualified as unusual. Also unusual? The dozen people scattered along the sidewalks watching and *not doing a damned thing to stop them*.

Well, they were idiots. Bad citizens. Pussies. All of the above.

He put his fingers between his teeth and whistled. Flynn was at his side in a second, with Kellan just a few steps behind. For half a second, Rafe appreciated how they were a unit again. "K, you call the cops. Flynn?"

"Yeah." Resignation mixed with excitement in his voice as Flynn took off his watch and shoved it in the pocket of his jeans. "I'll take the long-haired one."

They both broke into a run to catch the fleeing thieves. Skinny, in head-to-toe black but with brown knit caps, they lugged backpacks that dragged on the ground behind them. Slowed them down in a way that marked them as rank amateurs. It also made it almost too easy to catch them.

Almost.

Rafe grabbed the unzipped pack. Yanked hard. It slid almost to the wrist of the shorter, stockier guy. It also pulled him back and Rafe stepped out of the way so momentum would carry the idiot burglar off-balance. The stumble happened—predictably—but he came out of it swinging.

It was cute. Like a Chihuahua barking at a Newfoundland. Rafe had at least half a foot on him, if not more. Not to mention that Rafe also knew not to tuck his thumb inside his fist. This was becoming less of a fight and more of an insult to Rafe's years of experience. No point letting it drag on.

His arm shot out, straight from the shoulder. His knuckles connected with a satisfying crunch to the thief's nose. One and done, if you did it right. That'd been how he was taught, back in the day, by his dad. Good old life lessons that stuck with Rafe no matter what life he assumed.

The man's feet came out from under him. He landed on his ass, with both hands immediately going to the river of blood flowing down his face and black tee.

Checking on Flynn, Rafe was just in time to catch

his brother deliver a fully extended roundhouse kick to the chest of thief number two. It was perfect. A thing of beauty. And it was a damn shame Flynn didn't have anywhere to show off his MMA skills anymore.

"You good?" he asked, more out of habit than actual necessity. Flynn wasn't even breathing hard. The thirty-something thief, on the other hand, had the wind knocked out of him and was flat on the ground, gasping, his hat knocked clean off.

"Please. I've kicked the asses of nightmares harder than this little twat." He high-fived Rafe. Which was the best connection he'd had with Flynn in six months.

Who knew that doing their civic duty would bring them back together?

Kellan hovered on the balls of his feet less than a foot away, clearly itching to jump in and help. The shit-eating grin on his face betrayed his pride in how easily the Maguire brothers took down the pair. All Rafe had wanted was a family evening where they acted and felt like the tight unit they used to be.

Well, mission mostly accomplished.

Guess he just needed to be more specific in the *how* of his wish next time.

He and Flynn returned to their respective thieves and kicked away the backpacks, which left a trail of glass jars on the asphalt.

Weird thing to steal. Rafe looked up at the gilded cursive across the few shards left in the top of the window. Coffeehouse he got. He mentally filled in some missing letters to come up with bakery. But the last word looked a lot like dispensary. Since this wasn't a Gold Rush settlement in the 1800s, he had no idea what that meant.

He pulled off his denim overshirt, wadded it up, and handed it over. "Hold that against your nose," he ordered.

"You broke it." Shock—and the need to breathe—had the man's mouth gaping open like a fish and drew Rafe's attention to his eyes. The pupils were totally blown. The guy was high as a kite on something, which explained why he'd been dumb enough to attempt a burglary in broad daylight.

"Yeah, well, you broke the window first," he said, pointing with his elbow as he dragged the whimpering, quivering pansy-ass to his feet. He pushed him forward to line him up against the curved iron streetlight. A little pressure between his shoulder blades would easily keep him in place until the cops arrived.

Now that the excitement was over, people were rushing at them. Clapping. Whooping.

Weird.

People he didn't know. People banging out from nearby stores to stand around in a loose circle, jabbering away. Some filming him with their phones. A couple of people he recognized from the chamber meeting called him by name and even clapped him on the shoulder.

Rafe looked over at Flynn, who'd shoved his guy up against the light, too. "This feel surreal to you?"

"It couldn't feel any more surreal if I was stuffed into a shark costume and smoking a pipe."

"What is wrong with you two? You just apprehended criminals. You're heroes," Kellan shouted.

No.

Fuck, no.

That kept repeating in his head on a loop as the cops pulled up, handcuffed the men, and started in on more than a dozen witness statements. Rafe and Flynn were instructed to go nowhere—after being thanked profusely by a deputy and a full-blown sheriff.

Less than ten minutes later, Mollie ran down the street, full tilt right at him. Talk about a come from nowhere surprise. Good thing he'd been cooling his heels against the black-and-white, or she'd have tipped him over.

Not that he minded. An armful of the doc, even in her scratchy scrubs, was a damn fine way to pass the time.

"Oh my gosh, Rafe, thank you so much." The words peppered out of her as fast as pellets from a BB gun. Mollie rained kisses up his throat and across his cheeks.

Again, no complaints. But he wanted to know the cause so he could do it again. "For what?"

She pointed at the scene of the crime, now draped with yellow tape. "That's Gran's store."

"Store? I thought you said she ran a coffee shop."

"Yes . . . and no. I mean, that's what it started out as. But she, um, expanded as soon as it became legal."

"What did?"

She put the toe of her sneaker onto one of the glass

jars still on the street. Rolled it back and forth underfoot. "Marijuana."

"You're fucking joking." Flynn dropped into a crouch. He almost picked up the jar, but froze with his fingers curved right above it. Guess he'd realized putting his fingerprints on the evidence was the mother of all dumb ideas. Then he grinned up at Rafe. "You're dating the family of a drug dealer. Now who's in trouble?"

Kellan snorted. Turned to the side and covered his mouth with his hand as it morphed into a gut-puncher of a laugh.

Why had he given up everything to keep these two safe?

"It's not like that." Mollie dropped to her knees next to Flynn. "Remember, it's legal here. Gran used it a lot for the phantom limb pain of her amputation and wanted to make sure others could get the same relief. Oh, and I have to thank you, too." She threw her arms around his shoulders in a tight hug. "You're Flynn, right?"

"Yeah." He swiveled to get a better grip on her waist. "You're really welcome."

Enough was certainly enough of his younger brother copping a feel. Rafe took Mollie's elbow and lifted her out of their way-too-long embrace. "How did you know what we did?"

"The security company called as soon as the alarm went off. Well, once they couldn't get a hold of Gran. She's at the mall trying to buy Jesse some clothes he won't grow out of in a week. I got one of the nurses to drive me over. My phone was blowing up the whole way. All about the hero Maguire brothers who stopped the robbers."

"Hey, I called the cops." Kellan sauntered forward. Did he actually think Rafe would let him have a turn hugging Mollie, too? Not in this lifetime. "That's called engaging in due process. Equally important to the bigger picture."

"All three of you have my unending gratitude. And Gran's." The corners of her mouth flattened. "She'll probably bake you something, ah, *extra* special in thanks. Be sure not to eat it in one sitting."

"No worries. We don't touch the stuff." No drugs wasn't just a WITSEC guideline. It'd been a lifelong rule in their house. Trouble could be around any corner. You didn't need to be strung out when it came at you.

Hands jammed into his jeans pockets, Kellan flashed a smile. And that damned dimple that he swore got him crowned homecoming king in high school. The same one he used on the marshal. Come to think of it, Delaney was the only woman whose bra didn't unsnap by itself at the sight of it. "Aren't you going to introduce me?"

"This is my baby brother, Kellan." He dropped extra emphasis on the word *baby*. Might as well draw the line in the sand as thick as a NASCAR skid mark. "Doctor Mollie Vickers."

Kellan didn't take the hint. He did take Mollie's hand

and sandwich it between his. "Are you sure a board-certified medical professional wouldn't rather dump my monosyllabic, uptight brother and hang out with me?"

Putting a hard edge into his voice, Rafe said, "We'll never know. Because if you tried anything, I'd have to kill you."

The smile dropped off Kellan's face.

Jesus Christ. They used to be able to joke around.

Rafe knew, in his gut, that his brother didn't believe for a second that he'd do him real harm. It made him wonder, though, if Kellan truly believed that Rafe had never killed anyone for his job.

His reaction made it unlikely. Or did he just not like the reminder that Rafe had worked for an organization where killing people was a reality? Either way, it sucked that after less than half an hour of feeling normal, a huge wall was back up between them.

Mollie went up on tiptoe to kiss Rafe on the forehead, the nose, and then a far too short stop on his lips. "You'll get a more thorough thanking later. When there's no crowd watching us."

"Or family," he grumbled. The cock-blocking going on was unmistakable.

"Given your living situation and mine, that might take a little longer to arrange. But there's no expiration date on my gratitude." She put both hands on his face. Rounded those forest green eyes and looked—he'd swear—right into his heart. "You really impressed me,

Rafe. Other people would've done nothing. You put yourself at risk to help."

Wow.

This felt great. Being a good guy had some kick-ass perks. The sincerity coating Mollie's words, shining on her face, made Rafe feel easily twelve feet tall. Invincible. And yes, for the first time in his life, a little heroic. It made him want to commit to being the version of himself that she saw.

Maybe it didn't suck so much not being a bad guy anymore.

"No big deal. It seemed like the right thing to do."

"THIS WAS NO big deal. It seemed like the right thing to do," Rafe yelled. Then he thumped his hand on the rickety metal table in what passed as an interrogation room in the Bandon police station—although he'd bet they called it a conference room any other day of the week.

Marshal Evans clicked her shiny stilettos over until she was so close that his breath fanned the almost invisible blond hairs along her forehead. "I gave you strict instructions. No, back up. I gave you strict *written* instructions when you first joined the program."

"Yeah, but I seem to recall them self-combusting after one minute." Kellan patted his stomach and trotted out that damned dimple again. "Or we ate them. Either way, those eighteen pages of rules are a little hazy."

She rounded on Kellan. "Do not start with me. I know everything about you. I know your grades for every semester in law school. I know you were on track to graduate among the top five in your class. You've never forgotten a single word you read. And your two and a half years of legal education most certainly covered ignorance of the law not being an acceptable defense."

"It rings a bell." Kellan jerked one shoulder, then slapped an ass cheek onto the table.

He was backing down? The one time Rafe needed him to go toe-to-toe with the marshal—or even do that annoying flirting thing she pretended to ignore—and he fucking backed down? Unbelievable.

She barreled right the hell along. "I gave you explicit instructions to lay low. To stay under the wire. Do you realize that I have a team now scouring the internet to make sure that none of those videos get posted?"

"We're not idiots. We turned away." Rafe had claimed Flynn was embarrassed by the attention, then he'd asked Mick to go around to the few people filming and get them to stop. There was no doubt in his mind that Mick had not only made the request, but scared everyone into complying. Rafe was pretty proud of how he'd worked the small-town system to his advantage with that one.

The bell of her hair swung around Delaney's face. It was the first time they'd seen it down. In fact, she looked entirely different today. Softer. High heels, a black leather skirt so short that Kellan was probably at half-wood right now, and a fuzzy pink sweater. Had they pulled her off a date?

Finger in his face, Delaney said, "You know what happens if we find a single frame of you online."

A whole storm of shit that'd ultimately raise the odds that what was left of McGinty's crew would find them.

"We didn't audition for a reality television show. The videos were an accident. And they've been contained."

"Let me make this clear: laying low does not mean attracting a crowd and being hauled in to make an official statement to the police."

Rafe had done a lot of questionable things in his life. More than a few that were flat-out wrong. So he knew, without a shadow of a doubt, that this wasn't one of those times.

His own index finger came out to jab at Delaney. "You didn't just tell us to lay low. You also told us to blend in. Which is fucking hard to do both at the same time in a small town, by the way. You ordered us to make this place our home. To care about it."

She scrunched her eyes shut. "Yes."

Flynn gave him a thumbs-up from his seat at the opposite end.

"This is our home now. So we're treating it with respect. That means not standing around with my thumb up my ass when I see a fellow citizen being screwed."

Kellan cleared his throat. Guess he wanted to formally announce that he was jumping back into the argument. "Those scum suckers damaged property. They were fleeing with hundreds, if not thousands, of dollars worth of . . . well, retail goods. My brothers apprehended them so that they can make full restitution to the store owner."

Delaney whipped her head so fast toward Kellan, her neck actually cracked. The sound ricocheted off the stucco walls. "Don't try to sugarcoat it. I'm well aware of what got stolen. I'm up to speed on the narcotics aspect of this crime."

"How?" For that matter, how had she even known to come down and read them the riot act? They hadn't been arrested. Hell, at this point, Rafe got the distinct impression that he and Flynn might get a medal.

She tapped her toe. Then she crossed her arms. Classic defensive posture. Whatever she was about to say? They were going to *hate* it. "The Marshals Service has a contact here. He fed me the information."

"Nobody is supposed to know that we're not who we say we are." Kellan paced around the conference table in a few fast, long steps. "Not a single fucking soul in this town. That *is* laid out in those eighteen pages of rules, by the way. Which I do remember word for word. Especially the words that protect us, protect our secret. Why don't you tell us what the fuck's going on?"

Kellan aiming his anger at somebody besides Rafe for a change . . . well, that was just the cherry on top of the night.

Delaney's downcast eyes and hunched shoulders added some extra righteous whipped cream. Kellan had nailed her to the wall with her own damn rules. Rafe hooked an ankle around the chair and yanked it out to sit and watch. This was just *fun.*

"There are exceptions to every rule. Circumstances where what's always worked before simply does not apply. You three are the epitome of a special case. This is your fifth protection placement. In six months. More than a few people argued for at least Kellan to be kicked out of the program. The only way I kept you all in was by coming up with a solution that kept eyes on you."

Back braced against the closed door as if keeping out the world, Kellan demanded, "How is our safety guaranteed if our true identities are known?"

"The sheriff knows me. Worked a case with me before coming to Bandon and trusts me. He agreed to let me place my protectees here. And give me a cover as his date to get me in and out without being tied to you."

That explained the sex-kitten clothes. Rafe winked widely, jaw cocked. "You two kids be sure to use protection. The last thing the world needs is another law enforcement type."

His lawyer-ish brother did not look appeased. Or like he saw any of the humor in the situation. Maybe it was just the pain of hiding what had to be a raging hard-on at Delaney dressed sexy for once. "What does he know about us?"

"Nothing substantial. More to the point, nothing real. I told him you were completely innocent witnesses in a trial. Period. Nobody here knows your original identities, the true details of your case. You have my word. McGinty won't find you through Mateo."

Rafe wasn't thrilled with the face-to-face lecture. But it did give him the chance to press on the issue that got them moved to Bandon in the first place. The one Delaney never mentioned. "Is the bastard still in the hospital?"

"He's . . . *back* in. A complication from his heart attack."

Flynn tapped his fingers on the table. "You sure he isn't faking it to get a better bed than the Cook County Jail provides?"

"He's in the jail ward at the hospital. It's not a cushy situation. Now stop worrying about McGinty. We've got eyes on him at all times. And we won't let the bastard die before he gets eviscerated by the courts."

They could only hope. Rafe jumped back to the more immediate problem. "If the sheriff thinks we're good guys—which would be bolstered by what we did tonight—why'd he drag you down here?"

"He didn't. Mateo knew that as soon as he inputted your names into the system on the police report, I'd get a ping. He gave me the heads-up so I wouldn't panic. So I wouldn't race down here." She bared her teeth in more of a grimace than a smile. "But he doesn't know the Maguire brothers like I do."

Thanks to Kellan's relentless poking at the marshal, Rafe felt secure that they weren't in danger of being exposed. Secure with their handler? Not so much. And if they were going to have any success here, he needed this spelled out.

"Hang on, Marshal. Do you really think we did the wrong thing tonight? That we should've let a harmless little old lady have her shop vandalized by bullies?"

Two quick swipes of her hands had her hair behind her ears. Her lips firmed. Thinned. One hand reached for the gun belt missing from her waist tonight. Delaney tip-tapped the length of the room before whirling around to brace both arms on the table.

"No. Damn it, you did the right thing twice over. You 'acted' like model citizens. And the fact that you even felt the desire to do so means I wasn't crazy in giving you one last chance. Deep down, I believe you're good guys at heart. I always have. So thank you for helping."

He respected that she didn't keep fighting with them on principle alone. Rafe thought he'd toss her a bone. That way the trip down here—and the dinner with the undoubtedly boring sheriff—wouldn't be a total loss. "You have no idea how good we are. I signed all three of us up for the community service you suggested."

Flynn's voice was grim. "You did what?"

"Not a fan of you making decisions about my life." Kellan swung his head side to side, slowly. "The last one you made has turned out for crap."

In contrast, Delaney beamed at him. Right now, she was the only one who mattered. He'd deal with his brothers later. When he wasn't doing his damndest to make a good impression on the one person responsible for keeping them alive. "That's excellent, Rafe. You're truly making strides to fit in here and connect. Even if you did go a bit overboard tonight. What are you doing?"

Oh, she'd fucking love this. "Ever heard of the world-famous Cranberry and Cheese Festival?"

Chapter Twelve

MOLLIE NEVER GOT a long lunch break. Oh, it was marked off in her schedule. But most days the string of patients was too long to ignore without feeling guilt over enjoying a sandwich. Her patients came first. They were her priority.

Except today.

Rafe had done a drive-by on her at the hospital. Two could play that game. She'd stop by the garage. Unzip what, in her fantasy, were grease-stained blue coveralls, and give him a blow job that would roll his eyes back in his sockets.

Then she'd leave. With the upper hand. Over him, and over her emotions. Then she'd call Karen and Elena to see if she could talk them into a celebratory happy hour.

It was a solid, well thought-out plan that probably wouldn't even take up the extra time she'd blocked out.

Today's priority was proving herself right. Proving that she knew herself better than her friends did. Proving that this fling with Rafe came with no strings and no emotions. It was all she wanted. All she could handle. And, for the record, all she asked for from him.

When she ordered a hamburger, that's what she got. Not a slab of prime rib with a side of crab cakes. When she paid for a five-minute spin in the massage chair at the mall, that's all she wanted. Not to be stripped down, oiled up, and rubbed for an hour by two hot hunks.

Okay, maybe Mollie wouldn't say no to *that*.

But she and Rafe went into this thing with guidelines. Eyes wide open. Both of them on the same page. A page that her friends, no matter how well-meaning and concerned, had zero license to try and edit.

The triple-time flutter in her heart at seeing him last night, all rugged and confident and leaning against that cop car like a super hero, meant nothing. It was gratitude, plain and simple. Gratitude that he'd stopped the thieves in time so that Gran was able to recover all of her merchandise. Gratitude that he and his brothers unexpectedly came back with sheets of plywood, hammers, and nails to board up the broken windows. Rafe had said that stopping the burglars was only half the job. Keeping anyone else from getting in was the other half.

He didn't have to do that. She'd already been on the phone with her gran to get the name of her preferred handyman. They would've taken care of it themselves.

But it was so nice that Rafe did it, instead. So thoughtful. So responsible. So . . . sexy watching him flex his muscles.

As long as it stayed at gratitude, she'd be safe. Anything else was too dangerous. Too much of a risk that her heart would get involved . . . and then shattered when he inevitably left her.

But gratitude and respect and a serious case of the hots and genuine *like* and—

Mollie slammed on the brakes. On her plan and on the car.

She was still blocks from the garage, but there was Rafe, right in front of her. *Right* in front. As in crouched at the edge of the street with a measuring tape in his big hands. In gray coveralls with the top unzipped to show a plain white tee stretched to its limits against his perfectly bulging pecs. She pulled over onto the tiny strip of grass that edged along the water and parked.

The measuring tape made a metallic whizzing snap as it reeled back into the case. By the time she approached, Rafe was on his feet, with a huge smile to greet her.

Nope. No emotion whatsoever. No flutters in her heart. No butterflies in her stomach.

None that she'd cop to, anyway.

"Do your patients know you're playing hooky, Doc?"

"Does your boss know that *you* are?" Mollie lobbed back.

Rafe tapped something into his phone, then slid it and the tape into his pocket. "She knows I'm out here. But it's a legit errand. I'm on official business."

"Is Frieda trolling the streets for business now? Having you listen to cars that drive by to see if they've got knocks or clunks?"

"Stick to the day job, Doc. You're lousy at business development." Rafe snaked out an arm to pull her close. "Better yet, stick to me." His other hand tugged at her ponytail. Just enough to tip her head back so that when his lips came down, Mollie was at the perfect tilt to receive them.

Heat burst through her. No slow and steady sizzle. No polite but short kiss in deference to being on the edge of a busy street. Rafe devoured her like they hadn't touched in days. When, in fact, he'd kissed her good night after boarding up the windows just last night. Mollie matched him in hunger. In selfishly taking everything she could from his questing tongue and firm lips and pressing against every rock-hard muscle possible.

They fit together . . . well. Perfectly. His mouth gave the flawless amount of just-this-side-of-bruising pressure. Even his low hum of appreciation? Lust? Whatever it was, the throaty buzz ratcheted up her need. It sounded dark and dangerous. It was a sound that really only belonged let out of its cage when Rafe was naked and they were on tousled sheets.

He set her back on her feet before Mollie realized that he'd lifted her off the ground. Whew. At least he hadn't actually made the earth move.

As he brushed gravel off the legs of her scrubs that

must've transferred from his coveralls, Rafe said, "Nice to see you, Doc."

"Same goes for me. But you're crawling around the street why exactly?"

"I'm measuring the width of it for maximum float size for the festival. Bigger is always better," he said with a wink and a sexy smirk, "but we want a wide margin on either side. To accommodate for little kids running in the street, emergency personnel needing to get by. Looks like this town has been eyeballing it on a wing and a prayer in past years. Time to get safety conscious."

Mollie was more than a little surprised. Yes, he'd signed up to help with the parade, but he'd made it clear at the C of C lunch that he thought the festival was stupid, nutty, and way too full of cranberries.

"As a health care professional, that's an improvement I am definitely behind. I'm in no hurry to treat float-squished toes."

"I figure my new blood brings a fresh perspective. It's easy to get in a rut and always do things the same way."

Mollie squinted up at him, haloed by the bright—for once—noon sun. "Why are you going to such lengths to improve the parade when you've got nothing good to say about the tart red star of our festival?"

Rafe crossed his arms over his broad chest. All the teasing glints slipped from his eyes. The little smile crinkles deepened into something far more serious. "Because when I commit to something, I give it one hundred percent."

"Even if you don't believe in it? Or hate it?"

"You bet. I gave my word. That matters."

Some people gave lip service to that phrase. But Mollie had no doubt that Rafe meant it. Stood behind it. Geez, it gave her goose bumps, the way he said it like a solemn vow. People with that kind of integrity were rare in this world.

"Does that mean you've decided to commit to Bandon?"

His blue eyes widened. She grinned back and mouthed *gotcha.* Then he laughed. "The truth? I'm not sure—but I'm sure as hell trying."

"Well, your newfound hero status should make it easier to integrate with all the locals."

"Stop it with that bullshit." Rafe turned sideways. Rubbed at the back of his neck. Shifted his weight between his feet. Really, he could not have looked more physically uncomfortable if he'd been trying not to pee. "People who shouted that out last night were just caught up in the moment. When fists fly, you want to be on the side of the guy who's still standing."

A modest man with biceps like steel and blue eyes that could melt you with a look. Rafe Maguire had to be too good to be true.

"That's not why it happened at all. And the compliments are still flying. You're the talk of the town. Everyone's calling you and your brother a hero. I heard it in Gran's coffeeshop this morning. Then over at the bakery. All the nurses and the patients have your name on their lips."

His look of astonishment also surprised her. No, it was more *confusing*. Who would turn down an accolade like that? Especially when he knew good and well that he'd earned it?

Then his expression hardened. She could crack a hazelnut on the line of his jaw.

"Well, they need to quit it. We don't want to be the latest gossip. No attention, in fact, would be great. We prefer to keep a low profile."

Now it was Mollie's turn to laugh. Really hard. Doubled-over hard. He was about to learn a very important lesson about living in a small town. "Impossible. There *is* no such thing as a low profile in a town of three thousand people."

"Why not?"

Dismissing it with a joke was one way to go. But Mollie got the impression that Rafe genuinely did not know what he'd gotten himself into moving from whichever big city—*and why didn't she know which one?*—to Bandon. And it was an important lesson to learn. One that she was uniquely qualified to share.

Taking his hand, she drew him over to the strip of grass that ended in a protective curve around the edge of the marina. Nobody else needed to hear their conversation. Walking slowly, she said, "Do you remember I didn't want to be with you when I found out that you live here?"

"Yeah. I won't ever forget it." Rafe snorted. "The weakest attempt at a brush-off ever."

It wasn't . . . for crying out loud. It wasn't personal. It wasn't a brush-off. It was her *preference*. No different than saying she wouldn't date a smoker. Or a man who didn't share her deep and abiding love for the creamy goodness of fettuccine alfredo. A preference that Rafe overcame with his sexy swagger, anyway.

"We'll argue about that some other time. My point was that I didn't want you learning all about me from the people in town. I didn't want them to give you a one-dimensional impression of me."

Voice low and hot against her ear, Rafe said, "I like the three-dimensional version. A lot." He butted her hip with his own, to press the point. Or just because it was fun. Mollie didn't really care why. She just cared that the feel of his hip bone driving into hers made her imagine them doing that again soon—but naked . . .

Good thing a seagull squawked and got Mollie's brain back on track. Otherwise she'd have been down the rabbit hole of sexual fantasy for who knew how long.

His compliment made it that much easier to share her story. *Her* story, and thus one that should only be told by her. Not by any and every other random person in Bandon who had ever had even a minor role in it . . . *as they were wont to do.*

She angled to look up at Rafe. "You haven't asked about my parents."

"Was I supposed to?" One dark eyebrow lazily winged upward. "You didn't ask about mine."

"Touché." Oh, but it was fun when he challenged her. Why didn't more men realize that women craved a back-and-forth, a give-and-take? That should be the headline to a *Cosmo* article: Get Your Girlfriend Between the Sheets by Keeping Her on Her Toes. "But since I live with my grandmother, it's kind of an obvious oddity, hanging out there waiting to be picked off in a conversation."

"I figure if and when you want to tell me something, you will. If you want to keep things close to your vest, that's your call."

Wow. Rafe was so willing to let her keep her secrets. That was *definitely* a rarity here in Bandon. "Thanks, but I want you to know. I think it'll make this transition to small-town life easier for you."

"Okay." He stroked a hand from the crown of her head down her ponytail to end in a caress that rubbed his rough callouses across the nape of her neck. To be precise, it ended in an explosion of goose bumps from one shoulder to the other. "Are your parents exiled Russian royalty?"

Mollie giggled. "Aaaand the award for most random guess of the year goes to . . . Rafe Maguire."

"Just trying to make you smile before we get into something that I'm sensing is pretty heavy."

There he went being thoughtful again. Which, once

again, just increased her urge to strip off his pants and jump on top of him. "It is and it isn't. I never knew my father. When my mom told him she was pregnant, he left. Never came back. His name isn't even on my birth certificate."

His thumb moved into a back-and-forth caress right at the curve of her neck. It was gentle, tender even. But Rafe's voice was as harsh as broken glass. "He doesn't deserve it. People who abandon their kids are scum. Doesn't matter if it was his choice or not. When you have a kid, you have to be all in."

"I happen to agree. It's why I've never looked for him. If he doesn't want anything to do with me, I'm just fine without him. Better than fine, actually."

"*Very* fine."

"Thank you." Mollie switched sides, to put the stiff ocean breeze at her back. It had a tendency to make her eyes water and she didn't want Rafe to think this story was making her cry. She hadn't cried over her parents—or lack thereof—in at least, oh, a decade. Except for her med school graduation when there'd been a moment of welling up, wondering if they'd be proud of her . . . "Anyway, my mom tried to raise me. But she was only nineteen when I was born. That's a hard age to give up everything for a screaming, pooping bundle of full-time responsibility. She tried for three years."

"Do or do not." Rafe scrunched up his face in what she assumed was an approximation of Yoda's wrinkles. "There is no try."

"Nice. I like a man who can work a *Star Wars* quote into a confessional. Can you do it with, oh, I don't know, *The Godfather*, too?"

"No. Not at all. I don't watch movies about the mob."

His response was both fast and weirdly abrupt. "Don't worry. I'm not going to judge you based on your taste in movies. Not when I drop everything to watch the Hallmark Channel Christmas cheese-fests."

Rafe half spun away, shielding his face as if warding off any potential romantic movie contagion. "Thank God it's only May."

She wouldn't mention their whole Christmas in July run of movies. Because this . . . fling with Rafe would be over by then. Probably. Definitely. Wasn't there a time limit on how long a fling could last?

No matter how fun and casual, if it kept going for a measurable amount of time, it would turn into something. Something more concrete. There was an expiration date on their casual fun—Mollie just didn't know when it was. And didn't want to think about it right now.

"So my mom fell for a new guy. A rich one. She followed him back east. Didn't take me with her, as a three-year-old tends to impinge on romantic moments. They married. Started their own family. One that didn't have room for me."

"She left you behind?" He hooked a thumb over his shoulder back toward the town. "Like a beat-up dresser that didn't fit the décor in the new house?"

For all of his thoughtfulness, she also appreciated

that Rafe didn't beat around the bush. Although Mollie wasn't loving the analogy. "Essentially, yes."

"That's unforgivable. It's fucking illegal. Child abandonment."

Hugging her arms tightly around herself, Mollie said, "It wasn't the Dark Ages. I wasn't left on the side of a village well in a basket. She left me with Gran. Who had a full-time business to run and was still adjusting to life as an amputee. Full-time insta-motherhood was a lot for her to juggle. But luckily she didn't have to. The whole town stepped in to help."

"It takes a village."

He was quick with the quips, which Mollie appreciated. "Yes. In this case, quite literally. We didn't have daycare, so they set up a rotation between twenty different families to watch me in the afternoons. I belonged to all of them from then on. The high school math teacher taught me the multiplication tables. Lucien's dad sent me to summer camp with his son. Your boss's husband taught me to drive."

"But not how to change a tire? The owner of a garage?"

Apparently there was no slipping anything past him. "I only agreed to learn so much. The attention span of a teenaged girl is a tenuous thing."

Spreading his arms wide, Rafe said, "Everyone helped you. I get it."

No. He couldn't fathom the depth of it. Mollie looked out at the bobbing boats. Remembered riding on each and every one that didn't belong to a tourist. Helping the fishermen. Gassing up boats at the marina. She knew a little bit about every single part of what made this town tick. Her extended families had made sure of it.

"They didn't just help. They accepted me into their homes, families, and lives. I wasn't a chore. I wasn't charity. I was theirs. All of theirs."

Rafe dipped his head in acknowledgment of her correction. Then moved behind her, folded his arms around her waist, and just held her for a moment.

It felt really good. It settled her. Mollie took a few long, salt-tinged breaths before continuing.

"So, no, I don't want to date the men whose parents made them dance with me at the middle school father/daughter dance. I don't want to see the pity in the eyes of people who are convinced that I'm forever broken inside from my mother's abandonment. But that's a small price to pay for staying here in a town chock-full of big hearts and generous spirits."

"I feel like you're circling in to a point."

"Bandon might latch on to gossip, spread it thicker than hot fudge on ice cream, but they are good people, wonderful people, through and through. It's why I gave up a lucrative and prestigious career in Chicago to come back and work here. I *owe* this town. It is as important to me as . . . as your brothers are to you. They all drive me crazy sometimes, but I care for them, and will spend my life doing so."

"That's quite an endorsement."

"Too much? Did I oversell it?" Because Mollie felt like she'd been talking forever. And might've scared him off with her exuberance.

"Nope. You gave me a new way of looking at this place. Put a different frame around it. Loyalty that strong is impressive. Sure as hell makes an impact on me."

Whew. Rafe really did get it now. "Bandon is just a bigger version of a normal family. They've got their quirks, but you love them all the more for it."

"You think they'll take Jesse on as a project the same way they did for you?"

Her heart double-thumped. He'd made the logical leap. Proof he wasn't just listening, but absorbing her point. "Are you worried about my cousin?"

On a grimace, Rafe said, "Worried about my potential slave labor."

"With your generous intervention and the help of the town, yes, I'm hoping he'll be over his troublemaking phase by the time the festival rolls around in September."

"You think they'd take a chance on me? On an idea I've got?"

Mollie spun around in his arms. "After yesterday? I'd be surprised if they don't make you the grand marshal of the festival this year."

"Bite your tongue, woman."

"Make me." They stood there, just grinning at each other for a minute. There was always a low simmer of sexual tension between them, but that wasn't what hung in the air. It was just . . . *fun.* She had fun sparring with Rafe. The utterly relaxed, being totally herself kind of fun she had with Lucien and the girls. Her best friends, in other words.

Wasn't that startling?

Rafe tugged on her ponytail. "I'm serious. I have an idea to expand business at the garage—if Frieda will let me. Restoring classic cars."

"Is there money in it? If so, I guarantee that Frieda's in," Mollie said with only a hint of snark. The woman was notorious for wringing every last cent out of a dollar. Probably how she'd grown two businesses simultaneously. But she also had a heart bigger than Mt. Hood.

Flipping his hand back and forth, Rafe said, "There can be. At first, it'll just be a nice bump, but it has the potential to grow into something bigger."

"So, a passion project that produces?"

"Hopefully. I think it could turn into a real moneymaker. End up employing a couple of more people. Bring in more tourists, maybe grow it into a classic car rally."

It was a solid idea. And so great to hear the enthusiasm in his voice, see it light up those blue eyes. Mollie skimmed a hand down the outside of his arm. "How long have you been thinking about this?"

"It was my dad's big dream for retirement. He wanted to do it with me. We'd talk big about it while working on his car, or his friends'. Didn't hit me that it could really happen until I settled here. You're the first person I've mentioned it to."

Funny, the dazed smile on his face made it look like it hadn't hit him until about five minutes ago. "I'm so glad you did." She went up on tiptoe to brush a kiss over his lips. Men didn't share easily. He deserved a reward. "I think it's a stellar idea, Rafe. I'm sure you'll turn it into a booming business."

"You're *sure*, huh?" Rafe cupped her cheek, keeping her face a breath away from his. His eyes smoldered darkly. "How is it you see the best in me, no questions asked?"

The question pinched at her heart. How sad was it that he felt he had to ask? "Why wouldn't I? Maybe wait to broach it with Frieda for a few months, though?"

"No kidding. I need time anyway, to work up a solid business plan. Research who else does it in the area."

"Sure sounds like you've made up your mind to commit to Bandon."

Another grimace. "I'm never going to like cranberries."

Mollie could overlook that character flaw due to his flawless kissing technique. "How do you feel about ice cream?"

"Two thumbs up."

"How about I buy you a cone as a thanks for listening?"

"I'm buying." He dropped a featherlight line of kisses

from her forehead down to her lips. "You've given me enough today."

Uh-oh. The whole point of this lunch jaunt was to prove to herself that she wasn't falling for Rafe. Instead, she'd shared a deeply personal story she almost always kept under wraps—and been completely bowled over by his righteous indignation on her behalf and implied willingness to let the town grow on him.

All the ice cream in the world could not cool her off.

Which was a problem . . .

Chapter Thirteen

Wick's Garage, 4:00 p.m.
Mood in the service bay—surprisingly good.
Chances it'd last? Slim to none.

Rafe pointed at the stack of tires in the corner with a lug wrench. "Today I'm going to teach you how to change a tire."

"How come?" Jesse sounded curious. Not like he was pushing back just for the hell of it. Which had been the way of it the first two afternoons the kid had spent here. He was sulky. Ready to argue that the sky was polka-dotted if Rafe called it blue. But it was nothing Rafe couldn't handle. Hadn't handled a million times each between Flynn and Kellan.

Today had been different, though. He swept the whole garage without being reminded. Checked the list on the computer to see who needed a courtesy call about their car being ready. Again, without being asked. He'd done a one-eighty from being a pain in the ass to at least tolerable.

Maybe he'd gotten laid.

If so, that'd be Mollie's damn problem to deal with.

Thwacking the wrench against his palm—*and wasn't* that *a familiar feeling that shot him right back to a deserted Chicago forest preserve, scaring the shit out of some double-crossing scum*—Rafe said, "Because it's something you'll need to do a lot while you're working here. Because you can drive, which means you ought to be able to do it." Dredging out of his memory what *really* motivated teenagers, Rafe kept going. "And mostly, because your cousin doesn't know how. Thought you might enjoy rubbing your new skill in her face."

Something that, if you knew how to read teenaged boys, could be interpreted as a smile ghosted across his face. "It wouldn't suck."

"Good enough."

Rafe crossed to the iPod dock to take a shot in the dark at spinning tunes that wouldn't double the kid over in fake nausea—which had been his reaction to everything from old school head-banging rock to country to some weird electronica shit that Kellan must've loaded as a joke.

"I heard about what you did." Jesse took a deep breath, and then all the words spilled out faster than cereal into milk. "Mollie and Gran wouldn't tell me, but I heard about it at school."

In Rafe's old life, *I heard about what you did* was usually said in a hushed whisper. It happened after a big beatdown on someone trying to horn in on McGinty turf, like an out-of-towner trying to recruit and getting booted ass-first out of Chicago. Or the time they relocated an entire truck of cash headed to the casino in Wisconsin. Said in a whisper because those things were never official. Never acknowledged—unless you counted the victory ribeyes at Gene & Georgetti's.

At most, Rafe would stare for an extra beat or two. Long enough to make the person piss their pants in fear for bringing it up at all. Then he'd slow-slide his gaze away.

Jesse, though, was almost bouncing in his unlaced high-tops. The statement had burst out of him like the explosion of water when someone uncapped a hydrant on a hot summer day. And Jesus H., the kid lived with a pot dealer. He ought to be dialed in. Not hearing it secondhand.

He turned on Kanye, then angled back to face Jesse. "You mean us getting into it with the idiots who broke into your gran's shop?"

"You caught the guys. You punched one." Excitement and yeah, a little awe lit up those eyes the same color as Mollie's.

Tongue in his cheek, Rafe said, "I didn't have my lasso with me. Had to think fast."

"Your brother kicked the other guy all the way across the street. How'd he do that?"

All the way across the street. Flynn would snort beer out of his nose at hearing that his legend had grown. Guess his new, bad-ass rep would come in handy if he needed to bounce anyone from the Gorse.

"Lots of practice. Not to sound too much like a pain-in-the-ass adult, but practice almost anything enough and you can get good at it." He jerked his head at the boring, ten-year-old sedan in the middle of the shop floor. "Changing tires, for instance. We can time me doing it, then you. See if in a couple of weeks you come close to catching me."

"Catch you? I'll beat you," Jesse boasted, with a rare grin on his face.

"Big talk. I'll let it slide this time. Because you haven't yet witnessed my mastery of lug nuts." Relief washed through him. This was working. Jesse was, if not excited, then at least engaged.

"Could you show me how to do it?"

"Kid, that's the plan. Haven't you been listening?" Rafe plucked the top tire off the stack and started rolling it across the floor.

"No. Could you show me how to punch? How to beat someone up?"

Holy fuck. Thank God the tire gave him something to hold on to. Or Rafe might've raced right out the door.

This was what happened when you tried to be a good guy. When you stuck your neck out to help someone. Rafe thought having a gofer around the place would make his life easier. Make Mollie worry a little less about her cousin and allow some of Rafe's ruggedness to rub off on a kid being raised by women. Win, win, win, and he could put his feet up and assume angel wings were his.

Yeah, that was the dumbest thing he'd done in a long time.

Because Jesse needed real help. Rafe remembered Mollie mentioning that he'd not only been kicked out of school, but picked up by the police a time or two. And that was serious shit.

His problem was that he needed direction.

Rafe had never met a problem that he didn't fix. It was second nature to him.

If he didn't step up and give Jesse that help? Then Rafe would be the one with the problem. Because he wouldn't be able to live with himself.

What should he say?

What would Mollie want him to do?

Shit. Rafe let the tire fall. Dug a hand through his hair. "Do you want to learn how to punch? Or how to defend yourself?"

"What's the difference?"

"Intent. What you do with the muscles and fists. Do you want to be able to beat someone up? Be a bully?"

"Not a bully. But I wouldn't mind scaring a few assholes. Like those guys you beat up."

"Hey. That's not what happened."

"Go on. Take the credit. Everyone's talking about it."

"Doesn't mean they're saying the right things." Never, ever before had Rafe needed—or wanted—to downplay his actions. But mob life, and the reputation he'd built for being tougher than everyone else, was the *old* way.

This . . . this town of parades and the sourest damn fruit on the planet and people who genuinely wanted to know an answer when asking how you were . . . this was real life now. One he'd chosen to embrace. A life where people didn't beat each other up every other day. A life where fists shouldn't be the solution.

"I didn't beat anyone up, Jesse. That's giving extra licks, as punishment. I used one punch to stop a crime. Period."

"They deserve more than that. For upsetting Gran." The kid practically vibrated with the need to act. To avenge his pot-smoking, amputee vet of a grandmother. Rafe wanted to meet this woman who inspired so much loyalty in a child who'd only recently moved in with her. "If you teach me, I could show them how wrong they were."

Oh, Rafe understood the impulse. He was proud of the kid for wanting to stand up for his grandmother, do right by her.

He was damn sure Mollie wouldn't agree, though. Not if it ended with Jesse getting kicked out of another high school. That definitely wouldn't get Rafe in her scrub pants any sooner.

He'd talked to the police two nights ago, after giving his statement. Jawed with them. That'd been surreal. Cops sharing info with him out of gratitude. Talk about a mind fuck. And something that never would've gone down in Chicago. But sharing what they'd told him might get Jesse off the revenge train.

"The criminal masterminds who broke into the shop

had been high as kites. Said they were bored and that it'd been a dare. Something to do." He grabbed two sodas from the mini fridge in the corner and handed one over. It'd give Jesse something to do with his hands besides pumping them into fists. "They're going to pay plenty for a pretty low-key bad choice. You don't need to pay for making a different kind of bad choice."

"I still want to do something," he said, low and fierce. "To help her. To make her feel better."

No wonder Mollie wanted to help Jesse. Beneath all the sulking and smart-ass, there was one hell of a big heart. The idea of doing his part to keep even one kid from going down the wrong path, the one that he had, resonated with Rafe. He could do this. For Jesse, for Mollie—who believed in him enough to make Rafe believe he could be the guy she saw. And yeah, he needed to do this for his own sake, too.

"How about I give you an advance on your paycheck?" Rafe walked over to the till, pulled out a Hamilton, and pressed it into Jesse's hand. "Buy her some flowers at the grocery store. Nothing big or flashy. Just something bright to put on her counter that'll distract her from the boarded-up window. You'll be a hero."

"You think?"

Wow. Someone really needed to show him the ropes. "Kid, flowers can get you out of almost any scrape with a woman. We'll call that your number one lesson learned today. That's even more important than knowing how to change a tire."

"Thanks." After the bill disappeared into Jesse's back pocket, he took a long swig of his soda. "Does this mean you won't teach me how to fight?"

Stubborn, too. Rafe didn't know if he should sigh or smile or swear.

"Let's start with the tire. We're still on the clock. Gotta make sure we don't let Frieda down." That was the right thing to do, as the mechanic Frieda had entrusted with her husband's beloved garage.

As a good guy.

As a responsible citizen.

It wasn't enough, though. Who else would teach Jesse how to handle himself? He'd already gotten in trouble over and over again. He needed a way to channel that loose energy and frustration.

Rafe sure as hell wouldn't step in as the missing dad. Or even a big brother. But he could be a . . . a guide. Try to help him stay on the straight and narrow.

So as he popped his own can, Rafe continued, "Once you've pulled your weight here for a whole week? Then, yeah, I'll teach you the basics. Of how to defend yourself. Including a long lecture about not beating people up just for shits and giggles."

"Really?" Jesse's face lit up like a firecracker. "Thanks. You won't regret it."

"I'd better not."

"Maguire." A man's voice hollered from the front office. "You want to help me knock a few heads?"

At first, Rafe's pulse kicked up into overdrive. Who

could resist the fun of an offer like that? God knew he never had in the past. He actually set his can on the floor and had taken two steps before his brain caught up to . . . well, the rest of him.

No head-knocking. He'd just laid down the law to Jesse all of two stupid seconds ago. And? Not so much that he *knew* better . . . which he did. More that he'd sworn to change. Sworn to be different. To be a better person. Rafe had turned over a new leaf. No matter how hard it was, he'd stick to it. Even if he'd only given his word on that to himself? It mattered.

So no head-knocking. Period.

Son of a bitch, that was still a hard pill to swallow.

Less hard, though, when Mick walked through the door. Any call to action from a guy rounding seventy was probably something that should be ignored, regardless. For his own safety. Although the old guy sure looked ready to kick some ass and worry about taking names later. His USMC ball cap was crushed in a white-knuckled fist. The thin strands of his hair were all over the place. And the fury spitting from slitted eyes could torch the joint if anyone lit a match.

"You got a problem, Mick? How can I help?"

"I've got one hell of a problem. My car's a mess."

Man, people had been bitching about this all week. Like as a mechanic, he had some magical way to constipate birds when they flew over a car. This was his new life. A discussion about where not to park your car so the birds didn't shit on it. There'd better be sex or whiskey or both for him tonight, because he deserved a god damned medal for not rolling his eyes.

But he liked Mick. So he'd let him rant a little. No skin off his nose. "Apparently the birds are back early and leaving their marks everywhere. You can't park under a tree. That's the secret."

"You think I don't know that? That I'd come to a garage for that advice? My problem's not the birds, Maguire. It's him." With a rustle of his blue nylon windbreaker that had to be an actual relic from the eighties, Mick pointed at Jesse.

Shit.

"What happened?"

"That hoodlum messed with my car. Covered it in shaving cream."

Rafe shouldn't be surprised. You didn't go cold turkey and change your personality overnight just because you moved across country.

Well . . . maybe he and Flynn and Kellan had. But that proved cold turkey didn't work, seeing as how they'd been booted from so many different cities for *not* falling in line. They hadn't been able to change on a dime, not even with their lives at stake. It'd been six long months of trying to adjust and this new reality was still a far cry from feeling natural. From being effortless. And they were adults who knew the stakes.

It was pretty much a miracle that it took Jesse this

long to backslide. Believing the kid was guilty wasn't hard at all. Especially when his face had turned the color of Bandon's famous fruit. Berry. Whatthefuck-ever.

He deserved a chance to be heard, though. And then, if he had any spare brain cells rubbing together, he'd take responsibility like a man.

"Jesse? Did you mess up Mick's car?"

After a beat, Jesse straightened. Rubbed his hands through hair gelled into a shape that was probably the same as whatever pop douchebag had the newest video out. "Why do you think it was me? Do you always pick on the new kid in town?"

So he didn't cop to it right off. No surprise at his defensiveness. Rafe was kind of impressed at the way he played it cool without actually lying. Back in Chicago? Rafe would've filed those things away as potential reasons to recruit the kid for McGinty's operation.

Now? They were a story to tell his brothers at dinner tonight. And a big danger flag that he intended to take down. Mollie would expect him to nip all this in the bud.

But then Mick rushed forward, grabbed a handful of Jesse's shirt, and shook. "Listen here, I don't care if you're from Mars or wackadoo Sedona. My neighbor saw you do it. Recognized you as Norah's grandson. Don't even think of trying to skate out of this."

"Let him go, Mick." Rafe barked out the order, knowing the vet would respond to his tone. Even though it was tempting to let him keep scaring the bejesus out of Jesse. Fear could go a long way toward teaching a lesson.

So would hard work. And that way would no doubt be Mollie-approved.

He strode over to them. Crossed his arms and easily pulled on his old, ass-kicking, hard-as-nails mask. "Yes or no. Did you do it?"

After a swallow so hard Rafe swore he could hear the Adam's apple grind its way down his throat, Jesse nodded. "Yeah."

"Why?"

"I was bored. Thought it might impress some guys at school once I posted the photos. Maybe they'd be nicer to me."

Seriously? Here he'd thought Jesse was smart. But posting photos under his name of even misdemeanor behavior? Made him dumber than dirt. "Kids who are impressed by low-rent vandalism aren't the kinds you want to have as friends. You know why? They'll want you to keep pulling stupid stunts. You'll end up in jail."

"No way."

"Remember what I said about the idiots who broke into your gran's shop? They were bored. You know they got taken to jail. Booked. And you said they deserved more punishment. For upsetting her. Well, you were bored. You did something stupid. Now Mick's upset. What do you think you deserve?"

Another hard swallow. But Rafe had pressed the right buttons, because the cocky attitude slid right off of him. Jesse turned to Mick. Those green eyes identical to Mollie's met the older man's. "I'm sorry. I'll take whatever licks you want to give me."

Mick's frown lines—the ones not etched deep by time, anyway—smoothed out. He shook his head. "This isn't ancient Rome. No need to throw you to the tigers."

"A word?" Rafe jerked his head at the garage door. Mick followed him outside. A glance over his shoulder showed that Jesse looked like he was about to puke.

Good.

All part of the painful medicine Rafe planned to force down his throat.

Then he bit back a laugh. Because the shaving cream job on the black sedan was . . . weak. Almost embarrassing. No curse words. No cock and balls, no slurs. Just a couple of wavy lines and what Rafe planned to describe to his brothers as polka dots. Basically, it was the worst attempt at vandalism ever. Good thing it didn't get posted. This wouldn't raise his street cred in the eyes of the high school. It just would've gotten him mocked.

But it still could've damaged Mick's car if it sat too long. He stuck a finger in it. Not yet hard. The paint underneath was no doubt fine. "Must've been a kick to the nuts when you looked out and saw it like this."

Mick patted the fender, wobbling a bit and favoring his hip. Just barely. Rafe noticed, though. He always noticed. Any hint of weakness, anything that might give him an advantage if things went south. It was a habit he had no plan to shake.

The older man squinted against the sun and jammed his cap onto his head. "It's just a car. The paint job doesn't matter. What I don't like is people thinking they can mess with me."

Rafe admired the way he cut straight through to the heart of it. To the same thing he'd care about, if their roles were reversed. "If anyone thinks that, they're idiots."

Turning around to look back at the corrugated metal of the garage door, Mick said, "Jury's still out on the kid."

"Yeah. He could go either way."

He'd seen it happen hundreds of times. Not to say everyone that joined the mob was a bad seed. Plenty of good men. Men he respected. Men with a strong moral code. Ones who just did what they had to in order to provide for their families. Or out of loyalty.

But there were plenty of others who joined for the thrill of a fight. As an outlet for their violent natures. Those men were the most dangerous. Because to them, it wasn't a job. It was *fun*.

Hurting people, scaring them? That was never fun for Rafe. It was deadly serious business. He didn't want Jesse to think that bothering a man he'd seen as defenseless was *fun*.

And he didn't want Mollie to think for a second—by whatever he did or didn't do next—that he condoned what Jesse did. Mollie seemed to see him as a stand-up, play-by-the-rules, good guy. Rafe didn't want that image in her brain to tarnish even one bit.

Shit.

Mick aimed a raised thumb and first finger at Rafe. "Do you plan on keeping your hand on the scruff of his neck until he picks the *right* way?"

"Me? Not my job." Not long-term, anyway. He'd teach Jesse a few practical things. Not be his keeper. Or his conscience.

"Looks like it. You're the right person for it. Right place, right time."

The right person for it? That was debatable. Laughable. But at least he could see through Jesse's bravado. Could see there was a good kid still in there, ready to be yanked in the right direction. Flynn and Kellan could help, too.

That ought to count as a community service way more than measuring for floats.

Might even start to ease his guilty conscience about the eight thousand . . . *questionable* things he'd done in his old line of work. Rafe didn't regret his past. It was what it was. It put Kellan through law school. Had kept him safe until six months ago. But he still knew, bottom line, that he'd crossed lines. Hurt people, worked the system the wrong way, and broken laws. So, yeah, there was a part of him that hated, had *always* hated being bad.

He slapped the taillight of the car. "Do you want Jesse to pay for it? Which would probably just mean Mollie or his grandmother forking over the cash?"

"Depends." Mick jutted his bottom teeth out over his top lip, thinking. "Got a better idea?"

"Sweat equity. More painful for him. Lasts longer.

You'd have to be willing to let your car stay here a couple of days. So I can teach Jesse the basics on it. You'd get it back with a full tune-up, washed and waxed, tires rotated, all for free."

Mick clapped him on the shoulder. "See? You do know what to do with him."

"Maybe. Maybe it'll just piss him off more and he'll cream my car next."

After a beat, they both burst out laughing. "Nah. He's already shaking in his shoes about whatever you're going to do to him. That boy won't sneeze in the wrong direction around you."

"Here's hoping."

"I'll get him put on a festival committee. That weekend in September is the biggest thing that happens in Bandon. It matters to everyone who lives here. Now that Jesse does, too, he's got to learn how important it is." As he pulled the key off its ring, Mick asked, "Can you give me a lift home? It's a ways down the road with my bum leg."

"No problem." He'd been about to offer, for that very reason. Rafe was glad pride hadn't kept the old guy from asking.

Mick looked at his watch, then back at his car. "I was going to pick up a pizza for dinner."

"Call in the order when you're ready. I'll make sure Norah knows that Jesse's got to deliver it to you. That way she's dialed in to what went down today."

"Sneaky. He'll catch heat from all sides."

Rafe sure knew what that felt like.

Chapter Fourteen

MOLLIE HAD NEVER been one of those students squirming impatiently for the final bell to ring. She loved school. And, as a flag-flying overachiever, she never left a single thing undone, even if the day's bell had metaphorically rung. But tonight? She'd been counting the minutes to the end of her shift.

At first she told herself it was because the vending machine chips she'd called "dinner" were far from satisfying. Hunger pangs fluttering in her belly. That's all.

Then she dragged because there wasn't much to do. More than half the beds were empty in the hospital. Sure, that could change at any second. But now all her charts were done. She'd brought patients warm blankets. Even nipped over to sing—horribly—a lullaby to the lonely little girl with a double leg fracture. At least the crappy singing brought a smile to her face.

The truth, though? She wanted to see Rafe. Talk to him. Touch him. *Be* with him. After the walk along the water on Tuesday, their schedules hadn't aligned again. They'd texted a little. But she'd pulled the overnight shift on Wednesday. When he got off work, she was at her busiest. And when things slowed down for her at 4:00 a.m., well, she didn't have the heart to selfishly wake him up for sexting.

Now it was Thursday. *Thursday*. Mollie picked up her pace, soles squeaking against the tiles. For people who were supposed to be having a sex-heavy fling, where was the sex? How long would she have to wait?

Waiting was no good. Waiting gave her time to realize that they were talking and laughing and evolving into an actual relationship. One where she shared her feelings with him—even if mostly through texts. One where she actively wanted him to fall in love with her town. To be happy to stay here. Maybe be happy to stay with her . . .

No.

Nonononono.

So what if her dramatic oversharing hadn't scared him away? The problem was that it hadn't scared him away *yet*. It would. Or something else would. Eventually. Just like her mom left her. Like lots of unexciting men that she hadn't necessarily *wanted* to stick around, but it would've been good to have the option. Mollie knew that for some reason, people didn't stick with her. Except for the residents of Bandon. They were her only constant.

Was she being overly dramatic? Placing too much emphasis on *that one time her mother chose a better life over her own flesh and blood daughter*? Probably. But emotional hang-ups didn't have to be logical. They just *were*. And Mollie happened to believe that hers was a doozy.

She stripped off her gloves and dropped them into a biohazard container. She'd like her sex now, please. Right now, before things got any stickier and before she started to like Rafe any more.

Mollie checked her watch. Five minutes to ten. She'd handed off her patients. Even helped the nurses restock the crash carts. There was nothing left to do but tap her toes for five more minutes until she was free. Free to sprint to the car and try to catch Rafe before he went to bed.

It was the first time she'd been tempted to leave early. Hooking up—or trying to, at any rate—with a rough-and-tough-looking bad boy burbled to the surface all the rebellious urges she'd suppressed growing up. After decades of goodness, wasn't she due a few disobedient moments? Say . . . five of them?

"Hey Doc, wanna examine me?"

The cheesy come-on snapped her head up. But when she met Rafe's laughing eyes, Mollie relaxed. For a split second. Then her body went back on alert for a whole different reason.

A *lust* alert.

But as usual, concern for a potential patient took priority. Mollie ran her practiced gaze over him. No obvious cuts or bruises. He stood straight, not favoring anything. He could be feverish, though. She reached for his forehead. "Rafe, are you okay?"

"Isn't that for you to decide?" He snagged her hand and redirected it to his lips. Threw her a smoldering look from those bedroom eyes as he dropped a kiss on her knuckles. "You're the doctor."

"I mean, why are you here?"

"*You're* here."

Aaaaand her pulse kicked into overdrive. Because that was both the hottest and most romantic comment she'd received in, well, months. A too-good-to-be-true comment. Mollie pulled her hand back. "That's it?"

"Yep. I missed you, Doc. Didn't want to wait any longer to see you."

"I get off in four minutes."

His dark eyebrow winged up. Those fast, clever fingers undid her watch and tucked it into his jeans pocket. "Live a little. Let me get you off right now."

Okay, that was the best offer *ever*. But no. No way.

One quick glance through the open doorway and he tugged her into the empty patient room, kicking the door shut with his foot. The only light in the room was from the full moon shining in the window. "I mean, it'll take more than four minutes. I did promise you that for our first time it'd be an all-night marathon. But I can make these the hottest stolen four minutes of your life."

Mollie didn't doubt that in the slightest. Especially since their laundry room escapade had probably lasted no more than three. His hands were already running underneath her lab coat. Up and down and all around.

She slapped at him. Just enough to get some space between them. Because, uh, no way was this happening right here. With no lock on the door. "I'm working, Rafe."

"Not anymore."

"This is a patient room."

"Without a patient in it. Unless you count me. I've got a serious case of blue balls here, Doc. Something only you can treat." He grabbed her waist and picked her up like she weighed no more than an IV bag. Four steps had them next to the bed. Rafe put her down, then whisked the curtain to enclose them. The added layer of privacy was just enough to make Mollie marginally more comfortable with the idea of them truly doing this.

"Look, I'm totally on board. But we should go."

"Why wait any longer? We should stay right here. Get all dirty in the bed that moves into interesting positions."

Mollie's hand flew to her mouth. She'd never, *ever* contemplated a hospital bed as being adjustable for sex. It was . . . brilliant. Intriguing. Exciting.

So, *so* bad.

He ran a finger across the green embroidery spelling out her name. A name that conveniently ran right across the swell of her breast. The man could make a monogram sexy. "I wasn't planning to lead with this, but you owe me."

Well, if he got to touch, so did she. Mollie slow-walked her fingers from the bottom of his sternum up to his clavicle. "Oh, this ought to be good. For what?"

"For dealing with your cousin. The one you sicced on me."

Huh? Mollie remembered the conversation. The one where Rafe *volunteered*, out of the blue, to have Jesse work at the garage. But now didn't seem like the best time to remind him of the way it actually happened. Not since his kindhearted gesture now had him running herd on an out-of-control hooligan. Being around Rafe, soaking up all the good qualities of a real man—loyalty, strength, honor—was Jesse's best chance at getting back on the straight and narrow. She didn't want to do anything to make Rafe change his mind about the part-time job.

Dipping her head, she said, "Gran told me what happened to Mick's car."

"Not what *happened*," he corrected with a frown. One finger beneath her chin, Rafe tipped her head up to meet his hard stare. "What Jesse *did*. Don't whitewash the blame even a little. It's all on him."

It stung, but he was right. Her word choice had sprung from Mollie's mushy heart. The one that adored her cousin and still remembered him as a moppet who crawled onto her lap for hugs. "I'm not. Truly. He utterly screwed up."

"Yeah. He did." Rafe crossed his arms over his chest. "Something I hear he did a lot back where he used to live. Seems to be a bad habit of his."

"This was the first time it happened here, though," she rushed to point out. The comment sounded hollow, even to Mollie as it came out of her mouth. They'd all hoped that a new environment would curb Jesse's troublemaking tendencies, but this incident didn't bode well. Maybe it had been naïve to assume that Bandon would work its magic on him and he'd be instantly transformed into a valedictorian who helped little old ladies cross the street.

But Mollie still believed that his heart mattered. Not just his actions. People made mistakes. Everyone made mistakes. All the time. With a good heart, there was always hope for a fresh start. Not just for Jesse, but for anyone.

She refused to give up that belief.

Rafe, however, looked as serious as an aneurysm. It showed in the lines bracketing his thinned lips and the furrow in his brow. "It's a turning point, Mollie. Either he gets scared straight right the fuck now, or you lose him. To other bad kids, to jail, or worse. Moving here to live with you and Norah—and hopefully give a shit about what you think of him—is his last chance."

"I know. I'm grateful that Mick didn't press charges. Presumably that was as a kindness to Gran and me."

"Maybe." Rafe smirked. "Pretty sure it was more that he didn't want to hand over responsibility for his problem to the police. He's got a lot of pride holding up that steel backbone of his."

Rafe had him pegged already. Mick could be prickly, at first. It delighted her that they must've hit it off because she adored the colonel. He had his quirks, just like everyone else in town, but he was loyal down to his core. And he didn't put up with any posturing or bigheadedness. Which, after training with pompous surgeons, was a refreshing change.

Then she read between the lines. "But Mick was fine with handing it over to you?"

"We came to a mutual agreement on next steps."

Was Rafe trying to be modest? Because it didn't take her handful of degrees to connect the dots. "One that wouldn't expose what happened to his car to the entire town. So people wouldn't realize that a teenager got the jump on him."

"That's right."

What a softhearted sweetie. It was so darned easy to see right through Rafe's bluster. Mollie grabbed both of his hands. Felt a smile stretching her cheeks sideways. "You saved Jesse *and* Mick."

"Don't stick a halo on my head or anything. It's the smart solution. Period." His usual gruffness was there. Along with a shift of his eyes, barely discernible in the shadows, that made her wonder if the praise embarrassed him.

Oh, well. Too bad. Because he deserved it. So if Rafe didn't like hearing the words, she'd just have to find another way to thank him. Considering the reason he'd popped by, the answer was obvious. "You should come up with one more smart solution. To our present dilemma."

"What's that?"

Mollie put one hand on the bedrail and plopped onto the mattress. Swung her legs in what she realized too late wasn't a sexy move at all. Especially with a gap showing between her scrub pants and white crew socks. Not exactly fish nets and black stilettos designed to seduce. "One skinny bed. Two bodies. How on earth are we going to both fit?"

"Guess I'll have to get on top of you." The fire in his blue eyes seared through her as Rafe bracketed her thighs with his own. "I guarantee that will work. It'll be a tight fit, but tight's good."

"It's very good," she said, on more of a breath than an actual voice. Because now he had her thinking about just how big he was to make it a tight fit.

Inside of her.

Holy hell.

Rafe interlaced his fingers at the ultra-sensitive nape of her neck. Circled the pads of his thumbs in the hollows behind her earlobes.

God.

That was all it took. Two thumbs at the spot where her earring posts often stabbed her. How did that set her blood on fire? How did those tiny nerve endings somehow zip all the way down to spread heat through her entire pelvis like a pool of hot wax?

Clinically, she knew they didn't. She'd spent hours memorizing the anatomy of what connected where.

Clearly, when it came to Rafe, all bets were off. Everything Mollie thought she knew about the human body needed to be chucked out the window.

On a moan, she let her head fall back a little.

Because it felt that good. Already.

Rafe removed her stethoscope and placed it on the tray table. Turned on the light mounted high over the bed. "I've been fantasizing about stripping you out of your scrubs ever since you told me you were a doctor."

"How'd that fantasy play out?"

He winced. "Usually ended with me rubbing one out. Tonight's going to have a better ending."

"Yes." Oh, yes.

"See, I already know what you feel like. Your curves." He scraped his palms down over taut nipples not at all concealed beneath the lace of her bra, scrub top and lab coat. Nope, he'd brought those suckers out to *play*. "Your straightaways." He skimmed back up from wrists to shoulders. "Your wetness."

The tip of one long finger teased along her lips. Mollie sucked hard, swirling her tongue around it. The motion locked Rafe's thighs into pure steel in response. She ended with a sharp nip, just to let him know that she was more than ready to move right along.

"My fantasy is about peeling away all these serious, dull, unisex medical layers to reveal the woman underneath. The woman that you're hiding away just for my eyes only."

Rafe eased the lab coat off her shoulders and left it tangled at the crook of her elbows, pinning her arms slightly back. Then he lifted the hem of her top to reveal her stomach. One hand pushed her flat onto her back while the other traced lazy circles around her navel. Slow, teasing circles that made her quiver. And clench everything, inside and out.

When would he *really* touch her?

How on earth would she survive when he finally *did*?

The circles turned into zigzags that went from the cinched waist of her pants all the way to her sternum, and then back over to the opposite hip. Mollie shivered, arching up when he replaced his finger with his tongue and laved a long, wet line from side to side.

"So pale." His breath feathered over her skin, lips a scant hair from actually touching her.

Crap. No seductive clothing, *and* no sexy tan lines. Clearly she should've started prepping for this fling with the same intensity she'd studied for the medical boards. And long before she'd even met Rafe. "It's only May eleventh. We don't break out bikinis in Oregon until July."

"Not a complaint. You're so pale and soft, it's like licking my way across milk." Rafe lifted his head and threw her a wicked grin. "I fucking love milk." He shoved her shirt up, above her breasts. Clamped one hand on each breast and slowly squeezed. *Just* hard enough. *Just* perfectly enough to have her mouth fall open on a gasp.

"You're so beautiful, Mollie." Rafe nibbled his way across the lacy edge of her bra. "I thought I wanted you. Before. Now I know I've *got* to have you."

"Ditto." To the nth power.

"Glad that's settled." He dropped his mouth over one nipple and sucked. Sucked hard through the swirl of lace. Pinched her other nipple with corresponding pressure.

It was like he'd flicked a switch into sexual overdrive. Because now his hips rolled against hers. His breathing hitched and he shoved his other hand roughly underneath her to knead her ass. It was hot and wild and amazing.

"Let me touch you," Mollie demanded. Wanted. Needed. Vibrated with the burning urgency of the desire to feel those muscles beneath her fingers. Whatever.

"We'll get there. Once you come the first time, then you can touch me."

"What sort of evil, twisted game is that?"

He slid his hand beneath the waistband of both her scrubs and her panties. There was nothing between his big, calloused hand and her ass. Well, nothing except the goose bumps he'd raised. "One where you're guaranteed to come multiple times before we even take your shoes off."

How could she possibly argue with the logic of a statement like that?

Down came her pants. Fast. Before Mollie could even lift her hips to help, the harsh cotton raked across the backs of her thighs.

She loved it.

Loved the heightened sensations. Loved how the scrape of the waistband contrasted with the ungodly softness of his tongue still toying with her nipple. The uneven bumps of the blanket under her ass versus the much softer sheet touching her bare back. How the stiff seams of his jeans dug into her legs.

"The plan's to take the edge off. Like only giving the top of a soda a half twist. It releases the pressure of the bubbles so that you can take your time drinking the whole thing."

Well. If Mollie was soda, then Rafe had to be a neat shot of twenty-year-old whiskey. Smooth and oh-so-powerful. Thoroughly destructive to her inhibitions.

Because she didn't care that she was still, technically, at work. That there was an outside (okay, fairly remote) chance that a janitor could barge in to check the trash or mop the floor. That if they weren't very, very quiet then someone would most definitely come in and find them.

Mollie only cared about getting Rafe inside her.

Now.

A loud, electronic hum alerted her a moment before the bed began to move. The top half chugged into a half-seated position.

"Might as well make use of the amenities." Rafe winked at her. Then his head shot downward to nuzzle her inner thighs. His ten o'clock shadow chafed gloriously as his tongue traced the seam full of nerve endings between her pelvis and leg. But these were only fast brushes, quick pit stops on the way to his actual goal. Which was to peel her open with his thumbs and lick right down her center.

One long lick.

One slow, drugging, dragging lick.

Mollie held her breath, waiting for the next one.

There wasn't *one*. There was a sudden flurry of pointed flickering right across her clitoris. An explosion of heat flashed through her.

Mollie almost yelled but remembered herself at the last second and turned it into a low, choked-out, "Rafe! God."

"Make up your mind." He hovered, only his breath touching her.

"You. Definitely you."

His tongue started that magical, fast, and flitting motion again. At the same time, he drove two fingers into her.

Boom.

There.

Done. World tilted. Ultimate orgasm achieved with a single inward thrust. Mollie pulsed around him. Satisfied. Boneless. But she wanted more. She wanted the thickness of his dick inside her, not just his fingers. She wanted to feel *taken*. Used. Mindless.

So she consciously pulsed and tightened again. And again.

"You're doing that on purpose."

"Yep."

"You want me in you?"

"Yep."

"Are you ready for that? You don't need time to recover and build up slow from scratch again?"

"I'll tell you what I'm *not* ready for. I'm not ready for slow. At all."

Rafe pulled his wallet from his back pocket and removed a condom. Funny how the snap of rubber in a hospital room sounded the same whether it was hand gloves or a love glove. He threaded his legs through hers, then cinched them up around his waist. "No problem. I'm ready to drive into you so hard this bed will go right through the wall."

"Big talk."

"You've got the big part right." And in he went. No hesitation. A single thrust that did, indeed, feel as though he'd push her right through the mattress.

So. Good.

The residual slickness from her orgasm made it work, but Mollie still felt stretched as full as she'd ever been. Like she'd be perfectly happy just lying there, wallowing in that near-painful tightness.

Rafe dipped his head to work on one breast with his mouth. He alternated the sucking pulls of his lips with hard, powerful, possessing snaps of his hips. It was a matter of moments before Mollie began to spiral toward another climax. It was so dirty. So raw. So primal.

So unbelievably fantastic.

Mollie moved with him. Rolling, arching, aching in every cell for *more*. More hardness in the slam of his pecs against her chest. More heat pooling where their bodies merged. More brushes of the steel of his forearms against her sides. More of his low, guttural moans that she could barely hear over her own panting and sighs.

With a deep sigh, Rafe pulled back to look at her. Not just her face, but her exposed breasts and stomach, and *then* back up to meet her eyes. "You take my breath away, Mollie."

The depth of feeling in his gaze shocked her. Scared her more than a little. And lit an answering warmth in her heart that scared her even more. So she retreated to the safety of teasing. "That's from all the sexing."

"I haven't taken the time to tell you how special you are. Feels like I should before we finish this."

"We've flirted a ton, Rafe."

"And now I'm being serious. Because you deserve it. You're healing me in places I didn't know were broken." He followed up the uncharacteristically romantic words with a kiss.

A real kiss.

Not an I'm-about-to-come kiss. No, this kiss was tender. Soft in the way his lips explored, but still passionate.

It was a kiss Mollie felt in exactly one spot in her body. Her heart.

He started moving again, still with purpose, but

with less speed. His thrusts were deliberate. His hand on her breast a caress, his kiss still so achingly sweet it almost brought tears to her eyes.

A slight hiking of her legs brought him deeper. A twist of his hips put him in contact with Mollie's heretofore undiscovered G-spot. With her hands still not free, all she could do was sink her teeth in the ridge of muscles along the top of his shoulder as she shuddered and quaked and, once more, dissolved into a million pieces.

Two more thrusts and Rafe grunted much louder before stilling.

Whereas Mollie's heart immediately began to race once more.

What was *that*?

It sure hadn't been just fling sex. It started out that way. But then it morphed into what had to be called real relationship sex. Bordering on making love.

Omigod.

Panic started to set in. What should she say? What should she do? How did you thank a man for the most mind-altering sexual experience ever while also accusing him of acting like a more than decent boyfriend?

Or what if she was wrong? What if the key to the best sex ever was the hybrid nature of it? Maybe he didn't mean to let that emotionally naked sentence slip.

It was the sweetest thing anyone had ever said about her.

Which put her on the verge of breaking out into hives. This could not be a relationship. They had an agreement. An understanding. Mutually beneficial friendship, *period*. No real feelings.

Mollie was suddenly, horribly afraid it was too late to make that case.

Rafe trailed kisses up her throat to her ear. "Well, Doc? Still want to find out where my tattoo is?"

She wasn't an idiot. Nobody passed up an offer like that. Not even a woman on the verge of a panic attack. "Can I look for it with my fingers? Feel everywhere until I find it?"

"You can try." Gently, he released her arms and removed her lab coat and top. "I can't promise how long I'll be able to keep from jumping you again."

"Fair enough." Because she'd never ask Rafe to promise her anything.

Mollie knew all too well that some promises were too hard for most people to keep.

Chapter Fifteen

RAFE FISTED MOLLIE'S oh-so-soft hair. It pulled her head back, extending her neck so he had more access to kiss it. Might even leave a hickey. So that people *knew* she was off-limits. That she was *his*. That Mollie was in his heart, his brain, his dreams.

She was on her knees. He was behind her, his other hand clamped tight on her fucking perfect breast. It was a toss-up—should he move and get straight to the orgasm already tightening his nuts? Or stay frozen, just *feeling* every inch of skin where they touched? Rafe had never been tempted to do that with any other woman. But when he was with Mollie, it wasn't just about coming. It was about absorbing her pleasure, too. Enjoying being together, in bed and out.

Besides, it'd drive her crazy if he stayed still. Make her wriggle and breathe through those sexy little moans . . .

"Wake up!"

Shit.

As he rolled over, Rafe's arm pinwheeled, fist cocked to hit whoever was in his room. Whoever had pulled him out of the dream that had been such a fanfucking-tastic reality a few hours ago.

A strong hand at his wrist stopped him mid-swing. "Rafe. Stop."

Sounded like Flynn. Except Flynn wouldn't be dumb enough to wake him up predawn for anything.

Anything but trouble.

That thought brought him fully awake and alert. He scrubbed the heel of his palm over his eyes. "What's going on?"

"Someone's banging on the front door." That harsh whisper came from Kellan. With the dim light bleeding in from the hallway, Rafe could see both of his brothers now. Since they were both naked, he wasn't too thrilled at the sight.

Now he heard it, too—a repeated, dull, fast thumping—and adrenaline shot through him so fast that Rafe jumped to his feet.

Also naked.

Guess they needed to make a *wear pajamas in case we're about to be ambushed* house rule.

"What do we do?" Flynn asked.

Good question. They didn't have any guns. Rafe kept a butcher knife in the top dresser drawer, a baseball bat under the bed, and a tire iron in the corner. Things that the marshal wouldn't officially classify as weapons and boot them out of the program for having—but things they could damn well use to defend themselves.

Wait. Rafe cocked his head. Listened. "Is it just at the front door?"

Flynn nodded. "Sounds like it."

"You didn't look?" Had Flynn forgotten all the basics in their six months out of the business? You had to assess a threat before figuring out how to deal with it.

"We came to get you. No time to waste peeking through blinds. We need a plan. Fast."

"Do you think they found us?" Kellan came closer. The kid looked scared. Hunched over. Frowning. Way younger than his twenty-five years.

Damn it, Rafe never wanted him to feel that way. Never wanted anything about McGinty's organization to touch him. Here they were, two thousand miles and five sets of names away, and the ugliness of it was still hurting his little brother.

"No. I don't." The words weren't just to calm Kellan the fuck down. Rafe grabbed two pairs of sweatpants off the top closet shelf and tossed them at his brothers. "I think if McGinty sent people here to kill us, they wouldn't knock. We'd already be dead in our sleep."

"Then who is it?"

He tugged on his jeans. Jammed his feet into sneakers. Did the mental math and came up with only one answer. "My best bet is Marshal Evans. She's the one with the sick habit of dragging us out of our beds in the middle of the night. Did either of you do anything?"

Flynn whipsawed his head back and forth. "Anything that would set her off? No. I play it clean. Just like I always have. *You're* the reason we got pulled from the last town. What did *you* do?"

"Nothing."

Pretty much. Unless there were security cameras in the hospital? Was it illegal to have sex in an unassigned room? Like they were squatters? Wouldn't Mollie have said something if there were cameras?

Shit.

Mollie. She . . . complicated everything. He needed more. More time with her. More doses of her seeing him as a good guy. More quick, needle-sharp pokes of her wit. More kisses. More laughs. More of everything.

Just to see what happened next.

No way could he let Delaney yank them away from Bandon, away from Mollie without a word.

Not without a fight.

Rafe walked down the hall. He didn't creep. He didn't go on tiptoe. He just walked. Even though he could hear his brothers behind him trying to be all quiet and sneaky.

It was their damn house.

Whoever was pounding on the door at oh-dark-thirty should be the one on guard.

Kellan grabbed his elbow. "You're just going to open the door?"

"Only way to find out who's on the other side." But he did pause to open a drawer in the table they used to hold their keys and pocket crap. He removed a long knife and held it vertically along his leg.

Rafe sucked in a breath. Hoped he wasn't wrong—and therefore dead in thirty seconds—and opened the door.

It was Mick. Same cap and windbreaker as always. The pissy expression was also, by now, familiar. "About damn time. My fist's raw from beating on this door. Do you boys know how long I've been knocking?"

"Yeah." Flynn grunted the word. But next to him, Rafe literally felt the tension leak out of the crowded hallway. Kellan's hand dropped from his elbow.

God, he was glad it was the colonel leaning on the doorjamb and not the marshal. Or three goons with Berettas and extra clips. Glad . . . and annoyed. Because it was still four fucking a.m.

Mick jabbed a finger at him. "Why the hell didn't you answer sooner?"

Let's see, go with the truth? That it took time to mentally run through their makeshift weapons stash? To think about and then reject running out the back door, full bore, for the car and escape?

Nah. If he went down that road, it'd keep him from getting back to bed anytime soon. So Rafe patted his bare stomach. "Had to put clothes on. Oh, and decide if we wanted to bother talking to whoever would surprise us before the sun's even up."

"If the sun was up, it'd be too late." Mick pointed up

at the still inky black sky, full of more stars than Rafe had ever seen in all of his years in Chicago put together.

"For what?"

"Fishing."

He and Mollie had left the hospital at around 2:00 a.m. Rafe was dog tired now, but he'd been wide awake on the drive home. He was sure there'd been no half-asleep call to make these crazy-ass plans. Especially since he didn't touch a damned fish unless it was deep fried and covered in tartar sauce.

Flynn made the half-wheezing noise that always meant he was trying not to laugh out loud. Not that Rafe blamed him. Because he was torn between swearing and laughing, too.

Scratching the top of his head, Rafe asked, "Did you tell me we were going fishing?"

"Nope. Woke up to pee." Mick frowned. "That's what you do at my age. Saw that the conditions were right to drop a line. Thought you should come along. Try out a different side of Bandon."

Well, the damage was done. Rafe was awake now. Clearly a guy who showed up, uninvited, in the middle of the night wouldn't take no for an answer. Plus, he did appreciate the invitation. In a weird sort of way.

"Fine. I'll go grab a shirt, be right back."

Flynn stayed at his heels all the way back to his bedroom, whereas there was no doubt Kellan had stayed by the door to keep Mick company. The kid had manners as polished as the Stanley Cup at Game 7.

"You're fucking joking. You're going out on a boat? Now?"

"Scared to be left alone?" Rafe taunted as he tugged on a sweatshirt. Yeah. You grow up with a guy, you learn their weaknesses. Flynn's was that he didn't like to be teased. At all. Teasing him was twice as effective as a dare. Way better than reverse psychology. He didn't doubt that Flynn was still jittery from their scare. Totally imagined, no reason to be scared, scare.

So as a good, caring big brother, it was Rafe's duty to tease the fright right out of him.

Fun, too.

"Shut the fuck up with that." The Bears starting linebacker didn't throw as much defense as Flynn was putting off right now. "But Kellan won't be able to go back to sleep. Which means he'll bug me to stay up and play video games with him."

"Consider yourself lucky. The couch and coffee sounds like a better deal than smelly fish and a boat."

"So why go?"

Mick wasn't anything like the club-hopping, heavy drinking players he'd rolled with in Chicago. He liked the guy. Putting down roots meant making friends, and Mick was the closest Rafe came to having a real friend here in Bandon. "Could you say no to the colonel?"

"Probably not."

"It's a nice offer. One I've got no reason to refuse. Aside from being fucking exhausted."

"Fucking exhausted?" Flynn punched him on the arm with a sly grin. "Or exhausted from fucking?"

Not a hard thing to figure out. Nothing else in this town would've kept Rafe out so late. Didn't mean he was ready to talk about it. Or have Flynn talk like that about Mollie. Like she was just a way to pass time. Like she didn't rate a name.

No, that wasn't okay at *all*.

"Enough. Don't talk about the doc like that."

Flynn froze, mid-stretch with one elbow cocked. "For real?"

He wouldn't get into this now. Laying down the law was enough. Rafe shoved his phone into his pocket. "Delaney told us to get to know and like Bandon. You two are slow off the mark at that, so I'm picking up the slack. Taking one for the team."

"By fishing at the crack of ass."

"Yeah. You can thank me later."

"THIS HERE'S YOUR basic, six-and-a-half-foot, medium-action spinning rod." Mick gave a final tamp with his foot. The thing was jammed into a pyramid of sand, just like the one he'd done for Rafe.

"Will there be a test?"

"You have to know the names of your tools. Doesn't matter if its rods and reels, lug nuts and wrenches, or guns and ammo."

The specifics of that list put him on edge. Hopefully it'd been a callout to the colonel's own military service and not a dig for info on Rafe's blacked-out past.

"Sorry. You're right."

He pulled something dark and small out of a pouch at his waist, then attached it to the line. "We put a motor oil grub on the hook for bait. Surfperch are partial to it."

"That's what we're fishing for? Not salmon?" The only things Rafe knew about Oregon before moving here was that it had salmon and wine. Nobody fucking mentioned cranberries, that was for damn sure.

"Not salmon. Have to head into a river for that. Or go out on a boat."

Rafe looked out at the darkness churning as far as he could see. His stomach did its own churning at the thought. "No boat. No thank you."

"You got the sissy stomach?"

"I like boats in general. I don't like the idea of being out on the ocean in the dark."

"Roger that." Mick eased himself into a camp chair with a grunt. "Beach fishing's easier all around."

"We're just going to leave the rods standing there?"

"You'll see it bend when you get a bite. Until then, take a load off."

This wasn't nearly as bad as he'd envisioned. Cold, with the wind blowing straight at them off the ocean. But, yeah, with the constant ebb and flow of the surf, it was peaceful. Rafe sat and crossed his legs at the ankles.

"Thanks for bringing me out here."

"The beach is different this early. You see another side of it. Like watching a woman in her sleep. I like it."

"Me, too."

Mick swung his head to look at him. "Here's the straight shit. I can tell you don't want to be in Bandon."

Wasn't that a kick in the nuts? After all the work he'd put into being a good citizen? He'd mowed the Wicks' lawn so Frieda's husband wouldn't worry about it. Joined a festival committee—and stopped short of slapping Floyd silly. Eaten at restaurants. He was mentoring a teenager. Not to mention sleeping with the freaking unofficial town daughter.

Rafe opened his mouth to deny it. Then again, why bother? A little honesty wouldn't blow their cover. The Maguire brothers had been pushed to their limit by all these moves and probably radiated way too much attitude. Mick was observant. Just because he'd figured out that Bandon wasn't their bucket list town didn't mean he had any chance of figuring out the rest.

"It wasn't our first choice." God's honest truth.

"Still, you've got to find a reason to like it here."

He thought back to what he and Mollie did in that hospital bed. Didn't even try to stop the shit-eating grin that stretched across his face. "I'm working on it."

Mick took off his cap and ran the brim through his hand a few times to re-crease it. Then nailed him with the kind of look that McGinty used to give a client who claimed they were short with their monthly payment. The kind of look that said *I am not buying whatever you think you're selling.* "A reason *besides* Mollie Vickers. Unless she's enough."

Rafe hadn't thought about it from that perspective. Hadn't thought about what would or could happen with Mollie long-term. Mollie, who he'd spent more time texting than even seeing in person. *That* was a first.

Was that the secret? After all their insistence on friends with benefits, was the key to why he couldn't stop thinking about her that they'd become friends? Gotten to know and like each other instead of just fucking each other's brains out?

Still. Rafe knew, deep down, that nothing serious, nothing lasting *could* happen between them. Not when she deserved a man who didn't lie to her.

"I can also tell that you're either running or hiding from something. Lots of us are. This is a good place to stop running."

The best defense was a good offense. Rafe fired right back. "What are you running from?"

For a minute, there was only the crashing of the surf. Too early for any shore birds. No answer from Mick, either. Finally, he sucked in a couple of breaths through the side of his mouth. Slapped his palms against the canvas arm rests. "Oh, the usual. I saw bad things in all my tours overseas. Watched a lot of good men die. Horribly. Because of orders I gave."

Rafe knew exactly what he meant. Not to the same degree, to be sure. But guilt weighed just as heavy for every single life you watched blink out. And even though he'd never been the one pulling the trigger, watching it happen still weighed heavy on him. Because life freaking mattered.

It was a strong, brave admission. He couldn't let it sit out there without offering something in return. "I've been through something similar."

"Have you?" Mick didn't sound the least surprised. A soldier always recognized another soldier, no matter the trappings or circumstance.

"Nothing as large-scale as what you went through. Enough to wake me up in the middle of the night, though. Sweating and shaking the guilt out." He'd been in some turf wars. Just as bodyguard to McGinty, but he'd still seen men he knew get shot down right in front of him. Had watched, arms crossed and jaw clenched, as a lower-rank soldier carried out whatever hit McGinty deemed necessary.

He'd absolutely fucking hated it.

But it kept a roof over his brothers' heads. Let Kellan follow his dream and—almost—become a lawyer. So Rafe wouldn't do a damn thing differently.

Another long pause. Rafe figured that Mick was battling back the faces of the dead flashing through his head now, same as Rafe. They both stared out at the blackness in front of them.

The chair creaked as Mick rearranged himself. "You can't change your memories. You just have to learn to live with them. Somehow."

"Bandon fixed that for you?" Because Rafe would give just about anything for the same fix. It was true he'd thought a lot less about the past in the last twelve days. Wasn't that just because he'd been so busy? Getting settled, the new job, taking on Jesse, keeping watch over his brothers, joining the festival fucking committee, falling into a habit of these chats with Mick, and of course, Mollie.

Mollie of the big laugh and bigger heart.

Mollie, who thought everyone deserved a second chance.

Mollie, who didn't know jack shit about the old version of him and seemed to really like the new version.

Mick riffled through the backpack he'd stashed between their chairs. Pulled out two thermoses and handed one to Rafe. "My wife and I talked for years about where we'd live once the Corps spit us out. When you're posted to the ass-end of nowhere, it's a nice escape to dream. We thought the mountains would be nice. North Carolina, where there's enough military folk for us to feel comfortable. But Barbara died before my retirement papers came through."

"I'm sorry." He'd assumed Mick was a widower, from the lack of mention of a wife coupled with the ring on his finger. Still sucked to be confirmed.

"She was my rock." The older man took a long, noisy slurp. "Suddenly everything I knew was gone. My wife, my job, my friends, my whole life. Nothing made sense."

Yeah. That was exactly how Rafe felt when they first

joined WITSEC. At least he'd had his brothers. As pissy and unhappy as they were with him, it'd been a million times better than going it alone.

"Sounds hard."

"Living our dream by myself . . . well, it just didn't work. I tried three or four other places across the country. Nothing felt right. Nothing worked for me. Until I got here."

Was the guy inside Rafe's head? Digging out his own carefully blocked off feelings about their other pit stops across the country? And was he acknowledging that Bandon *did* feel right to him now?

Rafe unzipped his jacket, needing the coolness of the wet breeze. "Everyone's friendly here. A little too friendly and nosy, sometimes. But accepting."

"They don't care that I talk to my dead wife."

Rafe froze, the top only half unscrewed from the thermos. "Okay. That's pretty accepting."

"I'm not crazy. I know Barbara won't answer me. But I spent so many years running things by her, the habit's too hard to stop. It makes me feel better."

"Whatever works." Because who was he to judge?

"The people here don't give me any guff about it. Don't try to lock me up, either. They let me be who I am. That's why it works. That's why Bandon is home."

"I miss my old home." Rafe hadn't intended to say that. But he had to hide that pain around his brothers, around the marshal. It felt good to say it out loud. Like ripping off a Band-Aid to give a scab some air.

"I miss what was, too. Doesn't show it any disrespect to like where you are now, though."

Was that it? Had Rafe spent all these months making himself miserable? Fighting to not let go of Chicago? Even though it was his own idea to jump ship and leave?

He twisted sideways to look at Mick. "I want to make it work here. You have no idea how much I want this to work for us."

"So stop with the comparisons."

Shit. "Is it that obvious?"

"I see you watching. You size everyone up. Size every situation up. The only explanation is that you're comparing every thing, every person, every place against your old life. You're putting what used to be up on a pedestal. Throw a tarp over that thing. Move on."

It was damn good advice. The same thing the marshal had been yammering at him this whole time, but from a different tack. He wasn't cheating on Chicago. They'd broken up. For all the right reasons.

"I want to like Bandon. I don't like cranberries, though," he admitted.

Nodding, Mick took back the thermos. "You hate the jelly stuff in the can, don't you?"

Finally. Somebody in this town who hadn't drunk the cranberry-flavored Kool-Aid. "It's disgusting. Like eating snail slime."

"Ever had cranberry apple pie?"

"No."

He slapped a palm on the canvas arm of his chair. "I'll ask Norah to make you one."

"I don't want any—"

"Don't worry. She won't add her secret ingredient. She's a good baker. I'll bet it changes your mind. And if it doesn't? So what. You like fishing at dawn now, don't you?"

This wasn't the worst morning he'd passed by a long shot. Rafe took a big swig of coffee. And almost spit it right back out, surprised as hell by the hefty dose of whiskey in it. No wonder Mick was in such a good mood. "I think I could get used to it, yeah."

"That's the spirit."

"Thanks for bringing me out here."

"Thought you'd like it. It's nice to have some company for a change."

Rafe thought back to all the hours he'd spent shooting the shit in the back room at McGinty's headquarters. He'd missed that. And he hadn't bothered to look for a replacement. Maybe that was his big mistake. Because it *was* nice to have company.

He took another swig of coffee. "Do I have to eat the fish we catch?"

Mick laughed so hard it turned into a coughing fit. "You're a hard case, aren't you, Maguire?"

"You have no idea."

Chapter Sixteen

> RM: You know how to treat food poisoning, right?

Mollie frowned down at her phone. Are you sick? Throwing up?

> RM: Not yet. Those fish I caught with Mick—Kellan's cooking them. Trying to, anyway. Figure I'll get sick from whatever he does to it and Flynn'll probably get a bone stuck in his throat that K missed digging out.

It was pretty adorable how Rafe complained about his brothers. Because Mollie didn't think he realized just how often he brought them up. Good, bad, or infuriating, they were always in the forefront of his thoughts. It was nice to see how close the three of them were.

Do you have tartar sauce? That fixes every kind of fish, no matter what he does to it.

RM: A woman after my own heart. But from the smell coming out of our kitchen, it may be past the point of tartar sauce reviving it.

A loud barrage of knocks had Mollie hurrying to the front door. Maybe you should call a code on the poor thing. Just go order a pizza.

RM: Can't. Flynn and Kellan are tickled I actually caught fish on my first try. They want to turn this into a big deal.

See? She knew that, given time, they'd come around. Rafe still hadn't told her exactly why they held a grudge against him. Something to do with moving here—which, come to think of it, he'd never explained. Not how or why they chose Bandon.

Mollie paused in the hallway. Feels good, doesn't it? Them being proud of you?

RM: Yeah. Good enough I'll choke down whatever he puts in front of me.

Keep me posted. I'll have a syringe full of anti-emetic at the ready, just in case.

RM: What's that?

Stops the puking.

RM: Best present ever . . . He signed off with an emoji of a bucket. Funny guy. Slipping her phone into her jeans pocket, Mollie opened the door.

"Do you hear that sound?" Instead of bothering to say hello, Lucien put a hand to his ear. "It's the sighs of all the women down at the Gorse who won't have a chance with me tonight because I'm here."

Mollie stopped Lucien near the table where she and Norah tossed their keys to give him a huge hug. "Thanks for coming over."

"I'm your best friend. Why wouldn't I come over and hang on a Friday night?" He handed her the bottle of wine so he could shrug out of his coat. Mollie hoped he'd followed form and "liberated" something ridiculously expensive from the club's wine cellar. After all, she'd saved him a trip back to the hospital by taking out his stitches at his office. That deserved a little quid pro quo in the form of a decadently complex Shiraz, right?

"Because you'll be sharing the couch with a very pouty teenager." God knew she certainly didn't want to do it, at this point. Not after dealing with two straight days of huffed-out sighs and conversations consisting solely of grunts. Rafe swore he was behaving at the garage as he detailed Mick's car, so it seemed Jesse saved the attitude for his nearest and dearest.

None of which managed to take the sparkle off of her mood, however. One night with Rafe Maguire had a . . . rejuvenating effect. Mollie felt like she'd spent a week at a spa. Like there was caffeine in the air. Or champagne. Or both.

Lucien tugged on his French cuffs. Only he would pair a starched pinstripe shirt requiring cuff links with jeans and a movie night. "I thought you said Jesse felt bad about what he did to Mick's car?"

"He does." Mollie believed that with all her heart. "But he also feels bad for himself. For being grounded."

"Ah. The remorse/resentment combo. Been there, done that."

Mollie, too. She understood her cousin's attitude. Didn't make her any less sick of it, though. Still, just like she told Rafe every time he complained about his brothers, family was worth the effort. No way would she let Jesse down. If living with her was truly his second chance, Mollie would darn well make sure he took to it.

She kept Lucien crowded by the coatrack with a hand on his arm. "He's responding well to spending time with Rafe. I thought bringing you over would give him exposure to another solid, stable male role model."

His eyebrows shot up. "That's a lot of expectation riding on how well I park my ass on your sofa."

"Well, if you're saying you're not up to the job . . ."

He twitched his forearm out of her grasp. "Don't try to reverse psych me into it. Jesse's your cousin. Of *course* I want to get to know him better. I'm just saying all this," he swooshed his hand up and down his body, "can't be taught in between the previews and the closing credits."

"Lucien, I literally shudder to think what you might teach him. You treat women like they're disposable forks."

"Forks? Seriously?"

Definitely. "They're only meant to be used once, and you don't care if you break them because there's always another to be grabbed."

"Ouch."

"Do you deny it?"

He had the grace to stay quiet and think about it for a long moment. "I don't break women."

"You break their hearts. Because they fall for you hook, line, and sinker. Every woman is sure she'll be the one who can turn you from friend into fiancé."

The line of his jaw hardened into pure steel. "I don't make any promises. I certainly don't break any."

"I know. That's exactly the sort of thing I want Jesse to pick up from being around you. Your inner code." Lucien's loyalty was unshakeable. His work ethic remarkable, especially for a man being handed the keys to a very large kingdom. And although he didn't always draw the line *right* at black or white, when he did, he stuck to his guns. Mollie squinted at him. "Don't you dare actually try to teach him about women or dating or how to dress or how to mix a Manhattan."

"You've just wiped out every conversational gambit I had lined up." Lucien grinned, hip-checked her, and loped into the kitchen.

Jesse and Gran were side by side at the butcher-block island, with all the makings for cookies set out in front of them. When Jesse saw Lucien, excitement lifted his features and sparked in his eyes for a full five seconds before the pouty mask slid back on.

"Hey, Lucien."

"Hey, juvenile delinquent." He faked out a couple of punches. Probably just for the fun of irritating the boy.

Jesse shot an accusatory glare at Mollie. "You *told* him?"

"I tell Lucien everything. That's what best friends do." She picked up her ancient apron edged in pink ruffles and dropped it over her head. "It doesn't matter that he knows. Lucien will still like you no matter what, just like me and Gran. Right?"

"Absolutely. You're part of our weird little family. You can't shake me. However . . ." Lucien crooked an elbow around Jesse's neck and winked at Mollie, "if you stop acting like an idiot for a month, there will be rewards. Involving golf."

Another surge of actual happiness lit his face. "You'll teach me how to play?"

"It's a travesty you don't know already. Good thing you moved to the better coast. It'd be my honor to pass on my knowledge of how to spoil a good walk."

Mollie pulled down wine glasses from the glass-fronted cabinet. "Just like why you're getting a movie tonight. You pulled off a *B+* on your trig test, so you earned the reward of any two horrible movies you want to watch back-to-back. With popcorn. And the added bonus of getting to condescendingly explain things about these film epics to me."

"If you saw Transformers 1–6, I won't need to explain anything in 7 to you."

Amazing how he said that with utter sincerity. As though he firmly believed the entire world stopped to watch a movie franchise based on cartoons and toys. Jesse might think he was a grown-up, but his youth shone through in the funniest ways.

But it was his night. So instead of a lecture, Mollie took the blame on herself. "I've been a little busy watching myself transform into a doctor. Not a lot of movies under my belt since, oh, high school."

Jesse winced. Even patted her hand. "That's worse than me not knowing how to golf."

"Which is why I'm excited to let you school me tonight in all things cinematic. After we make cookies." Mollie handed him a measuring cup.

Which he gawked at as though it was a two-tailed turtle dropped in his palm. "Is this like the waffles all over again? You're teaching me instead of just making them?"

"I'm teaching you *and* making them. Because most of them will be a gift, so I need to add my own elbow grease."

Norah trailed her fingers along the line of ingredients. "Who earned peanut butter cookies? *And* chocolate chip oatmeal?"

"Rafe." Yes, it was opening a can of worms to admit it. But she couldn't ask them to help with the cookies under false pretenses.

"What'd he do to deserve all this?" Lucien's tone was loaded with skepticism.

Matter-of-factly, Mollie said, "We had a . . . date. It went very well."

Behind Jesse, Lucien made a circle with his thumb and index finger. Put his other index finger in and out of it a few times with a questioning grin.

Okay. She knew it was blazingly obvious that these were *thank you for all the awesome sex* cookies. Nobody baked as thanks for a normal date. But they wouldn't discuss that in front of Jesse, for goodness' sake. So Mollie gave an almost imperceptible nod of her head.

Which resulted in Lucien thrusting his hips violently, eyes screwed shut and teeth biting his lower lip. It lasted about three seconds before he convulsed in laughter.

Three seconds during which both Gran and Jesse noticed his gyrations.

"Ewwwwww." Jesse clapped his hands to his eyes and reeled backward.

Simultaneously, Gran clapped *her* hands together. "Oh, well done, Mollie. He's impressively large—I'm assuming that carries through in all the right places."

Mollie loved her family. She didn't at all mind living with them to help Gran out with Jesse—in theory. The reality, though, made her wish desperately for her own apartment. A place where she could talk to Elena and Karen and Lily without a peanut gallery. A place where she didn't have to watch her words around impressionable young ears.

A place she could bring Rafe.

A place where they could stay up, laughing and talking all night in more than a whisper.

A place where they could eat dinner naked.

A place where they could just *be* together.

"TMI," Jesse yelped. "That's my boss you're talking about."

Right. No mention of, you know, his flesh-and-blood cousin. Obviously he'd fallen head over heels into hero worship for Rafe, if *his* dignity ranked higher than Mollie's. She'd overlook it. This time. But she'd definitely file it away to tell Rafe later to make him crack up.

First, she'd take a tiny morsel of personal revenge. Mollie grabbed another apron from the hook on the back of the door. This one said *This recipe stumped me!* with a picture of a prosthesis. She'd custom ordered it for her gran, who'd laughed so hard opening it on Christmas morning that she'd snorted eggnog out her nose. Mollie dropped it over Jesse's head and tied it behind him.

"I'm not saying anything. Help me bake these cookies. You'll get exactly half of each batch. I'm giving the other halves to Rafe. Period. The why of it is unimportant." She thrust the recipes at him.

Jesse took them but didn't move. Norah swatted

him lightly on the butt to get him moving. He looked at Mollie. *Really* looked at her, not from the corner of his eye or with his head half ducked. And then even reached out to touch her upper arm.

"Is he nice to you?"

Omigosh. Mollie's heart melted into a puddle. These glimpses of the wonderful man Jesse *could* grow into were why she put up with his sulks. "He's very, very nice to me. Thank you for checking."

"'Cause if he doesn't treat you right, I'd send Lucien to go kick his ass."

"Nicely played, J." Lucien high-fived him. "But I'm sure that won't be necessary. Mollie can take care of herself—and any associated necessary ass-kicking."

Norah pointedly held out a wine glass until Lucien lurched to open the robin's egg blue drawer where the corkscrew lived. "I've sold Rafe and his brothers coffee. But I haven't gotten to know him yet. They aren't chatty. Where's he from?"

"Um. I don't know. I think he's moved around a bunch." They'd sort of skirted around that when they first met, and never got back to discussing it. He'd definitely lived in a big city. Funny, how it was such an obvious first-date question, but after two weeks and a ton of texting and conversation, she had no idea.

"That's odd." Using her pincer prosthesis, Norah pulled out cooling racks. "Mechanic doesn't seem like a job that would send you schlepping around the country."

"Hmmm. You're right." Mollie pushed the brown

sugar container at Jesse, keeping him rolling forward with the recipe.

His brothers had jobs that also gave zero reason for their move to Bandon, or anywhere else, for that matter. A mechanic, a bartender, and a glorified factory worker. None of whom, from what she'd gleaned from Rafe, seemed anything close to thrilled to be here. If Bandon wasn't their dream spot to settle down and raise their families . . . why *were* they here?

"Did he used to do something else? Is this a new career for him? A stress step-down? I hear lots of people are doing that. Heck, you could call my change in careers a stress-down. Making pot brownies is much more relaxing than getting shelled by enemy artillery."

Lucien chuckled. "Low bar, Norah."

"I'm not sure." Doubt . . . uncertainty . . . *unease* crawled over her like a bad rash. Mollie grabbed the wine Lucien had just poured and walked it to the French doors. She looked out at the tidy row of houses she knew like the back of her hand. Watched a big winged Caspian Tern swoop down from the top of the towering pine tree at the corner. And drank the entire glass of, yes, *ridiculously* fine Shiraz down in four big gulps.

"I don't know." She braced her forehead against the glass, needing its coolness as the enormity of what she did not know about Rafe barraged her mind. "I don't know where he went to college. Or if he did. I don't know why the Maguires decided to leave wherever they used to live. There's a lot—so much—I don't know about him."

Norah refilled her empty glass. "Sometimes actions speak louder than words, dear. If you're baking Rafe cookies, I'd say he's been a man of good action. You'll get around to swapping life stories instead of spit."

"Gran. That's horrible." Laughing, she spun around to scowl at her grandmother.

"I've been letting Jesse choose what we watch at night. I'm trying to pick up the current lingo."

"Don't. Just . . . don't." Mollie picked up the wooden spoon. To heck with the beaters. She'd mix this batch by hand, and hopefully stir out some of her sudden frustration. "The thing is, we have talked. Rafe's easy to talk to, and we never run out of things to say." Even though, as she ran it through in her mind, it was lots of him listening to her. Or talking about his brothers, her family. Favorite bands. Nothing, however, that showed up on a basic resume. "It hasn't been all kisses and cuddles." There. Acceptable teenager-proof euphemism for sex achieved.

Nevertheless, Jesse made gagging noises and clutched at his throat. Maybe she should suggest he go out for the summer school play, if he insisted on being this dramatic. Yet another way to keep him occupied and out of trouble. Dragging Rafe to watch high school theatre would be hysterical.

If they were still doing this whole friends-with-benefits thing by July.

It sure felt like they were waaaaay more than friends with substantial benefits. She cared for him. A lot. Which was not at all what she'd signed up for. Of course, given everything Mollie *didn't* know about Rafe, maybe her assumption as to the depth of their, um, infatuation, was incorrect.

She might have to make an extra batch just to sit on the couch and eat raw. No better way to combat a boy problem, in her highly specialized medical opinion.

Norah shook in the bag of chocolate chips while Mollie stirred through the growing burn in her forearm. "Well, what *do* you know?"

Okay. Good question. Focus on the positive. "I know that his first car was a *380Z*. That he's not a fan of cranberries. He loves Bond movies and therefore wants to go to Monaco someday. His dad taught him everything he knows about cars. That both his parents are dead."

Lucien leaned against the refrigerator, ankles crossed. "That sounds like the intro for a Jeopardy contestant. And . . . ? What else?"

Damn it. Now that Mollie actually thought about it . . . she didn't know that much more. Rafe had a habit of teasing information out of her. And then deflecting almost every question she lobbed back at him.

"Well?"

Mollie stabbed at the thick dough, leaving the spoon standing upright in the middle. Facts weren't the be-all and end-all of what made a person. She *did* know things about Rafe. "I know he's loyal. Responsible. That he'd do anything for his brothers. That he views his word as his bond. That he's a gentleman. That even though he's got a wild streak, he's got a good heart. I know I trust him."

"I thought this was movie night. How long are we going to spend talking about your boyfriend?" Jesse complained.

He had a point. Even though Rafe was *not* her boyfriend. Even though he wasn't *not* her boyfriend. Oh boy. "You're right." She handed him an ice cream scoop. "While you ball these up and put them on the cookie sheet, you can start explaining the wonders of the Transformers franchise to us."

Sipping his wine, Lucien leaned against the counter and crossed his ankles. "Some of us haven't been living under a rock and are already well versed."

"Good. Then you can make the pizza."

Lucien looked pained. "I would've brought pizza from the resort if you'd told me."

"I know. But then I wouldn't have the fun of watching you work so hard not to get a speck of food on your snazzy duds."

Norah stroked her hand down Mollie's back. "It sounds like you know everything that matters about Rafe."

Did she, though? Did she truly?

Chapter Seventeen

Wick's Garage, 3:30 p.m.
Mood in the bay—not half-bad

RAFE STOOD IN the open doorway to the garage, watching Jesse run a chamois over Mick's now shiny paint job. "Have you ever applied wax before?"

"Gross. No. What do you take me for? Girls do that to their legs. And eyebrows. And other parts, if we're lucky."

Rafe didn't bother to hide his laugh. Because while teenagers were a pain in the ass, they were also fun. "Got me there. But I hear surfers put it on their boards. And we put a thin layer of wax on a car after washing it to make the water bead off."

"Is this a real thing or just more of my punishment?"

"It's real. And this isn't punishment. You're learning how to take care of a car. You never know when that'll come in handy." Rafe, for example, had never expected to turn it into a career one day. Not that he hoped Jesse would fall into a life of semi-crime and join WITSEC. But if the kid stayed in school—without skipping—and made it to college, mechanic was a great part-time gig. Everybody needed beer money.

He pulled the tin of wax out of his back pocket and tossed it to Jesse. "You dab the chamois in it. Rub it in. Small circles. It'll take a while, but it also lasts a good long time. With how much it rains in this state, you'll get plenty of cars to practice on."

"Today?" The worry in Jesse's tone matched his wide eyes.

"Nah. Once you finish Mick's car, the rest of Saturday is all yours." And then Rafe pushed off the wall, dropping his arms and almost, *almost*, reaching for his nonexistent gun out of habit. Because both of his brothers were running full-out down the street toward him. Arms pumping, faces strained, like they were being chased by a guy in a mask wielding a chainsaw.

Shit.

He'd never seen them run like that before.

Especially not in sleepy, peaceful, middle-of-nowhere Bandon.

"What's wrong?" he shouted.

Flynn straightened one arm to point at the garage. "Inside. Now."

"Jesse, you keep going with the wax." The kid had the smarts to realize something bad was going down, because he nodded and didn't say a word. "Come and get me if there's a customer." Rafe pulled the chain to drop the wide corrugated door behind Flynn and Kellan. They both bent over, hands on their knees, panting. "What the hell's wrong with you two? We're supposed to be acting fucking normal. There's nothing normal about grown men *not* in running gear hightailing it through the middle of town at three o'clock on a Saturday."

Flynn swiped at the sweat on his forehead with his arm. "Emergency."

No panic. Nope. Every inch of Rafe turned ice-cold. Handling a crisis had been his specialty back in Chicago. Whatever it was, he'd get his brothers through this one. He grabbed two water bottles out of the mini fridge and handed them over. "So why didn't you call me?"

Kellan took two long swigs before answering. "After Delaney admitted the Marshals Service bugged your laptop, we were worried that they might have bugs in our cell phones, too."

Oh, shit. "Good thinking." Kellan really was the brains of the family. Rafe's mind shifted to the sexting he'd been doing with Mollie. Or, even more embarrassing, the tender things he'd sent her right before going to sleep last night. He didn't want anyone to know about that. Especially not the freaking U.S. government.

Flynn closed the door between the garage and the outer office. He even checked the bathroom and locked the back door. "Somebody knows we're here."

"Somebody who?"

"Somebody in McGinty's crew."

The sharp ends of the hook and pick set made him frown. Jesse was in for another lecture. Those were too dangerous to not put back in the tool box after every use. The kid was wicked book smart. But street smart? He'd pretty much lose a fight to a pigeon.

He tapped them against his shirt pocket, thinking. Who else did know? "Why don't they ask for more money?"

Flynn patted the pocket where his wallet sat. "We're not rocking high-powered careers here. That's a lot of money to scrape together in five days."

"Not to someone who knows how much we—" Rafe broke off with a grunt. The door from the office opened right onto his funny bone. It slammed the sharp end of the hook through his shirt, right into his muscle.

That didn't feel funny at all.

Blood poured over his hand, down his shirt to drip onto the ground. Jesse's head peeked through the half-open door. Then he turned white. "Oh crap. Did I . . . Rafe, I'm so sorry."

"Not your fault, kid." It was. Hundred fucking percent. They'd come back around to that when his chest wasn't pumping out blood. Having Jesse pass out would only make this already complicated moment a thousand times worse.

"I'll call an ambulance."

"No!" Flynn shouted.

Good thing Rafe agreed. An ambulance would get written into the day's official record, and it'd zip right

It was what he'd figured since he'd seen them sprinting down the street. But Rafe refused to accept it. He gave a slow shake of his head, left to right. "Bullshit."

"There's no other explanation," Kellan said earnestly. He'd stopped panting and paced in front of a jacked-up F150.

Kellan didn't pace. Not unless he was pee-your-pants nervous. He'd paced before getting his wisdom teeth pulled and before his interview to get into Northwestern. That was it.

Until today.

Seeing Kellan this shaken pierced Rafe's subzero calm. "For what?" he snapped. "What the fuck has you two literally running scared?"

"This." Flynn pulled a folded envelope out of his back pocket. "I went to check the mail. This was in it. Addressed to all three of us."

Problem solved. Everybody could simmer down. Rafe whapped the envelope with the back of his hand. "See, that proves it's nothing to do with McGinty. He'd never address something to Kellan. He was never a part of any of it."

"Just wait." Flynn unfolded the single sheet of plain white paper. "It says—"

If this was a real emergency? They'd be dead three times over at the rate Flynn was getting to the point. "Oh, for fuck's sake. Hand it over. I can read."

Rafe had to work not to crumple the flimsy thing in

his fist. Whatever it said, he knew he wanted to throw it out. To ignore it. To forget it. To just go back to their daily fight to scratch out a new life here.

To call Mollie. Hear her voice and let it soothe him better than a whiskey shot with a beer back.

He laid it out flat on the hood of the black truck.

I know who you really are. Give me $100,000 within 5 days. Or else I'll expose you to the world. Instructions tomorrow.

Rafe shoved it away. Didn't go far, but it felt good to do. "This is the worst blackmail attempt I've ever seen."

Kellan barked out a harsh laugh. "Not to insult you guys or anything, but who says professional mobsters are that well-schooled?"

"Really, counselor?" Flynn rounded on him with fire in his eyes and fists half-cocked. "You think now's a good time to poke at us for having fewer years of school under our belts than you?"

It was a sore subject. Flynn had wanted to go for his master's and McGinty paid for his bachelor's, but that was it. Declared it was time for Flynn to start earning back that tuition and put him to work full-time the day after graduation.

Rafe didn't . . . well, it wasn't that he didn't *care*. College would've been nice, sure. But he didn't *regret* the choice he'd made to join the organization instead of joining a frat. It'd provided for his brothers. Put a

roof over their heads and food on the table when bo[th] of their parents were gone. And Rafe was more proud [of] that than getting any degree in the world.

Kellan held up his hands. "I'm not starting anything. But calling it badly written doesn't automatically discount mob involvement."

Was he going to make them diagram it next? Rafe jabbed his index finger at the huge font filling the middle of the page. "I'm calling it *too* well-written. 'Expose you to the world' is a stupid thing to say. How about 'gimme the cash or I'll kill you.' That gets the point across."

Kellan took a step back. Eyes wide, he asked, "How many of these have you written?"

One of these days he'd have to sit down and actually explain what daily life was like working for McGinty. Or some of it. Enough so that his youngest brother's imagination didn't make him flinch away from Rafe at any and every mention of mob activity.

"None. Blackmail's not worth the time it takes to write the note. You don't know how other people prioritize things in their life. If they don't give a shit about whatever you threaten, you're left with no money and having to whack someone for no good reason."

"It could be a ploy. Just a way to disguise who sent it."

Flynn shook his head. "Nobody else knows that we're here living fake lives, under fake names. If not McGinty, then who?"

Just to have something to do with his hands, Rafe started picking up the tools strewn around the truck.

over to the marshal. Who'd undoubtedly take a couple of strips off of them for all the attention the siren and flashing lights would draw.

"Kellan will drive me to the hospital. Mollie's working. She'll fix me up. Flynn, you clean everything up here and wait for us at home. Don't do anything else."

Blackmail. Blood.

Another kickin' Saturday night in the making.

MOLLIE TIED THE last stitch off and finally exhaled. Not that Rafe had been in danger of bleeding out. But it had scared her to death when he stumbled in, his entire shirt covered in blood.

Luckily, the jagged tear down his pectoral muscle closed well. It was similar to injuries she dealt with from deep sea fishermen—or rather, the day-trippers who knew nothing and weren't careful when they went out to fish.

Even though he wouldn't feel it through the lidocaine, Mollie gently stroked a finger down his skin, reassuring herself that the rest of it was fine. "You're all set. A bandage and a tetanus shot and you'll be on your way."

Those bedroom eyes of his half lidded in invitation. Rafe curled a finger under her waistband to pull her closer. "No lollipop?"

Geez. Hospitals were like Viagra to this man. Not that she was complaining. At all. "Maybe I'll find you something better to suck on . . . if you're healing well when I check on it tomorrow."

"What the hell?" Rafe jerked up, indignation in his tone and pouty, aggrieved man painted all over his face. "You're taking sex off the table because of three lousy stitches?"

It was five. The fact he wouldn't let a trip to the ER take down his sex drive even a little . . . well, it was hot. Also, flattering.

But she knew what was best for him. Mollie taped a square of gauze over his wound. "You don't feel it now. But you'll feel it plenty when the numbing medicine wears off. That tool of yours went pretty deep into your pectoralis. You don't work tomorrow, right?"

"Nope." Rafe pulled free the dangling tatters where she'd cut his T-shirt away. "The only things I had lined up were baseball, beer, and hopefully a certain hot babe."

"You'll be fine to go back to the garage on Monday. Especially if I treat you to some TLC tonight." Taking pity on him—no, taking pity on her *own* now-stifled need, Mollie dropped featherlight kisses down his chiseled cheekbone to his lips.

To her surprise, he turned his head away. "I've got a thing tonight."

"A hot date?" she teased. Mollie wasn't worried one bit about his answer. Because even if it wasn't supposed to be a real relationship, they'd promised to not be with anyone else while this ran its course. The one thing

Mollie knew, down to her core, was that Rafe Maguire was a man who honored his promises.

"A . . . well . . . it's just a thing with my brothers. Not sure when we'll be done."

Mollie ran a hand through his hair, then slowly stroked it down the side of his face. Stubble scraped her palm. She couldn't wait for that same burn on other, more intimate patches of skin. "Be sure they take good care of you. I don't want you lifting anything heavier than a remote on that side of your body."

"How about a beer bottle?"

"Well, that's simply medicinal. I was going to insist on it." She grabbed the Tupperware container of cookies from the cabinet beneath the sink. Mollie had intended to drop them by the garage at the end of her shift. Handing them over now might chase away the shadows that flitted across Rafe's eyes when he'd mentioned his brothers. Which made her wonder what they were doing that he wouldn't tell her . . . "These were supposed to be a thank you for the other night. Now they can make you feel better, too."

Rafe peered through the clear plastic. Then his mouth dropped open. "You baked me sex cookies?"

"That sounds . . . disgusting when you put it like that." She set the container on her instrument tray and grabbed a wipe to remove the yellow Betadine stain from his skin. "We'll call them thank you cookies. End of discussion. Eat two whenever the pain bothers you."

Rafe grabbed her hand. Kissed the back of it. Kissed each individual knuckle with such tenderness that her heart practically burst. Then he flipped his hand, still in hers, to splay her fingers wide. He pressed the absolutely softest, velvetiest kiss right in the center of her palm. "Thanks for taking care of me, Doc."

Wow. *Wow*. Mollie tried desperately to play it cool. Even though that was a lie. She was anything but cool, anything but composed. She was falling to pieces. Or rather, the wall of resistance she'd put up to keep anyone from getting too close was currently crumbling to pieces.

"I have a vested interest in your muscles looking amazing."

Rafe shook his head. A thick, dark strand of hair fell adorably onto his forehead. It softened him. If anything could soften solid granite. "I mean it. I'm not used to anyone fussing over me. Or taking care of me."

"You've been hanging out with the wrong people," she said tartly. Mostly to hide the depth to which she was struck by how sad it was that Rafe didn't know the simple comfort of being coddled when sick, or blue or just *off*.

Laughter burst out of him. And not the way he'd laughed when she'd told him about the whole front line of the Chicago Bears coming in with food poisoning on her first shift in the Northwestern ER. No, this was something harsher. Like gravel scraping up and out of his lungs. Like what she'd said was actually the *least* funny thing in the world.

"You have no idea, Doc."

"Well, you have me now."

Uh-oh. That simple assertion had just slipped out. Slipped through the enormous cracks in the shattered wall that was supposed to protect her from hurt and inevitable abandonment. From someone deciding she wasn't enough, wasn't worth sticking around for.

Rafe's head cocked to the side. His expression blanked out, as though this were a test and he didn't want to give any hints away. "Do I?"

Mollie couldn't—*wouldn't*—lie. Not to herself. Not to Rafe. She'd mentally castigate herself later for the errant slip of the tongue that got them into this conversation. Especially since after the conversation with Norah and Lucien, she'd been ready to keep Rafe at arm's length until she finished interrogating him.

Then he'd shown up in her exam room covered in blood and quibbling about which life facts he had yet to share flew out of her mind. Relief that they'd have more time together filled her heart, without even a second thought about her paranoid phobia about being left. It made her realize just how important he'd become in an impossibly short amount of time.

Mollie stuffed her hands into the deep pockets of her lab coat. Took a deep breath of the overly sterile air. "I know it isn't what we agreed to, what you signed up for. There's no bait and switch going on here. I swear that I had no intention of this turning into a real relationship. But despite my best intentions, it appears that I'm falling for you."

"Is that so?" Still expressionless. Still not giving anything away. The man had one heck of a poker face. Was he mad? Ready to walk?

Mollie's defenses kicked in. The rest of it all came out in a rush. Because no way could he blame her for this. "After what I explained on the boardwalk the other day, you've got to believe that this isn't what I want. Being crazy about someone isn't in my plans at all."

"Mine, either."

"You can make all the plans in the world, but then life happens. *You* happened."

Rafe's chin dropped to his chest. "Shit."

Oh. Great. Not that she'd known what sort of reply to expect, but that one really didn't bode well. "Excuse me?"

His hands fisted on the exam table, making the paper crinkle. "You're smarter than me, Doc. By a whole hell of a lot. I hoped that you'd be the smart one in this. That you'd keep us from getting too involved. Because . . . I can't. I can't resist you."

"Did you try?" Mollie sure had. She'd tried over and over again to talk herself out of it since they first started texting. To remind herself that no good could come of getting in deep, not just with this man but with any man. Even the red flags that bloomed last night while baking the cookies didn't stop her heart from its unswerving tumble right into his hands.

"Hell, yes. As soon as you told me that you wouldn't have sex with me unless we could be friends, too. I saw it as a challenge. I don't back down from a challenge.

I'd make the friend thing *and* the sex happen. Then, despite my best intentions to protect you, things changed between us."

"Does that mean . . ."

"Yeah." His head came up. His eyes were practically black, they burned so deeply. "I'm fucking crazy about you."

It might be stupid, it might be reckless, it was definitely dangerous. That was the word. Falling for Rafe was dangerous in the extreme. But it was done. A *fait accompli*.

Bunching her scrub top in his hand, Rafe pulled her down to meet his mouth. This kiss was as tender as the one he'd placed in her palm. The soft exploration of her lips felt like a sharing of his heart. Like he was trying to kiss these new feelings into her, rather than stumbling through any more words.

Mollie didn't need the words. She'd heard enough. And right now, she was feeling *everything*. The uncertainty rolling off of them about how to handle this mixed with the utter certainty that this was oh-so-right. Behind it all, the heat that seared down to her core every time they touched.

She grabbed his biceps to steady herself . . . which was a smack to the medical part of her brain. Rafe was still her patient. Before things went any further, she needed to finish the procedure.

Mollie pulled back. "Let me do one more very necessary and doctorly thing. Then you go home and we'll pick this up tomorrow. Kellan stayed, right? He can take you?"

"He should be out in the waiting room. If he knows what's good for him."

"I'll send a nurse for him when we're done. He can walk you out, in case you get a little woozy when you stand up."

Rafe glowered at her. Dark and broody and dangerous. God, it was hot. "I don't get woozy, Doc. I can handle anything you throw at me."

"Yes, you're big and brave and strong. But you left a trail of blood two miles long between the garage and here. So humor me and let your *almost* as big and strong brother stick close to you." She shoved up his sleeve and prepped his arm for the tetanus shot with another antiseptic wipe. And then her hand stilled.

Rafe had a scar. A scar she hadn't noticed the other night. They'd turned off the lights after the first time, to cut down on the chance of detection.

This was a very big discovery. Because that scar was unmistakably from a gunshot wound.

"What's this?"

"Hmm?" Rafe cranked his neck around to look. "Just an old scar."

"I can see that. I don't need a specialty in plastic surgery to recognize a scar. What's it from?" Because she needed to know. She needed to hear the truth.

The truth about why and how her mechanic boyfriend whom she knew very little about got a GSW. Only four explanations came to mind. Three of which Mollie assumed he would've told her about right from the start. Either he'd been a police officer, a soldier, or a spy.

Or, option number four and the one that explained his secretiveness?

A criminal.

"I got it from a nail gun." Rafe reached over. Brushed his thumb back and forth as if to rub it away. "Flynn's great with his hands. He built an addition to our old house. I surprised him one day, and pop! Hole in the arm."

She re-swabbed the scar. The unmistakable scar. "That's not from a nail gun."

"Sure it is."

"That's from a gunshot." Mollie picked up the pre-loaded hypodermic from the tray. Despite her growing anger at his obfuscation, she still slid the needle into his skin as gently as possible. Pushing in the vaccine, she asked, "How'd you get shot?"

"Don't you think I'd know if I got shot?"

Smart-ass. That was pretty much her point. She let the syringe clatter back to the tray. "Yes. Yes, I do."

"It doesn't matter, Doc." Rafe spoke much more slowly than usual. As if trying to add extra weight to each word. "It's in the past."

"A past where people shot at you." She slapped on the bandage. Ripped off her gloves and tossed them into the biohazard can. Mollie wished she could rip an answer out of him just as easily.

"I don't want to talk about it."

"Tough." He didn't get a choice. Not anymore. Not after admitting that he cared. People who cared? Shared. Period. "I'm tired of you not telling me anything about yourself. I'm not asking for your computer password. Or your college transcripts. If you have any. Which I don't know because you don't talk about yourself." Mollie took a deep breath. "Where exactly did this happen?"

He pulled the denim shirt back onto his shoulder. Each motion was slow. Strained. Fighting for time, or fighting himself? Finally, he muttered, "Pittsburgh."

"Don't lie to me, Rafe. Don't disrespect all my years of medical training and think I don't know exactly what I'm looking at. This is a gunshot wound, isn't it?"

Eyes scrunched shut, he nodded. "Yes."

"Were you in jail?"

"No."

"Ever?" Because that brought up a whole host of medical complications, things that she deserved to know as his sexual partner.

His eyelids popped back open. "No. Never. I swear."

"Tell me what happened. Tell me how you got this," she demanded.

The expression on his face wasn't argumentative. No, the grooves around his eyes and mouth looked . . . sad? With a slow shake of his head, Rafe said, "I can't."

Well, if he couldn't, Mollie sure could. She could go digging. If she had to. But she'd far prefer the man who professed to care deeply about her to come clean on his own.

"Everything's electronic now. I can do a search of every hospital in Pittsburgh until I find your admittance record with a couple of clicks of the mouse. GSWs have their own protocol. Police have to be notified. Is that how low you want me to stoop to find out what the heck happened to you? Something that you should be willing to tell me of your own accord? Because you know I care and want to know all about you?"

Rafe pushed up to his feet. He fastened one button on his shirt, right in the middle. Then he stood in silence for a minute. Looking at her, no, staring at her with an intensity that was tangible.

Finally, he said, "Look all you want. You won't find anything about me."

He walked out of the exam room without another word. Let alone any hint of an explanation.

This was why Mollie had been worried about having a real relationship.

Had he really just walked out on her?

Chapter Eighteen

Maguire living room, 7:00 p.m.
Mood in the room—too fucking jittery. Everyone.

RAFE DID GO home and take a nap. He was stubborn, but not dumb. He'd seen how much blood he left on his shirt, three towels, and a ton of gauze. So he drank two bottles of water first, hit the sheets for an hour to let the pain meds do their thing, and figured that was enough treatment for his injury.

Except that the moment he came out of the bedroom, Flynn started taunting him. Bobbing and weaving around him like they were in the ring. Rafe had to employ some serious Matrix moves to avoid Flynn's air jabs.

"I can't believe you got stabbed by a kid."

"I didn't." Another fast lean to the left to avoid an uppercut that Flynn pulled at the last second. His brother had incredible control. That's what led him to win so many MMA fights. But being on the receiving end of a fist that looked like it was coming at him at Mach 4? Yeah, Rafe flinched. Every time. Because, again, not stupid.

"Oh, that's right." Fancy footwork had him circling Rafe, the scarred wooden coffee table, and side-stepping a pile of shoes and earbuds. "You stabbed yourself. Thanks to a kid. Not with a knife, not even on purpose. You've lost your edge, Rafe."

"Shut the fuck up with that."

After a feint to his face, Flynn did land a soft thump on Rafe's belly. "Remember that fight with Sean Sullivan's crew? When they tried to horn in on McGinty territory three years ago? Sean had two knives and brass knuckles, and you walked away without a scrape."

Not his proudest fighting moment, though. And about as difficult as a cooldown stretch after a run. "Sean Sullivan fights like a baby. He wouldn't know an offensive move if it came up and gave him a hand job."

From the kitchen, Kellan laughed. He was in there on attempt number *toodamnmanytocount* of making the food they missed most from Chicago. All these months, and his deep-dish pizza was still either a slime pit of grease or a concrete block. Maybe Rafe's injury was a good enough excuse to beg off eating whatever it turned out to be.

Flynn got his arm around Rafe's neck long enough to grind his knuckles into the top of his head. "Jesse got you to stab yourself with . . . what the hell was that thing?"

"You use a hook and pick to disconnect electrical connectors in cars." And you use your own center of gravity to bend at the waist, flip your idiot brother over your head, and slam him into the floor. Good thing his numbing medicine hadn't worn off yet. "Enough."

Flynn heaved for a minute. Rafe must've knocked the wind out of him but he felt zero guilt. It served him right. Finally, he said, "Hey, it's my job to make fun of you, bring you down a peg. Especially when you make it so easy."

"Fun's over." Yeah, it was nice to act like normal brothers again. But tonight was not the night to be normal. Was their good mood relief? Since the last time they saw Rafe he'd been spurting blood? "Christ, it's hotter in here than the salsa at Los Camales. Flynn, open all the windows."

"Sorry. That's my fault." Kellan opened the back door while Flynn popped the front one and all the windows in the living room. "I've got the oven on, and, well, the sun finally came out. Who knew this state even had a real summer?"

"Who knew this house wouldn't have an air conditioner?" Flynn grumbled.

"The house is free. No bitching. If you want some A/C, earn bigger tips and buy one." Then Rafe remembered it was still Saturday night. "Shouldn't you be at the Gorse?"

"I told them I had to take care of my dumb brother who got taken to the ER."

Rafe hunched over, clapping a hand to his thick padding of gauze. "This is how you take care of me?"

"You're fine." Flynn made a big show of ushering Rafe back to the plaid recliner. Then he took extra care to gently push it back so the footrest was up. "I really took the night off so we could have a war council."

"Don't call it that." The words snapped out of Rafe like a whip.

"Why not? We always used to."

Rafe—and the marshal, for that matter—must've gone over this problem dozens of times with Flynn and Kellan. Yet for some reason, it still wasn't sinking in with them. Not all the way, which was dangerous as hell.

But between stabbing himself and the fight with Mollie, Rafe knew he was on the edge. Ready to go ballistic over something as small as a half-twisted-around sock. So he made an effort not to yell. Or swear. Or at least not both at the same time.

"That's exactly why not. We always *used* to. That organization, that way of life? They're gone. Over. Nothing from our old lives can cross over and taint our new ones. Especially nothing to do with the mob."

Kellan banged a spoon against the counter. "Except for my perfect replication of the Lou Malnati's Chicago Classic pie with extra cheese."

If only. "News flash. You don't need mob ties to get good pizza. If you end up making a good one—someday—we'll call it the Maguire Classic."

"Sorry." Flynn brought over an uncapped bottle of beer that was guaranteed to be from an Oregon microbrewery. He'd taken Rafe's order to heart to keep drinking their way through local brews until they found something they liked. And if he treasured his life, it'd be an IPA and not any of that fruit-flavored crap. "That was a slipup. Habit. Not on purpose. I stayed home so we could talk about the blackmail letter that came in the mail today."

"Oh, that's much better. Blackmail doesn't make me immediately think of the mob *at all.*" Kellan's sarcasm was thicker than the neck of a Bears linebacker.

"Ordinary people do it every day." Rafe waved his beer toward the big-ass plasma screen TV in the corner. They may be on the run, but they were still men and they had standards. Needs. "David Letterman was blackmailed. By a guy who was sleeping with one of his mistresses. No mob ties at all."

"How do you know that?"

"He admitted it on his show. A long time ago. When you weren't allowed to stay up late enough to watch it." Rafe loved rubbing it in that Kellan was the youngest. For some reason, it set him off like nothing else. Even though there was jack shit he could do about it.

"Hard to have a conversation about the mob threatening us without mentioning, you know, '*the mob.*'" Kellan made air quotes with his fingers.

Damn it. He had a point. "Fine. For tonight, and

only tonight, we'll ignore the rule. We'll name names, come up with theories, and make an action plan." Rafe pointed at Flynn. "Start your damned war council."

Flynn jabbed his fingers through hair that looked like he'd been doing that all night. He paced along the braided rag rug behind the sofa. "Theory number one. McGinty wants us dead. This is a way to draw us out. Make us go someplace private to drop off the blackmail money. Next thing you know, we're six feet under or in the trunk of a car on our way to being six feet under."

Yeah. That'd been Rafe's first theory, too. "They know we'd put up a hell of a fight. But with a silencer, and more than one person, they could do us right here in the house. Or get us out of the house at gunpoint and into a trunk. No need for a blackmail scheme."

"I'm going to remind you again that we're not necessarily talking about the sharpest tools in the shed," Kellan said.

"Is that a dig at Rafe impaling himself on a sharp tool? Nice." Flynn expanded his pacing to high-five his little brother across the counter.

"It wasn't intended to be. But it can pull double duty."

His brothers were a laugh riot. Rafe was so glad he'd turned his life inside out to keep them safe. "I don't think this theory works. It's more complicated than it needs to be."

The pause followed by a sharp nod showed that Flynn agreed. "Okay—on to theory number two. Someone on

McGinty's crew knows we stole the money. Correction. *All* of McGinty's crew knows we stole the money."

Kellan dropped something into the sink with a clatter. He was in the living room in a handful of long strides. "Stole what money?"

Oh, for fuck's sake. Rafe leaned forward, resting his elbows on his knees and letting his head fall into his hands. The leg rest snapped back under with a bang. "That was a secret," he ground out between gritted teeth.

Or it was supposed to be, anyway. That was something he and Flynn had agreed on before they let the marshals pick up Kellan.

Here he'd thought his fight with Mollie would be the worst part of the day. And it still was—by a slim margin. Because there was no way his nine-tenths-of-the-way-to-a-lawyer brother would let that sentence slide by without one hell of a fight.

A hot flush spread up Flynn's neck. The kind he got when he was good and mad. Instead of apologizing, he crossed his arms. "It *was* a secret. Doesn't mean it still should be."

Rafe shoved up to his feet. And was rewarded with the zing of pain that Mollie had promised would kick in by now. Everything about this night was in the shitter. "You swore to me, on Mom's grave, that it'd stay between just the two of us."

"Yeah, well, we're all in this together, aren't we? The three of us against the world? Kellan deserves to know.

What if something happens to you and me? He needs to know he's got a backup plan."

"What. Did. You. Steal?"

Shit. The cat was definitely out of the bag. Kellan would keep pestering them for details until his dying day. He had a way of picking and arguing a thing to death. It would've made him a magnificent lawyer. It sure made him a royal pain in the ass of a brother, though.

Rafe met that glacial blue stare head-on. "We—me and Flynn—took some of McGinty's money. Right before we all went into protective custody."

"How much?"

A lot. "Enough. Enough to make that lying cocksucker who planned to throw Flynn in a cell to cover up his own fuck-ups squirm and hurt."

Strangely, Kellan looked pleased. "Doesn't that mean we could pay off the blackmailer? You have the hundred grand he's asking for?"

Rafe almost laughed. A hundred grand was nothing. They'd grabbed close to two million, but that was a conversation for another day. Since the amount was sure to send Kellan into a raging fit about right and wrong and ethics and a hundred things that just didn't fucking apply to the hand they'd been dealt.

Flynn finally found the balls to put in his two cents. "We don't have any of it, K. It's hidden. Back in Chicago."

"Don't you think that explains why we're being blackmailed? And by whom?"

"No." When Rafe walked out of the hospital, he

couldn't suck in a full breath. It hurt too much to think about what had gone down with Mollie to even breathe. To think about the disappointment on her face, the shock. The pain he'd put there. So Rafe had shoved thoughts of her down and basically spent his whole time in bed going over the possibilities. And he'd come up with the answer. "I don't think this was sent by anyone to do with McGinty."

"Why not?"

He flopped back into the chair. Braced his hands on the armrests—and then realized it was the same position he always used to command the table at war councils in Chicago. Shit. Old habits. When would he be able to shake a lifetime of them?

"Number one, like I said before, they could just kill us."

Flynn's eyebrow shot to the ceiling. "That's it?"

"If they figured out we took the money—and that's a big if—they would've asked for all of it. But the biggest red flag is that they didn't use our real names." As he dropped that logic bomb, Flynn and Kellan both sucked in short, identical gasps. "There'd be no reason for anyone to do with McGinty *not* to use our real names. In fact, they'd be sure to do it, to scare us more."

Kellan sat on the edge of the coffee table, knees spread and wrists dangling over them. "You think it's an inside job. A local one, since our last move. The Marshals Service?"

"Maybe. Or the FBI. That explains the low—for blackmail—cash amount requested. It explains how they found us after all our hopping around the country, with a different name in each place. Whoever this is? They don't know who we used to be. Where we're from. They only know our current case file. Who we are now, and that we're bad guys on the run."

Quiet fell over the room as his brothers let it sink in. Rafe heard the brush of pine leaves against the side of the house. Kind of an eerie sound to someone who'd lived with sirens and horns as the only background noise for most of his life. But he was getting used to it.

He was getting used to a lot of things here in Bandon.

A job he liked. One that rewarded a lifelong hobby with a paycheck.

The kid he could actually make a difference mentoring.

People he surprisingly liked. This town was full of people with not quite straight edges. Just like him. He'd spent most of his life outside the boundaries of normal society.

Scenery that made him look up and take it all in every time he walked down the street.

Mollie.

So much about Mollie that he liked. That he'd gotten used to so quickly.

That he didn't want to leave.

Rafe hadn't felt this way about any of their other WITSEC pit stops. Not even the ones where they'd stuck it out longer. And it wasn't just because this was their last chance. Sure, the cranberry festival was way too much hoopla over a freaking piece of fruit. But it made him laugh. He liked how excited it made Mollie. If it made her happy, it made him happy.

Oh, shit.

Rafe was even farther gone over her than he'd realized.

More than he'd told her. More than he'd risk admitting to his brothers in the middle of this blackmail crisis, for sure.

"Okay." Flynn nodded. He sat down on the couch so they were a tight unit. "Say that's true. That it came from a rogue law enforcement asswipe."

Kellan butted in with a lopsided grin. "Which means no death threat's attached to the letter, so we're already in better shape than we were ten minutes ago."

Flynn looked to Rafe. "Do we cut and run?"

"Hell, no."

If they were going to run, they would've done it day one instead of joining WITSEC. The marshals were supposed to protect them. Not to mention that the Maguire brothers could do a damn fine job of protecting themselves.

"Do we pay?" Kellan still seemed stuck on the money. They obviously wouldn't be able to stay away from finishing that conversation anytime soon.

"No," Flynn said. He thwacked his palm onto the coffee table. "You don't pay blackmailers. Because they never stop. Also, they're fucking cowards who don't deserve it. Thirdly, because *we don't have the money.*"

"Okay, okay. Geez, give me a minute to catch up. I've

used the word *blackmail* more times in the last five minutes than I have my whole life. It's like I've stepped into an alternate universe."

Rafe reached over to drop a heavy hand onto his shoulder. He hated that he'd opened a door to that alternate universe for his little brother. It was everything he'd devoted his entire life to preventing. "I'm sorry, Kellan. We tried our hardest to shield you from all of this."

"I know. I've been too pissed off to show my appreciation. But I know that both of you gave up a lot so that I could live my dreams. It means everything that you tried."

Another weighty silence. Then Flynn asked, "How do we trap this pansy-ass douchebag?"

There was only one answer. One that Rafe knew wouldn't go over without a fight. "We have to call Delaney."

Kellan sprang to his feet. He sort of jittered over to the potbellied stove in the corner that none of them had any idea how to use. "Hang on. You know I enjoy any excuse for a visit from the delectable Delaney. But this is a bad idea. She said that if we get in even a little bit of trouble, we're out of Bandon and out of the program. No more subsidized rent. No more perfect fake IDs and transcripts and job references. No more future."

With a sigh, Flynn stretched his arms out along the back of the sofa. "Dial back the dramatic speech. You're not in front of a jury."

"But our lives *do* hang in the balance."

Right. 'Cause that was dialing down the drama. But Rafe did have to give Kellan credit for not panicking. For everything that had been thrown at him tonight, a little overreacting wasn't so bad. Knowing they'd distracted the shit out of him, however, Rafe did get up and make a quick check to be sure he hadn't left the oven or stove on.

He went to the side window. Suddenly, the soothing, cool rustle of wind through the pine trees sounded like just what Rafe needed to keep his temper under control. Because it was right there, under the surface, like a million fire ants trying to tunnel their way out of his skin.

Someone, some dickwad, had scared Kellan. Was making them wonder if they'd have to leave their home. So what if it had only been their home for thirteen days? Sometimes you just *knew*. About Bandon. About Mollie. Getting this letter? It had flipped the switch on his knowing. On his accepting this as their home, for good. And now someone was threatening his whatever-thefuck it was with Mollie.

And for all of that, Rafe wanted to pound some faces.

Break some bones.

Use every low-down, dirty fighting trick he'd picked up working his way up through the biggest mob organization in the Midwest and fucking *whale* on whoever was responsible.

But that wasn't how the Maguire brothers rolled anymore. Now they played it by the book. Which would hopefully keep them alive. But it'd also be as unsatisfying as jerking one off in a bathroom.

Rafe braced a hand against the window frame. He was in charge of this family. Of keeping them all safe, despite his brothers' annoying and identical stubbornness. "Turning everything over for the Marshals Service to handle is the best solution. Better yet, it's the only one that keeps us under their protection. We all agree Delaney's clean, right?"

"Absolutely." Of *course* Kellan answered first. He was so into their official protection officer he'd probably turn over the two million just to get a smile from her. Yet another reason to hold off telling him all about the hidden money.

Flynn gave a slower, more measured nod. Like he'd actually put thought into it, instead of thinking with his dick like Kellan. "She's kept us alive this long."

Good. They were on the same page. Rafe pushed through the rest of his points. "She's smart. And as ferocious as a pit bull. If we tell her this, we'll get a gold star for honesty. It'll prove to her that we really are the good guys. She'll frisk every agent within a hundred miles, search their desks and computers until she finds who did this."

"Agreed. Except . . ." Flynn trailed off.

"What?"

He scrubbed a hand over his mouth. Looked to Rafe, then Kellan, then back again. "Except what if you're wrong? What if we're overthinking this and McGinty *is* the one behind it?"

No chance. It was good for Flynn to work through all

the possibilities, but not to fixate on the worst one out of fear. "I'm not wrong. I know Danny. I know how he thinks. How he plans a takedown. I'd put my life on it not being him." Actually, he was putting all their lives on the line. But Rafe knew this was truly the best solution.

Following his gut had gotten Rafe out of much more dangerous situations. No way would it let him down now. This might not be the most dangerous spot he'd ever been in—but it was the most important.

"Okay." Flynn stood. Held his hand out. "We stay hands-off. We put it on the Marshals Service. Or at least, on the one marshal we trust with our lives."

Kellan put his hand on top of Flynn's. "Agreed."

Putting his arm in as the third spoke, Rafe said, "Done. I'll make the call."

"Hang on." Flynn put another hand on top of the pile to keep them in place. "There's something else to discuss. While everything's still on the table and we don't have to watch what we say. This decision leads to another one, that you and I never settled. Now it's crystal clear. We can't leave the two million dollars we stole from McGinty hidden in Chicago. We have to get it when we go back to testify."

A noise, like a sharp thud on the porch, made all three of them tense. Their eyes met, and locked in place. Rafe's mind raced. Was it a coincidence? Or was it the only warning they'd get before bullets shattered the door and their bodies?

Nah. That was Kellan infecting him with his own

fear, so easy to read in his stark white face. But he didn't run. Didn't make a sound. No, he kept his head, and Rafe had never been prouder.

Still, whoever—or whatever, because there were a whole bunch of animals that ran free through this town like it was a zoo with no fences—was on the porch probably heard what Flynn said. About stolen money.

Or maybe they'd heard more. Who knew how long they'd been out there? And if their cover was now compromised, well, a blackmailer would be the least of their problems.

Rafe ran to the door. On the opposite side of the screen he saw Mollie. Face even paler than Kellan's, eyes even wider.

Just as scared looking, too.

Chapter Nineteen

OMIGOD. OMIGOD. OMIGOD. Mollie wasn't sure if she said the words out loud or just thought them. It felt, in her brain, like they were ten feet tall, bathed in scarlet floodlights and cranked loud enough for people up in Coos Bay to hear.

And what she'd just overheard the Maguire brothers say? *A hundred times bigger and louder.* Which was why she'd dropped the stupid cookies. Mollie looked down at the container, and then her head snapped back up at the heavy footfalls.

There was Rafe.

Rafe, the man who made her heart flip-flop. The tender, loyal, generous, sexy, caring man she'd been ready to break all her rules for and take a chance on. The man who made Mollie believe that she was actually *enough* to give him reason to stay with her.

The man who she didn't really know at all.

The criminal who apparently stole a lot of money and had to testify about . . . *something.*

The man who'd made a fool out of her.

"Mollie. What are you doing here?" Rafe sounded normal. He sounded exactly how she imagined he would when she appeared with his cookies. A little surprised, but not offended by the unscheduled drop by. Just mildly curious.

Was he playing it cool? Or did he not realize that she'd overheard the obviously-meant-to-be-secret conversation with his brothers?

While she figured out what to do about that, Mollie answered normally, as well. The way she'd planned on the way over, churning with frustration and more than a little bit mad. "I came to check on you because I care about you. I came by because you left without your cookies, which Jesse and I worked very hard to bake. But mostly I came by because I hated the way we left things at the hospital. Unfinished. Unanswered. Confused."

"How long have you been here?"

Aha. Rafe was worried that she'd overheard. Mollie had zero intention of allaying those fears right away. Her heart was racing as if she'd just gotten eighty cc of adrenaline in a needle straight to the left ventricle. He deserved to feel just as breathless and anxious and, well, *bad.*

"Odd question. Is that how you usually greet visitors?"

"Why won't you answer it?"

Aha again. His usual suave smoothness was gone. Rafe wasn't bothering to go through the back and forth of eluding her question. Or sidestepping the list of reasons that she'd stopped by. He'd done the mental math on the number of open windows and doors. Added in her presence as a variable. Then made a subset out of the knowledge of just how steady her hands were, since she'd literally sewn his skin together, and that she hadn't dropped anything at all in the times they'd been together. Divided it by the fact that she hadn't knocked or made her presence known.

That equation added up to 1) overhearing way too much, and 2) being so shocked by what she heard that the cookies had fallen from her numb fingers.

A little stubbornness and a lot of sheer bravado had her jutting out her chin. "I'll answer it after you answer my question from before. After you tell me how you got that bullet wound."

"Mollie—"

The fact that he didn't so much as blink at her demand drop-kicked the shock from her system and catapulted her right back into righteous anger. "No, I've reconsidered. I'll answer your question after you also tell me why you don't trust me enough to tell me the truth. Why you don't respect me enough to be honest with me. How you can claim to be so fond of me and yet hide from me who or what you really are."

It was like talking to a statue. On the other side of the screen, he didn't move. She didn't even see his chest rise and fall beneath a dark green pajama top. "You heard us talking. How much did you hear?"

Okay. Now they were at least confronting the elephant on the porch. "Enough."

"Enough . . . to what?"

"Enough to scare me. To put me off. Enough to know that I've got the moral high ground. Enough to know that I get to stand here and demand that you explain exactly what the hell is going on with you and Flynn and Kellan."

That made him move. He looked over his shoulder. Was he checking to see if they gave him the go-ahead to spill . . . whatever? Getting them to weigh in on a conversation that Mollie very much intended to be only between the two of them?

Not. Okay.

If Rafe had to wait to get buy-in to talk to her? Well . . . Mollie wasn't going to wait around for that to happen. She stomped down the steps. It was loud, but it wasn't loud and forceful enough. This weird, partial bombshell and non-conversation deserved one heck of a dramatic exit. So she ran.

When she heard the metal clap of the screen door, Mollie changed course. Rafe would catch her before she got into her car, so she veered back behind his house, into the forest.

A real forest. An untended forest. No neatly trimmed and flattened trail. Just bushes with luckily soft leaves that she used to be able to name. Along with the odd giant fern in the more heavily shadowed sections. The mat of pine needles on the ground made running soft, but there were still pinecones, chunks of rock to dodge, or else she'd have a turned ankle. Birds squawked and evacuated the treetops above her with a fluttery whoosh.

Mollie had spent her whole life fearing that people would get tired of her and run away. Just like her mom did.

And damn it, she wasn't waiting for Rafe to pull that shit on her. *She* was the one running away from him. Running away from the hurt and the distrust and God knew how many lies.

"Mollie, stop!" Rafe's voice bounced off all the tree trunks like thunder. More birds raced through the sky away from all the noise they were making.

"No!" It felt good. It felt good to be the one making the choice. Aside from the panting and the stitch in her side that reminded her walking to work didn't come anywhere close to qualifying as aerobic exercise.

His fingertips grazed the back of her arm. Mollie tried to go faster, but her rubbery legs just wouldn't obey. This time, when he reached for her, he got a firm grip that bounced her back a step and off-balance. Only his quick grab of her other arm kept her upright.

"Why did you run from me?" It was shadowy and gray amidst the tight network of towering pine trees. Still, Rafe's eyes blazed at her brighter than the blue flame of a Bunsen burner.

Fine. If he'd bothered to follow her, maybe, *maybe* he

was ready to talk. So Mollie hurled her answer at him. "Because you won't tell me the truth."

"Are you scared of me?"

Interesting. A different spin on the same old "what exactly did you overhear" interrogation. Still out of breath, she just shook her head and gave a simple, "No."

"Are you sure?" His fingers tightened, digging in to the soft flesh right below the short sleeve of her scrub top.

"What the hell, Rafe? Do you want me to be?"

His face twisted into disbelief and shock. Probably a mirror of what she'd looked like standing on his porch. "Of course not," he shouted. Squeezing his eyes shut, Rafe continued in a quieter tone. "That's why I chased after you. Because I want to be sure that you aren't scared of me."

"Well, I'm not." Even with the new and disturbing puzzle pieces she'd learned about him in the last five hours, it didn't matter. Okay, it did *matter.* That was why they were having this confrontation. A few bad puzzle pieces, though, didn't change the whole picture. They didn't negate all the good qualities she'd witnessed in him.

Mollie waited for his eyes to reopen. Then she laid the rest of the truth out for him. "Actually I am scared. I'm scared of what I feel, how much I feel, for a man who I apparently barely know."

"Does it matter?" God, the intensity of his eyes seared her. The harsh gravel of his voice scraped against her heart. This man clearly still wanted her to care.

How much she cared for Rafe was exactly the problem. Exactly the reason why she needed the truth. Not to decide whether or not to run from him or leap into his arms. Just to know.

"Yes. Yes, I need to know who I think I'm falling in love with."

His whole body stiffened. "Is that what you're feeling?"

"Yes." Mollie didn't want it to be that way, but apparently her brain didn't get a vote. Her heart had already cast the die. She'd known that without any hesitation the moment he walked into her emergency department covered in blood and pale as a ghost.

Rafe pulled her roughly to him, moving his hands so that one was in the small of her back, grinding her against his erection. The other fisted in her low ponytail, jerking her head into position for his kiss. "Then feel more." A hip thrust pushed him against her belly as his legs moved to the outside of hers, caging her in. "Feel more of that. Let yourself only feel me."

His mouth ravaged hers. Owned hers. Forced her to instantly give in to his demand, because there was no ignoring the passion he ignited with every swipe of his tongue. With the way his teeth nipped and pulled at her lower lip, sending little shocks of needle-sharp pain that somehow morphed into needle-sharp flares of arousal by the time the sensation traveled down through the network of nerves to settle in between her legs. His tongue surged in and out, tangling with hers in an interplay that was a promise of what was to come.

Mollie had never been so aroused, so fast. Especially never when she was this mad. This confused. But the heat of their argument, the uncertainty she felt, ratcheted up every sensation. He wanted her to feel more? Well, it was impossible not to. But he'd damn well better feel the same thing.

So she didn't hold back. There was no need to be quiet like in the hospital and Mollie moaned her arousal. She met every twisting taste of his tongue with her own. Used her teeth on his lip which immediately caused another circling grind of his hips into her. If this was a competition? They'd both win. Period.

Rafe whipped her top over her head. Didn't bother to undo the clasp of her bra. No, he just ripped it apart with a swift downward slice of his hand. The lace hadn't even fluttered to the ground before his mouth was on her breast. It was a direct hit, too. Right to the nipple. Right to sucking it so hard Mollie felt her eyes roll back in her head. She'd never believed that anyone could actually orgasm just from having their breasts fondled. In three seconds, though, Rafe had almost changed her mind.

The callouses on his big hand scraped against her other nipple as he palmed it in a fast circle. The combination of the sucking and the circling on both sides at the same time was . . . holy crap, but it was good. It was rough and wet and there was every possibility she could feel every single tiny bump of his taste buds as they laved her ultra-sensitive nipple.

Mollie leapt up, wrapping her legs around his waist.

Why wait for him? She rocked back and forth against the waistband of his pajama pants. With how hot he'd already made her, it wouldn't take much to push her over the edge. Rafe didn't get to say. He didn't get to be in control.

As though he'd read her mind, his head shot up and he murmured, "No."

"No, what?"

"No, you don't get to come yet. Not without me." And right when she was about to tell Rafe exactly where he could stuff his controlling tendencies, he continued. "Please, Mollie. I want us to be together. I want us to do this together. To share it."

Okay. That was tender and romantic and utterly at odds with their almost angry fight-sex vibe. She dropped her feet back to the ground and unwound the arms she'd tightened around his neck.

"Why? What is it that you feel, Rafe? If you can't tell me anything else, at least be honest with me about that. We dipped our toes into it at the hospital. This—" Mollie waved a hand to indicate the pajamas he'd run out of the house in "—this whole thing going down right now . . . you wouldn't do this if we were as casual as we initially said we would be. You wouldn't have chased after me. Forget saving your pride and being cautious and just tell me, no-holds-barred, what you feel."

Rafe paced away from her a few steps. More than a few, actually. Enough that Mollie started to wonder if she'd been wrong, and if he was just washing his hands of the whole conversation.

He braced his right hand high up against the thick bark of a pine tree. “I feel like I’m in a new country. One where I don’t speak the language or know the roads. And then you appeared and you’re my map. My translator.”

So much for romance. “You can hire someone to do all that.”

“No. Listen. I don’t tell people what I feel. Ever. I’m going to suck at this, so if that’s what you want? You have to wait and be patient as I try to get it out.”

Fair enough. “Go on.”

“That’s how it started. I mean, you’re hot as hell, so I noticed the total package. But you made me feel less alone. You made me feel like I belonged, when I thought I’d never feel that way again. You made me feel happy. Feel important. Two other things that I thought I’d never feel again. Most of all? You made me feel like myself. That’s huge. You don’t know how huge.”

Mollie hadn’t expected that much from him. Each word had been slow and halting, as if Rafe truly was digging up secret emotions never intended to see the light of day. It wasn’t poetry and flowers and compliments.

It was better.

It was *real*. Raw. Exactly what she’d asked of him. Exactly what she needed to push away the anger and remind her of the remarkable strong, vivid, caring heart at the center of this multilayered man.

Her sneakers crunched over the mat of pine needles as she crossed to him. Mollie put a hand on his shoulder. “Rafe—”

Dropping his arm, he turned around, hands hanging at his sides. "I feel a hell of a lot. I feel things I've never felt before and don't know what to do about it. Don't know how to integrate the sunshine you pour into my life with the other shit that's piled up in it. Selfishly, though, I want to. I want you in it. I want you with me. I want to show you all of me. Even the ugly parts."

"I want that, too."

"Trust me, you don't. You really don't. I'm asking you to feel more because I already do. Because I want you to feel as much as I do. Which, yeah, is probably love. How the hell would I know? I just know that it's new and more and different and irresistible." Rafe laced his fingers with hers. "So I want you to feel exactly what I do. That's why I want you to come with me. I want to feel you ripple around me as my dick pulses into you."

It was perfect. Rafe was perfect. That unpolished honesty pretty much sent her heart into an emotional orgasm. Which did put her one ahead of him, but that'd be Mollie's secret. "Together," she breathed, squeezing his hands.

His head whipped back and forth, scanning the gathering darkness for she didn't know what. "Come over here." Rafe led her past a vibrantly yellow gorse bush, past a cluster of enormous tree ferns, to a tree lying on its side. From the padding of deep green moss all along the top of it, it must've fallen in a storm years before. He sat, but put his hands on her hips to keep her in place.

Rafe hooked his thumbs into her scrub pants, but didn't pull them down. First, he licked along their edge, drawing a straight line of wet heat across her belly. That wetness caught the hint of breeze swirling through the forest and magnified its chill.

Goose bumps erupted from shoulder to wrist, neck to hip, but not in a bad way. It was just more sensation, more overload of awareness of every inch of skin on her body. Awareness of the rough stubble of his cheek right next to the softness of his firm lips. The tease of a few strands of Rafe's hair brushing against her hip. Her nipples tightened into aching, hard points that almost screamed with need for him.

Slowly, *torturously* slowly, he dragged down her pants. As every inch that was exposed, Rafe nibbled his way down each thigh. Each time he switched legs, he brushed against the lace of her panties. Thin lace that in no way prevented her from feeling the shock of his touch against her most sensitive flesh.

Mollie grabbed for the string tie at his waist. "Let's do this."

Rafe batted her away, but then took her hands. Pressed the backs of them, one by one, to his lips. "You don't understand. I'm ready to go off here like a teenager just from touching you. From being with you. Just you, Mollie. From the fucking awe that you want to be with me. Until you're screaming with need for me, until you catch up to how I'm drowning in the need to be in you, my clothes have to stay on."

It was the most romantic come-on she'd ever heard. But she didn't think it was just a line. Mollie truly believed that he was at his limit and she reveled in being the one who'd pushed him there. They were far closer to being on the same page than he knew. "I'm barely treading water here, Rafe."

"Not good enough." He locked his teeth in her panties, cranked his head away from his hand fisted on their seam, and ripped them right off. The sound seemed overly loud in the clearing, filled with only the faint rustle of leaves and an occasional chirp of a sparrow. That sound, that tiny, fabric-rending sound brought home to her that they were not in a bedroom, not anywhere with doors. That they were the interlopers in this lush overgrowth.

Rafe pushed her pants to her ankles at the same time that he raked his teeth down her slit. Mollie threw back her head and screamed as pleasure jolted through her. Pleasure. Need. Lust. Want.

Rafe.

All of it came down to him.

Her whole world centered on him. On his tongue licking her open. At his two fingers crooked inside her slightly against her G-spot. At the strength of his shoulders braced between her quivering thighs. At the sensual sight of his dark hair against her pale skin. At the bruising grip of his hands on her butt.

Mollie raked her nails across the thick ridge of steely muscles along his shoulders. And then jerked back from him two steps as she remembered his injury. "Rafe, are you in pain? Are you sure I should be touching you?"

"I'll be in more pain if you don't touch me."

A quick push of her heels against each other had her sneakers off. Mollie stepped out of her pants and sat on Rafe. She locked her ankles behind him. "I don't have a condom. Do you have a plan?"

"I don't have one, either. But I'm clean. I know you may not feel like you have any reason to trust me right now, but I wouldn't lie to you about that. You're the only person I've had sex with in six months."

"I'm on the pill. And I do trust you. And when we're done, you're going to explain to me why you think I shouldn't. Okay?"

"Yeah."

With that, Mollie lifted his penis out of his pajama pants, tucking their edge under his tautly plumped balls. Then she sank onto his length. Naked, inside and out. Which was yes, a little weird with Rafe still essentially dressed.

A little weird, but a lot amazing. Fantastic. Mind-blowing. The feeling was similar to the first time she'd gone skinny-dipping in the ocean. It was so freeing. Nothing held back. Nothing covered up. Except for where Rafe touched her. And those patches of skin vibrated beneath his hands.

"Mollie. Mollie, I . . . I can't wait."

She pressed her heels more tightly into his back. Kept her chest arched away from his injury, but worked her hips faster and scrunched even closer as she rubbed and lifted and worked him in and against her. "Don't wait. You told me, Rafe. Just feel."

A groan ripped out of his throat, long and low. His fingertips drilled into her butt and his head tipped back, mouth open. Mollie had the glorious and entirely new sensation of each pulse of wetness as he spent inside her, which kicked her orgasm over the edge into an explosion of light and heat and tingly pure joy shooting through her body.

She slid between his thighs to sit on the edge of the soft moss-covered trunk, still keeping him inside her as aftershocks made both of them quiver. There was only the sound of their panting. Rafe tipped his forehead to touch hers.

"Thank you."

"For what?"

"For trusting me." He wedged his hand between them to rest on her heart. "I have to say that now, before you change your mind. So thank you."

"You're welcome." It seemed an oddly formal response, but Mollie didn't know what else to say.

"We need to talk."

The four words most hated in the entire history of relationships. Not what anyone wanted to hear with their lover's penis still hot and thick inside them. But if he was finally willing to come clean and fill in the innumerable blanks of his life?

Well, that was just what Mollie had requested.

She really ought to be more careful what she wished for.

Chapter Twenty

Somewhere in the forest at dusk
Mood on the tree trunk—scared to death

RAFE HAD SPENT his whole adult life technically operating outside the law. Breaking one more legality shouldn't be a big deal, right?

Business as usual.

Situation normal . . . all fucked up.

He'd tried to be good. He'd followed each and every one of Delaney's rules about how to live their new life. Or tried damn hard, anyway. Turned over enough new leaves to fill this forest.

But he couldn't—*wouldn't*—lie to Mollie anymore. He wouldn't hurt her like that. She deserved the truth. Hell, she'd deserved it from the start. Sex was one thing. Friendship another. Where they stood right now, though, was deeper than either of those.

But naked wasn't great. A serious conversation with

his balls hanging down on something green and squishy? Talk about distracting.

Hands on her ass for support, Rafe stood, and then gently let Mollie unwind herself from him. Wordlessly, he picked up her clothes and handed them over. At least, the ones he hadn't ripped to shreds. If she was still talking to him after tonight? He'd make sure to buy her a replacement bra and panty set. Maybe an even dozen. That way he'd have license to rip a few more off.

Not that he put the chances of Mollie still being on speaking terms with him after the next half hour at anything better than hundred to one odds. Might as well bet against the Patriots in the Super Bowl. Just as little chance of winning.

Once her scrubs were back on, and Rafe had both legs in his freaking pajamas—not what he would've chosen for this moment, but her cut-and-run routine hadn't given him time to put on a suit—she came closer. Used her fingertips to smooth the edges of the tape down around the gauze on his chest.

"I don't see any seepage from the wound. Do you feel okay?"

Her concern blew him away and Rafe didn't think he'd ever get used to it. Or the tender smile that absolutely destroyed whatever scraps of a wall were still up around his heart. "After sex with you? I feel like I could pick up this log and surf it straight over to Hawaii."

A different kind of a smile ghosted across her face. A mix of humor and disappointment. Like teachers used to give him when he'd offer a funny as hell response to cover up when he didn't actually know an answer. "You know, Hawaii isn't actually across from Oregon. Or you would know that if you were from around here. Which I'm figuring out that you probably are *not*."

"Yeah."

Mollie dropped her hand. "Should I bother asking where you're really from? Or would you just evade the question again?"

"I'm going to tell you the truth." Rafe pulled on his top. Hoped to hell that wasn't the last time she ever touched him. "I'm going to tell you everything. Right now."

This was it. The moment that might change everything. The moment his brothers very well might end up cursing him for. Because taking this leap, telling Mollie, didn't just violate the most basic rule of WITSEC. It put all the Maguires potentially at risk.

It could play out a bunch of different ways. Mollie might freak out at the truth of his less-than-respectable past employment. Run straight to the US Marshals office and rat him out. Or she might tell her nearest and dearest in confidence, and then *they'd* decide to tell the Marshals. Or the police. Or the newspaper, which in today's internet-based society could lead to McGinty's crew tracking them down in a day.

His choice to tell her risked *everything*.

Except that it wasn't a choice. It was the only option. Rafe believed Mollie cared for him a whole hell of a lot. So if they were going to move forward at all—not that he'd ever imagined that happening with *anyone* once he joined WITSEC—he owed her the basic respect of the facts. The real facts about himself.

"That sounds ominous."

It sure as hell was. Rafe had no idea where to start. If he eased in slow with the whole life story, he might lose her before he got to the *why* of it all. If he started from today and went backward? That was starting with a lie and trying to excuse it.

He decided to go with a piece of advice from his dad. One he'd heard him say hundreds of times. *When you're in trouble with a woman, start by apologizing.* The old man had taught him lots of things. How to throw back a shot and a beer. How to pick a lock. Not to telegraph a punch. The apology thing, though, that was the most important. Probably the only thing that could save his hide right now.

"I'm sorry. I'm so sorry, Mollie. So sorry that I won't even ask you to forgive me. I only ask that you'll listen. Listen to it *all*. Starting with how sorry I am."

She didn't back down one bit. God, he loved that she wasn't scared to stand up to him. No other woman had ever gone toe-to-toe with him the way the doc did. Crossing her arms, Mollie coolly asked, "For what?"

"For lying to you."

"About?"

Everything? Rafe caught himself right before that word escaped. That answer probably wouldn't be a good start. No sarcasm. No short answers, either. Long explanations were the way to go. All the facts. Even the ones that made him look like a dangerous dick.

Rafe shoved his fingers through his hair. And combed out something he hoped to hell was a leaf and not a giant-ass spider. "For lying to you from the moment we met. Not because I wanted to. Not because I was playing you. But because I promised the United States government that I wouldn't tell the truth to *anyone*."

"The government? You're . . . what? A spy?"

God, what he'd give to be able to nod and cop to being the American James Bond right now. "I'm in the Witness Security Program. WITSEC. Under the umbrella of the U.S. Marshals Service."

"You're in witness protection?"

"Yes."

Her arms sort of morphed from just being crossed to hugging herself. Not a good sign. "Did you witness something bad? Or did you *do* something bad?"

That was a . . . decent way of easing into it. "Both."

"Did you kill someone?"

Wow. That question was the equivalent of burning rubber and peeling out at eighty miles per hour. So much for easing into it. "No. No! Shit, that's what Kellan asked, too. I'm no killer, Mollie."

"I don't know what to ask next." She walked in a slow, tight circle. "I . . . Is Kellan really your brother?"

"Whether he likes it or not. For the past six months,

he hasn't liked me much at all." But if this whole WITSEC thing worked out, he'd have the rest of their lives to convince Kellan to drop the attitude. That was worth it.

"Flynn, too?"

"Yes. To really being my brother and, coincidentally, also being pissed at me. Flynn's the reason why we're here."

Her eyes shifted down and to the side. "Did *Flynn* kill someone?"

"Shit." Rafe slid to the ground, back braced against the mossy log. He bent his knees. Spread his legs wide. "C'mere." This whole thing would go a lot better if he didn't look at her. If he couldn't see the twitches around her mouth, or the rounding of her eyes, or each and every little tell that screamed at him how freaked out Mollie was right now.

She sat, her sweet ass tucked up against him. Rafe wanted to hug her tight. But he didn't want to have her think he was trying to hold her in place. So he deliberately just rested his palms on her thighs. That was all for him. He needed the connection, the touch. In case he lost it forever.

"My dad was in the Irish mob in Chicago. It wasn't a secret. We didn't talk about it at the dinner table, but I knew. I knew from the day I went into the basement to look for a baseball and saw my dad with six of his friends. They all had guns either in their hands, or shoved in their waistbands. One guy held a bat. It wasn't pine colored, like the bats I used at school. This one had red streaks down it."

Mollie jerked against him. "You were a child?"

"I was seven." Easy to pinpoint his age because Kellan had still been a baby in his crib. "They all noticed me. One of them fished a fifty out of his pocket, handed it over, and told me to be a good boy and keep my piehole shut."

"What did you do?"

"I went back upstairs and asked my mom if we could have pie for dessert. The next day, my dad asked me to help him out. Carry a note in to the bakery for him, and wait for them to give me a box of donuts. What I eventually found out was that the monthly payoff to the mob was stacked under a half-dozen chocolate glazed. And a kid like me doing the handoff took all the risk out of it."

Mollie's hands slid back until they covered Rafe's. "Your father turned you into a criminal."

"No." Dad didn't stop it, but Rafe wouldn't let his father take the blame. That all, one hundred fucking percent, lay at the feet of exactly one person. The blame for getting him into the mob, and the blame for what eventually sent him running out of it. "Danny McGinty did that. He was the boss. It was his idea to use me. Dad wouldn't say no to him. Never did. McGinty reeled me in, little by little. More after Mom died. Being in his organization gave me a place to go, people to be with, a way to let off steam and work off my grief. I was twelve. Until last year, I thought her death was a random accident. Then I found out a bullet took her down that was intended for someone else. She got in the way of a turf war on her way to pick us up from school. She died because of Danny McGinty."

Rafe's head felt light and spinny, like he'd just gotten off of a roller coaster. Sure, he'd planned to tell Mollie everything. Just not in one big long breath. He hadn't even told the FBI and the Marshals about his mom. Guess he'd been waiting to get that off his chest for a while.

"That's . . . that's absolutely horrible, Rafe." Mollie twisted a little to lay her cheek against his chest. The side without the stitches. Because she was careful and caring like that.

"That's the tip of the iceberg. See, I thought McGinty *saved* me." Rafe remembered the rush of gratitude he'd gotten for years whenever he was with McGinty. When he didn't know any better. When he woke up every morning thinking that the sun rose and set on his *hero*. "He gave me responsibility. Money. Turned me into a man. When Dad died, when I was too fucking young to be in charge of my brothers, let alone keep a roof over their heads and food on the table, McGinty stepped up. Made me a full member. Eventually made me his right-hand man. Gave Flynn a job, and even paid his way through college."

"You didn't have a choice."

"Not really." He'd done a lot of thinking about that, over the past six months. If he'd taken the easy way. If he'd knowingly broken the law, hurt people, again and again in the name of his fucking hero, because it was easy. Easier than working three minimum wage jobs and not having health insurance. Easier than stealing shoes for his brothers to wear to school.

Maybe it was. But Rafe didn't regret it. It allowed

him to give Flynn, and much more so Kellan, a decent life. That was worth *everything* in his book.

Mollie's hands squeezed tighter. "That's unconscionable. He used children."

"McGinty uses everyone. Man, woman, child, you name it. It's how he works. He used my dad until the day he caught a bullet, too. And I'm pretty fucking sure that McGinty's the one who pulled the trigger that day. Something else I didn't find out until it was almost too late."

That turned Mollie all the way around to face him. It was getting harder to see in the twilight haze beneath the thick tree canopy. But it wasn't at all hard to see the horror in Mollie's wide eyes, wetness gathered at the corners. "The man who was a father figure to you *killed* your actual father?"

It wasn't any less of a punch to the gut, no matter how many times Rafe went over it and over it in his head. "I didn't know it at the time, trust me. Right before I left, I went through McGinty's desk. To take anything that could be evidence. I found my father's watch. And the St. Christopher's medallion that Danny gave him when I was born."

"Those both sound like common—"

A swift shake of his head cut her off. "They were both inscribed. Danny liked you to remember where the expensive presents came from. Definitely my father's. Which was weird, because I was told that Dad died in a shoot-out with another mob crew. McGinty and his bodyguard barely escaped the hail of bullets. When they went back to get Dad's body later, it was gone. Pretty convenient story to cover up killing someone off, isn't it?"

Mollie squeezed her eyes shut, then swiped the moisture away underneath them. "Is that why you left?"

It'd been enough to send him running when he put the pieces together, that was for damn sure. He remembered the jolt as his stomach turned to lead. As everything he thought he knew and cared about turned out to be false.

If Rafe hadn't already put in motion the plan to join WITSEC? At that moment, sitting in McGinty's green leather desk chair, he'd been genuinely torn between hunting him down and putting a bullet between his eyes . . . and shooting Danny in the kneecaps and balls *before* putting a bullet between his eyes.

No, Rafe hadn't ever killed anyone. But, as he held his father's watch in his hand, Rafe had been primed and ready to break that rule.

The watch he hadn't touched since the day his father died fourteen years ago.

He pulled in a long breath of the fresh, pine-scented air. It helped wash away the bitterness of that day. It would never leave him, but Rafe woke up less often, angry and burning with vengeance, here in Bandon.

"No. I'd already made the decision to quit the mob and testify against McGinty because of Flynn. I did it to keep Flynn out of jail."

Mollie resumed her previous position, back to his front. Hell, maybe she didn't want to look at him after all he'd just dumped on her. In a steady voice, as if ordering a soda, she asked, "What did he do?"

"Nothing." Since she hadn't cut and run yet, Rafe allowed himself to loosely hug her. He needed it. And if she was as shockingly sympathetic as it seemed so far? Maybe she needed it, too. "Well, that's not entirely true. Flynn was in the mob. He headed up the legit construction business that allowed us to have health insurance and launder money and look like regular citizens who worked and paid taxes. But when one operation went south, McGinty picked Flynn to take the fall. Even though he hadn't done anything wrong. Hadn't been a part of it, at all."

"Then how—"

It was harder to get this part out. Harder because Rafe's teeth automatically gritted shut. Hell, every inch of his body clenched and cramped, resisting the urge to get up and kick the shit out of a tree trunk, just to let out some of his anger.

But he wouldn't scare Mollie like that. Rafe just hoped he made it through the trial without jumping out of the witness stand and pounding in McGinty's face.

"Danny—the guy who took me under his wing, gave me everything I had, from a job to a purpose to a house—asked me to plant evidence. In my own house, against my own brother. 'For the good of the organization.' He promised that the lawyers would make sure that Flynn got off easy. That he'd only be inside for a handful of years. Promised a big bonus when he got out as thanks for his loyalty."

"He wanted you to put away your own brother?" Her voice was slow. Halting. "I'm sorry. I feel like I'm repeating a lot, or asking stupid questions. But this is all so different. Different from my life, different from anything I know. Even different from the movies. And yet so much more real."

God. Mollie sounded . . . off. Like he'd spun her world upside down without giving her an anchor. That was the last thing he wanted to do.

It was getting cooler in the forest as the sun dropped, and Rafe rubbed her upper arms for warmth. But he wanted to soothe her, too. Reassure her that the reality she knew was the one that mattered.

Not his fucked-up version.

"That's saying something." Rafe tugged on her earlobe with his teeth. "Coming from someone who literally deals in life and death every day."

"Most days, here in Bandon, it's more vaccines, stitches, and broken bones. But I get your drift." She batted him away, but finished by stroking his jaw. "Okay. I'm going to suspend freaking out and just listen. Like you asked."

"Each time Mom came home from the hospital with a baby, the first thing she did was put it in my arms. Tell me that he was my responsibility. I took it seriously. That jacked up a whole lot once she died. And once Dad was gone? Keeping Kellan and Flynn safe, healthy, and happy was my entire focus. I never once thought about trying to work out a way to go to college. Staying with Danny meant they were taken care of—simple as that."

"Your relationship with them is admirable."

God, if only. Rafe swore under his breath. Kicked at the leaves and twigs under his foot just to hear the harsh scrape of it against the ground. "Our relationship turned to shit since I yanked them out of their lives. Because it's my fault. *I'm* the one who decided to turn state's evidence. *I'm* the one who made the deal with the government. Contingent on putting not just me, but all three of us, in protective custody."

There was silence.

Or what passed for it in the middle of a forest. Rafe still noticed every damn rustle and hoot and squawk and scratch. Maybe he should put Kellan into research mode. Both because it'd make the brainiac happy, and because they should probably know if there were bears or cougars or whatever out here.

"It sounds like it was the only way to keep Flynn out of jail. And, I'm assuming, to protect Kellan from whatever ugly reprisal your former boss would have carried out."

"Reprisal. Yeah. That's an understatement." It wasn't often he let himself think about what might've happened if he and Flynn had left Kellan back in Chicago. Alone. To finish off law school and live a normal life.

But the few times he did think about it? It was with one hundred percent god damned certainty that McGinty would've plugged holes in Kellan the moment he found out the other Maguire brothers took off.

Or worse.

"You did the right thing, Rafe." Abruptly, Mollie

stood. Brushed off her ass and stared daggers at him. "You did the right thing. For you. I get that. I absolutely get that. I get what a hard decision it must've been. How brave and strong you are to have done that for your brother. To give everything up just to keep them safe. It makes me respect you so much more, makes me ache for what you've been through. It literally fills me with awe. And it also makes me want to push you off of Weber's Pier right into the ocean."

"I don't understand." Not at all. How was it she sounded so sincere and so pissed at the same time?

"First, tell me this—what was all that I heard through the door about millions of dollars?"

Oh, yeah. That probably didn't fit into Mollie's reality, either. But they didn't take it for shits and giggles. Or for a Ferrari. They took it for survival. "It's our insurance. We took it from McGinty in case things didn't work out with WITSEC."

In sharp, furious motions, Mollie pulled out her hair tie and smoothed everything he'd mussed up during sex. Then she yanked it back into a ponytail so tight he didn't think her forehead could move.

Until she frowned. At him. "This talk about retrieving the money. Does that mean you're leaving Bandon? Leaving me?"

Shit. The whole reason he copped to the truth was to give them a *chance* at a future. "God, Mollie, that's the last thing I want." How did they get here so quickly? Now Rafe was scrambling. Because telling the story of his life was easier than figuring out what was supposed to happen next.

"Which one?"

"Both of them." He got up. A little slower, because his chest had started to throb. Rafe took her hands. "I don't want to lose you. That's why I'm telling you all this. Because I won't lie to you. Not anymore. Not ever again."

She didn't look convinced. Not by a long shot. "You say it's the last thing you want. But you don't come out and promise that you *won't* leave."

His super smart doc had picked up on that, huh? "It's not entirely in my control. And like I said, I won't lie to you. We might have to leave. To keep you safe. To keep everyone in Bandon safe. I won't put anyone else at risk for our sake."

"Then maybe you shouldn't have come here in the first place."

That hurt more than the stab to his chest. Yeah, he got that Mollie was mad. Blindsided. So she got to lash out. As long as she followed it up with an explanation of exactly what she was pissed about so he could apologize right. "What's that supposed to mean?"

"I'm so mad at you, Rafe. Because there's no guarantee you won't be found. The way you describe him, Danny McGinty is sure to be scouring the country for you. To get *you*. To stop you from testifying. That means that you brought a significant potential for danger to my town. To my home."

There wasn't a good answer to that. He hadn't chosen

Bandon. Hell, he'd never heard of it before last month. It wasn't a strategic escape spot. It was nothing more than chance they'd ended up here.

Damn it, of all the bad things he'd seen and done, coming to Bandon was the only thing that wasn't his fault. *That* was what pissed her off the most? Not that she'd slept with an ex-mobster. Not that he was bad for her. But the threat of danger to the town had her up in arms? How the hell did he diffuse that?

Grabbing at the only straw he had in his arsenal, Rafe said, "The marshals say they've never lost anyone who follows all the rules."

"Do you?" She threw her arms wide, exasperation flowing off of her. "Do you and your brothers—men who've operated with little regard for at least some rules their whole adult lives—do you three follow all the rules?"

God. He scrubbed a hand across his mouth. Mollie definitely had his number. Especially since he was violating rule number one right now. As earnestly as he could manage, Rafe said, "We try."

"You know how much this town, these people mean to me. Yet every day you get up and stay here, knowing that you're literally the personification of danger."

"No danger." Not if everything worked according to plan. "Just three brothers trying to make a life. A new life. I swear to God, we don't want trouble to find us. And we sure as hell don't plan to start any. Please, Mollie." Rafe stopped, because he wasn't sure what he was asking from her.

She'd already given so much more than he expected—or deserved—with her sympathy and understanding. Could he really ask for forgiveness for the one thing that wasn't his fault? Coming here was entirely out of his control.

If she asked him to leave, would he uproot his brothers again? Convince the marshals to move them one more time?

"I need time to think, Rafe."

"I need your word that you won't reveal us."

Her face just . . . crumpled. Her whole body sagged inward. "Are you kidding me?"

"What?"

"That hurts. That piece of steel you took to the chest today? That pain's nothing compared to what you just did to my heart. For God's sake, don't you know you can trust me?"

He opened his mouth, but nothing came out as Mollie turned, with tears streaming down her cheeks, and jogged away from him.

His knees bent, without him even realizing it, until Rafe was back on the ground. Being blindsided did that to a guy. Trusting people hadn't gone so well for him in the past. What it *had* gotten Rafe was a one-way ticket away from his home, his friends, and the only life he knew. He didn't jump right to assuming every stinking level of trust. Probably never would again. Trust was pretty damn far in his rearview mirror.

On top of that? It just didn't occur to him that Mollie

would care enough to keep the secret without being asked. Especially after all the revelations about how bad he'd been before coming to Bandon.

No, it absofuckinglutely had not crossed Rafe's mind that she would choose *him* over her precious town's safety. That's not how the world worked. At least, that's not how the world he knew worked.

Rafe was the one who always put himself through the ringer to keep everyone else safe. Being on the receiving end of that never occurred to him

Except . . . that's *exactly* what Mollie would do.

She'd folded him under her umbrella of caring and wouldn't, no, *couldn't* rat him out. It wasn't in her nature. She'd told him that she was falling in love with him. The ultimate gift of trust. And he'd repaid her gift by doubting it.

Rafe dug his fingers into the dirt. The whole thing floored him. Her reaction to his life story. To learning that he was, essentially, a criminal on the run, if on the government's dime. Mollie had listened to it all, put aside his criminal past and automatically known, without question in her heart, that she'd keep his secret.

If she knew that, why didn't he?

Did he not trust himself to follow the rules and survive in this new life? To be a good guy? One who deserved a wonderful woman like Mollie at his side?

No good answer to that. Because his brain was consumed with a far bigger question.

How could he prove that he *did* trust her?

Chapter Twenty-one

Beach, 6:00 p.m.
Mood on the shore—still jittery as fuck

"We should have a beach day," Kellan announced. He kicked off his flip-flops and left them propped at the edge of a tide pool. "A cooler full of beer. Chips. Tunes. Ogling girls in tiny bikinis. Everything from the movies."

"Beach movies are about California, not Oregon." Rafe turned in a circle, spreading his arms wide. "You see anyone in a bikini?"

"I don't see *anyone*."

Damn straight. It was why they were at the beach at six o'clock on a Sunday night. "Hang on. You want to spend a day at the beach? With me? I thought you were busy giving me the cold shoulder for the rest of our lives." He untied his boot laces, feeling a twinge in his chest as he bent over. Yeah, it hurt.

But not as much as the memory of Mollie's tear-stained face as she ran away from him last night.

"I'm reserving that right, oh, forever." Kellan plunged his hand into the rocky pool and toyed with a couple of striped shells. "But what happened yesterday made me realize something. I've been going through the classic Kübler-Ross model."

Kellan never *tried* to make his brothers feel dumb. But with all those extra years of learning packed into his brain, it sure happened often. Rafe dug his toes into the cool sand, then squatted next to him. "Gonna need more than that."

"You know it as the five stages of grief. Terminally ill patients—and their loved ones, to some extent—go through them." He spread five shells out and pointed at each one in turn. "Denial, anger, bargaining, depression, and acceptance. That's what I've been going through. Because the person I was, for all intents and purposes, died back in Chicago. I had to process it."

Yeah. Rafe had heard of that before. And damn, if it didn't make a hell of a lot of sense. The Marshals Service had offered to send them to shrinks. Over a video chat, due to the need for secrecy. Maybe they should've. Nobody wanted to, and Delaney didn't push it, but maybe it would've gotten them back to really feeling like brothers again sooner.

The way he saw it was that by joining WITSEC? In shrink terms, Rafe had more or less killed off all three of them. Great. No guilt there at all. "Does that mean you accept it now?"

"Don't really have a choice, do I?" Kellan bumped

Rafe's shoulder with his own, almost unbalancing him. "But *you* did. That's the part I was too stubborn to hone in on. You could've let Flynn go to jail. Or you and Flynn could've gone on the run and left me to live my life. The thing is, you chose *us*. The three of us, sticking together like always. Sure, I got dragged away from my life. It pissed me off. You, though. *You* made the choice to give up everything to keep us together."

"There *was* no other choice." It was all of them or nothing. Because Rafe would have nothing without Kellan and Flynn.

"You're an awesome brother, Rafe. I should've thanked you months ago for saving me. For saving us."

"Are you yanking my chain?" This was the last thing he'd expected to hear tonight.

"I'm serious. You're not off the hook for lying to me my whole life. That's not going to sit right for a long time. But I've been an asshole. You raised me to be man enough to admit it. There will still be plenty of days when I'm a total prick because I don't know how to start over again, or I miss the chestnut glazed at Doughnut Vault. I'm going to work on having less of those, however."

Rafe didn't know what to say. Hearing Kellan's thanks was almost enough to make him throw his arms around his little brother.

Almost.

Flynn announced his arrival by tossing his sneakers down close enough to Rafe to spray sand onto his jeans. "I helped close at the Gorse last night, and went back today. My feet hurt, I'm tired, and I need to shovel about five tons of pasta into my face. Why the hell did you make us come to the damn beach at dinnertime?"

"Because I knew we'd be the only ones here."

The sulk slid right off his face. Flynn crossed his arms. "We're finishing the war council, aren't we?"

Nodding, Rafe said, "Thanks to your work schedule, this was our first chance. I didn't want to risk talking in the house again."

"Christ, Rafe, we could've closed the windows and doors."

Clearly Flynn was off his game. Out of practice. "What if this is an inside job and someone from the FBI's got us over a barrel? Don't you think there's a chance they've bugged our house as easy as they bugged our tablets and phones?"

"Shit." Flynn rubbed a hand across the back of his neck as he scanned along the empty beach. Empty except for ten-feet-tall rock outcroppings and a few fat, lazy gulls looking for scraps. *That* wasn't any different from the lakeshore in Chicago. Damn sea rats.

"I'll take that as a yes."

They all started walking closer to the dark edge of sand that marked where the water stopped with each wave. Rafe pointed at the enormous rock, right off the coast, shaped like a man's profile. "Do you two like that?"

"Face Rock?" Kellan's whole expression lit up as he turned to face it. "Oh, yeah. It's cool."

"More freaky than cool," Flynn corrected.

Right. Because it would literally kill his middle brother to show that anything in his current life ranked anywhere above a total suckfest. "I meant the whole view. The ocean. The rock formations. Do you like it here in Bandon?"

Kellan swung back around. "Why?"

"Because it's time to take a stand. To claim Bandon as our home."

Kicking sand—but at least not *at* Rafe—Flynn grumbled, "Didn't know we had an option otherwise."

And that wasn't just a match for the fuse on his temper. It was an already burning stick of dynamite strapped on to it. "God damn it." He picked up a rock and threw it into the water with the speed of a fastball across the plate. "That's the kind of thing we've got to stop doing. Acting like we're here as a punishment. We're here as a god damned gift. It's time to stop fucking around and commit to not just pretending to be a new person, but actually being one. That's the only way we'll survive."

People used to fucking *cower* when Rafe yelled his way through a speech like that. Unfortunately, his brothers were immune to his temper. Kellan just lifted one eyebrow. "Meaning?"

"Kellan, if you don't like your job, find a better one. Bitching about it won't change anything. So what if you can't use your almost-law degree? You're still highly educated and smarter than probably nine-tenths of this town. Figure out what *else* you can do."

"That's assuming we stay."

"Yes. Yes, for fuck's sake, let's assume we'll stay here. The Marshals already said they won't move us anywhere else. We don't want to go on the run. So this is it. We've got to stop what-if-ing. Stop pining for Chicago like it's a supermodel who took our virginity. We're alive. We're together. That makes this home."

Eyebrows cranked together into a single line, Flynn said, "Hey, I show up at work. I'm polite. I'm starting that community service thing with the Cranberry Festival. What more do you want?"

"A wise man told me that I need to find something about Bandon to make me happy. Well, I've found a bunch of things. People, mostly. It's your turn. Just showing up isn't good enough."

"You just turned into an inspirational poster. There should be a cat hanging out of the toilet right next to you."

"Go on. Take your shots." Rafe dug his big toe in, then swept his leg to the right. "See this? It is a literal god damned line in the sand." He stepped over it. Away from the sea. Away from escape. Toward Bandon. "Take some time to bitch and moan. Call me every name in the book. After tonight, I expect you two to join me on this side. All in."

"I'm not waiting." Kellan backed up a couple of steps. Then he made a running jump to end up next to Rafe. "You've kept us alive so far."

"That brings me to my next point." Rafe barreled on

without waiting for Flynn to pick a side. He'd give him some space. For a few hours, anyway. "We said we trust Delaney to keep us alive. Tomorrow, we go to her with our theory that a fed is blackmailing us."

"It's the right call. She'll keep us safe," Kellan said.

"Is that your reasoned, lawyer-mind talking? Because I've gotta say, it sounds a lot more like your dick talking."

"Yeah." Flynn pinned his younger brother with a warning glare. "We've put up with your nonstop flirting with Delaney. We get that she's hot, and you're horny. But don't forget—the marshal is off-limits. Big time. There'd be hell to pay with the Marshals if anything happened between you and Delaney."

"The way she gets all pissed every time you try to flirt with her? There may be hell to pay even if nothing happens. You behave, K." Rafe shook a finger to show his seriousness. "Let me do all the talking."

"I don't have to talk to flirt with a woman," Kellan said smugly.

"Christ. I'm not sticking around to hear made-up stories of all the coeds you seduced out of their panties." Flynn started to walk away, then paused without bothering to turn back toward his brothers. "I'm with you. All the way. Always. No discussion necessary."

That was . . . something. Enough, anyway. Enough to set wheels in motion. As good as it felt to have that momentary unity, though, Rafe needed to shatter it. Potentially.

"Hang on, Flynn. We're not done." As Flynn trudged back, Kellan squinted at him in confusion.

"There's nothing else we can do, if we're leaving it up to the gorgeous marshal."

"There's something else you have to know. Because I promised I'd never lie to you again."

"Uh-oh." Kellan and Flynn said it simultaneously.

"I told Mollie. Everything."

Flynn's jaw dropped. He advanced on Rafe, one hand clenched into a fist at his side. "You texted us last night that you took care of it. We thought that meant she hadn't actually heard much, or you made up some flimsy-ass excuse for whatever she did hear."

"I wanted to tell you in person. To explain."

"Explain what?" Kellan pushed against Rafe's shoulder, hard enough to send him reeling back a step. "That you recklessly put us in jeopardy? Christ, Rafe, if she tells anyone else, I'd be yanked from WITSEC. Separated from you and Flynn. And if you idiots decide to come with me, and we lose our official protection, we could lose our fucking lives."

It figured that Kellan would be the most scared out of all of them. And Rafe knew he deserved their anger. Not, however, that he'd deserved Mollie's. He'd stewed on that all day. Her anger over their placement in Bandon—which wasn't his fault at all—pissed him off. It wasn't fair.

But normal couples had fights. All Rafe wanted was

the chance to have that fight with Mollie, make up, and then keep going. Together.

"She won't tell anyone."

"How do you know? We keep the secret because our lives are at stake. She doesn't have that hammer over her head."

"She does. Because she's falling in love with me."

"Jesus fucking Christ." Flynn's words barely cleared his mouth before his fist connected with Rafe's chin. It wasn't full power, so Rafe didn't black out or go flying across the sand. It did, however, take all the strength in his body to hold his ground.

And he would. Flynn and Kellan were in their rights to take their licks. Wouldn't make him back down, though. "Go on. I won't fight you. Either of you."

"Damn right you won't," Flynn shouted, his words pinging off the giant rocks around them. "You did all of this—put us through all of this—to save our lives. Now you're risking them just for a piece of ass?"

"Don't call her that." Before Rafe processed the thought, his fist split the skin under Flynn's eyes. Because he'd caught him by surprise, Flynn's ass did hit the sand. "I'm fucking falling in love with her, too, you idiot." Then he immediately fell to the sand next to his brother as the truth and impact of his words registered in his brain and his gut. Who knew he'd say that for the first time in his life, tonight—and to his brother, no less?

Kellan plopped down next to them. "This'll be the

smallest wedding ever. Exactly three people on the groom's side. Including a marshal packing heat."

"Shut up." Rafe threw a handful of sand his direction, but the wind took it away.

Flynn touched his cut, then looked at the blood on his finger before looking back at Rafe. "You mean it? You love her? This is the real deal?"

"I think so." Rafe braced his hands on his thighs and sucked in a couple deep breaths. "Sorry I hit you."

"I'm not sorry I hit you. You had it coming."

"Agreed."

Flynn bumped his shoulder. "She's worth it?"

"Yeah. Definitely."

"Then I guess there's nothing more to discuss. She's one of us now, for better or for worse. Does she know how you feel?"

"Nowhere fucking close to it," he said fervently. Rafe had a couple more things to put in motion before he could fix what he'd broken between them. But at least nothing was broken with his brothers.

One step at a time.

This going good thing, committing to a new life, was more complicated than he'd anticipated.

A FEW HOURS LATER, Rafe was back on the beach. He still wore a jacket in May, just like he would've back home.

No.

He made a tight fist, disappointed in himself for

thinking like that. Not *home*. Bandon was home now. How could he demand his brothers get with the program if he'd already slipped up himself?

Shit. Good intentions wouldn't cut it. As punishment, he forced himself to walk closer to the inky black edge of the ocean. No way would he let some stupid fear of sea creatures keep him from putting down roots. He'd come out here every night, jog right along the crusty sand where the waves broke, just to show whatever *might* be out there that there was no scaring away Rafe Maguire.

"Rafe? Is that you?" Mick's voice came from around the side of a tall rock that got submerged at high tide.

"It's me, Colonel."

"If you came to try your hand at night fishing, it's for crap. Nothing to look at."

"I came to find you."

"Uh-oh." Mick took off his cap, creased the bill in his habitual gesture that Rafe now recognized as thinking or worry, and then settled it back on his crown.

"What's wrong?"

"Nobody comes out to find me on patrol at ten at night unless there's a reason. And it sure isn't just to shoot the shit."

Prickly old bastard. "It sort of is."

"Is that so?"

"I wanted to follow up on the last conversation we had out here. Let you know that I *have* found a reason to stay in Bandon. More than one, actually."

Mick's weathered face creased up into a wide grin. He clapped him on the shoulder. "That's good to hear, son."

Son.

Nobody had called him that in a long time. It felt . . . good. It felt like a couple of solid shovelfuls of dirt tossed into a deep hole in his soul.

Good—but not *quite* right. "It's, ah, funny you call me that."

Mick waved his hand back and forth. "I'm not looking to adopt you and ask you to keep me out of a nursing home. I just see something in you. Something I can connect with. That doesn't happen too often for this old man."

"Same here. It's actually why I came to talk to you." He wouldn't break the rules. Not again, anyway. But he needed to tell Mick the basics. If they were sticking around Bandon? Rafe was pretty sure the soldier in front of him was more than a little responsible for his willingness to do so.

"Sure we don't need a beer for this conversation?"

"Sorry. I'm not packing." He'd remember to put a couple of cans in his pocket the next time he wandered out to talk to Mick at night. "Look—I can't go into details. Not with you, not with anyone."

"Fine by me. Most people's life stories are boring as shit."

No wonder he liked Mick so much. "My dad? Before he died? More or less set me up for a bad life. Then my old boss screwed me over but good. So I don't want a father figure or a mentor—what I need is a friend."

"Done."

Rafe appreciated that it was that simple. A nod of the head, no questions, and they were good. "And I'd like to bounce an idea off of you. As a friend. As someone who knows the town better than I do. An idea that's been circling in my head ever since I helped out a pretty girl on the side of the road."

"You want to ask Mollie to move in with you?"

"Mollie's not talking to me right now."

"You screwed up."

Rafe laughed. He laughed so hard that he couldn't catch his breath. First, he bent in half, hands braced on his thighs. When that didn't help—or slow the fucking guffaws coming out of his mouth—he bent his knees and just fell to the sand. "So, so much."

"Fix it."

"I've got a plan to do just that. I promise." If it all came together. There were a lot of moving pieces outside of his control. Least of which was putting his faith and trust in the U.S. government. *Again.*

"How's your track record with that sort of thing?"

"I've never come up against a problem I couldn't fix. It's what I'm best at . . . or was, anyway. There's something else I want to be good at from now on. I need your take on it."

"What's that?"

If it worked? He'd be planted here for good. It was

too fricking big a step to take until after he testified at McGinty's trial. But that's what made Rafe want to do it so much. One last adrenaline rush of living on the edge.

"I want to expand the garage. Add on a business that restores classic cars."

"Do you know how to do that?"

"Some. Enough to start. It'd need to start slow, anyway." Rafe was already busy enough. But Jesse helped some, and he hoped once Frieda's husband recovered from his heart attack he could put in a little time restoring cars, as well. It might be just what Mr. Wick needed without overdoing it. "As it grows? It'll bring in people who come for the car but stick around for a long weekend to enjoy the beach. Classic car rallies get big crowds. This expansion would be good for Frieda. Good for the town."

"Good for you?"

"I think so."

"I like that you put the town first." Mick clapped him on the back. "It's a smart idea. I know it's a load off Frieda's mind since you started. She likes your work. What you're doing for Mollie's cousin. I'll bet she green lights it."

"Thanks, Mick. I needed to hear all of that." Needed to know that someone who wasn't related to him had his back. Someone he, yes, trusted.

"What are friends for?"

Chapter Twenty-two

THE DOOR TO Mollie's bedroom cracked opened just enough to let the brightness from the hallway assault her corneas. She didn't want light, or company. She basically wanted to wallow in her own misery. So Mollie squeezed her eyes shut. "What is it, Gran?"

Bracelets jingled with every step the older woman took toward the bed. "I brought you some medicinal tea."

"I'm not sick."

"Really?" A cheek brushed against her forehead. It was the technique Norah had developed to test for a fever once she lost her hand. "Your alarm went off fifteen minutes ago. You're still in bed. That's not like you."

"I'm having a slow start." Mollie pulled an arm out from under the covers to take the steaming mug, and then froze, midreach. "Define 'medicinal' as it pertains to this tea. Would someone else define it as perhaps illegal in thirty-nine states and definitely something that should not be ingested before I go start my shift at the hospital?"

"You're so suspicious. And judgmental."

"I prefer the term *law-abiding*. Can't practice medicine after taking drugs, Gran. The AMA frowns on it."

Huffy, Norah shoved the mug at her. "The tea is lemon-ginger. I thought you were sick, remember?"

"Thanks." Still cautious, Mollie took a small sip. It tasted . . . fine. Nothing like the coffee she craved and desperately needed, but beggars couldn't be choosers.

"What's wrong?"

"Rafe and I had a fight."

Sort of.

Not entirely.

Not specifically. Rafe opened up and shared the biggest secret of his life with her. Then she yelled at him. Which nobody would counsel as the proper way to reward such naked honesty.

But most people didn't have to strip down so far to get to the honesty. Most people weren't living a complete lie.

That she knew of.

Because heck, if the U.S. Marshals brought the Maguire brothers here, maybe they thought of Bandon as a safe haven. Maybe the rest of Mollie's neighbors were in witness protection, too. Maybe she was the only one living as herself.

These were the thoughts that kept her tossing and

turning for the past two nights. Imagining Frieda Wick as a globe-trotting drug mule who'd had a crisis of conscience and given up the dangerous life when she fell in love. Or that Floyd was really the witness to a triple homicide by a cadre of Colombian diplomats.

At least those ridiculous imaginings gave Mollie a reprieve from thinking about Rafe. About what he'd done. She didn't know the details, and truly believed it wasn't his fault for getting sucked in as a child, but it wasn't a big leap to assume he'd done some bad things and broken a bunch of laws.

Or thinking about who he was. How much of the man he'd revealed to her, the man she'd fallen for, was even real? How much was a carefully crafted persona? A costume? She thought/hoped/assumed that at least the majority of their interactions were real. That only his name had changed, and he still truly liked fast cars and fettuccine Alfredo and knew all the words to all of the Rolling Stones songs. But Mollie didn't know for sure.

Just like she didn't know if she could ever trust her own judgment again. If she could ever trust *him* again.

If he even stuck around. Because what if he left? Left Bandon? Left *her*?

So yes, Mollie had hit the snooze button. Twice. She'd earned it.

Opening the drapes on the other window with a dragging clank that woke Mollie the rest of the way up, Norah said, "I'll bring home some garlic bread from the bakery at lunch. And a half-dozen of their lemon cupcakes."

Following her Gran's logic was hard enough normally. Doing it pre-caffeine wasn't even worth trying. "Why?"

"I assume you're inviting the girls—and Lucien, of course—over for dinner. To call Rafe all sorts of names and then figure out exactly which sexy outfit of Elena's you'll borrow to drive him crazy until he apologizes."

"Aw, Gran. You're the best. But nobody's coming over tonight."

She cranked open the louvered windows. Sounding more than a little peeved, Norah said, "You're making conversation very difficult this morning."

"I can't talk with the girls about my fight. Or with Lucien." Not with anybody. Technically. Because Mollie stuck by her word. She wouldn't risk Rafe's life, or those of his brothers, by sharing what she'd learned.

On the other hand . . . Gran had seen a lot in her time in the Navy. Met lots of different people with different backgrounds. From all over the world. If anyone could give Mollie the answer to the central question buzzing through her brain, it just might be Gran.

"I'll bring home some wine if that'll cheer you up." After a firm pat of the quilt covering Mollie's feet, she turned for the door.

"I'd be a fool to say no." Mollie set the tea on the nightstand, then wriggled to a seated position. "But, can you sit and talk with me for a minute?"

"Of course." Instead of sitting on the edge, Gran

came around to join her. Back against the whitewashed headboard, and her uncovered stump resting on Mollie's hip like they had years ago.

The details of Rafe's ripped-straight-from-the-movies life weren't what bothered Mollie the most. They did bother her in principle. Wondering about them would circle in her head for a good long while. But given his reasons for staying in the mob after what was basically a childhood conscription, they weren't break-up worthy. Everyone had a story. Good, bad, wild. It was how you chose to shape your life *after* the excitement subsided that fleshed you out as a person.

What would his choice end up being?

Had he made it already? Had she fallen in love with the finished version of the new man Rafe was trying to be? Because the man she knew now was good. Mollie didn't doubt that for a second. But would he slide back into his old self? Or was he the same at his core and it was just his circumstances—and name—that were different? Doing bad things didn't necessarily make you a bad person. It might be semantics, but she believed they weren't the same thing. Mollie needed reassurance that was true before she moved on to her bigger fear about what could happen next between them.

"Do you think . . . have you ever seen . . . do you believe people can change?"

"Yes." Gran held up her hand and waggled it back and forth. "And no. It depends."

"Gee, thanks. Are you sure you haven't been hitting the medicinal tea already?"

"Yes. People *can* change. Drastically. Do a complete personality flip. Or ideology. Or something else. I've seen others who've tried to change, over and over and over again, and just can't do it. Not even for something small."

Mollie picked at a loose green thread along the border of a quilt square. She could keep tugging at it until the square came off. Then she could sew it onto a quilt and make a different pattern out of it. But when she looked at it, would she still only see the original shape? After having stared at it one way for so many years? Did Rafe *want* to be good now?

"What's the trick?" she asked in a low voice.

"It depends on their motivation. It's the same as beating an addiction. You can't change for someone else. You have to do it for yourself, first and foremost. That's the only way it'll stick."

Aaaand there went a direct hit to a much older burning question. One that also kept Mollie awake at nights. When she bothered to admit it. "You think that's why Mom never came back?"

Gran's neck audibly snapped, she twisted her head so fast. "Where's this coming from?"

"Mom left me to go find herself. I hear, that for normal mothers, doing things for the sake of their children is a fairly strong motivation. But in Mom's case, she changed—for herself—and that was it. She still didn't come back for me."

"Mollie Catherine, any fault, any blame, any lack falls entirely on your mother's shoulders." Norah's voice held a sharp, scolding edge to it. "I've told you that before, and I'll repeat it until my dying day."

"She left me. It seems obvious that there's something missing. That I can't expect anyone else to stick around."

"You're not listening. Your mother didn't choose to leave you. It was just a side effect of her own selfishness. She made the choice to move toward something else, not to leave you behind."

Mollie seriously doubted her gran had ever put it in quite those terms before. It was like a key turning in a lock, opening the door and letting her stupid, ridiculous paranoia drift out into the wind.

It truly wasn't her fault. Wasn't anything lacking in her.

Which explained why she had more friends than she could count at every hospital where she'd worked. Friends from college. An entire town of people here who loved her. Who'd turned their lives upside down to help her and continued to love her.

There wasn't anything wrong with her. Nothing lacking. There wasn't any reason to assume that Rafe would leave her.

Unless he was forced to . . .

Norah smoothed the hair out of Mollie's face. "I thought you said you were required to talk to a psychiatrist as part of your training? And that he helped clear all those old doubts of yours away."

Whoops. "I did *say* that. I thought it would make you feel better."

"You thought it would make me stop pestering you to talk to someone."

"That, too."

"You and Rafe had one fight and it brought all this back up? You think he's turning tail and walking out on such a beautiful, smart, sweet woman?"

"The thing is, for the first time ever, I didn't believe that. I had hope that we had a chance at something special. Now I'm just confused."

"Any reason why you have to figure that out right this second?"

Mollie barely stopped laughter from exploding out of her. "Yes. I'm quite certain there's a time limit on my pouting and navel gazing when it comes to Rafe."

Time was about to run out. Would Rafe and his brothers have to leave now that she knew their secret? Would he feel compelled to confess to his handler that someone else knew about them? Did that mean they'd automatically be relocated?

And when were they supposed to go back to Chicago and testify? Because that would undoubtedly be a dangerous trip, with no guarantee that he'd return. No matter what happened, it was sure to come to a head sooner rather than later. Mollie was shocked he'd left her alone for two days already.

Her bedroom door opened even farther and Jesse leaned in, both hands on the doorjamb. "I made waffles."

Mollie looked at the clock. Her heart sank. "It's Tuesday and you're still here? Are you cutting school?"

"No." He pulled his hood up over his head and scowled. "And your lack of faith in me is duly noted, by the way. I've got that dentist appointment this morning, remember? I thought I'd do something nice and make everyone breakfast."

Whoops. Mollie scrubbed her hands over her face. "That was nice. Thank you. I'm sorry that I jumped to the wrong conclusion. I'm having a bad week."

"It's only Tuesday," he said dryly.

Mollie pushed out a long, slow exhale. "Tell me about it."

"Did you and Rafe have a fight?"

"Sort of."

He came forward to awkwardly pat her foot. "You should make up with him. He's a good guy. He's patient with me. Doesn't yell at me for screwing up, only when I don't try. He gave me a second chance, remember?"

"He did, indeed. All his idea."

"I think you should give him flowers. That fixes everything." Then he left them alone.

Jesse was one smart kid. Rafe *was* a good guy. The things he'd lied about didn't change his heart. He was patient. He was loyal. He was funny. None of that was an act.

"He made us waffles. That's a big step." Norah patted Mollie's thigh. "I know you're staying here for Jesse's sake, but you should start looking for your own place.

Jesse's proving he can be trusted, more and more every day. The two of us will be just fine without you. I'll miss your smiling face, but we'll be fine."

Mollie needed reassurance on one more point. That she wasn't being a naïve, gullible fool. "Gran, do you believe in second chances?"

"And third and fourth and however many it takes. We all get them. Why shouldn't we be just as generous in giving them to someone else?"

That was exactly how Mollie had always approached it. She didn't know if Rafe was the one who needed the second chance, or if it was herself. Could she truly believe him? Give him a shot at a normal, new life here? How could she get him to trust *her*? Rafe had a big, secret stash of money to lure him away. How on earth could she compete with that? How could she be enough for him?

"HERE'S YOUR BLOOD money, Mateo." Delaney thumped a cardboard coffee tray down on the sheriff's desk. "Four triple shot, dark roast large coffees, as requested. I can't believe I have to bribe you to let me use your office."

"I can't believe you want to keep using my office when you've got a perfectly good one up the road. Any chance you want to tell me what this is about?"

Rafe knew that the cover story she'd given the sheriff would hold. But he still wondered, for a split second, what she'd say next. Because yeah, he still had a hard time trusting people. That wouldn't go away overnight.

But Rafe was trying, damn it. So he forced himself to hold his relaxed pose, leaning against the wall. Fake it 'til you make it.

"Be happy to." She winked at Mateo. "As soon as you're sworn in as a United States Marshal. Until then, my lips are sealed. What do you need four coffees from Eugene for, anyway?"

Mateo popped a lid and slurped in three long gulps. "The shop in Eugene is the closest one with Ugandan beans. And I need four because I'm down a deputy. Pulling extra shifts around the clock makes it hard to prop my peepers open."

"Don't you usually get a heads-up before someone transfers?"

"Not this time. Tricia got put on bed rest for her whole pregnancy. Didn't even know she was pregnant. Add in the maternity leave after that, and I'll be in serious trouble if I don't get staffed up before the Cranberry Festival."

Another thing Rafe was getting used to about small-town life was the slow easing into conversations. It actually tickled him now, most of the time.

Not today.

Not when he was itching to get back and make things right with Mollie. It had been two whole days since she'd left him in the woods. Two days of waiting to hear back from the marshal. Because he wouldn't go any further with Mollie until he knew there wasn't any danger—to her or to the rest of Bandon.

"At this rate, the festival will be here before you get down to business, Marshal." Flynn opened the door to the conference room and motioned her in. Nice that he'd played the bad guy. Kellan, as usual, was too busy ogling Delaney to probably even notice the long-winded conversation about the sheriff's staffing problems.

"There are days, Flynn Maguire, when I'm tempted to ask just how uncomfortable it is with that cactus stuck up your ass." But Delaney did lead them all inside. The moment the door shut, Rafe started throwing out questions.

"What's the story? Did you check your jailhouse snitches? Anyone connected with McGinty mentioning us all of a sudden?" Delaney usually kept them in the dark. Rafe jumped at every chance to pigeonhole her on what the Chicago crew might be up to. Find out if the old man was all recovered and still promising to rain down vengeance on them.

Delaney eased into a chair. Gestured to the others around the oval table and waited to speak until all three Maguires sat their butts down. "Danny McGinty is out of the hospital now, which made it much easier to get intel. Yes, you're still being talked about. But it's only to curse your name, and Flynn's. Well, along with promising to whack you when you go back to testify." She waved a hand through the air to dismiss the idea as easy as waving off an annoying waiter. "But we won't let that happen. The point is, there's no reason to suspect they have any idea where you are, or as to your new identities."

"Great." Rafe exhaled a breath he didn't know he'd been holding. With an opposite reaction, Kellan's knee started jiggling like crazy and he slapped Rafe twice on the thigh. Guess his little brother was more excited than relieved.

"It is great." Flynn laid his forearms along the table, leaned forward, then tilted his head to face Rafe. "Doesn't tell us who the blackmailer is, though."

Delaney tapped a bright red fingernail against the file she'd pulled out of her big purse. "Actually, that's why I popped down to your neck of the woods."

"Aww, and here I was sure it was because you wanted to see me." Kellan flashed her the panty-drop smile. Again. Rafe didn't know why he bothered, since it hadn't worked the first hundred times he'd tried it on her.

"We've pinpointed who sent you the blackmail letter."

Rafe all but catapulted across the table to grab the folder. The moment he flipped it open, his brothers' heads were right there next to his.

An ID photo was clipped to the top of an arrest warrant. Well, an ID card—one with FBI in tall blue letters. The man in the picture, the man who'd put them into a spin cycle of anxiety, had a bad comb-over. Rafe felt a little like Capone must have when he got arrested for tax evasion.

Flynn peered closely at the picture. "This is the dirtbag who scared us shitless?"

"Speak for yourself. I'm plenty regular. I think it's

the cranberry juice they've got around in big pitchers at the plant." Kellan must be a little giddy to be discussing how often he crapped in front of Delaney.

But damn, if it wasn't good to stop worrying.

"He looks like a middle-management nobody," Rafe said.

Delaney huffed out a half laugh. "That describes Special Agent Marvin Jessup to a *T*."

"Marvin?" Flynn shoved the folder back over to her. "Hell, no. I can't believe a Marvin did this to us."

Rafe asked, "Who is he?"

"Agent Jessup was brought onto the case locally as the FBI liaison to the Marshals Service. It gave him the authority to review all our joint task force cases. It was easy to track him down, since so few people have access to any level of your information. He assumed—which is shocking, given that he's a trained FBI special agent—that anyone in WITSEC was both guilty and hiding a ton of money. The same letter got sent to two other protectees under the umbrella of the Eugene Field Office."

"Okay." That was more proof that it wasn't personal. That it had been a wide net of a money grab. Rafe figured he'd have to light a candle and say a Hail Mary over this whole affair ending so fast and neat. It was what his mom would've wanted. It was nice doing things for his mom's memory every so often.

Kellan lifted an index finger. "Now that you've identified the perpetrator, what's the next step?"

Delaney wrinkled her nose. Like smelling a dead

fish washed up at the edge of Lake Michigan. "It turns out that he was already under investigation for stealing drugs from evidence lockup and reselling them. He's an idiot, and an embarrassment. But we don't believe he's a real threat. He only knows your current identities. Period. No way at all to trace you back to Chicago or the McGinty case."

Flynn high-fived Rafe, then reached over to do the same to Kellan.

"In case you didn't notice the arrest warrant when you purloined my confidential government file," she stared down her nose at Rafe, "Jessup is being taken into custody as we speak. We discussed your case with the Chicago team and don't see any point in relocating you."

This time Kellan started the round of high-fives.

"You also get a massive official apology from the Marshals Service. This never should have happened. We'll be reviewing personnel files of everyone connected to both the FBI and Marshals offices for the whole state, and adjusting the criteria for interagency liaisons."

Delaney looked both mad and embarrassed. It put Rafe right where he wanted to be to press this sudden advantage. "I don't think an apology is enough. For what we went through. For Christ's sake, we thought they'd found us."

"You did the right thing, bringing it to me. I always said you were smart. Following the rules is the smart call, every time. But I agree that you were subjected to undue mental anguish. What do you want? A trip to Oakland Coliseum the next time the Cubs play the A's? Pizza flown in from Giordano's?"

"I want something better." Rafe kicked back until his chair was only on the back two legs. Then he crossed his arms over his chest. Because damn, if it wasn't fun to be negotiating from a position of power one last time. "I want a favor."

Kellan groaned and clutched his stomach. "Dude. You're really going to turn down the pizza? She's worth that much to you?"

Delaney's head snapped up. "There's a 'she'? Rafe Maguire, what have you done?"

"Something I never planned on, I swear."

Chapter Twenty-three

Two coffees and three doughnuts later—the sugar made the caffeine work better, in her vaunted medical opinion—Mollie was still not in the mood. Not in the mood for the baby who vomited on her shoes. Not in the mood for the nurse who'd read a chart wrong, thereby leaving a dementia patient alone in a room with a tray full of hypos loaded with vaccines for Africa.

And now that it was *finally* her lunch break, she was definitely not in the mood to be paged from the clinic over to see a patient in room seven at the hospital. Most days, helping patients genuinely lifted Mollie's spirits. Today? The thought of her sandwich with ham, extra swiss, and grainy mustard was the only thing that dragged her through the morning. She didn't even remember the patient in room seven. Probably another charting mix-up that required zero actual patient care but would keep her tied up just long enough to make lunch an impossibility.

Because apparently, when you fell in love with an ex-mobster, everything else in your life got just as complicated.

Crappy.

Oh, and look. No chart in the holder outside the door. That translated to an automatic five minutes minimum of no-lunch spent asking the patient questions that were already answered and written down—somewhere. Mollie's stomach growled embarrassingly loud as she straight-armed the door.

"Good afternoon, I'm Dr. Vickers," she said to the pretty blond woman in the bed. "What's bothering you today?"

"Too many things to count individually. How about we lump it under one main pain in the ass?"

"All right. Is it a sudden onset, or has this been bothering you for some time?"

The door clicked shut behind Mollie as the woman grimaced. "It's been six months of constant pain and annoyance." She pushed the button that lifted the bed to a seated position. The covers fell down, revealing that she wore not a hospital gown, but a blazer over a pale blue button-down. "Sadly, I'm certain you're going to make it worse before it gets better."

Great. Now she'd lose another five minutes while the patient changed into a gown so that she could be examined. Mollie patted her on the leg, forcing a smile. "Well, that might be true. But I'd like to make you as pain-free as possible in the interim."

"Does that go for me, too?" Rafe stepped out of the darkened bathroom.

Mollie's head whipped around. "What are you—Rafe, get out of here right this minute!" She snapped her arm toward the door as she tried to shoot an apologetic glance at the patient. "Ma'am, I'm so sorry about this."

"I told you he was a pain in the ass."

The surprises just kept coming as Rafe's brothers lined up behind him while the patient got out of bed. Her blazer gaped open as she stood, revealing a holstered gun and a badge.

Mollie gasped as her brain started to race to conclusions. Was she a fellow mobster? If so, was she here to kill Rafe, or to ask him to come back? Friend or foe? Not just for the curiosity factor, but because Mollie's first priority was the safety of the patients in the hospital. She couldn't risk a hailstorm of bullets.

A quick peek at the Maguires didn't show any visible guns on them. But in the movies, weren't they always tucked down the backs of their pants?

"Don't freak out." Rafe moved slowly, one hand out, as if Mollie were the one with the lethal weapon. "You're safe. This is Delaney Evans, the U.S. Marshal in charge of our protection."

"Nice going, Marshal." Kellan made a tsking sound. "Doesn't it defeat the purpose of being undercover if you flash your gun five seconds after she walks in the door?"

She tugged her jacket into place, then buttoned it. "Doesn't it defeat the purpose of being undercover if you people share your life story with every pretty woman you come across?"

"Hard to tell. Seeing as how I only have eyes for you."

Flynn backhanded the side of Kellan's head. "Cut it out."

They all seemed very comfortable. Mollie, on the other hand, was about to jump out of her skin. Apparently she didn't handle being blindsided well at *all*. "What is going on here?"

The marshal crossed her arms. "Rafe's got something he'd like to say to you. I'm here to watch your reaction, so I can assess for myself just how trustworthy you are. Sorry about the audience, but that's just the way it needs to be."

Flynn spread his hands, palms up. "We're here because we're all in this together now." He threw his older brother a look more lethal than the gun in the room. "We weren't in it together when Rafe was feeling you up in the forest or deciding to put us all at risk by telling you who we really are, but we're in this together now."

"Do not talk to Mollie like that." Rafe's voice was threatening. But it was nothing compared to his thunderous expression and the way the cords along his neck popped out. Like skin and willpower alone were holding back the violence within him trying to get out.

He flinched and dipped his head. "Sorry. Honest. I'm pissed at my brother, not at you, Doc."

Mollie couldn't fix their obviously strained family dynamics, but she could put everyone's fear at ease. "I don't understand what's happening right now. I do, however, promise that I won't breathe a word of what Rafe told me. As a doctor, it's my responsibility to keep intimate details confidential every day. You can trust that I'll keep your secret, too."

"Thank you." Kellan gave a sharp nod. "You didn't ask to be dragged into this situation. Knowledge can be a burden. I'm, ah, well aware of how uncomfortable it is to have something like this—*exactly* like this—dropped on you. We're sorry about that." Then he grabbed Flynn by the elbow and dragged him back into the bathroom.

Rafe took her hands. Led her over to the bed and gently pushed on her shoulders until she sat on the edge of it. "Ignore them. This is about you and me, Mollie. You asked me a question Saturday night. You said, *don't you know you can trust me*?"

"I remember." That had been the most painful sentence she'd ever flung at a man. At anyone. It had ripped straight from her heart and out of her lips.

"I didn't know that I did. Hadn't given it any thought. That was disrespectful to you. Hell, everything I've done since we met has been borderline disrespectful. Kissing you on the side of the road. Lying to you day and night."

"Well, when you put it like that, you're quite the cad."

Delaney snorted.

His grip shifted to interlace their fingers. "I kissed you because I couldn't resist you. I lied to you because

I didn't have a choice. Not according to the federal government, anyway. I made fun of your town because . . . well, you've gotta admit it's a little strange. And if it made you worry that I didn't like it here well enough to stay, then I'm sorry about that, too."

"Can I make fun of Chicago to get even?"

Delaney laughed, and tried to turn it into a cough to cover it up. Rafe winced. "How about we hold off on that until the end of the negotiations? The point is that I said those things, even if they were over the top, because I felt like I could open up and say *anything* to you. Be myself. Even if I didn't entirely know who that was. Rafe Maguire's new to me, too. I'm still figuring out who he is. I'm figuring out fast that he's the man I've always wanted to be. Who I was meant to be. The man I'm most comfortable being."

"I like that man, too," Mollie whispered. That's what she kept coming around to. No matter what he had or hadn't told her about his past, they were living in the present. That's the Rafe she knew and adored.

Some people kicked drug or alcohol addiction. Learned to control their anger. Changed religions or political parties. Judging what they used to be was fruitless. Unnecessary. Accepting their present selves was the only answer.

He'd given up his criminal life, his *entire* life to save his brother. That single action spoke volumes about Rafe Maguire. Add in his determination to stand by his word no matter what, the way he helped Jesse, the fact that Frieda and Mick already liked and respected him, and the thoughtful way he treated her? It all added up to one heck of a man.

A man who'd reinvented himself, a phoenix rising from the ashes of his old life into something better and brighter.

A man she'd be proud to call her own.

As long as the government didn't drag him away. Because of what she knew now.

Rafe swallowed hard before continuing. "The man I used to be? The bad, dangerous one? That's part of me, too. Always will be."

Mollie didn't mind. She liked the rough edges. A lot. "Nobody's just one thing. It's how all the pieces fit together, the final big picture, that matters."

Rafe shot Delaney an incredulous, *can you believe this* look. Then he sat, too, thigh to thigh, one arm around Mollie's waist. "The fact that you believe that? It's huge."

"You're not as bad as you think you are, Rafe," she teased. Because she was trying to be sassy and strong in front of all these people. Trying very hard not to reveal that she was practically shaking with relief that her big, bad boyfriend was touching her again, talking to her again.

After talking with Norah, she'd been sure that Rafe wouldn't leave her. Not by his own choice. Not unless it was to save her life. But she was worried that the choice wasn't entirely his. The marshal insisting on witnessing this conversation didn't calm those fears one bit.

"Maybe not," he said with a laugh. "Not anymore, anyway. The big picture is that I love you, Mollie. I do trust you."

"Stop." She put her hand over his mouth. Now that they were in the same room again, Mollie couldn't wait another second to give Rafe the apology she'd figured out this morning that she owed him. "I know that. I should never have accused you of not trusting me. Once I calmed down and processed everything, looked past my own stupid issues, it hit me. Putting your new identities at risk, putting your *lives* at risk by telling me the truth was the biggest proof in the world that you trust me. I shouldn't have thrown it back in your face that way. I'm so sorry, Rafe."

"Thank you." He reached over and thumbed away a tear she hadn't realized was trickling down her cheek. "I didn't give you the choice. I did it all backward. I wish I'd told you the truth from the start, so you could decide if you wanted to even have this dangerous knowledge. So I'm fixing that. Right now. Proving I trust you more, giving you the choice now by including you in the planning for my new life."

Her heart leapt. If he didn't disappear in the middle of the night, as she'd feared constantly since the forest, they'd have a chance to keep going. To be together. Mollie hadn't exactly trusted Rafe from the very start. Or rather, she hadn't trusted herself, trusted in the possibility of a serious relationship with him.

"Does that mean you're staying? In Bandon?" She didn't look at Rafe when she asked. Mollie stared straight at the marshal in charge of him. Because this petite blonde woman was the one with the power to take him away. No matter what anyone else wanted.

"If it's okay with you."

She'd put to rest her fear of being abandoned. It was like having a five-hundred-pound emotional tumor excised. Mollie had carried it around her whole life without seeing the truth in front of her face—that nobody really abandoned her. That people made choices about what was right for them. It had nothing to do with Mollie. And now Rafe was giving her the power to make a similar choice. To choose who she wanted in her life.

That was easy.

"It's more than okay."

"You have to be sure. If you need time to decide, we'll give you, well, as much as Delaney can swing. If you think it's too dangerous for your town, or you just don't want a couple of ex-mobsters hanging around, we'll leave. The ball's in your court, Mollie."

Giving her that choice was the best present she'd ever gotten. Beaming, she said, "Then you're staying. That's the plan."

Delaney looked ready to kill Rafe. Her eyes snapped blue fire, and her scowl carved brackets around her mouth. "It's unorthodox. It breaks one of the primary protection rules."

"Tit for tat, Marshal. Seeing as how one of the primary protection rules was broken when an FBI agent used his knowledge to blackmail us."

"Agreed. That's the only reason this discussion was on the table. Are we clear on that?" She rapped on the bathroom door frame with her knuckles. "Flynn, Kellan, that goes for you, too."

"You mean are we clear that we're not supposed to tell anyone that we're ex-mobsters waiting to testify?" Flynn reached up and curled his fingers around the top of the door. "Yeah. That was always clear to me and Kellan. *We're* not the ones who can't keep our lips zipped."

"Thanks for not throwing us out of the program due to Rafe's slipup." Kellan threw so much gratitude and charm Delaney's way that Mollie could feel it, tumbling over her like a sexy mist of sugar and need. Guess he'd picked up some style points from his big brother.

"I'll admit, that was my first instinct. But you get a whole lot of credit for coming to me with your theory about the blackmailer instead of just acting on it."

"Hang on." Mollie went on alert, feeling like her eyes fired green daggers at Delaney. "An FBI agent who knew who the Maguires really are blackmailed them? Isn't that a huge breach? And a dangerous one? What are you doing to keep them safe?"

Delaney winced. Flipped her hand back and forth. "Yes and no. This particular agent does not know the *original* identity of the Maguire brothers. He only knows they're under witness protection and their *current* identity. He's been dealt with, severely, and is no longer a threat."

Flynn gave the marshal a nod. "Thanks for tracking him down so quickly." Then he extended his hand. The simple courtesy, for some reason, caused both Rafe and Kellan to do a double take.

Delaney shook Flynn's hand, albeit with raised eyebrows and a slight smile. "I give you my word, Dr. Vickers, that your safety and that of the town is of great import to the Marshals Service. The security here in Bandon, of the Maguires and everyone else, hasn't been compromised. Yet."

And then those ice-blue, assessing eyes slowly swung Mollie's way.

Mollie pulled her professionalism around her and met ice with ice. She respected the marshal for being wary. She appreciated that the woman spent her days making sure the Maguires stayed safe, but she wouldn't let the unspoken challenge go unanswered.

She stood, still keeping a tight grip on Rafe. "It won't be. I won't let you take him away. I have a vested interest in keeping Rafe's secret." Turning, Mollie aimed her next sentence right at those deep blue eyes and killer grin that had piqued her interest and then captured her heart. "I'm in love with him, too."

"I believe you. Let me be clear, this is a one-time courtesy. Only given to you because of the extenuating circumstances of the leak in our department." The marshal pointed at Flynn and Kellan. "Do I need to order both of you to keep your big mouths shut, officially? Or should I go bigger than that and order you not to fall in love like this guy, to cover all my bases?"

Kellan put his hand to his chest. "Too late, Marshal. You know my heart already belongs to you. Name any other part of my body, and it's yours, too." Flynn put him in a headlock and dragged him back into the bathroom.

Delaney shook her head, but as her hair fell forward to cover her face, Mollie saw a hint of a grin. Interesting. "You can't tell anyone else outside this room. Period. That includes your cousin and your grandmother, Dr. Vickers. And I've got a stack of nondisclosure forms for you to sign."

"Wait." Rafe stepped forward, one hand extended. "Just hang on before you bury her in red tape. Let me finish making my case."

Didn't he know that he'd already smoothed everything over with those three little but all-important words? "There's more?"

"I figure I should finish apologizing."

"For the record, that's always an excellent place to start. I'm also partial to calla lilies. And caramel chai cupcakes." The comfortable swing of their usual banter kept Mollie's spine straight. It kept her from launching herself at Rafe and smothering him in kisses. "But I probably haven't apologized enough, either. For assuming from day one that you'd leave me. For being too caught up in ridiculous, decades-old shadows in my brain to see you, and not judge you based on my own preconceptions."

Rafe's dark eyebrows shot up. "Mine'll be shorter." Then he grinned at her. And just like that, everything was back to normal. "I'm sorry I lied to you. It wasn't easy. Not one single time."

"I'll bet." She couldn't even imagine how hard it must be to have to think before speaking so often. To keep straight details that weren't actually your own. To figure out how to share who you really were, inside, without sharing, well, who he *really* was. It only proved all the more just how strong Rafe was—and determined.

Both extremely sexy traits.

"I'm sorry I hurt you. This whole relationship thing is new to me, but I won't use that as an excuse. I'll just promise to try harder."

"Me, too. I'm not blameless, either. I mean, not *living under an alias* levels of blame, but I didn't give you enough credit. Or myself. I'll work harder on believing that since we are good together, we can keep doing so. In perpetuity."

"Sounds like that belongs on a gravestone." Flynn's voice was echo-y from the bathroom. Mollie almost giggled at the utter lack of romance during Rafe's big romantic gesture. But that was kind of how they rolled. It worked for them. Even having an audience while they blurted out their love.

Two deep lines bisected Rafe's forehead. "My life is still complicated. There's a risk things won't go well in

Chicago when we testify. That's a big part of why I held back from you. It didn't feel like my life could really start over, for good, until the trial's behind us. But I don't want to wait."

"I can't wait."

"There's crap about my past you frankly don't need to know. I'll answer all your questions honestly, I swear—or tell you that I just can't answer."

"That's fair." Mollie didn't need all the sordid details. She assumed, given what little he had said, that there was a fair bit of violence in his past. Best to leave that as merely a hazy impression. Because that was another man's story.

This time, the other Maguires actually came out of the bathroom to interrupt. "How about you extend that same courtesy to your brother? You know, the one who shares your blood type and could give you a kidney if you ever need it? Because I've got a shit-ton of questions that need answers, too."

"Not now, K," Flynn said. "Give Rafe a chance to not be a total fuck-up."

Rafe framed her face in his big, calloused palms. "I know we'll have to start over from scratch. So that you can get to know the real me. But I also think you know more already than either of us realize. Because who I'm becoming in this crazy town, with you, is more real than anything I've felt before. Your caring for me opened my eyes and my heart. What I need to know is—will you let me care for you? Love you?"

She wouldn't waste any time playing hard to get. But Mollie did want one thing out in the open, if it was allowed. Better to ask before she screamed *yes* and lost her bargaining chip. "Can I ask you one question?"

"Sure."

"What's your real name?"

Rafe twisted to look over at the marshal. She put a hand to her forehead and sighed, but then she nodded. His head swung back. But when his mouth opened, Mollie changed her mind. She slapped her hand across his mouth. "Stop. Don't tell me."

"It's all right, Dr. Vickers." Delaney sounded resigned. "You're in deep enough already that it simply doesn't matter."

"It does. I don't want to scream out the wrong name during sex. I'm okay with switching our arrangement from friends with benefits to lovers . . . as long as *all* the benefits keep coming."

Rafe grabbed her into the tightest hug of her life. All her swagger vanished. Relief and rightness flooded through her. In his arms was where she belonged.

"I'll give you anything, everything I can Mollie, including my name."

"Your name doesn't matter. Your heart is all that matters, and I've seen that from day one. It's been hiding in plain sight."

"Just like me." He let go, and hurried into the bathroom. It had to be crowded in there now. Like a clown car. When he came back out it was with full arms. A giant box, and on top of it was a spray of at least two dozen red roses.

"I had Delaney bring these down with her from Eugene, so nobody here in town would get suspicious."

"You think I won't have to explain to my gran why I have a jillion roses?"

"She likes me. I'm sure she'll come up with a dirty reason behind them." Delaney full out giggled that time, as did Mollie. Rafe presented them with a hint of question still shielding his eyes. "We haven't done a lot of the standard date stuff. Sharing our life stories. Like how you don't know the details about my gunshot wound."

"Right. GSWs come up on all my other dates. Cross them off the list before I even finish my first cocktail."

"We'll get to that. I promise. For now, I'm starting with the old standards. Beautiful flowers for a beautiful woman."

Flowers *did* work, every time. Especially coming from the man who now held her heart. Mollie buried her nose in the mass of soft petals. "Thank you."

Rafe toed the box closer. "This is your real gift."

It was a plain cardboard box, not wrapped, and bigger than an EKG machine. Heart pounding, Mollie swept her lab coat behind her and knelt to lift off the lid. Inside was a long padded bag with handles. Still having no idea at what it was, she unzipped the top.

It didn't help much. She saw a flashlight. A shiny silver poncho. And a bunch of things she couldn't identify.

"It's a roadside emergency kit," Rafe explained. He pointed to each item. "Jumper cables, spare fuses, patch kit, flares—everything you need. So the next time your car breaks down, you won't have to accept help from some stranger."

It was offbeat, practical . . . and absolutely drenched in romance. A nod to their first meeting, while simultaneously fiercely protective.

It was *better* than the roses.

"I love it. Feels like I should give you a first aid kit as a reminder not to let any other doctor but me fix you up."

"No need, Doc. You've already fixed what nobody else could." Rafe took her hand and put it over his heart. "You helped me figure out who I am. Not who McGinty thought I was, not some made-up fake name living in a lie. You let me be myself—a little bit bad, but trying hard as hell to be good for you."

Mollie kept staring at the gorgeous blue pools of Rafe's eyes while she lifted her voice. "Fair warning. We're about to put this hospital bed to good use. If you don't want to watch, you've got about thirty seconds to get out. I need to show this man just how good I can be for him."

"But the forms—"

There was a scuffling, as if Flynn and Kellan were dragging Delaney out of the room. "Later."

And that thrilled Mollie. Because there *would* be a later with Rafe. He wasn't going anywhere. Except to bed with her. Which was right where she planned to keep him for a loooong time.

Flynn Maguire is the next Bad Boy to go good! Don't miss the second fun, sexy novel in Christi's new series . . .

NEVER BEEN GOOD

Coming April 2018!
Read on for a sneak peek . . .

Prologue

Seven months earlier
Graceland Cemetery, Chicago
11:30 p.m., October 31

"THIS IS NICE." Ryan Mullaney nudged Frank with his elbow. Flashed him a grin from behind the enormous fake white beard. "We haven't celebrated a Halloween together in years."

Yeah. His brother Ryan had lost his mind, no doubt about it. His brother, who was currently dressed like Santa Claus. On freaking Halloween.

Not that it was any better than his own off-season costume. Frank had flat-out refused—at first—when Ryan laid the leprechaun outfit across his bed. Until he pointed out the two best points of the costume. A big red beard and hat that would totally disguise Frank's features and a fake pot of gold. Aka something that wouldn't look weird for him to be carrying, just like the bag good old Santa had draped over his shoulder.

Since it turned out that just under two million in cash couldn't be stuffed in your pockets.

Especially not when traipsing through a cemetery. On Halloween. At almost midnight, surrounded by drunken, screaming people on ghost tours.

"That's probably because we're grown ass men. Trick or treating would just be weird at our age." Then Frank remembered that he'd skipped lunch. And dinner. Because Ryan had shown up at his front door with costumes and this crazy plan. "Although I wouldn't say no if you pulled a Snickers out of your pocket and tossed it my way."

Ignoring him, Ryan continued, his voice a little softer. "We haven't celebrated Halloween since Mom died."

Way to bring the mood back to serious-as-fuck. Grim enough to match the gravestones they were skirting. "You mean since she was *murdered*." Because Ryan had just shared that little bombshell with him. It was still rattling around in his head like a pinball. God knew it hadn't sunk in yet.

Ryan stopped at the edge of a replica of a Greek temple and dropped his sack onto the concrete foundation of the tomb. He fisted his hands on the red velvet and padding near his waist. "Can we not talk about that right now? One thing at a time. Let's get through tonight. Through the next couple of weeks. Then, I promise, we'll sit down and hash everything out."

Classic Ryan. Solving problems. Staying focused on

the long game. It was exactly what he did as the right-hand man for the leader of the Chicago mob.

Did . . . past tense.

Seeing as how today he and Frank had stolen all of the mob's cash. And then tomorrow they would watch their colleagues and friends be arrested in a sting—and hope the missing money would be attributed to the Fed's raid. After that, the Mullaney brothers would disappear forever, courtesy of the US Marshals Service.

Frank shifted his weight from one foot to the other. The frost-bitten grass made a crunching sound. Probably similar to the one his bones would make if this whole plan failed and the mob ever caught up with them.

"Are you going to talk to Kieran, too?" Because their little brother was out of the loop on all of it. He had no idea that his big brothers were even *in* the mob, let alone close to the top. He was balls-deep in law school.

Until tomorrow.

Until they ripped that away from him.

Just to save Frank.

How was that fair? God. Frank swallowed so hard he swore he could hear his Adam's apple scraping against his throat.

Ryan's blue eyes shifted to the side. Easy enough to see his discomfort at being pinned down, with the whole place lit up with spotlights and luminarias along the paths and footlights edging the most famous tombs. "You and I will talk first. Then we'll decide together how far in to dial Kieran."

"You think he'll hate us?"

Ryan's mouth turned downward into a bitter smirk. "Since it was all my idea to put us into Witness Protection, yeah, I'm sure he'll hate me. For a while. Pretty sure that you will, too. Once our new reality hits."

"No way. Not possible." The only way they'd survived the death of their mom was by banding together as tight as stucco on drywall. Their dad dying . . . wait. Being *murdered* by McGinty, according to the other truth Ryan laid on him today. Their dad's death had made their bond more unshakeable. Strong enough to get them through their worst days. It made them strong enough to survive anything, as long as the three of them were together. He could never, would never, hate Ryan.

"I'll check back in with you in a month when you're jonesing for an MMA fight."

How many more surprises were coming? Frank shook his head. "Hang on. I can't fight anymore?" His mixed martial arts training started as a way to prove to the other guys and to himself that even though he sat behind a desk, he was just as tough as everyone else in the organization. Appearances mattered. Respect had to be earned.

Kicking ass in the ring went a long way to making sure people stopped calling him a pencil pusher. To making sure that when he spoke, whether giving orders in a hard hat at a construction site or while making a point at a boring-ass Chamber of Commerce meeting, people listened. But he liked it, too. Liked teaching the skills to kids so they could defend themselves. A good fight worked out all his stress. And yeah, he'd cop to getting a thrill from winning the competitions, too.

"Keeping our noses clean is a pretty big requirement in WITSEC. I think an underground fight club wouldn't go over—" Ryan broke off before grabbing Frank by the neck and pulling him down behind the marble tomb.

"What?"

Ryan put his finger to his lips. Then he pointed at another tour group coming at them from the edge of the lake. This one was full of shivering women in skimpy versions of superhero costumes, hanging on the arms of already drunk and stumbling men.

Classy. And definitely making enough noise to scare away any ghosts that were stupid enough to hang around. Chicago's most famous cemetery was full of tours on a regular day. On Halloween it was as jam-packed as Wrigleyville during a Cubs home game.

Something else that they'd have to give up.

Shit.

Frank hadn't processed any of this yet. There'd been no time to think since Ryan burst on him at breakfast. Told him McGinty was a lying sonofabitch who intended to send Frank to jail to cover his own ass.

Before Frank had time to even break into a cold sweat of panic, Ryan told him that he'd fixed it. That he'd gone to the Feds and offered to turn evidence against McGinty and everyone else. That the Mullaney brothers would get a free ride and full protection as long as he lived up to the bargain and they played it straight.

Right after they socked away their "insurance" money.

Because neither of them fully trusted the Feds to keep them safe.

Yeah, that sweat was sure popping out now. It made the cheap polyester of his costume itch. Frank wasn't ready to give up his job, his clothes, his apartment, his fights, his *life.*

On the other hand, jail didn't sound much better.

His breath rasped out in little clouds. He realized how cold the marble was under his hands. Cold as death.

Jail—or a new life in the middle of nowhere—was definitely a step up from being cold in the ground.

After the tour group went down the slope to the lake, Ryan asked, "You got a date for tonight?"

"No." He tugged at the cartoonishly wide lapel of his bright green jacket. "No chance I'll get one dressed like this, either."

"You should get one. Go to a bar. Hook up. Live it up."

Was he serious? Their lives were the literal eye of a shitstorm of a hurricane right now. Frank could flirt half-asleep, half-drunk, only be half-interested and *still* score a girl. But tonight? His head wasn't in the game. Let alone his dick. "Not really in a pound-all-the-shots kind of mood, bro."

"Doesn't matter." Ryan stabbed a finger out toward the glow over the treetops, indicating the bright lights of downtown. "You need to be visible. Hit the usual spots. Make sure at least a half dozen of our guys see you having the time of your life. It'll keep them from being suspicious after the raid goes down. Can you fake it?"

That was a funny question. That's all that Frank did every day of his life.

He faked being okay with not being in on all the action. He faked being okay with not getting to choose his own damn college major, not being able to go to grad school. He'd convinced McGinty and the whole crew that he was fine with the choices made for him, the life they'd made and shoehorned him into.

Now he got to start over—and yet again, Frank still didn't get a say in it.

"Yeah. I can throw back some whiskey tonight, no problem." Probably the truest thing he'd said all day. The more he thought about it, the more getting shit-faced sounded like the only way to deal with all of this. No way he'd inflict himself and his weird-ass mood on a woman, though. "Want to grab one last deep-dish pepperoni at Lou Malnati's? Before we make the rounds at the clubs?"

"You bet."

Frank looked at his watch. The watch McGinty gave him the day he was promoted to vice-president of the construction company. Damn. That promotion had been a way to keep Frank under his thumb all along. A way to keep a convenient patsy close by. Turned out the job he'd worked his ass off for was basically the mob's version of a bench to be warmed. Just a placeholder in case McGinty needed someone who looked important enough—on paper, anyway—to take all the blame.

He planned to put this watch under the front tire of whatever government SUV drove them out of town. Crushing it, crushing the taint of its memory, would be his last official act in Chicago.

"We'll only make it if we wrap this up fast enough. Are we close, Ryan? Where are we stashing all this cash, anyway?"

"See that pyramid over there?"

Gray stone rose into a triangle of blocks, a sphinx on one side of the doorway, an angel on the other. Talk about a weird combination. It was cool and creepy and Frank had no idea how they were supposed to get inside of it. "The one with the giant black padlock on the door?"

"It's modeled after an Egyptian tomb." Ryan stood, slinging the red velvet sack back over his shoulder. "You remember the thing about all those ancient pyramids?"

"There was always a secret way out." Okay, maybe tonight would be a little bit fun, after all. Sure, a slice from Malnati's always scored in the top ten ways to end a night in Chicago. But a crazy-ass adventure with his big brother sounded like an even better way to spend their last hours in their hometown. A story they'd tell over and over and over again through the years.

Crap.

They'd only tell it to each other. Since this all had to stay a secret. From everyone.

For the rest of their lives.

Luckily, Ryan seemed oblivious of how often Frank's thoughts spiraled into near-panic. Gesturing for him to follow, his brother stalked in between the columns and zigzagged around a perimeter of six-foot-tall bushes. "Or, in our case, a way in. After this Schoenhofen guy died, his son-in-law took over the business. And he owed the mob a shit ton of money. He ran the biggest brewery in Chicago back in the day. Thought he'd gotten so big that he could skip paying protection money."

That was just stupid no matter what decade he was from. At least that stupidity erased the tiny bit of guilt Frank had been harboring about breaking into a tomb. "Let me guess. They took him out?"

"Drowned him in one of his own copper beer kettles." Ryan shot him a grin.

Frank couldn't help but smile back. It was kind of perfect. The Irish mob excelled at making their point in . . . creative ways. "Karma's a bitch."

"Whoever took over the business next wised up. He paid up. Fast. As a show of good faith, he offered this tomb as a place for us to hide . . . whatever we might need to keep out of sight. People. Money. Bodies. With Prohibition about to hit, we jumped at it. Settled his account right up. We used it for years. Nowadays a cemetery isn't so easy to go unnoticed in, so it just sits empty. I checked it out, oh, three years ago when I first learned about it. Nothing but cobwebs inside."

Suddenly, Frank didn't want to hear any more Chicago history, no matter how interesting. It just reminded him of the ticking clock hanging over his head. The one where he, Ryan, and Kieran were all leaving Chicago for good. That fact only seemed to clear out of his head for about two minutes, before the weight of it crashed back down again.

Shit.

Ryan was jumping through all these hoops for him. To save him. No way could he let his brother see how freaked out he was. It wouldn't be fair to lay that on him. Frank caught up in a couple of long steps. "How did I never hear this story?"

"Because you kept your nose clean running the legit biz. You didn't spend every day hanging out, shooting the breeze with lowlifes like me."

"Look what good that did me," Frank mumbled. Great. His clear head had only lasted twenty seconds this time around.

Laying a hand on his arm to stop him, his brother asked, "What are you talking about?"

"Ryan, you're the fixer for the head of the Chicago mob. You've done more than your fair share of bad things."

The fingers on his arm tightened. "I take care of bad people. There's a difference. Whatever I do, I guarantee they've got it coming to them. It's justice, Frankie. No different than handing out parking tickets. Our way's just faster. More successful, too."

Frank gave a quick thought to the parking tickets filling his glove compartment. Parking in Chicago was impossible on a good day. If by some miracle you found a spot, you kept it. The two-hour limit was a joke. Well, at least he was off the hook for a couple hundred bucks there. Silver lining. Get out of jail and get out of his tickets. Clearly, he owed Ryan a thank-you present. Something between a bottle of Blue Label Johnnie Walker and a boot to the balls.

He shook off Ryan's grip and turned to face him. He needed to bleed off some of the bitterness suddenly spurting up from his gut. "I toed the line. Ran the front. Paid taxes. Made sure all of your lowlifes had taxes and Medicare taken out of their paychecks. Made a construction company run even though half the people on the payroll never showed up to work. And yet *I'm* the one Danny McGinty wants to send to jail."

"You're not going to jail," Ryan said fiercely. "That's the whole point of this. You will *not* see the inside of a cell, Frank. I've got that in writing from the US Marshals. We turn evidence, we cooperate, we're free to go."

It was almost too good to be true. Nobody stood up to the mob and just walked away. "What if something goes wrong?"

Ryan put his head down, scanning the ground. Five graves down from the Schoenhofen pyramid, the earth rose into a low bunker. Tombs with pointed roofs that came up maybe to his waist were built into it. At the first one, Ryan dropped to his knees. He pushed at the cornice of each of the eighth-sized columns. Then he put his fingers around the starburst carved in the middle and twisted. The entire front swung inwards.

"That's why we stole all this money, isn't it? Best

backup plan in the world. Plus, it gives you your one shot at finally being a bad guy to the core. I call that a win-win." Shoving his sack in front of him, Ryan hit the deck and shimmied inside.

Frank looked around at the shadows from the pine trees, the full moon overhead, and the stark lines of the tombs. This was a pretty epic way to end things here in Chicago. Belly-crawling into a century-old crypt on Halloween? Come on. Classic Ryan, thinking to hide the mob's stolen money *in their own hiding spot*. So he'd have fun with this. No more sulking. No more freaking out. Maybe this new life was the best thing for all of them. They'd never intended to grow up to be criminals, after all.

Starting over would be good. Not just because it kept him out of jail.

And as long as he was with Ryan and Kieran, how bad could it really be?

Chapter One

Present day
The Gorse Bar
Bandon, Oregon

FLYNN MAGUIRE HATED a lot of things. As he slowly, carefully drew a pint of Guinness, he counted them. Starting with his brother, Rafe, who had the dumber than dirt idea to throw them all into Witness Protection.

He also hated his new life.

They were on version five of it now, having been planted and then yanked from four other towns and jobs. Their personal marshal, Delaney Evans, had issued the warning—aka threat—that if this one didn't take, they were out of the program. He'd hate her a little, too, if he didn't know she was just doing her job. Of all people, Flynn sure as hell knew what that felt like. Seeing as how he'd spent five years running a construction company he didn't give two shits about. But he'd run it and run it well.

For all the good it did.

Oh, another reason to be pissy had just popped up

today. Flynn hated that his new name—which he'd picked and actually liked, unlike the last two—was shared by the latest boy-bander to get thrown in jail for sniffing his paycheck up his nose. Now his name was on everyone's lips. Exactly what he—and the US Marshals Service—didn't want.

He hated this quaint fucking seaside village of a town. On principle, anyway. Because it wasn't Chicago. None of the towns they'd moved to were anything like the Windy City. The food, the people, the action—none of it compared. Flynn hadn't realized how much he'd miss his hometown. Mostly because he hadn't had any time to think about it between being told they were leaving, and disappearing.

Top of the list? That had to be how much Flynn hated himself. Or at least this sad sack version of himself he'd turned into since entering WITSEC.

"These should quiet down those thirsty backpackers. Thank you, Flynn," said a soft voice to his left. He whipped his head around to stare at the waitress as she picked up a tray of longnecks.

The *pretty* waitress.

The one thing in his life Flynn absolutely did *not* hate.

She was girl-next-door pretty, with long hair that fell in waves, the same dark brown as a good vanilla porter. Eyebrows that arched her face into a smile even when her lips didn't play along. Skinnier than his usual type back home. But it worked on her. She was small and fragile-looking. Made a guy want to be careful with her. Kiss her slowly. Thoroughly. Keep kissing her while taking off that blue shirt and finding out if her bra underneath matched . . .

The pretty waitress who drove him crazy. Because Flynn wanted her. He'd wanted her since his first shift here a month ago.

A month was a hell of a long time to want a woman and not make a move on her.

But he was no good. No good for her, no good for any woman. Flynn was a morose son of a bitch who lied 24/7 to everyone but his two brothers. He wouldn't inflict himself on anyone, let alone someone as sweet as Sierra.

Sierra . . . huh. He didn't even know her last name. Not that it mattered. Because a name didn't tell you jack shit.

At least, he hoped his name didn't tell anyone *anything* about him.

"Dude. My beer."

The outrage in Kellan's voice was enough to make Flynn tear his gaze away from Sierra and notice the foam pouring down the side of the glass. No wonder his little brother sounded pissed.

"Sorry, K." He flipped off the tap.

"You hear that sound?"

Flynn cocked his head. Since it was Sunday night, there was only the jukebox going instead of a live band, playing whatever bubble-gum crap topped the charts by his aforementioned, coked-up name-twin. Just a handful of the less than two dozen tables were filled. The pool table wasn't being used in the back room. No darts going on, either. All in all, even for a Sunday night in June, this bar was quiet. Which, to his mind, summed up perfectly this town of three thousand locals. "Hear what?"

"The sound of generations of our Irish ancestors rolling over in their graves." Kellan grabbed a stack of cocktail napkins and wiped off the glass. "Sure an' the fairies will punish you with bad dreams for wasting the mother's milk of our land," he said in a thick Irish accent.

"There's no fairies in Oregon."

Shaking a finger, Kellan gave him a look of disappointment. Something Flynn had gotten used to seeing from both him and Rafe more and more often. "Is there no magic in your heart then, young Maguire?"

"No," he said shortly. Then Flynn remembered that Kellan had volunteered to leave the house tonight so Rafe and his girlfriend, Mollie, could have some privacy. And he'd sat here keeping Flynn's sorry ass company all night. So he ratcheted up the corners of his mouth to a smile. Okay, nowhere close to a smile. Something closer to a smile than his usual scowl. "But there's no bullet lodged in there either, so I guess that's something."

"Jesus, Flynn." Kellan hunched over, then threw a lightning quick glance over each shoulder. "You can't say stuff like that. You know the rules. No discussing your old, um, *work* in public."

The only occupied tables were down by the doorway to the room with the pool table. Flynn could hear Carlos, the Gorse's manager, groaning over whatever baseball game he was listening to in his office. Sierra was still delivering that tray of drinks. He literally could've named every member of McGinty's crew and nobody would've heard a thing. Kellan was just overly paranoid.

Of course, Kellan hadn't been used to lying his whole life like Flynn and Rafe. They didn't come out and talk about being in the mob to their dates. But they also mostly hung out with women who knew the score. Whose families were involved, too. To everyone else they encountered—from doctors to bartenders to the kids he'd mentored—they stuck to their cover stories.

It'd been easier for Flynn, since he actually ran the legit business. The one they could launder money through when McGinty needed a fast influx of clean cash. The one that supplied paychecks on the up-and-up so that they all looked like tax-paying, law-abiding citizens, even if most of the organization only worked on Flynn's construction sites a couple of times a month. He was used to how it felt to say one thing and know there were three more things deliberately being left unsaid. And he'd honed an instinct about when it was safe to reveal more.

Kellan didn't have the luxury of those years of training. He was still in the paranoid phase, assuming that everyone who crossed paths with the Maguire brothers could see right through them to their dirty-dealing truths.

Probably because that's all he saw when he looked at his brothers. They'd pulled Kellan from law school with only a semester to go. He'd worked his ass off to learn everything there was about justice. About being on the side of right and might. Then he'd found out the rest of his family stood on the *other* side of the line.

"Relax." Flynn whipped his bar towel at Kellan's shoulders. "What did we tell you was rule number one?"

"Ever? Don't touch your shit without asking."

"Still true. But I meant the number-one rule of this." He circled his hand to indicate not just the cranberry red walls of the Gorse, but the whole cranberry-crazy town.

"Nobody thinks you're guilty unless you give them a reason to." Kellan winced. "That's abominable grammar, by the way."

"There's no grades when it comes to what it takes to stay alive. You either do or you don't."

"Great pep talk. Thanks, bro."

Shit. He really did feel guilty. Kellan was trying. But everything that used to get through to Flynn didn't work anymore. He didn't care about his clothes—and he used to buy every piece of workout gear between the covers of *GQ*. He didn't care about missing the fight club. He certainly didn't care about this job bartending that he'd been pushed into.

Instinctively, his gaze searched the room for Sierra, the one thing in this new life that made him feel . . . *anything*. Even if it was mostly frustration. Blue balls were no fucking fun. Working a whole shift with them? The worst. Just looking at Sierra, though, would smooth over the frayed edges of guilt poking at his stomach.

When he didn't find her, Flynn forced himself to look back at Kellan.

"Sorry, I'm being a dick." Add that to his list of things he hated. Because deep down, he really hated this fucking attitude that he couldn't shake. Now, though, it was comfortable. As easy to slip on as a pair of fleece pants.

But Flynn was worried that the day was coming when he'd lose the ability to ever take it off again.

"Oh, you mean tonight? Yeah. You've been a total dick. Pretty much every day for the past seven months, too. You bet." Kellan lifted his mug in a fake toast, then drained almost half of it.

Offering up as close as he could come to an olive branch, Flynn said, "This isn't as easy as we thought it'd be."

"Nope." Kellan cocked his head to the side. Those blue eyes, way lighter than his own, squinted at him. "Want to tell me what exactly you and Rafe were high on when you thought this might be easy?"

"You know we don't touch that stuff."

"Yet it's the only explanation I've got for you two thinking this would be a cakewalk."

Before he could defend himself, a loud shattering noise had Flynn jerking around just in time to see Sierra fall to the floor in a heap, right next to a knocked-over table with a spray of broken glass all around it that she was lying in the middle of.

He didn't bother going down to the end of the bar and lifting the hatch. Every second he wasted was another moment that Sierra might put out her hand to lever up and cut herself. So Flynn just planted a palm in the middle of the bar and vaulted over it.

Crouching next to Sierra, he heard the crunch of glass as Kellan rushed to his side. "Don't move," he cautioned her. Flynn put a hand lightly on her abdomen to drive the point home and tried not to notice the way she tightened at his touch.

"It's hard to serve beers from the floor," she quipped. And those blue eyes that almost never looked at him head-on lifted to meet his with what he'd swear to his dying day was an audible click.

Nah.

Had to be the crushed glass shifting.

Didn't it?

It was easy for Flynn to slip back into his take-charge mode. It was a mask he'd put on every day at the construction company. He knew exactly how much force to put into his voice to be sure people listened to him—and responded. "Where are you hurt?"

A self-deprecating smile ghosted at the edges of her pretty pink lips. "My pride's pretty well bruised."

"Sierra."

"My ankle." She sighed. "I landed on it and sort of twisted."

"Kellan, we'll need ice." His brother wordlessly left to carry out the order. Flynn splayed his fingers wider when he felt Sierra start to shift. "Does it hurt anywhere else? Are you cut?"

"No. Just sticky and wet from all this beer now on the floor."

Sticky and wet. If he didn't know better, he'd swear that the woman was trying to get a rise out of him.

But Flynn did know better. Because Sierra rarely spoke to him outside of what was necessary to get the job done. She sure as hell didn't *flirt* with him. Not ever.

"I'm going to pick you up now," he announced. "Once you're vertical, put all your weight on me. Then I'll brush off the glass."

"Oh, you don't have to do that." Sierra spoke so quickly all the words merged together into one.

Was she scared of him? Was that why she never looked him in the eye? Shit. Flynn put an arm beneath her knees and worked the other behind her neck and down her back. Glass nicked the back of his hand.

It didn't matter.

Because he was finally touching her. He might as well have been lifting a dandelion, she weighed so little. Even though he consciously held her away from his body because of the glass, Flynn noticed everything. The firm calf muscle against the back of his hand. The heat of her back through the sticky shirt. The way it pulled taut against her small breasts.

He watched to be sure she kept one foot off the floor, and then stood her up. Flynn grabbed the bar rag from where he'd stuffed it into his waistband and wrapped it around his hand for protection. Sierra white-knuckled his left arm.

Slowly, carefully, he brushed her off from shoulders to ankles in long, sweeping motions, keeping an eye peeled for any dots of blood on her shirt that might indicate a nick. Instead, it was just the blood from the back of his knuckles seeping through the towel. Flynn tried like hell to keep the whole thing professional. Medicinal. One co-worker performing a safety check of another.

Yeah. That angle sure as hell wasn't working for him.

When he finished her sides, Flynn came back around in front. Damn if her cheeks weren't pink. "I'm going to carry you into the back now."

"Oh, but Flynn, you—"

Whatever objection she was trying to get out he cut off by sweeping her back into his arms. This time, he did hold her close. Who knew when he'd ever have another chance? Flynn cradled her against his chest.

Holy hell. He almost stumbled in shock and decided that, if her ankle wasn't broken, this would now rank as his best day since they'd moved to this dot on the map. Maybe even his best day in the last four dots.

Holding Sierra was like holding sunlight. Her warmth shot through him. Reminded him how good it felt to be alive. How good it felt to be a man. Reminded him that maybe life wasn't a complete shitstorm after all.

This rush of goodness was the way he'd heard some of the mobsters talk about doing heroin. Flynn had no doubt that Sierra was even more addictive.

And dangerous. At least for him.

The trip around the bar and down the hallway to the

manager's office took too little time. He had no excuse to keep holding her. No excuse to keep rubbing his cheek against Sierra's soft hair. No excuse for inhaling deeply and appreciating the clean, floral scent that spurted want and need and full-out lust straight down to his dick.

So Flynn placed her on the rolling wooden chair that Carlos pushed toward him. Then he knelt in front of her and pulled her bad leg onto his knee.

Carlos put a hand on Sierra's shoulder. His thick eyebrows joined into a single dark line of concern. "*Dios mio.* What happened?"

"I was careless." She waved a hand, dismissing the whole thing. "A couple of the darts landed way off the board. I climbed onto a table to get them, but they were stuck into the wall so well that I lost my balance and fell."

"The drunk who threw them into my wall should've pulled them out," Carlos growled.

Sierra ducked her head. "It's no big deal. Really. I was just trying to be helpful. Instead, I've disrupted everyone and made a mess. I'm sorry."

The woman risked herself for stupid darts? Flynn's worry for her morphed into anger. "You're lucky you aren't cut from landing on all that glass. Why didn't you ask me to do it?"

In a low voice, not looking at him, she answered, "I didn't want to bother you."

A brick between the eyes would've hurt Flynn less. This was his fault. One hundred percent. He'd been avoiding Sierra for her own good, trying not to let his fucked-up darkness touch her in any way.

Instead, it made her awkward and jumpy around him, unwilling to ask a man who topped her by at least six inches for a basic, work-related assist. Flynn wanted to howl his frustration at his own idiocy. Actually, he really wanted to find a heavy bag and wail on it for a couple of hours until his knuckles ached, his lungs burned, and his muscles cried for mercy.

But now was the time to focus on Sierra. "I'm sorry that you didn't feel comfortable asking me for help. For the future, I'll do whatever you need. No matter what I'm in the middle of. Got it?"

She nodded, long hair still shadowing her face.

Flynn unlaced her black sneaker. It was streaked with different colors of paint. It made him wonder what she did in her off hours. Was she painting her house? Would she be climbing a ladder with a weak ankle? Would she let him help or refuse his not-yet-made offer?

Even though he was careful easing the shoe off, Sierra's sharp intake of breath made her pain at the movement obvious, which made Flynn's guilt stab into his gut even deeper.

Sierra's ankle was already swelling. He didn't even have to roll down her black and white polka dotted socks to see that. Frankly, he didn't trust himself to touch her skin again. "Ice," he barked at Kellan.

His brother handed over a dishtowel bulging with cubes. "I'll go out and clean up while you two take care of her." He grabbed the broom and dustpan from the corner on his way out.

"Thanks, Kellan." Carlos barely spared him a glance as he fussed over Sierra with little pats and frowns. He was acting like a grandpa instead of a hard-assed vet who'd seen multiple tours in combat. "Do you want a drink, Sierra? A couple of shots to cut the pain?"

"Oh, no. I've got ibuprofen at home. I'd rather take that than make myself feel worse with a hangover."

Flynn pulled over the trash can, upended it, and rested her foot on it sideways, ice draped across. Then he noticed the sparkly glints of glass in her hair. "Do you have a brush?"

"No." She looked up at that to give him an amused half-smile. "I'm not one of those women who reapplies their lipstick every twenty minutes and carries a whole makeup counter in their purse."

He'd noticed. He'd noticed everything about her look. Natural. Like hippy-natural. Which he found weirdly sexy. Weird because the women he'd dated in Chicago were all big boobs, loud makeup, and bigger hair. Sierra was just . . . herself. Which turned Flynn on more than he'd been willing to admit.

Until tonight.

Until seeing her crumpled on the floor of the bar had unlocked all the shit he'd kept tamped down for weeks now. All the interest. Lust. Attraction. Need.

Carlos produced a brush from his desk drawer. "Here. It's Madalena's." She was his sister who did the books for the Gorse. Flynn had only met her once but appreciated her no-nonsense personality. "I'll go watch the bar for you, Flynn."

"Thanks." He carefully pulled Sierra's hair over her shoulders so it draped down her back. "This should be the quickest way to get the glass out."

"Oh, but you don't have to—"

That was the kicker. After spending years doing what McGinty told him he *had* to, Flynn now did only the bare minimum of what other people expected from him. Sure, he could just hand her the brush. But this, helping Sierra, was a compulsion he couldn't resist. "I know I don't *have* to. I want to help. Let me."

"Okay." Her shoulders relaxed down at least an inch as she sighed. Then Sierra sighed again as the bristles made contact with her scalp. This sigh was different, though. It was pure feminine pleasure.

God, he couldn't wait to make her do it again.

Flynn made long, slow passes. A little more pressure against her head, because she seemed to like it, and then a pull through the long strands to shake out the glass. It was quiet. Intimate. Something he'd never done before for any other woman. The backs of his fingers grazed her neck as he gathered her hair in his hand.

Sierra shivered.

His dick throbbed at the sight. At her whole body shiver, and at the sight of her exposed nape. Right on the spot where, if he put his lips on it, Flynn knew he could tease another shiver out of her.

Then he noticed how her hair looked in his fist. He flashed ahead past a million impossibilities to a scene that he'd never let happen. Sierra on her knees. Naked. Looking over her shoulder at him with that shy smile while he fisted her hair and drove into her.

The ice slid off her ankle, tinkling as it tumbled out of the towel onto the floor. The moment was gone.

Although Flynn knew he'd never be able to get that image out of his mind.

Carlos reappeared in the doorway. "Flynn, will you take her home?"

"I can get myself home," Sierra protested.

"Did you ride that bike of yours here?" At her nod, Carlos fished his keys out of his pocket and tossed them to Flynn. "Here. Take my truck. You can load her bike in the back of it. I'll have Jeb drive me home once we close up."

"That's really not necessary."

"And it's not up for discussion." Unbelievable. First of all, a bike? Seriously? Secondly, he had to prove to Sierra it was okay to let him help. How had he never noticed the stubborn streak in this woman? "I'll grab my jacket and be right back."

Carlos shut the door to the office behind them, then rounded on Flynn. He brandished a stubby finger in his face. "Be nice to her."

What the hell? "I always am." He headed to his locker at the end of the hallway, right before the dry storage. Unfortunately, Carlos dogged his heels.

"No, you're polite. To everyone. That's not the same as being nice."

Flynn spun the combination on his locker. He didn't really get into personal conversations these days. Turned out that the easiest way to keep a life of lies straight was to say nothing at all. But he couldn't blow off his boss without a reason. "I don't want to give her the wrong idea."

"What? That you're a decent human being?"

"No. That I'm interested."

Carlos's swarthy features twisted into astonishment, then humor. His laugh boomed out, echoing off the pans hanging from hooks above the prep counter. "Because you're God's gift to womankind? One smile and she'll lose her common sense, her good taste, and her ability to resist you?"

"Something like that."

"So far as I can tell, you've got exactly one strength. Making up weird and wonderful cocktails. People go ape shit for them. You know what they don't go nuts over? Your looks and barely noticeable charm. If you can squeeze out a smile, I promise that Sierra will be able to withstand it. She's strong."

"She's fragile."

"Doesn't mean she's not strong. People are often more than just what they look like." Carlos cocked his head to the side. "Guessing you already know that."

"What you see is what you get."

"A guy with a chip on his shoulder?"

"Yeah. That's it." That's all he was anymore. Flynn couldn't risk being anything but the empty shell of a man. This move into WITSEC had hollowed him out. Hollowed out everything he thought he was, who he was. No point filling that back up. No point deciding on a new persona.

Because there was a good chance it wouldn't last long enough to matter.

About the Author

USA Today bestseller **CHRISTI BARTH** earned a master's degree in vocal performance and embarked upon a career on the stage. A love of romance then drew her to wedding planning. Ultimately she succumbed to her lifelong love of books and now writes award-winning contemporary romance.

Christi can always be found either whipping up gourmet meals (for fun, honest!) or with her nose in a book. She lives in Maryland with the best husband in the world.

www.christibarth.com

Discover great authors, exclusive offers, and more at hc.com.

A Letter from the Editor

Dear Reader,

I hope you liked the latest romance from Avon Impulse! If you're looking for another steamy, fun, emotional read, be sure to check out some of our upcoming titles. We have something for everyone next month!

If you're a sports romance lover, you are in luck! Lia Riley has a brand-new Hellions Angels novel for your reading pleasure. HEAD COACH is a sexy, fun story about a sports reporter who's determined to get an interview with a stoic hockey coach. He may hate the press—but he can only resist the tempting reporter for so long. Grab this second book in Lia's new series and become a Hellions fanatic overnight!

If you're in the mood for a quick, fun, light-hearted holiday romance, you don't want to miss the new Heartbreaker Bay novella from Jill Shalvis! In HOLIDAY WISHES, a carefree bad boy reunites with the girl he lost his virginity to a decade earlier during a friend's wedding weekend. But now their positions are reversed, because this good time guy finally wants something real—and his one-time flame is in the mood to be a little wild!

For historical romance fans, we also have a brand new Victorian romance from Christy Carlyle! HOW TO WOO A WALLFLOWER, the final book in her Romancing the Rules series, features a free-spirited woman who is determined to revamp her family's publishing venture . . . except the uptight, scowling, and irritatingly handsome editor has other plans. It's a charming, fabulously passionate story that you do not want to miss!

And finally, for a quick, sexy, suspenseful read, you'll want to one-click the new novella from HelenKay Dimon! THE NEGOTIATOR, about a woman who discovers her supposedly long-dead husband's body on her kitchen floor and must team up with sexy, savvy Garrett McGrath to uncover the truth before she's accused of murder!

You can purchase any of these titles by clicking the links above or by visiting our website, www.AvonRomance.com. Thank you for loving romance as much as we do . . . enjoy!

Sincerely,
Nicole Fischer
Editorial Director
Avon Impulse